THE SANDPIPER

By Susan Brace Lovell

Published by
KRisSCroSS Press
Grand Rapids, Michigan.

The SANDPIPER is a work of fiction.
The characters live only in the author's imagination.

Cover design and composition by Brad Hineline.
Author's photograph by Jody Price.
Editorial proofing by Diane Johnson.
Marketing by Sue Anderson.
Printed by Colorhouse Graphics.
Sold at Schuler's Books & Music.

Gratitude for other team members:
Ellen, Brandie, Cynthia, Suzanne, Diane, Linda,
Mark, Jill, Roger, Kaitlyn, Corey, Sophie, Julie.

Sold at Schuler's Books & Music.
Also available at Amazon.
E books at: Kindle, Nook, I Pad, Sony Reader

Visit the web site: thesandpiperbook.com
ISBN 978-0-9892874-0-1

Death puts life into perspective.

RALPH WALDO EMERSON

ABOUT THE AUTHOR

SUSAN BRACE LOVELL earned undergraduate and graduate degrees with honors in English from the University of Michigan; taught high school and college English; co-founded Cadence, a weekly newspaper in East Grand Rapids, Michigan; has written four non-fiction histories; serves as a consultant to The Wege Foundation; and sits on the Grand Rapids Salvation Army's Advisory Board. She and her husband Dr. F. Raymer Lovell, Jr., have three children, six grandchildren, one naughty Cavalier spaniel named Lucky, and live in Grand Rapids.

THIS NOVEL IS DEDICATED TO
EVERYONE WHO HAS EVER

LOVED … AND LOST
S O M E O N E

TO THE DISEASE OF ALCOHOLISM/ADDICTION.

FOR EVERYONE IN THE DISEASE,
THIS BOOK IS A PRAYER
FOR RECOVERY…ONE DAY AT A TIME.

LET GO AND LET GOD.

THE SANDPIPER

SUSAN BRACE LOVELL

The Sandpiper

PROLOGUE: JUNE 1968

"All the lonely people," Joan Baez's throaty voice on the radio, "where do they all come from?" Ellie punched the OFF knob. She didn't need any more sadness in her head. She lifted her damp thighs, one at a time, away from the itchy upholstery and scratched the skin below her cutoffs as Jim turned on to U.S. 31 south. The open car windows didn't help, the outside air steaming in. She pushed her dirty bare feet against the glove box and sensed the turn of her husband's head. He wouldn't say anything. Not today.

But, then, he didn't need to. He took better care of things than she did. Even the dashboard of his Nash Rambler that was old when they'd met four years ago. The orderly specificity of medicine. Dr. James Cameron. The new name would take getting used to. Loosening her jeans zipper, she leaned back into the seat and closed her eyes.

"Tired?" he asked, muffling his voice not to wake Katie.

Ellie shook her head, the silver dangles on her hoop earrings making a soft tinkling sound. She willed herself not to look at him. The sensuous grazing of his eyes might undo her, like slow finger strokes. Tired was for normal couples doing normal things. Ellie Cameron was light years beyond tired.

This Friday drive from the east side of Michigan to the west was his idea, not hers. But once the word "beach" had been spoken at breakfast and Katie began skipping around their hot apartment, Ellie was outnumbered. All she'd really wanted to do on this miserably hot morning in late June was curl up and die.

From the moment she'd first seen him in the Ann Arbor café, Jim Cameron of the ebony hair had snake-charmed her soul. In one blazing look, he'd ensnared her with his eyes—dark pools of brilliance like a holy man's. No, she'd really had no choice about this three-hour drive for an afternoon on Lake Michigan. Lifting her long auburn hair off her damp neck, she knew Jim hadn't come up with the idea that morning. He planned his moves. Whatever this trip was about, it wasn't swimming.

Until eight weeks ago, Jim and Ellie Cameron had no secrets. They held nothing back. His rotation on pediatrics and the little red-haired boy with a liver transplant. Her surprise ten-dollar tip one busy lunch shift at the P Bell. The busboy who got fired for grabbing Ellie's fanny. Sometimes they talked over early coffee, leaning in to lace each other's fingers as the black dawn swept around them like a mantle. Always later in the night, they shared each other's days as they made the studio couch into their bed. Afterwards, after the clinging into each other—the pooling of their separateness until neither could breathe without the other—they'd talk some more. Make plans. Spin their dreams.

It had all changed with the secrets. First his. Now hers.

Ellie jerked out of her thoughts when she felt gravel spinning under the tires.

"Sorry," Jim said, backing up on the shoulder of a road beside what looked like a forest to Ellie.

"But this isn't a public beach, honey." The last word caught in Ellie's throat. So natural to talk in lover's endearments, Ellie had almost forgotten. Those days when loving Jim Cameron was what she did—what she woke up for every morning. Who she was, really. Those days were almost over.

"Beach, Mommy?" a little squeaky voice came over their shoulders. "Are we there? Are we there?"

The small head gleaming with blue-black hair cut in smooth bangs appeared between them, her three-year old body already bouncing against the front seat. "You have sleepy breath, Katie," Ellie said gently pinching their daughter's perfect little nose.

"Wait here a sec," Jim said. Before Ellie could stop him, he was out of the car and jogging up a dirt road. That's when Ellie saw the sign with two hand-inked words on it.

"Oh, no way," Ellie said out loud, fumbling for the door lock to call him back. Katie was already out the car's back door running after her dad.

"Shit," Ellie said smacking her open palm on the now dirty dashboard. Anger and despair tangled into her until she wanted to scream and cry at the same time. Mostly she wanted to go back to Ann Arbor. To the tiny apartment in the red-brick mass of married housing. She needed to start getting used to it without him. "Shit," she repeated louder, flinging open the door, then slamming it behind her as hard as she could.

The little stones mixed into the dirt hurt her feet, but she was too mad to care. She could see Jim hadn't taken time to put his shoes on either. Ellie wondered if the soles of his feet hurt as much as hers. No, they wouldn't, she decided, picking her way around the bigger stones. He'd probably plopped Katie on his shoulders and sprinted up this road, no foot pain or oxygen sucking to slow him down. Ellie was breathing hard already, each step more grimace than walk. What the hell was she doing? She should have just stayed in the car on the gravel shoulder and cried. She was getting good at that. Taking a bath and crying. Sleeping and crying. Doing laundry and crying. She could break down just about anywhere.

A glimmer of bronze on her right stopped her awkward pace. A flash of sunlight hit three square windows in a log cabin, the fat timbers a burnished molasses under the red chimney. It was like a mirage, the wood shimmering behind the purple and pink wildflowers scattered through the beach grass around it. Impulsively Ellie began walking toward the cabin, her stinging feet forgotten.

In there she could hide, put away the secrets. In there the betrayals would evaporate like summer fog.

"Mommy." "Ellie." The two voices she loved beyond all sounds of the earth called down to her in one vibration—overlapping, blending, harmonizing until her heart filled warm and liquid. Ellie turned her back to the cabin and headed up the winding dirt road. Then, in a trill of intuition, Ellie had the sense she'd been here before—walked this path. She pulled her head up straining to see where she was going. Some unspoken part of her knew it mattered very much.

On a knoll beyond an emerald colony of pine trees, she saw an old clapboard house, its intriguing juts and angles painted two different colors. As she got closer, she could see Jim and Katie talking to an auburn-haired woman with tanned arms wearing paint-splattered blue jeans and a red tee shirt. Then Ellie realized the cottage's bleak grey was being covered over by a sparkling white. Clusters of hot-pink impatiens grew randomly around what seemed to be the back door and an attached shed. Ellie immediately liked whoever planted the flowers for doing it with no pattern, no symmetry. Like nature.

"That way to the lake," the woman, who looked to be in her thirties, was saying to Katie as she pointed around the house. "But not alone, Katie. Never alone." The woman smiled while she leaned down toward Katie. Ellie saw a smile spread into the woman's eyes, even into her body movements.

Ellie was startled to see Katie grab both the woman's hands and leap off the ground. "You come too. You come."

"Katie!" Ellie heard the scold in her voice and felt embarrassed in front of this gentle stranger. The woman's head came up, and Ellie was looking into deep grey eyes set wide with intelligence, their edges attractively nicked with laugh lines.

"Hey, Ellie Cameron. Your husband told me your name." She reached out a hand, "If you don't mind a little white paint. Helena Judd, but my friends call me Nina. That means you and the new doctor. Congratulations. It takes two to get one man through Michigan's medical school.

"Oh," the woman leaned back down to make eye contact with Katie, "and how about 'Aunt Nina' for you, pipsqueak?" She laid a soft hand on Katie's head.

Suddenly a familiar cramp of urgency hit Ellie. She had to urinate fast. "I need to…" she hesitated.

"I would think so after three hours in the car," Nina finished for her and took two quick steps toward the house. She opened a creaky spring door for Ellie and gestured toward a little bathroom just beyond the kitchen.

"The stairs to the beach are around that way," Nina called back to Jim. "Ellie will catch up with you two."

When Ellie came out of the bathroom, Nina was seated at a high-gloss, round white table. The smells of paint and turpentine blended with the sweet air blowing into the open galley kitchen from the living room windows facing the lake.

"I needed a break, and you looked as if you could use a little caffeine too."

Ellie felt tears strike her eyes as if this woman knew—but didn't hold it against Ellie. She sat down next to Nina, gratefully lifting the yellow mug to her lips.

"It's even got cream," Ellie said savoring the earthy flavor.

"You strike me as the kind of woman who takes cream in her coffee," Nina said. "Like the farmers."

"I didn't know farmers did," Ellie said, her muscles loosening in a way they hadn't for a while. Not since the first of May anyway. As Nina bent to sip her coffee, Ellie noticed the finely chiseled bones of her cheeks, her short wavy red-brown hair outlining the oval face.

"They do in Connecticut, where I'm from."

"How come you—" Ellie paused. She wasn't one to ask nosey questions. But this Nina Judd—she felt an unfamiliar tug of wanting to know more about her.

"Oh, it's a long story. But right there is the short version." Ellie followed Nina's eyes toward the living room beyond the kitchen and sucked air against her teeth at what she saw. Ribbons of cobalt edged in the white of the window frames, Lake Michigan filled the long room empty of everything but a stained canvas drop cloth and painting supplies. The lake's magic spilled over the paint cans and buckets of brushes and rags until the work scene took on an elegance of its own.

"I see," Ellie said nodding, her eyes scanning the flat horizon, blue on blue, a few puffy white clouds floating above. "Yes," she nodded. "I really do see." Ellie stared at the curls of silver lining the waves with a longing she couldn't name. Neither of them moved for a moment. Then Nina spoke.

"Jim told me, Ellie," Nina said with the natural intimacy of old friends. "I'm sorry for you. For both of you. All three of you."

"Four," Ellie said and shocked herself. She'd told no one.

Her daughter's laughing voice sang up from the beach where Ellie could now see Jim and Katie splashing their feet in the shallow water. She felt Nina watching her.

"Jim doesn't know. It's wrong of me." Tears came to her eyes so easily now.

"You want to keep him. That's not wrong, that's love."

"You don't understand." Ellie shook her head slowly. "I promised last time—with Katie. That we'd wait until he graduated to have a baby. Then I just quit, you know, using anything."

"And?"

Ellie looked down at her dusty feet. "I wanted to surprise him—but that wasn't all of it. I was only 19, when we met," her voice cracked, "a silly freshman and he was already in med school. I was scared he'd get tired of me."

"And you think you're the first woman on the planet to do that, Ellie? Come on."

"But the deceit—that's what hurt him. We'd agreed I should finish school too before we started a family. Then I...I tricked him."

"You're way too hard on yourself, Ellie."

"I promised him our second baby would be planned. Together, I mean." She raised her head to look out at the water. "I never imagined I'd break that promise until..." She couldn't finish.

"Until he volunteered to fight in a war you despise?"

"He told you that?" Ellie jerked her head toward Nina.

"Not really. Only that he was going to Viet Nam and I can't imagine a married medical student with a child is going to get drafted. But then you come hobbling up the road in your hippie cut-offs with that peace necklace on. I teach English, not math, but I still can put two and two together."

Ellie fingered the silver medallion, then dropped both hands to her stomach muscles, still hard and flat. "I'm not going to tell him."

Nina nodded as if she'd already known.

"How stupid is that? To get myself pregnant so he won't go and then—and then not tell him?" Ellie could not believe she was unloading a secret she'd kept so tight to a woman she'd just met.

"Because you love him and down deep you know he has to go." Nina pulled a paper napkin out of a table drawer handing it to Ellie to dry her eyes. "Look, I'm 32 and single, so I'm no authority on romance. But because I do teach at Spring Port High, I read lots of writers who are authorities on the subject. If you won't gag at an English teacher quoting poetry, there's a line in Shakespeare: *Love is not love that alters when it alteration finds.*"

"*Nor bends with the remover to remove.*" Ellie spoke without thinking.

"Hell, I knew I liked you the minute I saw you limp up my hill," Nina slapped her thigh. "The passion I heard in Jim's voice when he talked about Viet Nam—in his mind he *has* to go whether you agree or not. I hate this damned war every bit as much as you do, Ellie. I've already lost one of my students over there and he was just a kid!"

"Jim has to go sometime—every new M.D. gets drafted. But Jim got into the Berry Plan that lets him finish his surgery residency first—and this horrible war can't last forever. He might never have to go. I kept telling him that, begging him if you really want to know. But he'd just look sad and shake his head. I know he thinks it's wrong that college kids get exemptions while working-class kids get drafted."

"Hard to argue that, I guess," Nina said softly.

"But I didn't listen. He was trying to tell me what I wouldn't hear. Then one day Jim sees some asshole burn his draft card on the Diag and goes after him. He almost broke the guy's nose. The next thing I know Jim's signed up with the Army."

"His decision was not as impulsive as it might have seemed."

"But how…how could he do that to Katie and me?" Ellie had asked herself this a million times. Now, even though she'd just met her, she needed to know what Nina Judd thought. She covered her mouth letting the tears run free again.

Nina laid one palm on her arm. "Jim Cameron must love you as much—maybe even more—than you love him. That's why he's going. Twisted reasoning you think, and so might I. But the man you fell in love with and married is the man who has to do this."

"…my only sunshine." Both women looked up at the singing to see Katie waving through the front window from her dad's shoulders. "We're getting the car, Mommy. My suitcase."

"Suitcase?" Ellie looked at Nina who gave her a quick smile.

"Your handsome husband packed some overnight things for all of you—a little surprise. He was going to find a motel."

"But saw the 'For Rent' sign?"

"Put it up two days ago on a lark. Figured a little rent money for the back cabin could buy me some more white paint for this place."

It seemed to Ellie as if Nina's face lit from the inside when she looked out at Lake Michigan.

"You mean we're staying in the dear little cabin back there?" Ellie leaned forward on her elbows.

"Yours for the weekend. Jim and I have a deal."

Ellie turned toward the lake. "I didn't want to come today. Wouldn't have if I'd known about staying overnight. But…"

"It gets to you, doesn't it? The 'big lake'—as they call it around here. You and Jim could use some time listening to the waves. If you'll let me, I'd love taking Katie on a beach walk later on. The only little people in my family are my niece's two children, and they're way back in Connecticut."

"You are not babysitting for us."

"Heck, it'll get me out of painting. I'll show Katie how to find beach treasures. And she can meet my sandpipers. I haven't painted the sign yet, but I'm naming this cottage after them."

"I like the name."

"It was either that or The Alewives. I could never have bought this place if it weren't for the invasion of the alewives after we fished out the lake trout that fed on them. Our beaches can look like alewife mortuaries some mornings."

"I think naming this place after a bird instead of dead fish is nice, Nina," Ellie smiled, and suddenly felt okay. Even more than okay. "And Katie will love looking for beach treasures with you."

"Good. After teaching five sections of seniors this year, I'm over the top with adolescent hormones. Hanging out with a three-year-old will be a kick. I'm thinking she's a pretty smart little cookie."

"Like her dad," Ellie said, almost ready to actually be happy. Then she remembered what she'd done. For the second time she'd created a child to bind him to her. She laid both wrists below her navel. Maybe she would miscarry. A life conceived in such selfishness might not make it to birth.

She thought about their desperate passion the night Jim told her he'd signed up. She'd smashed every plate they owned, then flushed her diaphragm down the toilet. Their furious lovemaking over the following weeks had to conceive a boy. She couldn't imagine a little girl coming out of such tortured love making.

"You and the sonnet, Ellie—you don't strike me as too dumb yourself."
Ellie smiled wistfully. "My enthusiasm for freshman humanities decelerated the day he," she glanced toward the back door, "walked into a café on State Street where my roomates and I were having coffee. All that mattered to me after that was him."

"Mommie, Mommie," Katie burst into the cottage wearing a red bathing suit. "We're back."

"I guess you are, Munchkin," Nina said standing up.

"Daddy's got his bathing suit too. In the log house."

"Your mom's next, Cookie," Nina said carrying the cups to the sink. "And I must say you talk very well for three. First, though, your mom's coming with me to get a couple of my soft old quilts for you guys to snuggle under tonight. It can get cool when the sun goes down."

Katie began hopping her happy dance back outside to find her dad. Ellie trailed Aunt Nina down a long hall lined with boxes of books praying herself into holding this new sense of joy. She could not slip back into the darkness this weekend. For Katie's sake. For Jim's. She looked down at her belly and prayed for the tiny boy she carried. This child born of a broken promise would need all his mother's extra blessings. She laid first one, then the other palm on the bare skin above her navel. Feeling the warmth of her own flesh, Ellie guessed that one day she would have to pay for her selfishness.

T h e   S a n d p i p e r

JAMIE 1998

"You're not ready, Jamie."

"I'm going, Ann—with or without your approval." Jamie felt the dampness begin along her hairline, the air in the small office close. Barefoot, her long legs Indian style in the armless chair, she took a long pull on her water bottle, wondering how people ever got used to the desert. It was smoldering in April.

Jamie studied the incense burning in the open jar on Ann D'Amato's desk trying to resist the silent pull of the social worker's dark eyes. 'Lemon or sage?' she distracted herself. She held back as long as she could stand it, then raised her eyes to meet the older woman's. Ann's lips were pressed together, one hand resting on a closed manila folder in the middle of her desk. Her black reading glasses dangled on a silver chain around her neck.

Mrs. D'Amato hadn't needed to read the chart to get ready for this morning's exit interview. The social worker knew all about Jamie Cameron. The ceiling fan whirred overhead. Well, no. Not all. Jamie absently rubbed the tiny scar on her left ankle with her other foot.

"Jamie, you're so close. Before he left Dr. Summers told me—"

"No." Jamie shot her arm up like a traffic cop. "You're not my therapist, Ann. You have no right." Jamie thrust her legs straight off the seat and began swinging them back and forth.

"I am your caseworker, Jamie, and Dr. Summers thought it was important enough…"

Jamie jumped off the chair and shoved her feet into the black Birkenstocks, smacking each one hard against the wooden floor. "I need to finish packing. Thanks for all you've done."

1

"Dr. Summers did not give me details, of course. That is privileged," the woman with short grey hair continued in her soft, monotone. Jamie didn't move. Since she'd first walked into this office over three months earlier, Jamie had been gentled by Ann's calmness.

"Jamie, my dear," Ann leaned forward on her elbows, "post-traumatic …"

"Bullshit!" Jamie cut her off, stung by the betrayal.

"You didn't listen, Jamie," Ann said, her tone never modulating. "Dr. Summers shared his diagnosis only. Not the cause—the event. And he did that only because he was leaving and thought it was crucial to your recovery. What I know about you—from this room, from group, from your not letting anyone come for family week. Well, it could explain a lot."

"Can I have the car keys now?" Jamie's pulse throbbed in her neck.

The woman sat motionless ignoring Jamie's opened palm. The gurgle from the small zen fountain on the window sill sounded like a waterfall inside Jamie's head.

"One favor. May I ask one?"

"I can't stop you from asking." Jamie didn't move her extended hand.

"Your friend Jake, whatever I might think of him, did bring you to Saguaro and paid for six months. I called him yesterday about your leaving early and taking the car. He refused any refund for your treatment here."

Jamie couldn't smother the sneering snort. "That's his control gear, Ann. You know that. It's his mother's money, anyway, so what the hell. He's got nothing to lose."

"I don't disagree on his motivation. It's healthy for you to see it so clearly. But the fact remains you do have almost three months of unused time. And, let's be honest here, you and me. Relapse is a real possibility. I'm asking, if it happens, will you consider coming back to Saguaro and finishing your work?"

"Not a hot vote of confidence."

"Realism. Most people don't make it. You know that," her voice stressing the last three words. "The psychiatrist coming to take Dr. Summers' place has an excellent reputation. He could pick up with the therapy Dr. Summers was just getting…"

"I don't want to talk about that - any of it right now." Jamie felt a single drop of sweat slide between her breasts. "I'm not going to relapse, screw all the statistics. That's the bottom line. So thank you very much and now can I have the keys?"

Jamie saw a flicker of uneasiness tighten around Ann's eyes. Then she relaxed into a smile and nodded. "Of course, Jamie. You're an adult. It's your car." She leaned over to open a desk drawer, then paused to look up at Jamie, a little smile softening her face. "I can already see it. You'll put the top down before you get to the highway and there'll be one major traffic jam while the truck drivers check out the beautiful young blond in her fancy white convertible."

Jamie had picked out an all white Saab convertible in Aspen as her Christmas present. But then she lost Christmas—and almost herself. Jake had ordered the customized car delivered to a dealership in Tucson instead. "A recovery present," he'd said before flying back to their—to *his* high-ceilinged home on Aspen Mountain. But Jamie knew better. It was his tether to get her back.

Ann handed Jamie the keys. "Have a safe trip to Michigan, to home," Ann said with affection. "Maybe you and Kate can—sorry. Out of line. Counseling's over. Drive carefully, my dear. Please let us hear from you."

Kate. A wave if anxiety rose in Jamie. Once her dearest friend in the world. She wrapped her fingers tightly around the leather key holder. A sudden chill made her feel naked. Fragile. She stared down at the keys. For the first time in three months, she was free. A car. Money in her purse. A charge card. All high-risk stuff for an alcoholic. Worse, she was headed to a Spring Port mined with memories that could blow up under her.

Panic spiked her like an electric current. Ann was right. She wasn't ready. And Ann's tentative look said she knew Jamie knew it too. Reading Jamie's thoughts, Ann said quietly, "One day at a time. That's all you have to do now."

Jamie nodded but didn't move. Then she took a half step toward Ann. "If it weren't for Aunt Nina…"

"I know, Jamie. You're needed there."

Jamie hesitated, then forced a smile. "I will keep in touch."

Ann D'Amato blew her a kiss and smiled back. "I'd like to think so, but I won't sit by the phone."

The two women laughed at the same moment. Then Jamie left the office without looking back, and closed the door behind her.

Jamie slammed the trunk over her four crammed suitcases, three of them filled with clothes she'd never unpacked from Colorado. She'd given the skinny jeans and tee shirts she'd worn every day since January to her roommate. Roxie had two more months at the Saguaro Rehabilitation Clinic, and then she could dump them. Or pass them on to the next underweight addict. Jamie heard a commotion and looked up to see her friends from group coming across the parking lot toward the car.

3

"I told you guys not to," Jamie said feeling her eyes sting again. "I'm tired of crying. We said our goodbyes upstairs."

"Hey, nice wheels, bitch," Roxie said as she struck an angular pose to model the black nylon running suit Jamie'd left on her bed that morning. "Here. We got a present for you. Everyone in group signed it."

"Even Howard," Maxine said talking around a burning cigarette, "and he never signs shit for nobody."

Inside the cover of the navy Recovery Bible, Jamie saw the scrawls and good luck wishes from people whose deepest secrets she knew—and who knew most of hers. The signatures blurred, and she pulled her tortoise sunglasses down from the top of her head. "I said I am not crying anymore, you assholes. Now get out of here."

As she started to open the car door, Roxie handed her a brown paper bag. Stapled across the closed top was a sheet of paper typewritten in big letters: PLEASE GIVE TO JAMIE CAMERON. "This was outside our door this morning. We're dying to know what's in it. But, see," Roxie ran her finger along the staples, "in our new lives of absolute honesty, we didn't peek."

Without hesitation, Jamie ripped open the staples and looked down at a full cactus plant covered in fuchsia blossoms. She started to lift it out when she saw the familiar handwriting. *Jamie* in tight script on a small ivory envelope underneath the terra cotta pot.

"Oh," she forced a laugh and twisted the top of the bag closed. "I forgot about this. A cactus I gave one of the cleaning girls. She probably thought I wanted it back." Jamie looked at each of her friends with a shrug, grateful for the sunglasses.

"Shit. Nothing exciting ever happens around here," Roxie said grabbing Jamie in a big hug. "Hey," she whispered. Don't let your bitch sister bring you down. A harder squeeze. "Are you listening?"

Jamie dug her head into Roxie's shoulder, but couldn't trust her voice. They'd heard all about Kate in group.

"And don't forget about the wisdom," Tanya yelled out as Jamie climbed into the car.

Jamie looked over at Tanya and gave her the thumbs-up. "You got it, Tee. Serenity forever." Then Jamie held her new Recovery Bible out the open window and kissed the cover. "Thank you. Thank you. I love you crazy psycho addicts."

Out her rearview window, she could still see them waving as she pulled onto Mission Road. The white canvas top hummed overhead as it collapsed into itself on the back ledge. Ann had been wrong. Jamie was not waiting until she got to Interstate 10 before she put the top down. She'd also been wrong to bring up Kate. It reminded Jamie how much she dreaded seeing her sister again. But Ann D'Amato had not been wrong about anything else.

Jamie looked down at the brown bag on the passenger seat. Her instinct was to heave it over the car's open side and let the plant smash all over the desert road that was taking her away from to the Saguaro Clinic. But the plant couldn't hurt her. The letter was another story. The smart thing would be to rip it up without opening it. Jamie Cameron, however, had not been doing smart things for a long time now.

She grabbed the envelope from the bottom of the bag, and slid her scarlet thumbnail under the flap to open it. Pulling the elastic band off her ponytail and shaking her hair loose in the hot air, Jamie held it up by the windshield and began to read.

T h e   S a n d p i p e r

KATE

Pete and her mother didn't like it, but Kate loved running alone in the grey-pink edges of dawn. Joe O'Connor, her best reporter at the newspaper, had warned Kate about running alone at this hour. Even on the groomed bike path undulating along Lakeshore a sand dune away from Lake Michigan, bad things could happen. Joe had made a point of telling her the nasty details of his interview with a Muskegon woman attacked a block from her home.

But nearing the cross street where she would turn back toward her house, Kate could feel nothing but safe, even in the semi-darkness. It wasn't even a mile from The Sandpiper, the cottage where she and Jamie had spent their best summer days. Yes, she felt safe here. But also sad. Just thinking about The Sandpiper hurt because it was where her Aunt Nina lived.

Aunt Nina, her high forehead of intelligence, her thick auburn hair that refused to go grey. The strength of spirit modeled in her defined jawbone. But all overwhelmed by the pure grey eyes of Athena that sparkled with a rebel's love of mischief. The woman who'd helped raise Kate was dying. And Kate could not think of a world without Aunt Nina in it.

In ways, over the years since she'd left Spring Port, Kate often missed Aunt Nina more than her mother. Her mother's own wounds had left her vulnerable, and Kate knew to tiptoe around her. But not Aunt Nina. No, Helena Judd was as open and encompassing as the big lake she'd taught Kate and Jamie to love.

Only once had Aunt Nina let Kate down. "Nobody can get into Duke from Spring Port High, chickadee," she'd said. "And even if you could get in, they don't call them Blue Devils for nothing. They don't need to give scholarships for brains because they don't have to. And your mom can't afford it."

Kate could still feel the shock of hurt at Aunt Nina's response. From Kate's earliest memories of Aunt Nina, all she'd ever heard was almost embarrassing praise. Yet Kate had taken Aunt Nina's confidence into herself like a brook drawing from a river. And then the rejection of the dream Kate had wanted most of all. But Kate proved Aunt Nina wrong. And no one hugged harder than Nina Judd when the acceptance letter and academic scholarship from Duke came. How unimportant that all seemed now.

All the times they'd been together since then, every time Kate came home from school or Chicago, she saw Aunt Nina. But it wasn't the same. And Aunt Nina was too perceptive not to feel the nuance of distancing. How wrong of Kate to have held onto such an immature grudge. And now Kate was going to lose Aunt Nina. She could already feel the leak in her heart.

The whine of a passing motorcycle brought Kate back. This last stretch of path before she turned around ran along Sheldon, the shortcut street Michigan Power Plant workers took to their early shifts. So maybe some of these dawn drivers did check her out in the black running tights. She breathed in the mix of pine and spruce, the April lake breeze fresh on her cheeks. She wasn't worried. Nothing to fear from guys leaning out their truck windows to yell, "Nice ass." The loud ones might be jerks, but harmless. It was the ones you never heard coming.

Pete wanted a big dog she could run with these dark mornings. But, then, he'd been jaded by what had rolled through the ER doors of Cook County Hospital. She'd watched some of her husband's North Carolina innocence bleed away with the brutalized people he helped put back together. But it was for more than Kate's protector. As long as she'd known him, Pete had talked about the thick-shouldered lab he was going to have some day. A dog like Pogo, the black lab his neighbors had when Pete was growing up.

Kate slowed her pace as she turned away from the big lake and toward their Cape Cod house in the new Birchbark subdivision south of Spring Port. She pulled the headband off, rubbing one palm into her short black hair and watched the sparkles of gold ignite the tree tops. *I'll tell you how the sun rose, a ribbon at a time,* poetry she didn't know she remembered. But she did know why the line came.

Aunt Nina loved Emily Dickinson. Like Aunt Nina, Emily Dickinson never married—never had her own children, loved words. Aunt Nina was the one who'd filled Kate's soul with stories and poetry. Kate loved language because Aunt Nina had loved it first.

She stretched one leg to avoid stepping on a sidewalk crack. Since she and Pete had moved from their Chicago apartment to Spring Port and a home with a yard, Kate stalled about getting a dog. Dirt and shedding and how could they train a puppy when they both worked? But it wasn't the truth. The fear her rational Pete would never understand was that a puppy might jinx them. Kate knew too many childless couples putting Santa hats on their dogs for photo Christmas cards. Kate had to do everything right to get this baby. A dog felt like bad karma. Like giving up.

She hated how everything in her life was about getting pregnant. What she ate and did not drink. Most of all, when she and Pete could have sex. She missed the way it used to be—their heart-sweat passion at the barest touch of fingers ending up in the bedroom—if they made it that far. Her eyes stung in the brisk wind. Already those times seemed like an old love song they'd forgotten the words to. Now the calendar decreed their sex lives. Pete, God love him, still whispered the special erotic tease words. But it wasn't the same.

The startled call of a robin cut into her thoughts. A sign winter was over even while her breathing made white puffs in the cold air. The robin would lay her sky-blue eggs as surely as Kate had known she and Pete would have a baby whenever they wanted. But it hadn't worked out that way. Kate hit her shoe hard against the tarmac to fight back the remorse. Her career. Pete's ortho residency had come first. They'd taken no chances on a pregnancy. Now she blamed her nine years on the pill for her infertility. She'd wanted a masters and Chicago Tribune bylines more than a baby.

But if she couldn't change the past, why did she have to keep blaming herself for it? She thought of a story Aunt Nina once told her about a farmer who cleared all the rocks out of his field one fall. But the next spring, the farmer found new boulders the ground had heaved up over the winter. "Like regrets that won't stay buried," Aunt Nina had said.

Kate pulled a water bottle from the refrigerator and gulped until she had to breathe. Then she hit the button on her answering machine blinking three messages. Her mother's deep alto came on. "Hi, honey. Sorry to call so early. I wanted to catch you before work to see if—if you and Pete could maybe come for dinner tomorrow night?"

Kate wondered why her mother seemed hesitant.

"It's short notice, but I thought, well, I'd make Pete's lasagna. Call me when you can—please, honey."

"Kate, Joe here." Kate squeezed the bottle until her mouth filled with water.

"Hey, assuming you survived your jog in the dark, this is a heads-up about the old beach photos. Remember, bring me anything you got of Lighthouse Beach. The camp sites' story." Kate had forgotten. "Anyone organized like you are has scrapbooks—probably in chronological order. See you at the editorial meeting. Later."

The third message clicked in. "Oh, Kate, I forgot." Her mother was talking too fast. "Could you and Pete pick up Aunt Nina for me? The last chemo really knocked her down, but now she's ready for an outing. Hope that works. Thanks Katie."

"Katie!" The word stunned her. It was her little girl name—the one that had died with her dad. No one ever used it anymore. Certainly not her mother.

Kate pulled the day planner out of her purse sitting on the white formica counter. Pete was on call Friday night, but with any luck, dinner would work. If no one turned up at the Waters Hospital's ER with a broken arm for a few hours, Pete could count on one good meal this week. She loved her mother's face when Pete told people he'd married Kate for her mother's cooking.

Kate went into the second bedroom they used as an office—but not forever, she prayed. Her mother had no idea how hard Kate was trying to give her a grandchild—and how much that failure hurt. Pete thought it wrong of Kate not to tell her mother what was so important to Kate. But since the day the soldiers with stiff shoulders knocked on the door of Aunt Nina's back cabin, Kate's job had been clear. She had to protect her mother.

It was why she'd covered for Jamie so many times. Why she'd never told her mother about a midnight drive from Chicago to Ann Arbor to bail her younger sister out of jail for drunk driving. It was why she and Pete had borrowed money to quietly get Jamie into a 30-day program in Brighton—only to have Jamie walk away after a week.

Needing to think about anything else, she yanked a red vinyl photo album out of its exact spot on the shelf and thought about Joe's comment. She wished she could be more spontaneous—more fun. Like Jamie—at least like the old Jamie she'd loved so much. But to survive in that dark time when Katie grew into Kate, she'd learned to tighten her grip. She did not dare loosen it now.

The first page she turned to was a photo of Aunt Nina in an inner tube, laughing at the whitecaps splashing around her. And now dear Aunt Nina was fighting a recurrence of breast cancer. The damp of Kate's sports bra made her shiver. She was glad her mother wanted her to pick up Aunt Nina Friday night.

Since moving back to Spring Port, Kate had not helped Aunt Nina with the chemo, telling herself Helena Judd didn't want someone clucking around trying to be useful. Besides, Kate knew Aunt Nina's investment-club friends drove Aunt Nina to treatments and brought in dinner twice a week.

She watched a goldfinch—still wearing his winter greys—glide in to take the chickadee's roost. Kate could not rationalize her way out of selfishness. The truth was she couldn't stand to deliver Aunt Nina into the white-cold walls with their Lysol odors and IV stands. As long as she didn't go there, Kate could put off the future. Could avoid the unacceptable reality that Nina Judd, the one who'd carried the three Cameron women through the ripping tragedy of their lives, might not always be around.

Kate shook her head in shame. All she'd cared about was saving herself from pain she couldn't bear. She didn't like herself very much at that moment. But she made herself clamp her jaws tight against the rising guilt. She couldn't go there now, not with the new fertility drug bombarding her ovaries. In time she would make it right with the woman who long ago taught her to see with clear eyes. To accept the hardest truth of all.

In the black days after the soldiers came and Ellie Cameron turned to stone, Aunt Nina was the one who'd squeezed Katie's hand beside the coffin draped with an American flag. Later, their mother got better and remembered she had Katie and a new baby daughter. After that, Ellie Cameron worked overtime to make happy for her girls—to make up for leaving them those first months. Ellie Cameron's way of gentling their fatherless lives was to pretend away any painful subjects. And on the most painful of all, she was the most silent. So many years ago, Jim Cameron had died in a jungle on the other side of the world. And his widow still never talked about it.

Kate turned to a colored picture of Jamie and her in matching green velvet Christmas dresses sitting beside their mother and Aunt Nina. On the facing page, a muscular young man bare to the waist faked a grimace as he gripped two small calves dangling over his chest, his curly black hair fisted into toddler hands. The little girl with the same ebony hair grinning into the camera above her father's laughing eyes was called Katie. Jamie never could have such a photo with their father. Kate could not let herself forget how much more Jamie had lost than she had.

She quickly flipped the page over, riffling the plastic edges until she came to the snapshots of Lighthouse Beach State Park. One was in front of Gertie's Diner with Sarah Quinn, her best high school friend, Jamie, and a bunch of their classmates eating hot dogs at an outside picnic table. She slid the three pictures out of their plastic cases for Joe and started to close the book.

A photo she'd almost forgotten stopped her. She and Jamie, brown arms against their white Camp Arbutus tee shirts, leaned their shoulders tight together as if holding each other up. Then Kate saw her bandaged left knee.

* * *

Kate Cameron didn't hear but sensed her little sister creep away under the heavy canvas. Peering through the hot tent, Kate squinted to see the dim outline of an empty cot where nine-year old Jamie should be. It had been breezeless that day, the July sun on fire. Flopping on her cot after taps, Jamie had said she felt like one of Aunt Nina's roasted marshmallows and she'd never get to sleep.

Kate rolled off her cot and began crawling, furious at herself for not paying more attention to Jamie's comment. At twelve, Kate was already used to getting Jamie out of trouble. She slid between the tent stakes wanting to shake her sister like a naughty kitten. It was easy for Jamie to break the rules because she always had Kate to bail her out.

As she stood up on her bare feet, Kate realized she didn't have a flashlight. Luckily the three-quarters moon uncovered the dirt path winding down the dune to Lake Arbutus. Kate knew where Jamie was. The youngest girl in camp, Jamie was the best swimmer. She was also the camper who two days earlier had taken off on the camp's fastest horse during a morning trail ride. Leaping fences as they galloped cross-country, Jamie's blond pigtails and Black Diamond's flying tail had feathered out behind them like shared wings.

Later Jamie told the red-faced riding counselor the horse had run away with her. But no one who watched the poetry of animal and rider believed it. That wasn't the first trouble Jamie caused. Before that was her larkspur and lupine centerpiece for the counselors' table touched up with sprigs of poison ivy.

Kate felt her way down the uneven path, the moon's reflection on the water like liquid light. This midnight swim would get Jamie sent home, wasting the bar tips their mother had set aside all winter for the expensive Camp Arbutus. Kate heard the splashing before she saw Jamie's shoulders like a pair of silver fish knifing in and out of the water. From the shore Kate hissed snake-like at Jamie trying not to wake anyone. But Jamie was lost to her own world. In frustration, Kate pulled off her night shirt and went in after her.

Suddenly, like an absolution, the cool water washed away Kate's anger. When Jamie broke the surface for air and saw Kate swimming beside her, her younger sister's face glistened with startled pleasure.

Afterwards on the path, the warm night air caressed Kate's sunburned arms when she suddenly turned to make sure Jamie was still behind her. The quick move made Kate lose her balance and stumble, a sharp pain jabbing her knee. At once Jamie was beside Kate, patting the cut with the bottom of her wet tee shirt. Then, in the gleam between moon shadows, Kate was appalled to see Jamie dab her own forehead with Kate's blood. "Jamie" she started to blurt. But then she saw Jamie's upturned face, something sacred in her expression, and stopped. Wordlessly Kate leaned down to touch a finger to her knee, too, and marked her forehead like Jamie's.

In the simple language of innocence, they pledged a fidelity to each other beyond their bond as sisters. No one would ever know about the midnight swim. From that night on, neither would betray the other's secrets. No matter what happened. No matter what.

*   *   *

Kate's chest hurt. That had been another world. A time when Jamie was her dearest friend. All at once Kate knew. Her mother's nervousness on the phone. That kind of stress could be about only one thing. Friday night's dinner was about Jamie.

T h e   S a n d p i p e r

JAMIE

A soft rain redolent of Midwest farm country began falling as Jamie left Colorado and crossed into Nebraska. The pores of her skin felt renewed by the moisture. She was a water person, after all, the desert as alien to her as the moon. "Half fish," Coach Briggs used to say, punching his stopwatch.

She lifted her face to the last sprinkles, before the Saab's canvas top moved over her like a small cave. The rain felt like tears, as if the mountains she was leaving behind wept her departure—as if they sympathized with her dangerous journey. Every mile she closed between her speeding car and the small town on Lake Michigan tightened her vigilance. Listening to Celine Dion singing about "my heart will go on," visualizing the Titanic sinking, Jamie prayed for herself. Her own heart's needs. If she was to do this thing, she needed to stay focused. Clear. Vigilant. Otherwise she couldn't help Aunt Nina—or herself.

She glanced at the clock adding the hour to Tucson time as a silver semi outlined in yellow lights sprayed her windshield with dirty water. The first mistake she was not going to make was Omaha. She pinched her shoulders together gauging the soreness of a long day behind the wheel. The speed, she loved. The slipstream of landscape on both sides. But her need for freedom— for movement resisted the diagonal strap pinning her to the car seat for long hours.

It would have been smarter to take I70 through Kansas City and avoid Omaha altogether. Then there'd be no temptation to thumb the phone book and see if Merit Financial was still headquartered there. She didn't need to check Merit's small Michigan branch in Spring Port. It had closed abruptly when Jamie was eighteen. But instead she'd taken 76 north east out of Denver. Now she either had to stop this side of Nebraska's capital or get a good hour east of it.

The pressure of a full bladder decided it. She moved into the exit lane at 83. She had been confined long enough. Tomorrow she would speed around Omaha in the morning and spend the night near Chicago. Then she'd have an easy three hours on Saturday to reach Spring Port. Her mother wasn't looking for her before Saturday night.

She was following the Platte River toward a Holiday Inn sign when the car phone rang. For a moment she stared at the sleek black receiver. The only person who'd know this number was the person who'd given it to her. Another tether. If he'd called only ten minutes later, she wouldn't have heard it. Wouldn't have felt obligated to pick up. Jake Menard never said she owed him, which was shrewd. It made her own sense of indebtedness worse.

"Can't get away with anything can I? How you doing, Jake?"

"Lonesome, baby. How's the car working?" She felt the net tighten.

"It's a generous gift. More than I deserve—as we both know." She put on her blinker to turn left into the motel parking lot. Jake probably had saved her life, whether she'd wanted him to or not. In his own spoiled way, he had a good heart.

"Nothing's too good for you, sweetie. So what's this shit about us staying apart another three months. Hell, it's been three already." She heard him swallow and visualized the green Beck's bottle upended in his hand. It used to be fun, the two of them après-ski getting loaded on the wrap-around leather sofa looking out on Ajax Mountain.

"You know perfectly well, Jake. They told you the day you dropped me off. No relationships the first year sober. You want the car back, fine." He shouldn't have called when he was drinking.

"Hey, cool your jets, baby. I'm asking is all. The car's yours. The credit cards—all of it." She heard the click of another bottle cap popping off.

"It's just—well, who wouldn't get pissed for paying to get his girl dried out and then hearing he has to disappear? I mean what kind of shit is that?" He was slurring now. She used to think he was cuter when he was drinking. But that was because she was getting wasted with him. Right now she didn't need this.

"Jake, I'm in the Holiday Inn parking lot about to wet my pants. I really gotta go."

"I care about you, Jamie. Really care—like nobody ever, you know that, baby." Jake, attractive in a raw-boned, cowboy way, always went sentimental in his booze. Her drunks skidded into black depression.

"Jake, I really have to pee. I'll call you. Take care." She hit the 'end' button before he could respond. She could still hear the phone ringing as she went into the lobby to ask for a first-floor room. She wanted to park outside the door and not unpack.

The sting of the hot water on her face told her she'd left the top down too long in the spring sun. Tomorrow she'd use sunscreen and wear her Colorado Rockies baseball cap. She wasn't going to call Jake back. Maybe not for a long time. She pulled her damp hair back in a pony tail and threw on black slacks and a white cotton turtleneck. She hadn't eaten since breakfast. And the Saguaro Clinic's mantra was never to get too hungry, tired, lonely, or bored. A juicy hamburger rare sounded like the best thing in the world right then.

The waitress turned toward the small table Jamie pointed out in the far corner of the busy motel restaurant. Following the woman closely, Jamie kept her eyes on the green speckled carpet wanting not to be noticed. As a teenager she'd enjoyed—encouraged, actually—the male glances that stuck to her like lint on black velvet. "A tease" they'd called her in high school. How naive she'd been. And what a price she'd paid for it.

She took the chair facing the wall, her back to the room. The waitress brought her a carafe of decaf and went to put in the order for a blood-red hamburger loaded with fried onions. Jamie began reading the newspaper she'd picked up in the lobby when the long-stemmed glass appeared from nowhere. Jamie pulled back as if it were a living thing, her palms immediately sweaty.

"Sorry to startle you, but you look like a vintage merlot woman to me," a deep voice said beside her.

She whipped her head up to see a man in a pin-striped business suit, his graying sideburns too long, watching her from the next table. "I'm not," she said willing her hand not to shake as she picked up the glass and set it on his table.

"I'm usually right," he said giving a friendly shrug as he pulled the glass back. "Too classy for beer—maybe a chardonnay? Gin and tonic?"

Not reading a word, she kept her eyes on the front page and said, "No thank you." Her mother had pushed good manners; Aunt Nina, civility. "If you can't be polite, Jamie—"Aunt Nina had told her, "you can at least be civil." That quelled her impulse to heave one arm at the glass of merlot and watch it darken the man's creased pants like blood.

"Heading east or west?"

Jamie took a deep breath, then put the newspaper down. "I'm sorry but—" she paused to let the waitress deliver the hamburg encircled by fries. "I don't drink and my husband wouldn't appreciate…"

"No wedding ring," the man pointed at her left hand. "And no tan line from wearing one." Jamie looked down at the plate, her stomach suddenly queasy. She had to get out of there. Away from this man and his wine beckoning like a lost friend. "I'd like to take this to my room," she called after the waitress.

"Join you?" he asked, his voice now slippery.

Jake's boozy call had already triggered drinking thoughts. This man was dangerous. She shoved herself away from the table and stood up, suddenly aware she hadn't bothered with a bra. Pulling one arm self consciously across her chest, she leaned toward him, her flesh warm.

In a quiet whisper, she said slowly, "I just did three months of drug rehab because my heart stopped the day before Christmas from ODing on coke, and I never do drugs unless I'm drunk. And, yes, merlot is my drink of choice."

She grabbed her plate and left, but not before she had the kick of seeing tiny sweat pearls bead along the man's forehead. Inside her skull she could imagine Aunt Nina saying, "Sometimes, Jamie, with perfect creeps—civility be damned."

Her heart didn't quiet until she finally crawled into bed. She reached for the new Recovery Bible, desperate for some reassurance. She opened the book at random and read the first thing she saw. *Now no one in Israel was as handsome as Absalom.* Oh shit, she thought, then apologized to the open book. Of course she'd land on *that* family! The last place she wanted to go. She grabbed a thick chunk of pages and flipped forward into the New Testament.

She stopped at the Recovery Bible's headline, "Delayed Gratification." She began reading from James. *Resist the Devil, and he will flee from you.* That's more like it, she thought skimming the short book of letters. It wasn't until she came to the passage where James said to *get rid of all the filth and evil in your lives* that something hit her. She could not help smiling. The Book of James and Jamie. He'd grown up in the shadow of a perfect older sibling too. Maybe the Bible was written for her after all. She switched off the light and finally fell asleep.

Suddenly the tall figure was coming at her, the thick arms—the stink of wine breath as he pressed against her kneeing her legs apart, the sharp pain at her foot. Then the hurt, oh the hurt…

Jamie jolted up in bed, her heart beating wildly in the strange room. As she gasped for air, her fingernails dug at her left ankle. Her chest heaving, she knew why the old nightmare had returned. Ann should not have talked about 'post-traumatic stress.' Shouldn't have put in Jamie's mind the scum bag who'd bragged about flying jets. How stupid she'd been to think Roger Hamper was somehow like Lt. James Cameron because they'd both been in the military!

Dr. Summers was the first person she'd ever told—the only person who knew why a married Marine pilot had driven himself off a Spring Port, Michigan, bridge. She should have thrown the cactus away in Tucson.

The red digital numbers read 3:42 a.m. Her sleeping was done. It didn't matter that she had stopped short of Omaha. Or that she'd slammed the pages down on Absalom, the defiler. In the deep of her subconscious, connections had been made.

She hit every light switch in the room to drive the image away. She splashed her face with cold water and brushed her teeth. Then she pulled on jeans and an ASU sweatshirt. A large coffee and gas were all she needed before getting on I 80 and straight through to Spring Port. She could not risk another motel with a bar and some horny guy handing out drinks.

Within minutes she'd checked out and was turning on the highway, the power to her car phone turned off. She couldn't deal with Jake today. What she had to do was going to take every shred of strength she had. And even that might not be enough.

The first sight of Lake Michigan around Chicago, the white cresting on blue, pulled the exhaustion out of Jamie, her muscles softening like warm snow. By early evening she spotted the tall striped stacks of the Michigan Power Plant marking Sheldon Road as she passed Aunt Nina's cottage, her favorite place on earth, The Sandpiper.

Continuing north into town, Jamie breathed in the familiar spring scents of Lake Michigan, a rich blend of pine and cherry blossoms with a hint of fishiness. Aunt Nina told her the Ojibwas were the ones who named it "Michigan,'" Algonquian for "big lake." For Jamie, the "big lake" was home.

Dionne Warwick was singing "a little prayer for you" on an oldies station when Jamie parked in front of the small two-story grey house near downtown Spring Port where she and Kate had grown up. A white sedan she didn't recognize was parked in the driveway. Her fingers jittered as she picked up the cactus, its brown paper bag forgotten in a Starbucks wastebasket outside North Platte. With careful movements, she began walking up her mother's driveway. She could hear someone talking on the backyard deck that ran off her mother's kitchen.

"Jamie…" She heard her mother's voice. Jamie stopped moving and stared blankly into the familiar chaos of scattered coolers and dish boxes inside the detached garage. Kate always kept the door closed when they were growing up. Her older sister never wanted their mother to be a cateress.

"...Roger Hamper's death." Jamie held her breath as her mother's voice carried around the house. "That's when Jamie's drinking started to get so bad. Remember how Roger was, well, almost like a father to Jamie that summer before she went to Michigan? His death had to be huge blow to her."

Jamie exhaled a puff of gratitude. Her mother still didn't know what happened the night Mr. Hamper died. Kate had not betrayed Jamie's terrible secret. Her sister had honored their blood oath.

"Do we have to keep talking about Jamie's problems?" Kate's voice now, Jamie listening as the pink sky darkened above her.

"Well, I hardly know your sister, Kate," now Pete's soft Southern accent, "but what I do know is she set the curve in calculus her first year at Michigan. You told me that yourself."

"You're right, Pete," the unexpectedness of Aunt Nina's voice caught Jamie off guard, "and she kept making those grades until," a pause, "well, her senior year."

Jamie heard the drop Aunt Nina's tone with those last words. Now she could not wait another second. She'd come home to care for Nina Judd, to make up for all her alcoholic behavior. To make up it up for leaving Michigan that last semester and breaking Aunt Nina's and her mother's hearts. Breaking them once again.

She walked quietly back to her car at the curb, ran a brush through her hair, dabbed on lipstick, and then slammed the door hard.

She was almost at the back door when the wet nose kissed her bare calf. "Dear old Ginger." Jamie set down the cactus and kneeled to scratch the spaniel's floppy ears. The neighbor's dog yipped her welcoming bark as Jamie laid her head on Ginger's. Dogs and horny men can always smell me, Jamie thought, nuzzling into the wiggly blur of brown and white.

Then they were all coming out the door toward her, her mother in the lead, Aunt Nina close behind. Jamie's throat tightened as she embraced them both in one huge hug, trying not to feel Aunt Nina's sharp shoulder blades. "Kate, Pete," she called to them, unable to stop the tears.

"Hey," she surprised herself by saying, "I brought you guys a cactus from Arizona. It's over a century old."

She had wanted to dump the plant. Get rid of the memory. But typical Jamie, the impulsive alcoholic, she'd ruined her own plan. O.K. So now she would share plant cuttings with all of them, but nothing more. Somewhere east of Albuquerque the letter was blowing in scattered pieces across the spread of desert.

The   Sandpiper

KATE

"Editorial meeting in ten, Kate, but first the big boss." Marcia, the receptionist for Spring Port's Lakeshore News, pointed toward the publisher's office as she peered over red reading glasses. "And a man named Hal Carter called from Los Angeles. I told him to call back after your meeting."

"Never heard of him. Any message?"

Marcia shrugged. "That's all he said." Marcia's desk inside the newspaper's front door was squeezed between two thick ferns spilling out of brass containers. With her round cheeks and easy smile, Marcia was the first impression visitors got of the upstart weekly paper. It was a good one.

With no competition, Spring Port's only daily had loped lamely along for years. That made the nerviness of this little weekly more than galling. It worried the owners of the The Spring Port Daily News.

"I brought in an extra mocha lattee." Marcia cocked her head in a half-question. Giving up caffeine on her fertility hormones had been harder for Kate than she'd expected—the wine at dinner much easier. But, then, she knew too much about drinking.

She'd studied Jamie's vivid blue eyes the night her sister got home from Tucson. Jamie's eyes never lied. And, even after 14 hours of driving, they were clear as an eagle's. Her sister had made it home from treatment sober. Kate raised a no-thank-you hand to Marcia.

"Don't know how you live in this den of coffee freaks, Kate. Great outfit, by the way."

Kate had to look down to remember she'd put on her short red jacket over a black shell and plaid skirt. Growing up she'd always wanted to dress like her best friend Sarah Quinn's mother with her big-city styles of contrast fabrics and chunky jewelry.

Kate's own mother worked too many hours to dress up, except for church. But when Ellie Cameron did put on a dress suit and heels, with her high cheeks and wide-set dark eyes, she looked Italian enough for an Amalfi photo shoot. Aunt Nina always said Ellie Cameron had an inborn classiness other women would kill for.

"Kate, good, have a seat," George Lathrup said as she walked into his office. A husky man, Lathrup was an MBA who also valued solid writing. It was one reason Kate took the Lakeshore News job over more money from the Spring Port Daily. The other reason was that Lathrup let her work her own hours, a must for short-notice blood tests and ultrasounds.

"I'll get right to the point," as if he didn't always, Kate thought. He spread his thick fingers open on the desk. "We have an editorial meeting in five minutes. You're doing such a great job for us I'm getting sick of people telling me your damn *Ms.Cellaneous* is the first thing they read." George Lathrup's left eye had a tendency to wander when he smiled.

"I still vote not to have my picture run with it."

"You've been most accommodating about that," George acknowledged raising his palms.

"How could I not? The new kid gets her own column? It's a small price to pay even if it means getting stopped at Meijer's to hear how lakeshore developers are ruining Spring Port."

"I get that. It gets old. Look, right now what I need from you is to hand off your reporting assignments and become my executive assistant—be me when I'm not around."

She tilted her head like a robin trying to hear better.

"I've decided to buy two struggling weeklies up north, and it'll take time to get them up to speed. We promised we'd grow when we hired you. And I'm convinced the future of the newspaper business is local news and weeklies do it best. I'm guessing that's why you took us over the daily."

With a masters in journalism from Medill, experience copywriting for a media company, and stringing for the Chicago Tribune, Kate had been flattered, if not surprised, when both Spring Port papers made her offers. Kate Cameron Shane had a clear sense about what she could accomplish. She wondered if other self-assured people could name the exact hour their confidence kicked in. Kate could almost feel the textured envelope from Duke.

That letter had told Kate she could do anything she wanted if she just worked hard enough. That's how she got to be Spring Port's valedictorian. And the state swim championship senior year hadn't hurt either, even though she knew it was a fluke when Coach Briggs told her she'd qualified for the state team.

The night the Spring Port girls won the Class B State Swimming Championship had been one of Kate's happiest because it was freshman Jamie Cameron who'd done it. Jamie's two record-breaking times had pulled the whole team to the victory podium. Kate had never been so proud of her little sister. How long ago it all seemed.

"Joe's your back-up," Lathrup broke into the memory. "You know he's solid. We're beefing up our business coverage, and he'll need your help on the local angles." George Lathrup kept talking, not seeming to notice her flushed skin.

"I'm not so sure about local angles, Mr. Lathrup. I've lived away since high school."

"Yeah, but people out there," he pointed at the window, "give you leads because they remember you—Spring Port's shining star. Besides, everyone in town knows your mother."

With a whispering sadness, Kate realized Mr. Lathrup didn't even know she had a sister.

An hour later Kate rocked in her computer chair, the telephone pressed to her ear. The hospital operator came on the line to say Dr. Shane wasn't answering the overhead page. She'd hang on. Tossed like a dinghy on the big lake by Jamie's return the week before and now this job promotion, she'd barely tracked the discussion during the editorial meeting.

"Oh, Mrs. Shane," the switchboard operator came back. "Dr. Shane is finishing surgery. He'll call you in the next few minutes."

Kate thanked her and punched in the computer button, the booting sounds humming her to finish the column she'd started. As the computer ran through its screens, she gazed out the window. Her second-floor office overlooked the harbor where Angel Lake connected to Lake Michigan. Lighthouse Beach, with its signature red lighthouse at the end of a concrete pier, wrapped along the Lake Michigan shoreline beyond the distant sand dunes.

A few cars idled below, a scattering of pedestrians in sight. By Memorial Day, the street would be filled with SUVs pulling trailers with boats and jet skis. Tourists wearing Spring Port tee shirts and flip-flops would become moving patches of color gliding between the docks and the Harbor Street stores. Kate turned to pick up the ringing phone.

"Hal Carter out in California, Kate," a male voice said. "I called earlier. I'm trying to find your sister. Jamie."

Kate stood still at the window, the spring sun on her back suddenly chilly. Jamie had only been back a week, and it was beginning already.

"I knew her at Michigan," Hal went on, oblivious to Kate's silence. He had the glib speech of a lobbyist. "We partied together—you know how it is."

Kate knew far too much about how it is.

"Jamie left school all of a sudden our last year and I lost track of her. But I sure didn't forget her." Something musky in his tone repulsed Kate.

"You see a few of my buddies raise a little hell on the slopes every year. Last December, we hit Aspen and we're heading up the mountain one morning gawking at this blond in a purple one-piece boogieing over the moguls. Our chair gets closer, and I almost fell off. It's Jamie Cameron! My three buddies say fifty bucks I don't know her so we go looking."

"I'm sort of waiting for a phone call, Mr. Carter." Kate couldn't pretend to be interested.

"But you gotta hear this. We're on this steep mother when Jamie comes flying out of the trees over a bunch of rocks and does this helicopter spin—you know the ski thing." Kate remembered the ski poster in pure whites and blues Jamie used to have over her bed. For a moment she thought she might cry. What had happened to that Jamie?

"Jamie's a natural athlete," Kate heard herself say without intending to. She felt a pinch in her ribs seeing the grace of her sister's arms pulling through the water.

"I'm divorced, by the way, Kate. Just so you don't get the wrong idea about me." Kate almost laughed at him. But she did not want to prolong the conversation. At last Hal seemed to pick up on her attitude.

"Okay. Bottom line, we had a ball that day even though none of us could ski up with her. We closed the lifts, then Jamie and I had a few drinks. She said this guy she was living with—Jake, I think, anyway they weren't getting along. She was thinking of moving out."

To move right in with you! Kate felt herself getting angry. The old protectiveness for little sister kicked in.

"We were supposed to meet the next morning to ski, but she never showed. My only way to find her was through your newspaper. I remembered Lakeshore because Jamie talked so much about Lake Michigan. And she was really pumped about how well you were doing with your own column."

Kate felt her eyebrows go up in surprise that Jamie would care. She was probably high, Kate thought—and then felt a quick shame for assuming that.

"Maybe I can get Jamie's phone number? Some way to get in touch with her?"

"Hang on." Kate punched in the second line before the ring ended, exhaling in relief for the chance to think. "Oh, good, it's you, Pete. Hold on one second." She went back to the first line. "Look, Mr. Carter, that's my husband on the phone and he's hard to get a hold of. Sorry, but I don't have Jamie's number with me."

"Don't worry. I left my number with your receptionist so you can call when you have it."

"Pete," Kate came back on with an almost a physical need to hear his voice. Rich with notes of North Carolina, he sounded more like a preacher than a man who drills human bones.

"Hey, Honey, what's up?" His voice soothed her like a caress.

Then she heard the familiar squawk of the hospital's loudspeaker in the background. "Is that for you?"

"No. But I don't have much time."

She tapped a pen against the side of her desk. "Some guy from L.A. is trying to find Jamie. I didn't tell him she was in town."

"You can't control her life, Kate."

"Jamie's record with men stinks. Starting with a married pilot and father who kills himself because of her!"

The phone went quiet. "Is this why you paged me?" He finally replied, his voice somber. He wanted this conversation over. "You couldn't make her decisions then. You can't now. I need to go."

"She's not supposed to date at all the first year. And, no, it's not why I called."

Kate's shoulder blades under her silk blouse tightened in a painful spasm. Having Jamie in Spring Port was already causing trouble.

"Mr. Lathrup—he wants me to take over his job after he buys two papers up north."

"Good. Maybe now he'll pay you what you're worth."

She pinched her thumb against the gold wedding band she never took off. She hadn't even asked about the salary, and it was Pete's first reaction. Eventually Pete would have a good income. But for the moment, his medical-school loans and their mortgage ate up most of their paychecks. Her infertility bills took care of the rest.

His resistance to seeing the fertility specialist in Chicago had been about money. Even with Dr. Delgado's professional courtesy for a Northwestern resident, the tests had run into the thousands. Pete still believed they'd have a baby on their own. Kate was afraid not even the expensive drugs would be enough.

All euphoria about her job was gone. "I haven't accepted yet."

"Do whatever you want. It's your call." She heard Pete talk to someone nearby. "I really need to sign some orders now. I should be home by seven."

"I love you, Pete."

She'd waited too long. The line was dead.

T h e   S a n d p i p e r

JAMIE

Jamie pulled the windshield visor down against the early sun. The short block of small frame houses on Third Street sat close together behind patchy grass lawns separated by cracked concrete driveways. She looked for the white lilac bushes, bent with the weight of feathered blossoms, marking the narrow driveway. In the paved lot behind the converted home, she pulled her Saab into the last space, pleased with herself for a change.

In her two weeks home, Jamie had already learned only the early birds got to park in this former backyard, now a paved lot for the Alcoholics Anonymous Club in Spring Port. Everyone after that had to leave their cars down the street next to the post office.

At the back door she braced herself against the smell of cigarettes and burned coffee permeating the one-story house. The acrid stink of smoke so early in the day made Jamie feel so sick she had to make herself breathe through her mouth. She allowed herself a spark of pride for the ease with which she'd quit smoking when she had to. Or at least thought she had to because it seemed like the right thing to do. It hadn't been all that long ago. But she still let herself count smoking as one bad thing she didn't do anymore.

Over the ten years she'd yo-yoed in and out of AA, she'd watched her fellow alcoholics give up booze with the ease of letting a balloon go. But they couldn't give up their cigarettes. For her not smoking had turned out to be the easy part. It was the other stuff—the liquor, the coke—the brightness in her head that filled the black sucking spaces inside. It was those moments of high escape she yearned for. And she knew her craving to sail beyond the darkness could destroy the people she loved as surely as putting rat poison in their cereal.

She walked past what was once the living room, now the big room for smokers where muffled conversation blended with the rattle of metal chairs. The early arrivals at the main meeting were situating themselves around a long rectangle formed by several smaller tables. She could see little curls of smoke rising from the clear glass ashtrays scattered along the tables.

By the hour's end, all the ashtrays would have to be emptied so the next wave of Bill W's friends, the fraternal password for AA members, could fill them up again. One of the seated men looked up as she passed the open door.

"Hey, Jamie. Come in here for a change. We smoke, but we don't bite."

"Yeah, right, Ben," she called without slowing her pace. His look made her think of the Holiday Inn, the man with his slicked-back hair, and she felt debased, like a bitch dog in heat. It didn't matter she'd figured out how to exploit the erotic tug she had on men, she still despised it. She had been ruined by it.

At the front of the house, she turned left into a small, former bedroom with fading wallpaper of pink flowers in urns. A dozen chairs circled a long wooden table scarred with cigarette burns and coffee spills. In her short time back in Spring Port, she'd chosen this 7 a.m. women's meeting in a non-smoking room as her home group.

They were close, these women who met together most mornings of the week—as they had done for years. But in the way only alcoholics reach out to strangers, they'd made Jamie one of their own the first morning she came into the room.

They called their group "No Sniveling" and meant it. At her third meeting, she had begun wading into her old self-pity pond for the father she knew only as a handsome soldier in the leather-framed photo she packed up first every time she moved. An unsmiling Lieutenant James Cameron wearing green fatigues stood in front of a helicopter painted in camouflage.

"Least ways you know who your daddy was, girlfriend," the woman beside her, named Gloria Cook, had said that morning when it was her turn. Gloria's dark skin was illuminated by a smile full of big white teeth. But what captured Jamie were Gloria's charcoal eyes that saw without blinking.

In these early morning meetings, Jamie learned about Gloria's particular hell as an alcoholic and addict. She'd also knew that Gloria judged no one, but did not put up with crybabies. When the other No Sniveling women had ignored Jamie's poor-me-ism altogether that morning, Jamie got the point. She had not mentioned her dad since.

But in her savaged core, Jamie knew there was a military officer she did need to talk about. And these women would not call her down for sniveling if she told them about him—how he'd destroyed a part of her. But she wouldn't tell them. She couldn't tell anyone. In the ten years since it happened, she'd told only one person. And telling Dr. Summers about Roger Hamper had been a mistake. A catastrophic mistake. She would not risk that again.

Within minutes, the dozen women of No Sniveling were seated with their styrofoam cups of coffee, the meeting underway. Looking around the table, Jamie could have been in morning group at Saguaro. Once again she was surrounded by women seemingly unalike—but bonded into a family by their disease. Roxie should be here, Jamie thought missing her gum-cracking roommate.

At Jamie's left sat Michelle, a regally slim doctor's wife in a sleeveless pink Lilly, her makeup perfect. Somewhere in her fifties, Michelle had hidden her bourbon in the laundry room. Beside her was Kathleen, a young CPA who'd gotten hooked on cocaine. Kathleen was talking to Maudie, a brashly funny grandmother whose sagging jowls and baggy eyes testified to her decades of six-packs.

Two chairs down from Jamie sat a freckle-nosed young woman named Tillie whose husband was a youth minister. No room for snobbery in this place. To alcoholics, social status was a joke.

Today's topic was forgiveness. Marcie, a chubby blonde whose two children had been taken away by Child Protective Services, opened the meeting. She began talking about her alcoholic mother who'd made Marcie's childhood a nightmare. "I know I can't blame her for my drinking," Marcie's tone contradicted the words. "But it's so hard. All I remember is Ma hitting us for nothing and then passing out on the couch."

Some children are better off not born, Jamie reflected, not for the first time. "Like I know it's not my ma's fault I messed up again—and now I've lost my babies," Marcie's voice broke in a sob. "Today's one of my bad days. I'm in too damn angry a place to even talk about forgiving Ma for what she did to me and my brothers."

When her turn came, Jamie intended to talk about how she needed to ask her older sister for a favor. How humiliating it was going to be—how dangerous to her sobriety. But she wanted them to understand she was against a wall and had no choice.

Jamie needed the women around the table to know how wobbly the shelf she teetered on was. The abyss of relapse loomed huge beneath her. So far she'd managed to avoid the street where Merit Financial used to be. The place where a man she'd trusted like the father she never knew gave her a bookkeeping job the summer she turned eighteen. She loved the job—until that last day.

The underground explosions were going off again. Jamie struggled to keep her guard up. The memories—the images from the past nipped at her sobriety like a puppy underfoot.

On her right side, Edith, a pouchy faced, white-haired woman in a faded red sweatshirt, said quietly, "Today—today I really need to be here. The hole," she tapped wrinkled knuckles on her chest, "the one we drunks keep trying to fill but never can. I'm hurting today so I'm going to listen and pass."

Yes, Jamie thought looking at Edith's sad eyes, wanting to tell her she knew all about that black hole. Then suddenly it was her turn, and inside her head whispered what she already knew. These women knew pain. Lived with it. Accepted it.

The problem she had to face with Kate was just that. Her problem. If she told them why, these No Sniveling women would jump her ass for using her sister. For choosing the alcoholic's way out. The easy way.

Jamie could imagine their responses as clearly as if they spoke in the strophes of a Greek chorus. One after the other they would say to her the two words alcoholics despise the most because they are the most true. *Grow up.*

So, instead, Jamie heard herself say, "Your anger is never going to touch your bitch of a mother, Marcie. She didn't get it then, and she's not going to get it now." Jamie could almost see Marcie's pot-bellied mother in a yellow nylon blouse over double-knit slacks, her hair frizzed from a bad permanent, slapping a little girl with blond pigtails across the face. Jamie could smell the mother's whiskeyed breath as she leaned toward little Marcie, her drunken eyes dangerous.

All at once Jamie's words raged forth, no more stoppable than a storm on the big lake. "That woman never deserved a nice daughter like you, Marcie. And she doesn't give a rat's ass about your forgiveness. You are the one who needs it, Marcie. You have to forgive yourself first. Then the hate and blame and awful shame will start to go away."

Then come back here, Marcie, Jamie prayed, please come back here to this very room and teach me how to forgive myself.

T h e   S a n d p i p e r

JAMIE

The two lattees were still hot and the bagels warm as Jamie punched Aunt Nina's phone number in from memory. "Jamie from Starbuck's room service moving south on Lakeshore six minutes from the Sandpiper. Are you up for company?"

"Certainly not. But for family? What's taking so long?"

Jamie snapped the phone shut and accepted the truth. This visit was a favor not to Aunt Nina, but to Jamie. The AA meeting had wiped her out. Her projected 'forgive yourself' to Marcie had sucked away the emotional stamina she needed to fight down the dread of what lay ahead—Aunt Nina, Kate. Worst of all, early tremors of cravings were starting to move in her brain. She prayed an hour with Aunt Nina would bolster her spirit so she could go another 24 hours without a drink.

"Jamie from room service arriving," she called out as she juggled the paper bag and venti coffees toward the back door.

The vigor with which the Sandpiper's door was flung open made Jamie step back. "Well, what is this? The sick lady from hell dressed and combed and ready to bark like Badger. I thought you were supposed to be reclining on a chaise like what's her name Browning. And if you tell my mother I came this early, I'll have to kill you."

Aunt Nina held open the door. "Did you get bitchy at your AA meeting, or did you wake up this way? Elizabeth Barrett."

"I knew that," she kissed Aunt Nina's cheek. "Wanted to make sure you remembered. So my mother tells you every time I leave the house?"

"Pretty much." The two windows over the sink in the small galley kitchen faced south and were already open to the morning breeze. Jamie could see the jeweled purples and golds of small pansies filling the window boxes. As the sun got hotter into July, Aunt Nina would replace the pansies with puffs of crimson geraniums.

Jamie pulled two mugs and plates of colored Fiestaware out of the cupboard stacked where they'd always been. The wooden tray shaped like a turtle was in its same spot against the back of the shelf in the blue hutch.

Jamie assembled what they needed on the funny brown tray that had toted so many cups of Kool-Aid, the spills and drips had warped the wood. Yet the tray was still the fat mud turtle she and Kate had used to play waitress so they could be like their mother. That was before Kate got older and decided waiting tables wasn't good enough for Ellie Cameron.

"Now, Aunt Nina," she asked holding the door to the lake open, "tell the truth for a change. Can we sit on your deck or is it too chilly outside for you?"

"You know this deck and I have been companions in snow and storm, young lady. My only question is can you take the cool air? Here, I'll get a towel to dry off the chairs."

"If it were me—excuse me, Miss Judd, if it were I," Jamie emphasized the pronoun, "these coffees would be left in the paper cups." Jamie divided one of the lattes into two round-handled mugs, one orange and one turquoise. "But I know the New England elitist in you insists on china and linens."

"Cottage living is not an excuse for slovenliness," Aunt Nina said laying out fillagreed silver spoons.

"Oh, Aunt Nina," Jamie sighed looking out at the lake. Somewhere deep in her soul, she understood what memory could not name. This cottage, this deck of streaming sunlight, the lapis water had been her sanctuary. Aunt Nina's the embracing place that kept her safe from the darkness—a hideaway where despair couldn't find her.

*　　*　　*

It was to this place Jamie had fled when Alex Hamper came to see Kate the day after his father's funeral. Alex had been Kate's boyfriend in high school, and he'd gotten his dad to give Jamie a summer job as a favor to Kate. What Alex didn't tell his dad was that Kate had hoped a job would keep her little sister out of trouble until she left for the University of Michigan in the fall.

Jamie could hear Alex and Kate talking on the porch. "The police found this," Alex was saying. "Looks like a broken ankle bracelet." Jamie didn't have to see it to know what Alex was holding. It was gold with a 'J' on it. "It was in Dad's car when they pulled it out of the water. The cops assumed it was Mom's," his voice softened.

Jamie understood. In a town where everyone knows everyone, of course the policemen knew Roger Hamper's wife's name was Joyce. "Mom would never wear an ankle bracelet. But I've seen them on Jamie before." Jamie heard a small gasp from Kate.

Then Alex told Kate an insurance investigator had already questioned the police about possible suicide. Why a former Marine pilot like Roger Hamper never used his brakes when his car hit the bridge's railing?

"You know my mother's never had to work. We have a big mortgage and my younger brothers are still in college. Dad had a suicide clause in his policy." Jamie heard a tremor in Alex's voice. "Kate, please. Nobody needs to know."

Kate's face had been white when she slammed the screen door shut behind her, pitching the chain at Jamie as she ran into her bedroom sobbing. Jamie had driven straight here—to this shoreline and hurled the ankle bracelet as far out as she could throw.

After it happened, she'd been too ashamed, too degraded, too violated to tell someone she'd been raped. And now she never could tell anyone what Roger Hamper did to her that night. The gold had flashed into the water, Jamie doubled over with longing. If only she could disappear under the waves with it.

*   *   *

"Nickel for your thoughts, Jamie Girl. Inflation you know." Aunt Nina brought Jamie back "Do you remember how you used to tell me the sun was taking his nap when a cloud covered it up, kind of like that one over the water," Aunt Nina pointed a thin finger. "Of course it didn't work when I tried to get you to follow the sun's example. Kate was a good napper, but you were the pits. Never wanted to miss anything."

"So what's changed?" Jamie asked, shaking her head against the remembering.

"You, for one. You're not drinking."

"One day at a time. One long day at a time, Aunt Nina."

"Since you brought it up…"

"I didn't."

"Whatever. Have you ever read anything by a psychologist named Karl Levinson? From UCLA?"

"Aunt Nina, let's get real here. Which of the two Cameron girls begged to come up here and read books with you and which one kicked sand if she had to leave the beach?"

"You know I'm always on the look-out for any new info on alcoholism," she ignored Jamie's comment. "When I came across his book, it rang some bells."

"The Return of the Prodigal Daughter?"

"Subtitled, now that you mention it. At least look it over and see what you think, OK?"

"But Ms. Judd," she made a whiney voice, "you said book reports aren't due until next Friday."

"You didn't even have to practice that one." Aunt Nina took a nibble of the bagel. "Your best was when you told me your theme wasn't done because Kate used one of your library books to press her corsage. You didn't want to ruin her prom scrapbook."

"I thought I'd been a little more creative than that." Jamie made a disappointed face.

"Now, if we can dispense with the bullshit, pardon my Latin, tell me what's going on with you. Really going on—not what you think I want to hear."

A dog barked from the beach. Jamie turned to see a woman in a white sweatshirt and jeans walking along the big lake while a small boy and a Golden Retriever ran in front of her along the water's edge. The Golden's tail was a frantic metronome as the boy held a driftwood stick over his head. Then his small arm hurled and the dog bounded into the water after it. The boy's laughter above the quiet rhythm of waves made Jamie's lungs too heavy for her chest.

"So?" Aunt Nina continued.

"Oh, Aunt Nina. I love Aspen, the mountains, a few people there—certainly not a lot of them. But this—this lake is my home. It's where I want my ashes scattered when I die."

"A little morbid at your age, I'd think. But, in any case, stand in line, my dear."

"Don't say that."

"Oh, excuse me? I guess you can talk about your death and what you'd like, but I can't? Well, don't you worry, Jamie girl. I've got it all written down, and your mother has promised she won't let my niece override my wishes. But we were talking about you."

"If you must know, Mom's busy doing her chipper-cheery thing so Jamie doesn't get upset and take off for the bars."

"Might you?" Aunt Nina watched her with steady grey eyes.

Jamie took a big breath before answering. "I'm struggling, Aunt Nina. White knuckling it, if you want to know. Ever since I got back. Mom. Kate." The land mine she couldn't talk about. "But today I won't drink. That's as far as I can go." She'd almost told the knee-jerk lie she'd used so long it seemed true. 'No, I'm not drinking again ever.'

But this was Aunt Nina who kept a life rope coiled for Jamie. She'd thrown it when Jamie got suspended for drinking beer over lunch in the high school parking lot. Her friends had scattered when they saw the principal, but Jamie's back was turned. She could have gotten off by telling on them. But she didn't.

The suspension, her mother's embarrassment—Kate's outrage had made her feel worthless. Then Aunt Nina tossed the ring. "You nimrod, you!" Aunt Nina had crowed. "How could someone with an IQ in the upper stratosphere do something this stupid?"

Now Aunt Nina had cancer and Jamie didn't think she could make it without her.

"Aunt Nina, Mom has no idea how close I am to the edge. She still thinks she can save me."

"Your mother reads a lot about alcoholism and addiction, believe me. But she's always thrown herself in the breach to keep you and Kate from any harm or, God forbid, sadness. She can't accept the fact you have the one disease she can't help you with."

"The disease only the patient can treat." Jamie echoed quietly.

"So how's it going with Kate?"

"What can I say? Kate does everything right."

"Guess we are milking the prodigal theme today. She's the reader, you're the sand kicker." Aunt Nina slipped the barely touched bagel onto Jamie's empty plate. "So did it ever occur to you that you might have something your sister wishes she did?"

"Oh, let me see. Would that be multiple DUIs or a bad liver?"

"Have you ever thought how much energy it takes Kate to do everything right to meet her own high expectations? Can you imagine how taxing it is never to be allowed to fail?"

"Let me see if I can picture myself fatigued from yet another day of perfection."

Aunt Nina picked up one of Jamie's Birkenstocks and pitched it into the dune grass surrounding the deck. "Hope you get poison ivy trying to find it."

"Guess I'll be too busy looking for my shoe to run the vacuum for you." She stood up and held her hand out to pull Aunt Nina to her feet.

"Lucky for you I already did. See?" Aunt Nina opened the screen door and pointed at the wide-board pine floor and bright blue and green area rug. "Spotless. Oh, and look at your plant."

Aunt Nina's cuttings from the Christmas cactus spread out from a terra cotta pot sitting on its own little cherry table soaking up the morning sun.

"I move the table around in here so your friend's plant keeps getting light and thinks it's still in Arizona."

"I didn't say it came from a friend."

"Hey, don't go crabby on me. Look, you just don't buy a 100-year old plant. Someone had to give it to you. And presumably gifts come from friends, do they not?"

"I'm sorry for snapping." She was sorry. Not Aunt Nina—not anyone could know who'd given her the cactus. So many secrets. Too many. Too many. She touched the emerald notched leaves and knew she couldn't wait much longer to go see Kate.

"Lovely, isn't it?" Aunt Nina pulled the little table into a new patch of light streaming through the window. "One of these times I need you to scrounge through my high cupboards to help me find my Victorian urn. I want to plant your cactus in it. You've seen it—one of my estate-sale finds. White with raised garlands of grapes and leaves around the bulbous part. But we won't look today."

"Aunt Nina, if you don't let me do something for you," Jamie walked through the long living room into the kitchen, "my mother will be mad and I might go drinking. It will all be your fault." As Jamie began rinsing the plates and cups, she felt Aunt Nina's hand making soft circles on her back the way she'd comforted her when she was a little girl.

"Cookie, you and I know what's ahead for me. And you are the one I want with me because you will let me go when the time comes. Your mother would do mouth-to-mouth on picked asparagus."

Jamie got caught again in the swing of hysteria between tears and giggles.

"And I know, Jamie, that when the time comes, you are the one I trust to be honest."

"Please, no, Aunt Nina. Don't put any trust in me."

"Oh, I know you can lie through your teeth. That's part of alcoholism like spots and measles. You lie, honey, but you're not a liar. In ways, you're the most honest of us all. You accept your demons. The rest of us pretend we don't have any."

Jamie turned and pulled Aunt Nina into her embrace.

"That does it!" Aunt Nina pushed herself away. "Your dripping dish rag's getting my shirt all wet." She grabbed a soft-cover book from a shelf and handed it to Jamie. "Here's Dr. Levinson's book. Read it." She said in her English teacher's voice.

Jamie hardly glanced at the book as she took it. "When do you want me to come stay?"

"Not now. You'd be a pain in the fanny. I'll let your mother worry about you sneaking drinks for a while. When I need you to bring your toothbrush, Cookie, you'll be the first to know. Meanwhile, this visit was better than radiation."

"Why, you're just going to corrupt me with compliments, Aunt Nina," Jamie said in a Scarlett accent trying to keep from crying. She knew what Aunt Nina really meant was that her best friend Ellie deserved to have her younger daughter home so she could see her sober for a change.

"All right, you big smart aleck," Aunt Nina gave her a glancing kiss. "Go find your damned hippie shoe. Then get home and help your mom finish all those fussy creampuffs she's making."

"Yes, Boss," Jamie called over her back as she climbed the deck rail to retrieve her sandal. "But don't you forget that if I'm the big smart aleck, there must be a bigger and a biggest one. Comparative and superlative," she said pulling on her shoes. "See, I did learn something in your class after all."

"All right, genius child, who was the first poet who wrote about AA?"

Jamie stopped, and looked up at Aunt Nina. "Hemingway wasn't a poet, but he should have been in AA. How about one of the big Irish drinkers—Dylan Thomas maybe?"

"Welsh, not Irish. How about this," Aunt Nina began to recite slowly, "'*I taste a liquor never brewed...*'"

"Emily Dickinson!" Jamie held up a palm to stop her. Something whirred far back in her head. "Hang on. *I taste a liquor never brewed, Ta ta ta ta* ta—oh, it's right there," she touched her tongue.

Aunt Nina prodded, "'*Inebriate of air am I...*'"

"'*And debauchee of dew!*' Yes. Dickinson. I still remember thinking how cool to get debauched by dew! But, of course, I was just a good beer drinker back then—not a full-blown alcoholic." Not yet, anyway. Tissues around her heart seemed to crimp.

"There's the liquor never brewed," Aunt Nina pointed out at the lake before she opened her arms wide for a hug. "All you'll ever need, my dear. Right here in front of you. One day at a time."

"One day at a time, Aunt Nina," Jamie kissed her cheek.

She beeped goodbye on the Saab horn, the sound still reverberating when she reached the log cabin. Jamie looked over at the honey-gold logs, thinking that inside the coziness of those sturdy walls her parents had been together for the last time. Her name was meant for the son her mother was sure she was having. But she gave it to her baby girl anyway. A sort of benison, Jamie thought—a way of giving Jamie a piece of the father she never saw. Having his name made Jamie proud.

She'd been fists-fight ready to defend Lieutenant James Cameron as the decorated war hero he was when her classmates said it was a dumb war and everyone knew her dad didn't have to go. They were right. He could have finished his surgery residency before the Army drafted him. Her mother had begged him to wait—he would have missed the worst of the war. He would have operated on patients behind the lines like MASH instead of flying over enemy territory in med-evac choppers to pick up wounded soldiers.

But her mother's pleas didn't work. The April before he graduated from the University of Michigan Medical School, Jim Cameron had walked into the Army recruiting office and volunteered for Vietnam. Jamie and Kate didn't know much more than that about their dad. And they only knew that because of Aunt Nina. As little girls, she and Kate somehow understood they couldn't talk to their mother about their dad—certainly not to ask questions about him.

Jamie wondered how her mother had felt finding out she was pregnant while her husband was on his way to Vietnam. She could not have been excited about another baby when she was going to be alone for a year already busy with a three-year old. Had the idea of not having Jamie ever crossed her mother's mind? Jamie caught her reflection in the car's rearview mirror—her mouth tight, her eyes narrowed, and she knew. Ellie Cameron would never have even thought of it.

In a surge of the blackness that so often engulfed her, Jamie wished her mother had thought about it. She shouldn't have been born. Her mother did everything right and kind in raising her, but it hadn't mattered. From her first beer, Jamie was a partier. Liked the short skirts, the flirting. And then one lightning-blasted August night she had teased the wrong man.

After that, beer wasn't enough to numb the pain. She squeezed the steering wheel and took a deep breath. How she envied a woman who could be "inebriate of air." Jamie could almost feel the cocaine high begin in her nose. The craving jolted her. Kate *had* to help her.

She was picturing Marcie's mother passed out on the couch when her peripheral vision caught the full title of Aunt Nina's book on the seat beside her. She hit the brake and grabbed it in shock. "Addiction and the Power of Post-Traumatic Stress Disorder" by Dr. Karl Levinson.

How...how? What had Aunt Nina said about this UCLA doctor? That his book rang a bell for her? But Aunt Nina couldn't possibly know about Roger Hamper! Jamie shivered with goose bumps and shoved the book deep underneath the passenger seat where she couldn't see it. Then she pressed the accelerator hard to the floor.

The   Sandpiper

KATE

Kate lay still, comforted by Pete's arm stretched over her stomach as she listened to the spring peepers outside their window singing the air full of chirps. She stroked the ropey muscles of Pete's forearm and turned her head to nuzzle him, moved by the rhythmed breathing of his sleep. She touched the white-gold edges of his messy hair, and eased out from under his arm not to wake him. In one automatic move, Kate pulled her basal thermometer out of the drawer in her bedside table and stuck it under her tongue.

She'd learned how to read a thermometer the winter Jamie had scarlet fever. Kate had moved into Jamie's room so she could bring her little sister cold drinks of water when Jamie got thirsty in the night without waking their mother. Now, since Jamie's return from Tucson, she'd hardly seen her younger sister.

Kate read the normal 98.5 degrees and penciled an X on her temperature chart underneath "Day 12." It reminded her of a Bingo card, but she didn't feel lucky. "Relax more and worry less," Dr. Bauer said at every appointment. But all she'd known since Katie became Kate was "on duty." Help her mother. Take care of Jamie. Study harder than anyone else. Now what she wanted most was supposed to happen only by trying not to try! She felt her temples throb in frustration.

She went into the kitchen to grind Pete's favorite Colombian coffee beans, inhaling the rich aroma. She would again be the first person in and out of Dr. Bauer's small lab on Front Street to avoid running into someone she knew.

Not enough she grew up in Spring Port, now her picture ran in the paper every Wednesday. At least the Ms.Cellaneous byline was "Kate Shane," not "Kate Cameron." If someone did spot her at Dr. Bauer's, she was getting routine blood work. It wasn't anybody's business she was taking hormones tricking her ovaries into popping more eggs at a time.

She was brushing a streak of plum blush along her cheeks when Pete came up behind her, kissing the small groove in the back of her neck. "You smell lovely, Kate—but so does the coffee." His cobalt blue eyes met hers in the mirror, and he held a stare.

"What?"

He hesitated. "I was just thinking what a knockout you are and how much you and Jamie look alike. Even with this short black hair," he ran a soft hand over her head, "and her long blonde ponytail."

Kate thought about her own first reaction the night Jamie got home. Coming around her mother's house, she'd seen Jamie kneeling by the neighbor's dog in the driveway. Kate had almost forgotten how exotic her younger sister was with their father's melted-chocolate eyes and their mother's high cheekbones.

Kate didn't think she and Jamie looked alike. Jamie was movie-star pretty. Maybe it was the smiles that gave them away as sisters. Full lips over even white teeth, thanks to the braces their mother had to pay for over time. That first night Jamie had her honey-blond hair pulled back with only a few stray curls spilling on her forehead. It made her younger sister's Arizona tan glow like liquid copper.

"Do you think she's sober?" Kate finally asked Pete.

"She's been fine the few times I've seen her. Your mom says she goes to AA meetings every day."

"And relapses on a dime."

"Hey, that's alcoholism. All we can do is support her the best we can."

Kate began brushing her hair hard away from her face. She wanted him to be right. But she'd cleaned up Jamie's drunken vomit too many times. She'd listened to her mother crying on the phone too many times. She wouldn't trust Jamie's sobriety now.

Electricity clicked from her short thick hair as she turned toward Pete. She needed to tell him how terrified she was of optimism. Hope only made the relapses harder. But the blue-silk softness lighting his eyes told Kate he wouldn't understand. To Pete, Jamie wasn't bad, she was sick. And sick people can get well.

"Come here, you pretty thing." Pete pulled her into his arms, his lips nibbling her ear. "I'm having trouble worrying about your sister when all I can see are those great dark circles looking at me through your robe."

Kate tried to pull back, needing to protect Pete from Jamie. Warn him not to get his hopes up either. Then she felt her nipples grow hard under his slow thumb. Her words came out as a soft moan. Slowly, slowly she leaned into his moving fingers. Dear God, please let me get pregnant by this man, she prayed.

She was still blowing kisses at Pete as he stood in the back door while she drove her Mazda out of their driveway past the white lace of their Juneberry tree. Neither of them had mentioned her early morning appointment. Somehow they'd arrived at an unspoken agreement to steer around conversations about infertility. Pete knew the importance of blood work and ultrasounds to make sure the ovaries didn't get dangerously over stimulated. He'd taken exams on the subject.

But ever since the cold dawn in Chicago when he'd accused her of being obsessed with getting pregnant, Pete had learned. He knew how to avoid the subject. Kate could still see his bloodshot eyes from all-night call, the lines from his surgical mask pressed into his cheeks.

"I think I'm ovulating," she'd said as he came through their apartment door, his scrubs speckled in dark red stains.

"For God's sake, Kate, can't you think about anything else?" None of his apologies could stop her sobbing. They didn't have sex at all that cycle.

She turned north on U.S. 31 into Spring Port when a movement of brightness along the road caught her eye. In the center of a trimmed lawn, the branches of a majestic weeping willow flickered a yellow so strong the tree seemed illuminated. Aunt Nina had taught Kate about trees. The vibrant yellow meant the weeping willow was about to bloom.

Next to it the plump red husks of a silver maple budded like tiny garnets. She saw beyond the shimmering loveliness to the renewal. This would be her season too. Her body would bloom with new life until she glowed like the willow. She pressed one palm against her belly and said her silent baby prayer yet again.

And, God willing, maybe Pete would turn out to be right about Jamie. Maybe three months in the Tucson rehab had done what the Brighton treatment center had not done—either time. Nobody wanted the old Jamie back more than Kate. Jamie was the little sister Kate had watched out for and adored. They had been inseparable, fatherless against the world. If Jamie could stay sober this time, the two of them would find their way back to the closeness Kate missed more than she'd thought possible.

But she was scared. The 'if' was what she didn't dare let go of.

T h e   S a n d p i p e r

KATE

Joe O'Connor's penciled handwriting on the post-it note stuck to her phone reminded Kate to get him an interview with someone in a Spring Port investment club. The stock market had always interested Joe. So when he read an article about the National Association of Investment Clubs and discovered a man from Detroit named George A. Nicholson had started the whole thing in 1951, he was hooked.

Detroit was just across the state from Spring Port so it felt almost local. He would do the West Michigan angle by interviewing members of an NAIC club in Spring Port. But he needed Kate's hometown connections to make the connection.

And Kate certainly had one. For as long as Kate could remember, her mother, Aunt Nina, and all their best friends had belonged to The Sandpiper Investment Club. Her mother was an original member so it didn't start until she'd moved to Spring Port the summer before Jamie was born. Aunt Nina had started the club and was still its brain power.

She also became the perpetual hostess since the rest of the women had children and loved escaping to Aunt Nina's beach home where they nibbled munchies and drank wine and gazed at the vast majesty of Lake Michigan. In honor of Aunt Nina's hospitality, the women named their club after her cottage where they looked forward to gathering once a month to talk stocks and giggle in chorus with the sound of waves.

Nobody seemed to know—or care—if they ever made any money in the market, though they did know Nina had gotten them into Walmart early. Kate was pretty sure the main reason the Sandpipers still met was to have a night out together on The Sandpiper's deck in the summer and around Aunt Nina's fireplace in the winter. Kate's mother never mentioned the stock market after meetings, but she always brought home some tidbit of Spring Port gossip.

Ellie Cameron would not be the one for Joe to interview. She loved everything about the Sandpipers' meetings except the stock market. Aunt Nina, on the other hand, read the *Wall Street Journal* daily. But Aunt Nina was not well and didn't need a reporter peppering her with questions about the Sandpiper Club.

Kate decided Sandra Quinn, the mother of Kate's best high school friend Sarah, was the one for Joe to interview. Sandra Quinn picked up on the second ring.

The low, cultured voice called up the image of the slender blond who had favored Chanel suits and chain belts. Her husband Tom Quinn was the senior partner in Spring Port's oldest law firm. Kate remembered how Uncle Tom used to look at his wife with great, moony eyes. Besides their daughter Sarah, the Quinns had a freckle-faced son named Ryan. They were the perfect family. The kind she'd promised herself she would have one day.

She thought about the gold carpet that ran all through the Quinn's large home, so plush their sneakers left foot prints in it. In the Cameron house, bright rag rugs were strategically placed to cover up the worn patches of carpeting.

"A story on The Sandpiper Club? The Sandpiper Club?" Sandra Quinn repeated, almost as if she were stalling. Kate's journalism career had taught her how to hear a dodge.

"Oh, for heaven's sakes, Kate," Sandra Quinn finally said, her normal self-assurance restored. "You don't want your Lakeshore News reporter wasting his time on us old ladies."

Kate pictured the tiny crow's feet edging Aunt Sandy's eyes, the lone touch of time since she and Sarah had been in high school. "'Old ladies" wasn't even a good excuse.

"Here, hang on a sec," Aunt Sandy said. "I've got a name for you." Kate heard the rustle of papers. Then Sandy Quinn came back on the line. "I have just the person you're looking for. Esther Perkins. She's president of the WOWS— Women of Wall Street. The WOWs have been around a long time. And they are way more serious than we are!" She read Kate the phone number, then quickly said, "We have to have lunch, honey. You and Sarah and your mom and me."

Kate felt a poke of guilt thinking how little she'd seen Sarah since moving back to Spring Port. They'd talked on the phone—and Sarah had tried to meet.

But Kate always seemed to be busy. The honest obstacle was not Kate's work. It was all about Sarah's chattering on how hard it was to take care of three pre-schoolers. "You and Pete are so smart to wait."

"I'd love that, Aunt Sandy," Kate replied, hoping she sounded sincere. While her mother never said so, Kate knew how eager she was to have grandchildren of her own. Lunch with all the happy chatter about Sarah's three would make it even harder for Kate.

"Tell your reporter that The WOWS do their homework, Kate," Aunt Sandy went on. "Not like us. Those women follow the market and know what they're doing. We Sandpipers—well, to be honest, we just let your Aunt Nina do it. Always have, honey. And Esther will love bragging to a reporter about their portfolio.

"Now tell me about your job, Kate. Do you like it?" Aunt Sandy scarcely took a breath, switching topics with obvious abruptness. "And that drop-dead gorgeous charmer husband of yours?" She again changed gears not waiting for Kate's answer to her first question. "You should know all of us getting close to our 60s are saying it's worth breaking a hip to get Dr. Shane to take care of us."

"I'll tell Pete," Kate mumbled, curious about Aunt Sandy's diversionary conversation. "It'll give him an ego boost. But back to The Sandpipers, your group has been together so long," Kate tried again. She wanted to find out if Aunt Sandy really was trying to distract her from questions about the Sandpipers Club. "You must have at least one or two good stories on some lucky stock purchase you made that Joe could write about."

Kate heard the forced lightness in the low laugh filling the phone. "Don't we wish, honey. No, we didn't learn diddly about the stock market. You know your Aunt Nina—she kept trying to teach us. We were worse than her worst remedial English class she always told us. She'd try to talk stocks, but nobody paid attention. Enough boring stuff from me. I know Jamie came home to help Nina and I hear she's never looked so beautiful."

A patch of sunshine chased a shadow across Kate's desk. She wasn't imagining it. For whatever reason, Aunt Sandy did not want to talk about The Sandpiper Club. She'd had to resort to the Cameron family's most sensitive subject. "Yes, well, we're glad she's back."

"Jamie's what Helena needs right now."

"And vice versa."

"You're right, Kate. Helena loves Jamie—loves you both. You are the daughters she never had."

Kate rolled a pencil back and forth on her thigh. It was time for her to start acting like one. "I'm not sure we deserve her," Kate said softly, thinking not about Jamie's alcoholism, but about her own selfishness.

"That's not what she thinks," Aunt Sandy said in clipped syllables.

Kate thought about the closeness of her mother's friends, the bonds that had grown tighter over the years. Maybe it was the sacredness of their friendships Aunt Sandy wanted to protect. Writing a news story about the Sandpipers might diminish that—make them like any other stock group when their commitment to each other went far beyond a stock-market club.

Kate would honor that wish for privacy. It was this group of women who had once embraced a pregnant young widow and her three-year old daughter when they'd moved to Spring Port knowing nobody but their landlady Helena Judd.

"I appreciate having Mrs. Perkins' name for Joe," Kate said. "But I don't care if the WOWS made a million dollars and the Sandpipers lost their shirts. I know who has the most fun at their meetings!"

Sandra Quinn laughed, her voice relaxed for the first time. Kate the journalist was no longer pursuing the Sandpipers. "Don't forget our mother-daughter lunch before the summer gets too hectic. And we'll do it here so your mom doesn't cook for a change. Honestly, Kate, none of us can figure out how she does it all. But no Sandpiper would dream of having a party anymore without Ellie's Catering."

Kate said goodbye knowing Aunt Sandy meant it as a compliment. Kate wished she could see it that way too. She leaned back in her computer chair and thought about the Quinn family, about how long she'd envied them. She'd wanted a father like Sarah had. A father whose wife didn't have to wait tables to support her children. Then she felt the pain of shame for this disloyalty to her mother.

Kate never talked about what gouged her like glass shards in a glove. How it would hurt her mother to know her first-born had longed to be part of a real family like the Quinns. But her mother never knew because Kate was too good at hiding her own unhappiness, a collapsed umbrella to be opened only if her mother wasn't around.

She'd never told her mother how often her dad's death caught her off guard—like a head bump in the dark. Strong as her mother was, Ellie Cameron had endured enough, burying the only man she'd ever love under the red-and white stripes blanketing his casket. After Jamie's problems began, Kate had to work even harder not to be sad around her mother.

In the distance beyond her office window, Kate saw the turquoise triangle of a windsurfer lean toward the harbor's water, a dark figure in a wet suit outlined against the sail. Kate did not believe God would let her grow up without a father and then not let her have a child of her own. She rubbed fingers into her temples, seeing the square jaw, the blue-black hair of the father she'd hardly known.

Then her hands slid automatically to her flat belly. She had paid her dues. God would not bring her world down again. This would be the month, she told herself with a flex of will and a silent prayer. She closed her eyes to visualize Pete's sperm inside her like a swarm of commas wiggling their way to the egg that would make them a family. A real family.

A week later, Kate's temperature fell. When she went to the bathroom in the middle of the night, she was bleeding. She put one hand against her mouth pressing back the sob. She didn't want her crying to wake Pete.

The   Sandpiper

JAMIE

Jamie waited until she heard her mother's minivan, packed with four red coolers carrying a luncheon for thirty women, turn the corner. If her mother had sensed Jamie's agitation, she didn't show it. But, then, Jamie knew how to smooth her mother's uneasiness—to say what she wanted to hear. Ellie Cameron's overarching wish for her daughter to be "herself" again fuzzied her otherwise sharp perceptions.

Kate, on the other hand, would have picked right up on Jamie's restlessness that morning. Shifting her weight back and forth on the balls of her bare feet while she stood at the kitchen sink and pulled cooked chicken apart for her mother's salad.

Yes, Kate would have recognized Jamie's idle talk as staged, scripted to play her role in their mother's fantasy, her mother's dreamy hope that Jamie was back, recovered, all better now. So Jamie made herself Ellie Cameron's normal, stable loving daughter working cheerfully beside her mother in the kitchen as she once had.

While Jamie continued her fake small talk at the sink, her mother had moved around the kitchen with easy grace, checking off the puff pastries she was wrapping in foil, the washed lettuce already in plastic bags.

The white bib apron with *Ellie's* embroidered in bright green accentuated her mother's full breasts and tapered waist. Her mother had a heft to her figure, an earthiness Jamie knew men liked in women. Jamie'd been studying her profile, strong against the morning light when her mother caught her eye and grinned, exposing the tiny dimple in her left cheek.

A surge of affection had risen in Jamie's chest and almost buckled her knees with shame. Her mother loved openly and without judgment. She had never given in to the bitterness that would have corroded a lesser woman's spirit. Her mother had accepted the reality of a war she'd loathed—a war that had slaughtered the love of her life one rainy cold December day when she was twenty-two and pregnant with her second daughter.

For over 30 years her mother had worked as a single parent who didn't know self-pity. Jamie could not imagine how much worse it would have been if Aunt Nina had not stepped in to become their family. But, even then, a woman friend—no matter how close—was still not a man to curl up with at night.

Her mother should have married Mike, the Chicago architect with an authentic sweetness about him. Until the night he walked off their porch for the last time, Jamie had never seen a grown man cry. Her fingers tightened on the dishcloth as she wiped up the kitchen counter. Kate had ruined that for their mother. But Jamie couldn't go there right now. She could not give in to that old resentment starting to rise in her like a black ooze.

She listened again for the van in case her mother had forgotten something, then tossed the dishrag in the sink. She ran up the stairs, three at a time as she always did. What she had to ask her sister today—she could not let her festering bitterness get in the way.

Jamie knew only one way to stuff the rage. Just one small drink to calm her nerves so she didn't blow it with Kate by losing her temper. Asking her sister for help was humiliating. She needed just a tiny boost of alcohol to get through the next two hours. She would not count it against her sobriety, because she only needed one drink and just for this one morning.

Jamie felt the worn carpet under her feet as she reached the closed door to her mother's bedroom. The last time she'd come home from Aspen for a brief visit, the wine rack was empty. The small kitchen cupboard where her mother kept liquor for guests was filled with perrier. But the first chance Jamie'd had to search, it took ten minutes to find four wine bottles and unopened Scotch under a pile of blankets and scrapbooks in the window seat of her mother's bedroom. She'd made it to bed in a drunken stupor and slept until noon the next day. Her mother had to know, but never said a word about it. That was Ellie's form of denial.

For a moment Jamie stood still, her head leaning on the doorframe. Please, Lord, she prayed, please don't let me find anything this time. Sweat rimmed the edge of her bra. Almost four months sober—the longest stretch she could remember since Roger Hamper. Since her binge drinking at Michigan had stopped being enough. Since Aspen and coke and her drugged heart almost stopping two days before Christmas. "Cocaine will kill you," the Aspen ER doctor had told her with toneless finality.

She banged her head against the wooden door jam, willing the AA prayer to stop her. Alcohol was her gateway to coke. One drink would trigger the cravings. After that she'd do whatever she had to for the next high. For escape, to numb herself from memory, from shame. Death, at that point, would be irrelevant.

The bedroom's brass door knob seemed to turn by itself. In two big steps, she was on her knees at the window seat. She yanked off the gingham-checked cushion and pushed the lid up on its hinges.

Dear God, her brain heaved thunderbolts inside her skull. She wondered if this was what a stroke felt like. The crushing head pain and then all at once her shoulder muscles twitch in full spasm. Please don't let this be happening. She shoved her hand beneath a folded fleece blanket, its softness sinking like packed sawdust. Her hand found the padded baby books, Kate's pink on top of her own blue one for the son her mother was sure she was having. So instead, her mother had given Jamie her father's name when she was born a month after Lieutenant James Cameron got killed evacuating a wounded soldier.

Two big photo albums, a shoe box of loose pictures—all of it shoved to the back while her hands frantically searched the chest's flat bottom. Jamie's fingers explored the length and the width of the smooth wood before she sat back on her heels. She threw her head back in tears as the ceiling blurred above her. Her mother had found a new hiding place.

An hour later, the salty sweat from a hard run burning her eyes, Jamie sprinted across the expanse of sand at Lighthouse Beach, named for the cherry-red lighthouse at the end of a concrete pier. The blue-green water rippling in soft waves called, *Ja Mie, Ja Mie* in the rhythm of her name. She'd been able to hear the watery voice of the big lake since she was a little girl.

She lunged toward the lake, the scratchy sand grains rubbing at her ankles, seeping into her socks. She didn't stop to take her shoes off, but ran ten yards in full sprint through the shallow water until she came to a depth where she could dive under the freezing canopy of liquid.

The pleasant looking receptionist peered over red reading glasses when Jamie walked through the front door of the Lakeshore News office. "May I help you?" Marcia Kraft said from behind her tidy desk, her fingers lifted from an out-of-date computer keyboard. Catching Jamie's glance at the old computer, she patted it with a laugh. "All you young people look at this like it's from outer space. But my old friend here has carried me this far. I'm not deserting her now. So after more information than you need, what can I do for you?"

Jamie took a quick breath. "I'm, I'm here to see my sister. Kate. Kate Shane. I'm Jamie Cameron. She doesn't know I'm coming. But I was downtown, so I thought I'd see if she had time for lunch."

"Oh, I'm sure she'll make time for you. What a nice surprise! I didn't realize Kate had a sister." Marcia pushed on the nose bar of her glasses. "I mean, she hasn't been here long enough for us to know all that much about her. But I certainly can see the family resemblance. You are both beautiful like your mother." Marcia picked up the phone to buzz Kate, but Jamie stepped forward to stop her.

"Do you mind? I'd like to surprise her myself." She gave Marcia what she hoped was one of her convincing smiles. Jamie couldn't afford to give Kate time to find an excuse not to have lunch with her.

"Oh, of course," Marcia said standing up with surprising spryness. Behind the desk she'd seemed heavier, blockier.

Following Marcia down the hall, Jamie still felt tingly from the shower. But it had worked, the run and then the big lake and the peppering hot water. She had drained herself of everything but what she'd come for. She was as ready for what she had to do as she could be without a drink.

"Most people don't think I look like my sister," she said to distract herself from a growing anxiety. "The hair," she touched her head, "and Kate's is so black. And I'm a giant next to my petite sister."

Marcia made a scoffing hand gesture at Jamie as she came to a closed oak door marked Editorial. "Taller, maybe. 'Giant' is not a word I would use to describe you, my dear."

Kate would never know how many times Jamie had held her big sister's picture up beside her own reflection in the mirror, pulling her long blond hair back to compare faces. Their arching cheeks from their mother, the full lips like their dad's. But her likeness to Kate reassured Jamie. She could not be a change-ling child dropped like a black kitten on her mother's porch. Even if Kate's life turned on a star while hers hung over an abyss, they were still sisters.

A red-haired man in his late 30s hurried out the door, nodding toward Jamie. She heard his quick footsteps slow down and didn't have to turn around to know he was watching her. Stares from men pleased most women. Once upon a time she had been flattered too. Not any more. Now she tensed at the stares, as if their eyes could penetrate her without her consent.

Yet she knew she dressed to attract men, a typical Jamieism of not knowing who she was or wanted to be. Her white sleeveless cotton dress with a deep V-neck, a red pull-through tie scarf loose around her hips. But she could feel the angles of her body move against the fabric when she walked, her runner's calf muscle tightening as she followed Marcia Kraft into her sister's office.

"Jamie!" Kate said looking up from her desk, the shock audible. Jamie waited until Marcia closed the door behind her before she spoke.

"I was afraid you might not see me if I called first."

"Not much of a greeting, Jamie."

"Sorry," she shook her head, the old feelings of inadequacy around her sister kicking in. Everything in Jamie wanted to erupt—to tell Kate she'd overheard her talking about Jamie the night she came home from Tucson. How Kate's judgmentalism had kept Jamie from asking for help so many times when Jamie had needed her most. But she could not let herself. She dug her toes into her sandals, holding herself steady.

"I'm honestly trying, Kate, not to be obnoxious. I need your help and being rude would be a stupid way to start. I was hoping you'd have lunch with me." She knew her sister did not like to be caught off guard. Starting in grade school, Kate was a planner, her school clothes laid out the night before, her homework turned in early.

And the more compulsive Kate got, the more out of control Jamie got. It was partly to bug her big sister. But she knew it was also the alcohol. From sneaking her first beers in middle school, Jamie discovered alcohol was magic for her. She was prettier, brighter, way funnier with buzz on.

Kate had snuck Jamie past their mother's bedroom too many staggering nights after that not to know her little sister had a drinking problem. It was also one of the reasons Kate asked her friend Alex Hamper if his dad would hire Jamie at Merit Financial the summer before Jamie went to Michigan. Kate liked Roger Hamper and thought he would be a good influence on her wild little sister. The solid father figure Jamie never had.

Yet even if she'd wanted to, Jamie could not blame Kate for what happened. She knew she'd worn her skirts too short at work, her blouses too tight. What had happened was her own fault.

Jamie stood motionless in front of her sister's organized desk wishing she could tell Kate right then the truth about Alex's father. Almost ten years later, Kate still thought he'd killed himself because he was a married man having an affair with a teenager. Jamie trembled at the remembered pain, the sound—her arms beating at him, her screams lost in the thunder.

Jamie came back to the sound of Kate's voice. "Hey, we're good to go." Kate looked up from her day planner. "You all right?"

"Oh, sure. Just a mind wander."

"I'm free until two. I have to meet with my boss."

"The guy whose job you're taking over? Mom is really proud of you." Jamie hoped Kate heard the sincerity. She was glad because Kate's successes made their mother happy. Jamie knew one reason Kate pushed herself to excel was to make up for Jamie. The familiar cramp of guilt gripped her belly.

"We can go right across the street to Barry's," Kate said coming around the desk. "It's new since you were home. They have great salads." Kate grabbed her purse.

"I was thinking about Gertie's—for old time's sake you know?" Jamie asked. At the small diner on Lighthouse Beach, they could talk privately. Gertie's might even give Kate some nostalgia to make what Jamie had to say easier to hear. She did not want to eat at Barry's where Kate's reading fans might make Jamie feel like even more of a loser. It might stop her from asking at all. Mostly she could not risk being overheard.

"Gertie's is a dump," Kate said. Then she registered her younger sister's disappointment. "But that's fine if you want to, Jamie."

"You sure?"

Kate held her office door open for Jamie. "Gertie's is a great idea. I haven't been there since Pete and I moved back here. You drive and let's put that fancy white top down."

For a moment, Jamie remembered how much she had once liked her big sister.

The Sandpiper

JAMIE

Gertie Higgins began selling hot dogs and hamburgers at Lighthouse Beach when her husband joined the Navy the week after Pearl Harbor. Daryl Higgins came home on leave long enough to get Gertie pregnant before he was shipped overseas. He never came back from the South Pacific. Gertie kept the small summer restaurant going to support her twin sons Ed and Allen. Jamie remembered her mother talking about Gertie Higgins with the affection of a fellow pilgrim.

When Jamie was little, she always wanted to ask Ed or Allen what it was like for them growing up without knowing their father. But, by then, they were adults with children of their own. And even though Jamie was seldom shy, she could never bring herself to ask one of Gertie's sons about their dad.

She came close once, on a lazy summer night when her mother had brought them to Gertie's for a burger and fries. But when either Ed or Allen Higgins— Jamie never could tell them apart—moved toward their table emptying ashtrays, she'd known it would make her mom too sad if she asked.

Climbing out of the passenger seat, Kate told her Gertie had died, but Ed's daughter still ran the cement-block restaurant. The original pink neon light flashing *Gertie's* in huge letters now appeared on postcards. Since the end of World War II, Gertie's had gradually become a trademark of Spring Port's public beach. Half a century later, the neon sign's fame was second only to the red lighthouse itself dominating the far end of the pier.

Jamie looked through Gertie's spring-cleaned windows at the cracked vinyl booths in burgundy facing each other over tan formica tables. "How about we eat outside?" Jamie asked easily, thinking about voices carrying in tight spaces.

Kate nodded her agreement, and they walked toward the outdoor tables.

As certain as the daffodils, when Gertie's picnic tables appeared on the weathered deck, winter was over. Jamie wondered if her initials could still be read on one of them through the layers of polyurethane. Was it Ned Turner or Steve Knapp—or even that dirtbag Duane Carmer—who had gouged out J.A.M.I.E. trying to win her over? Trying to get her pants down, actually. But Billy had been the only one until—No! She couldn't go there. Not today of all days.

Kate walked ahead to the farthest table as if she understood the need for privacy. They sat across from each other under a red umbrella encircled with white fringe flapping in the brisk, off-shore breeze. On one side of the table, Lake Michigan tossed scallops of water on the darkened sand a hundred feet away. On the other side, across Beach Road from Gertie's, Jamie noticed many of the quaint old wooden cottages had been replaced by tall new homes with long windows.

"What happened to all those cute old cottages, Kate?" she asked, glad to put off her real question.

"Lake-front property values, I guess. That and taxes. People on the lake can't afford to use their places only three months a year. They end up winterizing or selling. The new buyers tear the whole thing down and build those huge places you see over there."

An older Hispanic woman with a catsup-splattered apron shuffled slowly toward them. The high school kids who hopped around the deck like water bugs trying to earn good tips wouldn't be available to wait tables until school was out in another month.

"We must be early," Kate said scanning the empty picnic benches around them.

"Or else the story of the E coli bacteria has gotten around. Remember how you and I used to beg Mom to bring us here for one of Gertie's greasies when we could eat steak free at the Harbor Inn because Mom worked there?"

Kate cocked her head and smiled at the reminiscence, making her pretty face even prettier. Kate's hair sparkled a luxurious blue-black. The waitress finally arrived to take their orders.

"I'd like a Gertieburger, please, with everything, Anita," Jamie said reading her name tag. "And a cup of coffee. Maybe you could bring out a pot so you don't have to keep running out here to refill our cups?"

She knew Kate had stopped drinking coffee, but she could use the whole pot herself. People in recovery need to keep their hands and mouths busy. But Jamie wasn't about to explain all that to Anita. Since she'd left Tucson, she needed her coffee even more.

Kate ordered the house salad with low-fat Italian on the side. She'd always complained about how much Jamie could eat and not gain weight. But Jamie had a good appetite—except when she did cocaine. When she *used* to do cocaine, she corrected herself.

Anita took the last dish off her tray. "So what's up?" Kate asked

Waiting for the waitress to leave, Jamie watched her sister tip the small styrofoam cup of watery dressing and make neat circles over her lettuce and tomatoes. Jamie took a bite of her own juicy rare hamburger, but could taste only a metallic fear.

"Kate," Jamie said finally, trying to stay calm, "I know this sounds strange, but I need to ask for our old blood-pact, remember?" In spite of the wall Jamie's alcoholism had put between them, she counted on Kate to respect the oath of loyalty they'd sworn at Camp Arbutus. She counted on it because she knew now that Kate had never told their mother about the broken ankle bracelet—about the affair Kate thought Jamie'd had with Alex Hamper's father.

Kate rolled her dark hazel eyes as she used to whenever her little sister said something stupid—which Kate had to do a lot when they were growing up.

"Not even Pete," Jamie said

Kate pushed her wrap-around sunglasses over the top of her thick hair. "I'll probably live to regret this, Jamie, but—okay. Blood-sister silence. Shoot."

"There's one more piece, Kate."

"Now why doesn't that surprise me?" Kate gave her the crooked grin of a childhood conspirator, and it turned the food in Jamie's mouth sour. Kate was trying to make some fun—be friends again. And Jamie was about to hurl lye in her older sister's face. Jamie knew she had to talk fast, or she'd never get it out.

"Kate, Kate—this is the hardest thing—the worst thing I've ever asked of you." She saw Kate's eyes narrow in apprehension. "Yes, far worse than getting me out of jail."

Kate stopped eating, her intensity focused on Jamie's face.

Jamie tapped her fingers nervously on her thighs wanting this not to be happening. Maybe Kate wasn't the answer.

"Well?" Kate asked, her tone now guarded.

Far beyond the lighthouse, Jamie watched a freighter move along the water like an upside down turtle. "Do you want the short or the long version?" Jamie finally spoke, her hand unsteady as she reached for the orange-handled coffee pot. Jamie had no idea what she meant about two versions. But it put off the awful words a few more seconds.

"Let's go with the short." Kate's conspirator's smile was gone.

"I'm pregnant and I need you to help me get an abortion."

High over their heads, a flock of white winged seagulls wheeled in circles making shrill squawking sounds. Kate sat motionless, rigid, reminding Jamie of their childhood game of statue.

"Kate. I know what you're thinking."

Kate yanked her sunglasses off her hair and pressed them hard against the bridge of her nose. "No. No. No, Jamie. You don't. You have no idea what I'm thinking,"

"Oh, yes, I do. I have no right to ask anything of you. Not after the pain I've caused you and Mom and Aunt Nina. We both know I'm a loser, Kate—that's why I'm asking you to help me. I don't want this baby—and I shouldn't have one. Ever. Kate, I don't have to tell you no child deserves me as a mother."

Kate didn't move, didn't seem to be breathing. Jamie sucked in her cheeks against the sick reality of what she'd just asked of the sister she admired more than Kate would ever know. The sister Jamie would have done anything for— and did once. Jamie toyed with the pickle on her plate. She had helped make Kate's dream of Duke happen. But Kate could never know about that either.

"What are you thinking to ask such a thing of me," Kate punctuated each word, "as if I somehow *owed* you something?"

"Owed…owed?" Jamie stumbled over the unexpected word. It was eerie— like when she and Kate used to guess what the other was thinking—and usually got it right. But Kate had no idea about what Jamie had done for her. Only one person knew, and Coach Briggs promised he'd never tell.

Jamie saw Kate's face grow dark, then a small cloud passed overhead and the color deepened.

"It's not about owing, Kate. You're the only one I can turn to because you know I hurt the people I love best. I'd do it to a baby too."

"That's a bullshit excuse." Only Kate's lips moved.

Jamie had to make her understand. "Kate, I went looking for Mom's liquor this morning. That's how good my sobriety is! Believe me, if I had anyone else to ask, I would."

"How—how far along are you?"

"Seven weeks." She could have told Kate to the day. Even the hour, after she subtracted the three-hour time difference. "And please don't ask me about the father because it doesn't matter."

"You don't know?"

Jamie flexed her thigh muscles against the bench for control. Kate meant Roger Hamper. How her promiscuous little sister had jumped in bed with the father of Kate's high school friend who ended up killing himself because of it. "If you need to think of me as an alcoholic slut who doesn't remember who she slept with, fine. But you're so wrong—so wrong about..."

Jamie stopped mid-sentence. She couldn't speak the man's name. Kate's chilling stare, her eyebrows narrowed told Jamie it didn't matter what she said. Kate wouldn't believe her anyway. A young woman in jeans shorts and her boyfriend in a Michigan State tee shirt sat down on the picnic table next to them.

Jamie leaned toward her sister. "Never mind. All I need is you to drive me to the Women's Clinic in Grand Rapids a week from Tuesday," Jamie controlled her voice. "Then get me back to Mother's. Mother doing a bridal shower that afternoon and won't be around. And I promise I'll never ask you for anything again. I'd drive myself if they'd let me."

"You seem to know the routine."

More than anything in the world, Jamie wanted to smack Kate across the face. Smack her for blaming Roger Hamper's death on Jamie when he'd been the one to destroy her. And hit her again even harder for loathing Jamie because she was an alcoholic.

But she had to stuff her urge to retaliate. What she had to do was too important. Jamie had to save this thing—she would not let herself think 'baby'—growing inside her from a life worse than none at all. She did not have the luxury of losing her temper.

"Finished?" The waitress appeared beside them.

"Yes," Kate said standing up abruptly. She pulled a twenty from her wallet. "Keep the change."

"It's too much," Anita started to protest, but Kate waved her off and moved away from the table toward the car. Jamie followed at a distance noticing the clipped movements of Kate's legs, the narrowness of her shoulders. As she heard Kate slam the passenger door of the Saab, Jamie remembered how Kate never had the fluidity or the build to be a competitive swimmer. Then it came back in a rush.

*　　*　　*

Jamie saw herself walk barefoot into the yellow cement-wall office beside the pool and close the metal door. "If my sister doesn't swim at state next week, Coach Briggs, I don't."

Without taking his eyes off her, Coach Briggs gestured over his head toward the back wall. Four blue-silk banners emblazoned in white block letters read, "MICHIGAN CHAMPIONSHIP CLASS B," the title year below. "I'd say my system works pretty good."

Jamie stared back at Coach Briggs.

"Look, I know Kate's a great kid. I've liked having her on the team. But she's no athlete. She could never be the swimmer you are, Jamie. But, heck, she's the smartest kid in Spring Port High. Isn't that good enough?"

"No," Jamie finally spoke. "You have me down for three events at state and Kate's a senior not even swimming. I can't do that."

"So tell me, Coach," Coach Briggs's tone took an edge as he went back to rubbing his hair, "what event did you put your sister in?"

"The freestyle relay. Swimming first. Put me last, and you'll get my personal best. I promise. Kate's always taken care of me—with my mom working and all." Jamie hated people feeling sorry for her. But this time she had play on Brigg's soft heart. She had no choice. "This is one thing I can do for Kate, Coach. It's either, well, both Kate and me or neither of us."

Jamie refused to look away as Coach Briggs studied her unsmiling face.

"Does Kate know about this?"

Jamie was shocked at the question. "Kate? Are you kidding? She'd never do it if she knew." The sound of voices drifted in from the hallway.

"What if I told you that if you don't swim at state for me, you won't swim for Spring Port High again?"

Jamie glanced at the door making sure it was still closed. Then she looked straight into his soft brown eyes. "This is something I have to do."

He leaned toward her, his eyelids rising. "You would give up a great high school swimming career—probably four state titles of your own—a college scholarship—to sit on the bench with your sister? Kate *would* know if you did that."

"I've already thought about that. I'll just do something stupid and get you to kick me off the team. Kate will have no trouble believing that."

Jamie felt the first flutter of hope when she saw the half moons along Coach Briggs' mouth crease into a smile. "You won't regret it, Coach. I promise I'll swim my heart out. And we'll never tell anyone. Never. You won't be sorry."

And he hadn't been. Ten days later, the Spring Port Girls Class B Swim Team came into the final event of the state tournament trailing the perennial power house team from East Grand Rapids. When Jamie Cameron's fingers touched in the last lap of the 200 freestyle, Coach Briggs pulled her out of the pool and wrapped her in a giant bear hug.

"You do keep your promises, Jamie," he said as her back heaved in oxygen-sucking gasps. "State title. State record. Number one all the way. You did it, Champ." Then he whispered close to her wet ear, "And you got your sister her state championship."

Over the screams of the other swimmers mobbing her, Jamie heard Kate's voice calling to her, "My little Jamie! You're the best. Blood sisters forever."

*   *   *

The whirr of air around the open convertible replaced conversation while Jamie drove Kate back to work. The cold silence told Jamie all she had to know. Kate would honor the bond she'd pledged her sister one hot summer night on a hill overlooking Lake Arbutus.

The   Sandpiper

KATE

Alice Graham burst through the door wearing a canary yellow tee under her long white lab coat. The room immediately felt lighter to Kate, the gust of rose cologne sweetening the air. "Kate," Alice began as if she'd been asked a question, "we are going to look at your budding ovaries right this minute."

Kate liked Alice Graham, a large-boned woman in her late 40s—Dr. Bauer's favorite OB nurse when he was delivering babies in Grand Rapids. Unmarried, smart, funny with patients, Alice joined Dr. Bauer when he gave up the unpredictable hours of obstetrics after a mild heart attack. Now he did only infertility, and Alice ran his Spring Port clinic.

He told his patients he was convinced his heart trouble was a God thing as he'd long felt a calling to help couples have children. Alice's former excitement helping deliver babies now spilled into helping infertile women get one of those babies. Alice's wanting it so much for Kate—and never using the word 'if' in talking about pregnancy—made her Kate's friend.

Like two dancers trained for this choreography, Kate pushed her heels into the steel stirrups while Alice chattily distracted her from the cold, lubricated metal she was sliding into Kate's vagina. Kate watched the monitor on a cart beside her as the transducer probe bounced sound waves off her left ovary in a grainy visual image on the screen.

The first time she'd had trans-vaginal ultrasound in Dr. Delgado's high-rise Chicago office, the procedure had repulsed her. Watching the nurse roll a condom over the transducer then rub it with lubricant before inserting it inside her had mortified Kate. Now spreading her legs for the unbending probe felt like a perverse way of opening her mouth for the dentist.

Dr. Bauer stood beside her, his steadiness soothing her apprehension.

"Your blood tests look good, Kate," he said studying the monitor. "The hormones are up—but well within the safe range. And," he pointed at the screen, "look there. Three nice follicles—Alice get a size on those, would you please?"

Kate stared at the black blobby objects on her ovary like three tiny ink spots as Alice measured. "Left and middle 12—far right, 14. Good work , Kate," Alice smiled down with her large white teeth.

"Nice response to Clomid," Dr. Bauer said. This early Tuesday morning he wore pinstriped trousers neatly creased. But she liked it that under his white coat, his tie was widely striped in horizontal band of bright reds and yellows. He was conservative in his medicine, but not too cautious to try new therapies when they got reported in the journals.

A silent prayer whispered through her heart as she stared at the tiny shapes on the screen. Like goat entrails, the uneven spots of gray held the secret of her future.

"Good follicles, Kate." Dr. Bauer tapped the screen, and Kate felt a surge of joy. Her left ovary had been duped into ripening extra follicles, each hiding the miracle of an egg. More eggs, more chances, more hope.

"And four here," he said looking at her right ovary, "none of them oversized at this stage." No dangerous overstimulation of the ovaries was what he meant.

"We'll start the blood work and sonograms now until at least one gets up to 16 millimeters. Then the shot to release the eggs—well, you know the routine. The next day and a half, you'll have your best chance to conceive. We'll all keep saying our prayers and see what happens."

Kate didn't feel worthy of their prayers knowing what she was about to do.

"I must say, Kate," he rested a hand on her shoulder, "you seem agitated this morning. Try to relax, and let me do the worrying for both of us."

The excitement of seeing the follicles evaporated as she headed out the clinic door. In its place flowed a misery, profound and bottomless. She was going to help Jamie destroy what Kate ached to have growing inside her.

Turning on the ignition, she rubbed her eyes, scratchy from a poor night of sleep. This morning she'd heard the peepers outside long before Pete's alarm went off, and she had not wanted the sun to come up. Not wanted this day to begin.

She turned east toward her mother's house, and the anger she'd suppressed since the lunch at Gertie's rose in her like hot smoke. Today, right now she had to face the brutal fact of Jamie's abortion. At some unconscious level she had believed the problem would go away. This day was never going to come. And if Kate Cameron Shane was good at anything, it was disciplining her mind.

Kate had begun that training the day the soldiers came. Watching her mother disappear into grief had forced her young psyche to wall off pain. Out of that wounding tragedy, Kate taught herself to isolate what she could not bear.

Now she was going to pick up the sister she'd loved better than the sun before Roger Hamper's funeral. The broken chain with Jamie's initial. The only way Kate had kept her promise not to tell anyone about the ankle bracelet was sealing it up in a vault of her brain. Now Jamie was asking her to do it again. Keep one more horrific secret.

She put on her sunglasses against the early sun, feeling the blood drain from her heart. She told herself women have abortions every day. None of their reasons justified destroying a life - but who was she to judge them? This wicked act of Jamie's would be over in hours. Then Jamie could never again ask for their bond of secrecy. Kate would be free of it forever.

Stopped for the light at U.S. 31, she wondered what her mother and Aunt Nina would do if they knew what she was doing. A car horn beeped impatiently behind her when she didn't notice the light turn green. No, she didn't really wonder. She could almost see the light go out in her mother's eyes. Almost hear the pitch of fury in Aunt Nina's condemnation. And Kate had already let Aunt Nina down in her neglect—in letting herself forget what Aunt Nina meant to her. Now this.

Her eyes stung like salt knowing Aunt Nina's only fault was loving Kate too much. She and Aunt Nina were the book worms—the poetry lovers—the writers. But then Kate proved Aunt Nina wrong about Duke and she had gloated like a spoiled child. She'd treated her scholarship as some sort of put-down on Aunt Nina. Kate had a lot of unkindnesses to make up for—and she didn't have a lot of time left to do it.

She double parked behind the Lakeshore News office and ran inside to pick up copy to proof. She needed to stay busy while she waited for Jamie. She could not let herself think about what was happening after they took Jamie away.

"Hey," Joe O'Connor called after her in the hallway as she hurried toward the back door carrying a manila folder stuffed with news articles. "Those women in that investment club your friend gave me—Women of Wall Street—they've made more money than the S & P average. Not bad for females, huh?"

Kate did not have teasing in her right then. "Can't wait to read it," she waved a feeble hand and turned to go. "I'll try to get back before you leave. I have to go—go out of town."

"The story's in your computer by five. And by the way, the WOW's president told me she heard your mother's group bought Walmart on the IPO and made a killing."

"That's great, really great. Got to run, Joe." Kate had no time or interest for this.

"Lakeshore development or the Indian casinos?" Joe stepped forward to open the door. "Any preference?"

"Fine. Whatever." Then hearing her own inattentiveness, she paused at the doorway. "They're both important stories. Your call on the timing."

Kate watched herself climb back into the car. She could no longer pretend the terrible mission was not going to happen.

The Sandpiper

KATE

Jamie was standing in the yard when Kate pulled in front of her mother's house. At the sight of her younger sister emerging from the door, a blaze of outraged envy made Kate's mouth go dry. Jamie half ran down the sidewalk and grabbed the door handle before Kate could turn the engine off. "Let's go before Mom hears your car," Jamie said at once.

But their mother was already walking down the driveway from the kitchen at the back of the house carrying a foil-covered paper plate. She got to the car before Jamie could close the passenger door. "A couple peanut butter cookies for the road," their mother handed the plate in to Jamie. "And I don't want to hear a word from either of you about calories."

"Mom," Kate forced an upbeat tone, "you'd think we were going off to camp." Kate hunched over the steering wheel so she could look up at her mother leaning on Jamie's open door. The yellow flecks in her mother's eyes sparkled like spun gold. It was all Kate could do not to blurt out everything.

Kate needed to stay strong. She had to deflect any intuition that something was not right here. Growing up, Kate and Jamie could never fool their mother. But too many years of fear over Jamie's addiction had forced their mother not to see what she couldn't stand to. Her mother's denial about Jamie was painful to Kate, but today she needed it. She could never let her mother find out where they were going.

"Our favorites, Mom," Kate said leaning over Jamie. "except we like to eat the dough first." Kate pulled a moist, warm cookie from under the tinfoil. Her mother's grin torqued her heart.

"I don't need to tell either of you how it feels," her mother tapped her own chest, "right here to see you girls going off together to have some fun. Like old times. Like you always did."

Kate looked down at the white rounds of skin where the knuckles of her left hand gripped the steering wheel. Jamie exhaled beside her. Kate recognized her sister's painful spasms of guilt. Kate put the car in gear just before Jamie pulled the passenger door shut with a grim forcefulness. By the time they reached I-96 east to Grand Rapids, Jamie had changed radio stations at least five times.

"You felt like a shit back there too," Kate finally said with enough volume to be heard over the jarring music. "And, please, could you turn it down a little? It's too loud."

Jamie jabbed her finger into the power button, the abrupt silence almost more disturbing than the noise. "If you're not going to eat any more of these," Jamie held the plate toward her, "I'd like to put them in the backseat so I can't smell them."

"Just one and make Mom happy—" Then it hit Kate. Morning sickness. The blessing of nausea—the sign of a miracle happening.

"Mom's been baking for me since I got home." Jamie said not hearing Kate's broken sentence. She leaned back into the seat. "She's working on the sugar thing."

"Sugar?" Kate rolled her window down a few inches to clear the peanut-butter smell she wished made her sick. And talking about anything—even sugar—was better than the only subject today.

"Alcohol turns to sugar in the body so when we alcoholics quit drinking, we crave sweets. At least in the beginning." Jamie made an unpleasant laughing sound. "I've had enough beginnings to know."

"Mother knows that about the sugar?" Kate looked at Jamie's dark lashes over closed eyes.

Jamie nodded without opening her eyes. "Mother and Aunt Nina are walking experts on alcoholism and addiction. Aunt Nina's read every book ever written on the subject." Then her voice fell to almost a whisper. "The one book Mom really needs is on letting go."

"And denial," Kate said, then instantly regretted it. She did not mean to pick a fight with Jamie. This day was going to be hard enough. But it was too late.

"Well, that's one thing you certainly don't need an AA book for. You have never denied what a hopeless drunk I am."

"Is that why we're doing this, Jamie? Because you can't quit drinking? A baby can't be born because you love booze and drugs more? Is that what this is? Because I'd kind of like to know seeing as how you've manipulated me into this." Kate could see a dark flush spread along her sister's neck. Jamie's hands began digging into her thighs until the material of her khaki skirt buried her fingernails.

"Shut the hell up!" Jamie's voice reverberated with stoked anger. "Just shut your mouth and drive and after today we'll never have to do anything together again ever."

"Jamie," Kate erupted, "you have to be the most selfish, immature person I've ever known!" She thought about Dr. Bauer's kindness an hour earlier telling her to stay calm, to *let me do the worrying for both of us.* "This is all about poor Jamie without one second of thought to what you're making me do."

"This," Jamie jabbed hard at her belly, "has nothing to do with you and is none of your business."

"I'm sorry, but that's my flesh and blood and Mother's grandchild!" Kate couldn't breathe for a moment. She'd finally said out loud what she'd tried not to name before now. Grandchild. Jamie was carrying the grandchild she couldn't give their mother. Jamie had succeeded at the one thing Kate wanted most.

"Unreal!" Jamie's voice shrilled into her thoughts. "The liberated editor who talks choice now turns sob sister when it's actually going to happen! Don't you think it's a bit hypocritical to believe in women's rights and then get upset if somebody's uterus has to get scraped?"

"You make it sound like no big deal, Jamie. Like you've—have you, I mean gone through this before?" She looked over in time to see Jamie's head fall forward as if the neck muscles had been severed.

Jamie sat still for a moment, then finally answered, her voice tired. "You know everything, Kate. Why ask."

Jamie's words caught Kate in the chest. Reflexively, she pressed the accelerator, her thoughts clarified. Until that instant, Kate had intended to try and talk Jamie out of the abortion. She'd planned to take her time driving to Grand Rapids—to say whatever she had to, but she *would* change Jamie's mind.

But not now. No, this angry, uncaring woman wasn't the Jamie she knew. The little sister she'd loved and watched out for was not someone who could abort a baby like an extra suitcase.

Now she had to agree with Jamie. Her sister was too sick to take care of a baby—especially one that might be damaged from Jamie's addictions. Kate pressed the accelerator.

Once, at Cook County Hospital having dinner with Pete, a neonatal nurse had walked them through the nursery and pointed out a newborn crack baby, its tiny legs in jerky kicks, the stick arms trembling. "He's in his little and forever hell," the nurse had told them, her voice sad with helplessness. Kate watched the Mazda's speedometer needle flutter up to 80.

Kate saw them blocks away. She was afraid they'd be there. They were the people who wrote angry letters to the Lakeshore News every week, the Right-to-Life protesters. This morning her own soul carried too much freight for any confrontation. Yet as she waited for the light at the top of Division Avenue, the sight of the dozen or so marchers waving red-inked signs above their heads hardened Kate's conviction. She would not let them intimidate her. She was not going to let the picketers stop her from doing what had to be done.

These sign carriers had no business telling an addict like Jamie she had to have a baby whether she could take care of it or not. Whether she'd abuse it in a drunken stupor or not. The stoplight turned green. Kate moved forward, looking sideways to see Jamie's eyes partially closed, her head back against the seat. She guessed Jamie was trying not to see the protestors as they began to bunch up at the clinic's driveway when the Mazda slowed down, and the left-turn signal started blinking.

The Women's Clinic was on Hill Street just off Division. Kate knew the protestors could not trespass on Clinic property. But from the sidewalk they began to chant something about dead babies as she drove past them into the long driveway. She turned on the radio, letting the loud music drowned out their words while she circled the small parking lot behind the one-story grey building.

The Women's Clinic was a grim series of concrete blocks broken only by three opaque windows sealed with chicken wire. Kate stared at the metal grids supporting the glass, and in a whirled vision, the steel shaped itself into a smooth speculum pushing into her own barren uterus. She could not count how many times she'd felt the shock of cold metal slide inside her.

Jamie sat forward with a jerk, her dead eyes staring at the building. Then, without looking at Kate, Jamie pointed toward red tail lights at the other side of the parking lot. "That van's leaving," she called above the jarring music.

Kate pulled her car over to give the van space to back around her. As she waited, she watched the distant mouths of the marchers moving like so many angry mimes at the end of the driveway. At least their threats of damnation were overpowered by the car radio.

The van finally began to move forward, and Kate wondered if the person sitting low in the passenger seat had just had her body emptied of humanity. How far along had she been? Was it going to be a boy or a girl? What could possibly be so wrong in her life that she couldn't let one little baby be born? "Keep saying your prayers," Dr. Bauer had said an hour earlier.

Suddenly Kate thought of a picture she'd seen in Pete's obstetrics textbook when she'd once had the arrogance to think she could have a baby whenever she wanted. And when it didn't happen right away, she dismissed it as bad timing. Pete's schedule, her work—their lives too crazy. Yet Kate had always been willing to dig deeper to get what she wanted. If she wanted a baby, she would simply *make* it happen.

The picture in the Pete's book was a twelve-weeks fetus with feet and fingers and ears. Kate hadn't looked at it in over two years. She knew part of that was superstition. But another part was penance. It was her self-imposed humility to make up for her presumption of pregnancy on demand. Having a baby was not a given, she'd finally understood. And now she was taking her own sister...

With a lurch, as if another driver had taken the wheel, Kate's car locked into gear and she hit the power locks on her door. The van's startled driver whipped his head toward her as she accelerated around him, racing through the lot and straight down the driveway, only half seeing the marchers jump out of her way. She knew the Right To Life people wouldn't grasp what was happening until they saw her speed away down Division Avenue, barely glancing at oncoming traffic.

"What the hell do you think you're doing?" Jamie screamed, the vein in her neck pulsating.

Behind them the cheering calls of the protesters mixed with the loud music and Jamie's curses, all the sounds crashing together in the car like a flock of crazed birds that couldn't land. Kate had no illusions she was stopping an abortion. Jamie would find someone else to drive her back. Her sponsor, maybe. Gloria something. Anyone, but not Kate.

And she would not lie to herself about doing this to save a tiny human being. Certainly the image from Pete's book was too fresh, too real. But right now she was running away from the clinic, the car doors locked around Jamie, out of selfishness. Something truer than reason whispered in Kate's ear. If she walked her sister through those clinic doors, God would never let her have a baby of her own.

The Sandpiper

JAMIE

"I ran into Dr. Madison today, Aunt Nina." Jamie came onto the deck carrying two tall glasses of ice tea.

Aunt Nina tilted her face toward the orange ball of sun suspended over the water. "So whatever happened to patient-doctor confidentiality?"

"Nothing," Jamie put the glasses on a low table between their chaises. "He wouldn't answer any of my questions, if you have to know." She stretched out beside Aunt Nina and held her tea glass in the air to watch the condensation refract the sun's rays into sprinkles of gems. Then she put it down next to a plate of marinated shrimp from a party her mother had catered the night before. She handed Nina a tooth-picked shrimp and popped one into her own mouth before she dropped her sandals on the deck.

"That's the first thing your mother does when we come out here," Aunt Nina pointed at the sandals.

"Bet you never threw hers in the poison ivy."

"Didn't have to because she wasn't a smart ass. So it looks like maybe you're getting it this time, Cookie?"

The quiet twilight lap of small waves seemed to Jamie like the lake's own heart matching hers, beat for beat, after a day of blazing sun and high winds. "Can we talk about something else?"

She felt Aunt Nina's eyes watching her. "Okay. For a minute anyway," Aunt Nina's voice blended with the water sounds. "So how many nights do you think we've been out here like this, Jamie girl, and watched the sun go down? *Bring me the sunset in a cup. Reckon the morning's flagons up, And say how many dew.*"

"Sounds like your Emily again." Jamie looked over at Aunt Nina's high forehead. The diminished flesh of her cheeks caught something in the underside of Jamie's ribs.

"Front of the class, Cookie."

Jamie gnawed inside her lower lip, then forced a laugh. "But your New England poet never saw our big lake's green flash."

Nina chuckled in the soft crackling sound Jamie could pick out in a noisy crowd. "You and your green flash. The reason you've never seen it when the sun drops under that perfect horizon is because there is no flash."

"You have always been my reality check, Aunt Nina."

"Never to kill the magic, I hope. I mean Merlin and Santa Claus—now those two fellows do live even if your green flash is a phantom."

Jamie smiled thinking how Aunt Nina had been the one person in her life who'd reminded her to laugh when all she'd wanted was not to breathe anymore.

"You know you're looking more like your mother all the time?" Aunt Nina asked looking over at her.

"How about my dad? I'd like to think I look like him too. At least from his picture."

Aunt Nina went quiet. "Your mom and I need to have a little heart-to-heart about that."

Jamie watched a lone gull hover in an air current, the black-tipped wings extended in pure float. "She'll never talk about him, if that's what you're thinking."

Beside her Aunt Nina sipped her tea, then carefully put it on the table. She spread her thin fingers apart on her lap. "I don't have that many talks left, so she'll humor me."

Jamie squeezed against a hiccup of sadness. Whatever else she did, she was not going to let Aunt Nina see her cry.

"He's been a taboo subject long enough. At least Kate knew him." Aunt Nina's voice quieted. "I knew him too. And Jim Cameron deserves more than silence. I don't care if I piss your mother off. It's time."

Jamie let her lungs fill back up. "I'll bet you never talked like that back in Connecticut."

"I never did a lot of things back in Connecticut. Like have a family who cared about me."

Jamie held her breath. "Don't start, Aunt Nina," she tightened her stomach muscles against the thrust of a sob. "You said no sentimental crap," Jamie put her fingers over wet eyelids. "I wasn't going to cry tonight and you are such a shit for making me."

Aunt Nina reached for her hand and gave one squeeze. Jamie looked over to see Aunt Nina's clear grey eyes on her—soft with kindness. How many times had Aunt Nina rocked Jamie in her arms and murmured, "It's going to be all right, Cookie. It's going to be all right."

Aunt Nina turned and punched her fist into the back cushion to soften it, then leaned back. "So now, my dear," she said as she bit into a shrimp, "if you're done talking trash, let's get back to the real topic. Your mom tells me you've been on a big downer since the shopping trip."

Jamie flinched.

"Oh, forget it." Aunt Nina shook her head. "You girls haven't fooled me for years. I know Kate didn't get a headache so you had to come back from Grand Rapids without shopping. You two had a fight and I don't give a damn what about."

Jamie had to talk about anything—anything at all but Kate and that day. As she struggled against remembering, she suddenly realized Aunt Nina had paused to press a discreet palm against her ribs. It was a gesture of pain Jamie knew she was not supposed to see. Aunt Nina wanted it that way—acceptance, not sympathy.

Once Nina's exquisite strength had carried Jamie's mother out of a bottomless pit. She'd stayed tight beside the young widow Ellie Cameron and dragged her back into the light. Now Aunt Nina needed that undiluted strength for herself. Jamie would honor her rules.

"You just better be friends when I'm gone," Aunt Nina went on as if nothing happened, "because you're mother's going to need you both. And you sober. So what's with the long face your mom's talking about?"

Jamie scrunched her feet toward her fanny until both knees were bent. Who else but Aunt Nina, an incurable cancer eating her bones, still worried about everybody else? Death, clearly, did not have the power to peel away her goodness. She wrapped her arms around her knees and watched two yellow Seadoos zip down the lake, their wakes making spray fins.

"Same old baggage, Aunt Nina. Guilt. Shame." And for reasons beyond the drinking—for reasons Aunt Nina didn't need to know.

"You're half-truthing me, Cookie. You're not happy."

Aunt Nina knew her too well. Jamie could not lie—but she didn't have to tell her the worst either.

"I know if I relapse, I'll end up dead. That's not a happy thought." Jamie pierced another shrimp with a toothpick festooned in pink.

"That's not what your mother's talking about. She says you can't sit still. That you were calmer when you first got home."

"Is that what you think?" Jamie stalled.

Aunt Nina shrugged. "I told her you'd just gotten done with three months at a Tucson rehab spa so who would be relaxed? Here you are back in the real world with a car and a credit card in your purse and the chance to drink if you want. Of course you're going to be strung tight."

That was only part of it. The twilight air took on a sudden chill. Jamie pulled her black sweatshirt over her head against the cooling air as the bottom rim of the sun touched the water.

"Okay," Aunt Nina finally said, her voice tired. "Your mom also told me you've been driving your sponsor Gloria to job interviews." Aunt Nina reached a weightless hand over to lay it on Jamie's arm. "Now that's the Jamie I do know." Aunt Nina hesitated a moment. Then, her voice low, she asked, "Did I ever tell you, Jamie, that Harley Briggs told me about the state championship?"

Jamie's shoulder blades tensed.

"What you did for Kate? Don't worry, I've never told anyone."

Jamie stared at Aunt Nina.

"No, not even your mom."

"Because it didn't matter," Jamie spoke fast. She didn't want to talk about Kate. "She'd have gotten the full scholarship from Duke anyway."

Aunt Nina let out a sudden hiccup sound, then coughed, a dry scraping rasp that scared Jamie.

"Are you all right?" Jamie jumped up.

Aunt Nina nodded vigorously, one fist pressed to her mouth. Jamie leaned forward, both hands extended toward Aunt Nina. "That's it. The no-seeums are out and it's time for me to go. Are you going to be offended if I offer to clean up and get you ready for bed?"

Aunt Nina ignored Jamie's outstretched hands as she eased herself out of the chaise, holding her back stiffly. Jamie had to squeeze her own fingers not to reach out and lift her. Aunt Nina used the back of the chair for support to stand up. Then, as soon as her hands were free, she used both index fingers to give Jamie the bird. The perfect inappropriateness of Aunt Nina's balancing so she could give the double finger tugged up a teary laugh Jamie could not stop.

"How graciously you decline," Jamie finally could speak. Not even bothering to wipe her wet cheeks, she gathered the glasses and barely touched shrimp plate. "I won't offer again soon."

"That's the point," Aunt Nina said over her shoulder. Jamie tried not to see the thinness of her legs as she followed Aunt Nina across the deck to the back door.

"Remember the Ugly Stepsister's Sandpiper Shuffle, Jamie Girl?" The name triggered memories of what Jamie needed most right then. Pure joy. At the oddest hours, Aunt Nina would appear at the Cameron house announcing herself as the fairy godmother. "Forget Cinderella," she'd tell the two giggling girls, "I'm taking these ugly step-sisters out to do the Sandpiper Shuffle."

They each had to grab a favorite book, no toothbrushes or clothes because they kept all that at Aunt Nina's cottage. The Sandpiper Shuffle was a short-notice slumber party—on the beach if it was warm enough.

It had taken Jamie years to realize Aunt Nina called it the Ugly Stepsisters' Sandpiper Shuffle instead of what it really was. The break their mother needed, but would never ask for. Waiting tables and raising two children alone, their mother needed time away from Kate and Jamie. But Aunt Nina understood that in the logic of childhood, they might have thought their mother's wanting to be alone for a night meant one day she would go away and never come back like their father had. So she named it the Ugly Stepsisters...

All at once it hit Jamie. "Are you saying?"

"No. Not yet, Cookie. Not quite yet."

"Oh, Aunt Nina, what if I can't do it when the time comes?" Jamie's heart began to pound in something close to panic. "Maybe—maybe you should let your niece—I mean you wouldn't have to worry about Cecilia going off to the bar."

"No, I wouldn't. But she might bore me to death before the cancer could get me."

Jamie grabbed the deck railing to laugh as she pictured Nina's over-permed and over-weight niece playing nurse with one eye on the soaps. She'd only met Cecilia once, but it was enough. "I still don't believe she's your blood, Aunt Nina."

"Her dad was a lot more fun." Harold Judd, who had died long before, was Aunt Nina's only sibling.

Jamie knew how many times Aunt Nina had invited Cecilia and her husband and two children to come visit, but they never did. Beyond thank you notes for the Christmas and birthday checks Aunt Nina sent all of them, Cecilia made little effort to keep in touch with her aunt. Only after Aunt Nina wrote

Cecilia about the cancer's recurrence, did her niece call to say she was coming to take care of her favorite aunt. Aunt Nina had graciously declined. They all knew Cecilia would come soon enough to cash in her inheritance by selling the cottage.

What Jamie suspected, and Cecilia could not, was that running The Sandpiper Club, Aunt Nina had taken on the stock market as she did King Lear. She would understand every facet of options and derivatives as she did every word Lear howled on the moor. Then Aunt Nina would apply her powerful intuition to grasp the nuances of market trades just as she understood the old king's tragic cries. Yes, Jamie was pretty sure Cecilia would inherit a lot more than The Sandpiper.

But whatever Cecilia did after Aunt Nina really didn't matter. The thought of her selling the Sandpiper would have crushed Jamie—except that without Aunt Nina, it was only a building.

"Sorry, Aunt Nina. I didn't really mean that about getting Cecilia here." What Jamie did mean was that this dearest of women needed to be surrounded by people who cared about her. Mixed up as she might be, Jamie loved her Aunt Nina with all the force of her being. Maybe as much as she loved her own mother. But that was all right. Her mother loved Aunt Nina that much too.

And so did Kate. Jamie couldn't help thinking about Kate because something had happened between her sister and Aunt Nina. Whatever it was, Kate needed to get over it before they lost Aunt Nina. She had to for Aunt Nina—and for herself.

"Cecilia means well," Aunt Nina said, "even if she's a little enamored with the sound of her own voice. Now give me a hug."

Jamie put her arms around Aunt Nina carefully, feeling the pointed bones under her thick sweatshirt.

The screen door snapped on its spring behind Aunt Nina as Jamie walked toward her car. Overhead, the twilight etched the tree limbs in grey-black angles. The dying sun sent ripples of pink across the driveway. She looked back to see Aunt Nina standing behind the screen, her hands at her waist as if she were holding up her torso. They stood still looking at each other for a long moment. Then Jamie blew one brief kiss from her finger tips. She held on until the car reached the log cabin. Then the sobs began to lurch out of her throat.

The Sandpiper

KATE

"Hey!"

Kate's head jerked up from her computer startled by the sudden voice.

"Woops." Joe O'Connor made an exaggerated grimace. "I think I scared you from that deep pool of concentration you immerse yourself in. Would that I had a quarter of your cerebral focus. Might make deadlines once in a while. But time to come up for air. I'm buying at Barry's."

"I can't," Kate said automatically. Since the day she'd driven Jamie away from the clinic, she'd buried herself in work. It kept her from obsessing on Jamie and which day she'd gone back. Which day Kate had lost a niece or nephew. Her mother a grandchild. She stared blankly at the computer screen and then tapped it with her finger nail. "Look, I'm editing your story," she pointed at the slug identifying the article. *Lighthouse Beach Campsites Filled For July 4ᵗʰ Weekend.*

"Copy guys don't need that story before two. We'll be back in lots of time for you to finish it. Look, you've been non-stop at this computer lately. And remember I told you when Lathrup moved you up, I wasn't going to let you turn into a work robot. And besides you need to give me, your best reporter, some strokes for the great job I did on investment clubs. Let's go."

Kate sighed, then hit the save key. Joe O'Connor had been her friend before she'd known it. And it was only by chance she'd found out.

She still felt embarrassed remembering how she'd given herself credit for the warm reception she'd gotten when she first arrived at the Lakeshore News. She'd been nervous that the staff, most of them older than she, might resent her walking in as the managing editor. But when they welcomed her from the first day, she'd told Pete she must have good people skills.

Al Ryan, one of the Lakeshore's more garrulous ad salesmen, slipped one day and told Kate Joe had threatened anyone who gave her a bad time. "I don't give a rip how young she is," he'd said to the grumblers. "The lady's got credentials. Consider ourselves lucky she didn't take the Daily's offer."

Joe was in his late 30s, barrel-chested with shaggy dark hair the same color as his horn-rimmed glasses. Smart and respected by the staff and readers, Joe wore his standard jeans and wrinkled plaid shirt—his "river guide" look Kate called it. She knew from Marcia that Joe and his wife were in marriage counseling. Because they didn't have children, Kate was sure. The absence of babies must have something to do with their marital distress. She knew she went overboard seeing too many things through the lens of wanting a baby; but she also knew the strain infertility put on a marriage.

"Stop," Joe raised a hand as they started toward the Lakeshore's front door. "Forgot my notebook. Never leave home without it." Kate was standing at the door to Joe's office when the phone on his desk rang. Fumbling through his top drawer with one hand, Joe picked up the receiver and tucked it against his shoulder.

"I'm out the door so this better be imp—oh, hello, Mr. Brocker. No, no, I need to talk to you too." Joe rolled his eyes at Kate, then pulled what looked like a rubber-banded poster off the bookshelf behind him. He waved her into the room and handed it to her, making a signal she should unroll it.

"Right. The Nortier property. Not long. Just a few questions," Joe shoved papers around. Kate never understood how anyone as bright as Joe could work in such confusion. The top of his desk was strewn with scattered pink sticky notes of phone messages, a wire basket overflowing with print-out copy, and an unworking clock with a brass plate she couldn't read. Jamie was the only other bright person she'd ever known who could function in such disarray. But Kate didn't want to think about Jamie.

Instead she thought how somebody's patient fingers had stitched the needle-point sign in primary yellows and reds and blues that hung behind Joe's desk. "An empty desk is the sign of an empty mind." She wondered if that wasn't simply clever rationalization. It was easy to make excuses for anything. Messiness. Alcoholism. Even abortion.

Kate had half waited for Jamie to jerk the steering wheel or grab for the power locks so she could jump out of the car. But she hadn't. Instead, after her furious outburst, Jamie had sat motionless, seemingly exhausted by the torrent of insults she'd hurled at Kate. Then she'd balled herself up against the passenger door, her head on the window, and never spoken another word.

Kate pushed back the memory and grabbed three books plus the clock, juggling them to the hardwood floor. She kneeled down to unroll what she saw was a huge aerial land map of Spring Port Township, using the weights to anchor the four corners. Joe walked around his desk and pointed down at two red circles on the grey-brown map. One was marked "Nortier Property." The circle next to it had a question mark in the middle.

"Just wondered about the status of your development, Mr. Brocker," Joe said. "Yes, I was at the planning commission meeting. Right. I understand your frustration. Of course. But they do have to wait for the DEQ's decision. You know, the sensitive dunes. Of course. I understand. Yes, I do know the township's engineers have approved it. Right." He flapped his fingers toward Kate in the sign of a talker.

"Actually, Mr. Brocker, what I called you about was to see if you've had any luck buying the second property. The piece directly north of the Nortier land?" Joe moved back to his desk and began scribbling notes, nodding his head as if Mr. Brocker could see him.

Kate turned the map so that north was above her, the only way she could orient herself. Jamie was the one who'd led the hikes at Camp Arbutus. She was like a woods creature instinctively knowing the unmarked paths to remote campsites. One day the counselors with their compasses had tried to fool Jamie with false directions, but she beat them back to camp.

Again Kate had to put Jamie out of her head—pay attention to what Joe wanted. What this map was all about. She tapped Lake Michigan on the west edge of the map where it belonged. Not in the east where she'd had to deal with it in Chicago. She never did get used to the sun rising over the big lake.

Now she found the Michigan Power Plant just off Lakeshore Drive not far below the two red circles. She traced her finger south until she located Olive Road off Sheldon Street leading to a dark speck that had to be Aunt Nina's cottage. From this aerial photo, The Sandpiper was a tiny pebble in fuzzy brown like an old sepia photograph.

"Sorry that took so long, Kate," Joe said leaning over her shoulder. "This guy Brocker is from Texas and runs a major financial firm in New York. He's impossible to reach, and then he never shuts up. I had to grab him while I could."

"I remember Bea and Frank Nortier from a long time ago," Kate said pointing at the red circle marked with their name. "They were old then so I'm sure they're gone. My Aunt Nina was a good friend of theirs. I'm surprised their children—maybe even their grandchildren—would sell the cottage. It's been in their family forever. Especially that they'd sell to some Texas developer."

"You wouldn't be if you knew their 200 feet of lake frontage is worth $15,000 a foot. Brocker doesn't care a rip about the cottage. It's the frontage with its two acres of land. If he can buy the adjoining lot too," Joe tapped the circle with a question mark, "which has another 200 front feet, he's going to tear down the old Nortier cottage and subdivide the two parcels.

"He'll put up four mega-bucks houses on the lake, with 100 feet of lake frontage each, then build as many smaller homes behind them as he can get. People will pay to live near the big lake even if they're not on it." Kate understood that. The lake's spiritual power had pulled her in for as long as she could remember.

"The real estate man who handled the sale told me the Nortier grandchildren were not happy when they found out about Brocker's plans even with his hefty offer. But Brocker's a wheeler-dealer so he sweetened the pot by promising to name the development "The Nortier Dunes" once he buys the neighboring lot."

"At least I like the naming part. I have good memories of the Nortiers. Frank and Bea. We used to take them blueberry muffins every summer after we'd gone picking. Aunt Nina drank coffee with them and my sister," Kate held her breath a moment, "well, we used to run up and down the huge dunes right next to their cottage. Wild asparagus grew there and we'd pick some for dinner.

"So this," she tapped the red circle with the question mark, "this has to be those same sand dunes. That's the piece of land you were asking Brocker about?"

"If he'd bought it, yes. The Nortiers sold it off years ago, but Brocker can't locate the actual title filing. It's in some kind of sealed trust. He's hot to buy it so he can develop both parcels into one luxury compound."

"He must have checked with the Spring Port assessor to find out who pays the property taxes."

"He and I both did. No luck. The checks are signed by the lawyer for a trust that owns the property. The T.T. Lane Trust," Joe said checking his notes. "Nobody around here remembers the Lane family—and certainly not with that kind of property on the big lake. You didn't happen to know anybody named Lane when you lived here?"

"Beyond Superman's girlfriend? Not that I can think of. It's a common enough name."

"Wherever they are, they got a gold mine with those dunes you and your sister cruised. Look," he leaned over to run his finger along the huge expanse of dark that was Lake Michigan, "this unknown Lane parcel also has 200 front feet on the water just like the Nortier's land with its four acres that Brocker now owns

"But here's what's big, and why he's salivating." Joe pointed at two parallel white lines running back from the lake. "This lot with the question mark—the Lane piece—is twice as deep. Almost eight acres. Four-hundred front feet and twelve acres on the big lake? If Brocker can combine them, we're talking some serious money."

Kate sighed thinking how she'd assumed those dunes would always be there. Free to run down. Pick asparagus on. "Pete and I dream about living on the lake—but who can afford it anymore? I doubt Aunt Nina has any clue how valuable her little cottage has gotten."

"Her property-tax bills must be telling her," Joe said looking down at the map. "Oh, but she gets the homestead exemption and if she's never sold it, she pays at the taxable value, not the assessed value. Show me where she is. What's her last name?"

"Judd. Helena Judd. I was three when I met her—she's not my real aunt." She's far more important to me than any real aunt ever could be, Kate thought with a chill of sadness. And I need to tell her that.

"I've heard about her. The English teacher from the high school everybody in town knows? And seems to love?"

"Yes," Kate couldn't help a twinge of pride. "She taught English at Spring Port High until a few years ago." Kate tapped the pebble she decided was The Sandpiper, the even tinier speck behind it the log cabin. "She's right here."

Joe leaned forward to look. "Well, she's sitting on a small pot of gold too. How long has she owned it?"

Kate shrugged her shoulders. "As long as I've been around. Actually, no, I do know when she bought it. It was just before she met my par—parents." Jamie and she once talked about stumbling on 'my parents.' It was a term they'd never needed.

"In 1968—during the Vietnam War," she said carefully. Joe's silence told her he knew about her dad.

"Well," he said after a deliberate moment, "the land was cheap in the late sixties because of the alewives and beach erosion—hey, wait a sec. Do you think maybe your Aunt Nina has an idea who Mr. T. T. Lane is?"

"Possibly," Kate said, grateful to Joe for not asking about her dad. "She taught for so many years, she knew almost every Spring Port family at some point." Then Kate sat back on her heels. "But if these Lane people want to be anonymous and Aunt Nina *does* know them, she'll never break a confidence." Kate thought about Aunt Nina's loyalty compared to her own. "She's that kind of person." She wondered if Joe heard the remorse.

"And Tom Quinn can't tell us because he has the whole client-attorney thing."

"Tom Quinn?"

"He's the Lane family's lawyer. Do you know him too?"

"His daughter Sarah was my best friend growing up."

My best except for Jamie, Kate didn't say out loud. "Sarah's mother Sandy Quinn is a close friend of my mother's and Aunt Nina's. They're all in the investment club I told you about. In fact, Aunt Sandy's the one I tried to get you an interview with. And I still don't get why she wouldn't do it."

"Could this be the same club that bought Walmart on the IPO, according to rumors among the WOWs?"

"The Sandpipers? Yeah, right! Listen, the Sandpiper women are like the bridge groups who meet every month and never get out the cards. I doubt they know what an IPO is. Except for Aunt Nina who does all the club's work. And has since she started the club.

"It was right after my mother moved here from Ann Arbor and it gave Mom an instant group of great women friends. I've often wondered if that wasn't half the reason Aunt Nina set up the club. The Sandpiper women have stayed close ever since."

"Sounds like an interesting lady, your Aunt Nina."

Kate looked past Joe's shoulder in silence. How could she begin to tell Joe about Aunt Nina?

"And Tom Quinn," Joe was taking notes, "what about him?"

"Tell you anything? No way. Uncle Tom—Mr. Quinn—wouldn't spill a client's business under torture. Lane's probably the married name of somebody in the Waters family or maybe the Amway people. They already own half the lakeshore in Holland. And they'd never sell—especially to a developer."

Joe held the front door for her as they headed to Barry's. "Knowing how keen Brocker is on that land—and how deep his pockets are, I'm betting he'll find out who owns those dunes one way or another. Once he does, since everyone has a price at which they'll sell, he'll own both parcels. But will you ask your Aunt Nina? It's worth a try."

She looked at Joe, a sudden twitch in her gut. Was her mother right about coincidences, she wondered as they crossed Harbor Street. Her mother believed coincidences were not accidents, but memos from God. The thing was you had to pay attention if you wanted to get the message. Kate already knew she couldn't wait much longer to bring Aunt Nina back into her life. Really in. Now Joe was handing her the perfect opening to begin a conversation she had not known how to start. A memo from God.

The   Sandpiper

JAMIE

The sweat in her armpits smelled raunchy. Of course she'd picked the hottest day since she'd been in Spring Port to move into Aunt Nina's. And she knew she was packing with the same impulsiveness she did everything in life. She'd upended the dresser drawers on the bed at her mother's and was stuffing the jumble of clothing into the battered blue suitcase she'd lugged more places than she could stand to think about. The rest of her things were already crammed into a black garbage bag in the back seat of the Saab, the hanging clothes piled on top.

Whatever hadn't been wrinkled before certainly was now. Looking at the mess she'd made of her old bedroom, she suspected her mother had felt a glimmer of relief when Aunt Nina called to say it was time. The protective mother and alcoholic daughter under one roof were starting to make each other crazy. Jamie didn't think she could take another day of her mother's forced cheerfulness—her careful conversations about anything but what really mattered.

The light banter could not distract Jamie from noticing the tension lines around her mother's mouth. Ellie's brave effort to disguise her worries about a relapse only made Jamie feel guiltier than she already did.

The worst of it was that Jamie knew how close to the truth her mother's fears were. Despite her mother's skill at not seeing what she didn't want to, Jamie knew she still had static-free antenna about her younger daughter. Her mother was straitjacketed by the fear Jamie was about to drink—or already had. But what her mother couldn't know was that Jamie was even more scared about it. One day at a time was too long right now. Jamie was counting her sobriety by the hour.

And the only people she could tell about it—the only people who under-stood her struggle—were the women from No Sniveling. Thank God for Gloria. Jamie dumped the contents of her medicine cabinet into a brown paper bag. Her sponsor's bulldog friendship had kept Jamie from slipping more than once since she'd come back to Spring Port.

Gloria Cook was a smart buxom black woman with a smile full of perfect teeth that Crest should photograph. Gloria was in her mid-30s with two daugh-ters by a live-in boyfriend who'd wanted to marry her. Gloria had refused. Even while she was "a drunk," as AA people often called themselves, he wasn't up to her standards of what a father should be.

Gloria had been sober over four years. Jamie's admiration was tinted in envy. Gloria lived with her mother, who had taken care of Sissy and Melinda while Gloria finished her GED and took business classes at the Ottawa County Vo-cational Center. Now Gloria was giddy with joy about her new job as an ad-ministrative assistant for a small architectural firm located in a lovely, restored Victorian house two blocks from the AA Club. Gloria had already bought a used car, the first she'd ever owned.

Jamie thought about Gloria's unruffled sobriety—her simple acceptance of the reality that she could never drink again. Like all those fortunate souls in recovery, Gloria's sobriety was woven into the texture of who she was. Even after Jamie's six months, her own sobriety was like Aunt Nina's story of Laocoon wrestling the sea monster to ground. Only that was a one-time fight. Jamie had to battle her monster every single day. More like Prometheus and the eagle. And the endlessness of her warfare drained Jamie, leaving her scared and depressed.

By the time she'd scoured the upstairs bathroom, run the vacuum in her room and the hallway, and put her sheets in the basement washer, it was late afternoon. The hot blue day had turned dark and blustery. Without saying so to each other, she and her mother had made sure her mother would not be home when Jamie packed up. Even if she was moving only four miles away, her mother did not handle goodbyes well.

Jamie guessed it went back to her father's leaving for Vietnam. Jamie's own gypsy ski life had only made it worse. Just the sight of Jamie's scarred blue suitcase at the front door would have made her mother sad, despite feeling some relief for the break. And Jamie's endless trips up and down the stairs in her disorganized fashion would have upset them both.

Yo, Mom, Jamie now scribbled on the back of an envelope in the kitchen. *Sorry I didn't get the clean sheets back on my bed—but left my room presentable!*

Jamie deliberately used the possessive "my." Her mother always wanted her daughter to feel it was her room in her home. *I'll miss our time together, Mom. I know I haven't helped you with the catering as much as I meant to. I'm finding that just staying sober is a full-time job by itself—and we both know I'm running out of relapses. Keep praying for me…as I always do for you. Call you later. I Love you, J.*

A large bang of thunder crashed above her overloaded car as Jamie pulled out of her mother's driveway. She hated that sound—would always hate it. Stupid, stupid girl. She'd let Roger Hamper kiss her, thunder booming in the hot August night. One kiss—for the hell of it. The wine had made her a little giddy. That would be all—only it wasn't.

Another clap of thunder, a stab of lightning in the distance, and Jamie did a U turn in the street heading away from the lake. She needed an AA meeting. Thinking about Roger Hamper was dangerous. She'd already brought herself down with the packing and moving she'd done so many times in and out of Aspen the past ten years. Her life's story written in black garbage bags. She needed a second meeting today. She could just make the five o'clock.

By the time she reached Aunt Nina's, the blowing rain had cleared away the sticky heat. She reached over the back seat to grab the paper bag of toiletries and the top layer of hanging clothes. The rest could wait until the rain stopped. Through Aunt Nina's back screen door, she smelled fresh coffee and what *had* to be melted chocolate. Aunt Nina was holding the back screen door open before she reached it.

"You can't imagine how I need that cup of coffee." Jamie kissed her cheek as she squeezed by. "Oh, I did smell it—you angel woman. Indoor s'mores! Nothing could taste better right now."

S'mores were Aunt Nina's best excuse for building a bonfire on the beach. Putting scorched marshmallows on Hershey squares and letting the gooey concoction melt between two graham crackers meant eating "some more." The indoor fireplace s'mores, which Aunt Nina could be talked into on rainy days, never tasted quite as good as the beach s'mores with a little sand in them.

"You know what?" she opened her mouth for the single Hershey square Aunt Nina held out to her, "I think I'm going to like it here."

Sucking the rich candy, Jamie smiled to herself. Of course just like Jamie's mother, Aunt Nina knew about sugar for recovering alcoholics. Feeling a new lightness, Jamie headed straight to the hallway behind the kitchen where three bedrooms ran along the north side of the cottage from the beach to the woods.

The front bedroom, still cozy in spite of the modern bathroom she'd added on, was Aunt Nina's where the lake sounds could be heard the best. The middle room was reserved for adult guests—usually Jamie's mother. The end room, with its low ceiling and ornamental iron beds, had been Kate's and hers as long as she could remember. But when they got old enough, she and her older sister began to beg Aunt Nina to let them sleep in the back cabin—each for her own reason.

Kate liked the cabin because she could remember bits of the days she'd spent there with their mom and dad. Jamie could never have that shine of memory. But she loved it because they had been there together when her own tiny life was growing inside her mother's belly. With its quilt-covered big bed and pine-redolent walls, the cabin was the second most precious building in the world to her. The Sandpiper would always be first.

For her mother, it was far different. The back cabin was where the soldiers in dress greens appeared a month before Jamie was born. Growing up, Jamie used to sneak looks at her mother whenever she drove up Aunt Nina's long road watching for a reaction as they passed the log cabin. Her mother's profile remained fixed, refusing to give even a sideways glance. Jamie couldn't remember ever seeing her mother inside the cabin.

Jamie dropped her bag of cosmetics on the tan-spackled linoleum counter in the little bathroom at the end of the hall. The old claw-footed, porcelain bathtub stood beside the metal shower stall. Jamie missed the shower curtain she'd loved as a little girl, the crinkly plastic covered with tropical fish. Aunt Nina had replaced it with boring dark green muslin.

The bathroom off Aunt Nina's bedroom was the only remodeling she'd done to the cottage since she bought it. They all loved the ramshackle feel of the cottage just as it was, the beaded wood ceilings and wide-board walls all painted the same dazzling white as the outside.

Jamie hung her clothes in the long bedroom closet as naturally as if she were returning from a long weekend away. An unexpected sensation of being home overcame her. She paused, bowing her head, absorbing the unfamiliar content-ment. She ran her fingers over the sweet-smelling quilts she'd always curled up with.

The hand-stitched coverlets in pale blues and whites covered the white iron twin beds whose springs gave a friendly squeak when she or Kate turned over. For a moment she almost believed Aunt Nina wasn't sick and she could live with her here forever. Aunt Nina's weakened voice from the kitchen shattered her fantasy.

"Your coffee's poured and waiting, Jamie Girl."

"I hope it's strong—I need a little recharge before I face unpacking," she said going back into the kitchen. Aunt Nina was already seated at the kitchen table painted white so many times it glistened. She sipped coffee from a yellow Fiestaware cup on a green saucer. Jamie saw her own cup was turquoise on a cobalt saucer.

In the middle of the table was the Christmas cactus, the deep green vibrant against the crackled off-white of the Victorian bowl. Jamie had finally found Aunt Nina's lost pot on the highest shelf in the back hall storage room. "The plant looks good in that container Aunt Nina," she said sitting down, "but when do the flowers come out?"

"*To every thing there is a season,* my impatient Cookie."

"Ecclesiastes 3," Jamie said showing off.

"Well, I'm impressed!"

"My Recovery Bible. The girls in my group in Tucson gave it to me the day I left."

"And you're reading it?"

"Every night. But...but how can I tell you this? It also helps me fall asleep."

"At least you're remembering some of it."

Jamie pulled the oval yellow platter closer and picked up another one of the graham cracker sandwiches, warm chocolate and marshmallow dripping out the sides. "Yes, and it helps. These s'mores are not quite the same without the sand, by the way, but pretty darn tasty."

"You already know that I know you need sweets to replace the alcohol." Nina spoke as matter-of-factly as if she were again handing out breakfast vitamins to Jamie and Kate. In the same nonchalant tone she added, "And just to save you some snoop time, if you get the urge, don't bother.

"I have no booze in this cottage or the back cabin. I do, however," she grinned, "have a pantry full of chocolate bars, Meijer's finest graham crackers, and bags of marshmallows. We won't run out of s'mores."

Jamie finished the gooey mess, its sweet warmth soothing her insides. If her mother had made the same comment about her searching for booze, Jamie would have been outraged and hurt. But Aunt Nina always put her thoughts out in plain sight—no hidden agendas, no need for guess work. If only her mother could be as open with her worries. It would be easier for both of them.

But, then, Jamie knew whose fault it was her mother had learned to be guarded.

Through the living room windows, they could see the swollen grey clouds suspended like whales over the lake, the waves dancing in whitecaps. "You know, Aunt Nina," she said quietly blowing into her coffee cup, "this is the first time I can ever remember moving anywhere without feeling hopeless."

"You're probably just on a sugar high," Aunt Nina nibbled at her own dripping chocolate. "The other times—when you've moved *without* s'mores waiting for you—why so hopeless?"

Jamie pushed leftover crumbs around her plate. "Can't you guess?" she finally responded

"Sure. But I'd rather have you tell me." Aunt Nina's grey eyes flashed. "Then again, if it's going to make you cry, forget it."

Jamie tucked her chin into a snorting laugh like a tickled colt. "You know me way too well. Yes, I *was* about to get teary. Talking about it makes me as sad as it does furious at myself. It's that—well, moving anywhere reminds me of how rootless I am. I'm not even sure where home is anymore. Oh, how I've wasted the last seven years of my life."

"So you're 28. You've got a few left to catch up."

Beside them the wind blew pebbles of rain against the windows over the kitchen sink. "Just pulling out that crappy old suitcase got me started again today."

She felt Aunt Nina watch her, listening with the purity of concentration she'd always given her. Of all the people who mattered to her, Aunt Nina was the one who took her most seriously. Once upon a time her mother might have regarded Jamie with the same respectful attention. But now she and her mom circled each other like seagulls over the waves instead of really talking. So much caution blocked anything like an honest conversation. Jamie knew her mother was terrified she'd say the wrong thing and send her daughter out the door to the bar.

"You know, Aunt Nina, I've filled out more mail-forwarding forms than most people send out Christmas cards. Do you realize the only real address I've ever had was Mother's house?"

She held up a protesting hand when Aunt Nina arched one eyebrow at her. "No. You don't have to say it. I know. And I'm not blaming anybody but myself. Believe me. But the shitty reality is how much money I've wasted on booze—how much men like Jake have spent on me. I could own several condos by now."

A thickness filled her throat, and despite her effort, tears seeped into her eyes. "Oh, Aunt Nina, I've screwed up everything." All at once her forehead was pressed into the table while Aunt Nina sat quietly, one thin hand moving in circles over Jamie's shoulders. Outside the waves hit the beach in a turbulent rhythm that pulsed through the cottage.

"Hope is the thing with feathers, That perches in the soul," Aunt Nina began in a soft croon. *"And sings the tune without the words, And never stops at all."*

Jamie felt Aunt Nina's hand come to rest on her rain-damp hair. "Emily Dickinson knew something about despair, Cookie, and still she could write that. But if you think you're the first homeless Cameron, it's time you heard about the day I met your parents."

Jamie lifted her head slowly toward Aunt Nina, her breath erupting in small gasps.

"First, what I'd really like is for my star camper to build us a little fire in the living room to take the chill out. The wood's in the copper barrel by the hearth where it's always been. I'll bring our coffee in there. Before anything else, though, go splash water in your face. You look all red and puffy."

The   Sandpiper

JAMIE

Within minutes, Jamie had an apple wood fire splashing hints of light into the corners of Aunt Nina's living room. Outside the wind pelted raindrops against the cottage. Jamie pulled the overstuffed loveseat she'd monopolized as a child closer to Aunt Nina's wicker chaise and the popping fire. Looking out at the stormy lake through the living room's wall of paned windows, she shivered in a frisson of textured memories. The only place she hadn't resented bad weather for sending her indoors was here—this cottage and the back cabin.

She could almost smell the buttered popcorn Aunt Nina used to make on those rainy summer days—along with a pitcher of red Kool-Aid. She and Kate and Aunt Nina would sit on the floor in front of a July fire and play Monopoly by the hour, the three of them content and warm and loving each other. Coming back into this cottage with its antique wicker, scattered wildflower bouquets, and smooth pine floors, she realized for the first time this funny old cottage was what the Martha Stewarts of the world labored to pull together.

Only The Sandpiper was the real thing and always had been. Low bookcases filled with paperbacks and hardcovers ran beneath the long width of windows fronting the lake. Standing on its skinny legs in the middle of a window ledge stood the wood carving of a beach-pecking sandpiper their mother had given Aunt Nina long ago. Aunt Nina cherished it, telling Kate and Jamie the darkening feathers around the bird's tiny shoulders meant he was getting ready for winter. The room's south wall, opposite the fireplace, was solid with more built-in white wooden bookshelves.

Displayed among the floor-to-ceiling books were Aunt Nina's shore findings of driftwood twisted by nature into miniature sculptures. The choice pieces were tastefully arranged like an art gallery. Aunt Nina's prized collection of unbroken old bottles washed up on the beach stood like small soldiers between small stands of books. The various sized bottles of turquoise, blue, green, brown, and clear glass were all worn to a matte finish by time and sand.

In a huge fishbowl on the long table behind the couch, Aunt Nina kept her colorful pieces of beach glass, the shards of smashed bottles sand-rubbed to a rich patina. In their years of daily beach walks with Aunt Nina, she and Kate must have contributed half the pieces of colored glass and, for sure, some of the old bottles.

The north wall in front of her was dominated by a high fireplace made of Michigan fieldstones piled to the ceiling in a comforting blend of pinks and greys. Along the mantel stood a cluster of old brass candlesticks and a fat pewter pitcher filled with red zinnias. In the center, and toward the front of the mantel where a visitor's eyes would go first, sat an old photograph of Kate and her.

From the sand, two little tan faces squinted up at the camera, Kate holding a yellow plastic pail, Jamie's hand squeezed on a red shovel. In front of where their round knees made small circles in the wet sand stood a lumpy castle surrounded by a moat and twig bridges.

As Aunt Nina eased herself into the wicker chaise, Jamie reached over to straighten the quilt over her knees. Of all her cherished antique quilts, this had always been Aunt Nina's favorite in its hand-stitched loveliness of Lake Michigan blue with yellow squares filled by pink tulips and winding green stems.

The quilt by itself was not a bad sign, Jamie tried to assure herself. Even without the cancer, Aunt Nina never had enough body fat to stay warm. Still, Jamie made a mental note to build a fire every night whether Aunt Nina asked for one or not. A fire would take the coolness out of the night air so Aunt Nina could keep the windows open the way she loved to, letting the lake's sweet aromas and musical waves fill the cottage.

"I was sitting right here," Jamie patted the loveseat's arm, "when you first read to me about Mole and Rat. *Wind in the Willows*—how I loved those stories!"

"And the myths," Aunt Nina smiled as if she could feel two squirming girls pressing into her from both sides. "You guys drove me crazy wanting me to hear the same Willows story and the same *Iliad* chapters over and over. And the *Odyssey*, of all things. Both you girls nagged me to read more about poor Ulysses's trying to get home from Troy. Your personal favorite was Polyphemus getting his eye poked out—all the gore!"

"Well, look who's talking?" Jamie sat forward and eyed Aunt Nina. "What about the Poe stuff you read us about cats locked in walls and people buried alive? It's a miracle Kate and I didn't have nightmares."

"You probably did. But by the time we got into Poe, you girls were sleeping in the back cabin so I couldn't hear you. And if you got your nightmares at home, it was your mother's problem."

Aunt Nina had set the turtle tray with two coffee mugs on the sun-bleached cable spool she used as a table. The heavy wooden spool had floated up on the Sandpiper beach one morning years before. The three of them pushing together barely managed to roll it in far enough to keep it from washing back out. Aunt Nina thought it made a great beach table. But she and Kate insisted it needed to go right in the cottage living room.

Once the spool dried out, Aunt Nina got her handyman to roll it up the dune and into the cottage. Countless games of rummy had been played on it, pictures colored—and enough juice spilled to create some interesting blotches of darkened wood.

"It was right around the time schools get out—like early June as your dad had just graduated from med school. That's when I met your parents." As Aunt Nina began, the singsong of her storyteller's voice filled Jamie's head with images. Even the unusual words "your parents" caught in her chest as she visualized the young couple side by side—a reality she knew only from a few photographs.

She knew Kate and she never referred to "my parents," but Kate must have said "Mommy and Daddy" sometimes because she was three and talking when their father left for Vietnam. Jamie never had a reason to put "my father and my mother" together in one sentence. For her, they were as separate as life and death. One was here. One never had been.

Growing up in the close-knit town of Spring Port had actually made it harder not to have a dad. Everyone knew Lieutenant James Cameron was killed in Vietnam, but nobody talked about it. Even in a conservative community where fire hydrants were painted red, white, and blue, nobody said anything to Jamie about the young father who'd been shot when he wouldn't abandon a wounded soldier.

She and Kate only found that much out by accident one winter day while they moved boxes around their mother's walk-in attic to clear space for a club-house. On the end wall, what felt like a big picture covered in brown paper blocked their way. As they slid it into the corner, kicking up sneezy dust, they found a large grey cardboard box held together by three thick rubber bands.

Underneath what looked like legal papers, Kate and she found what their mother hadn't wanted them to see. For a long time they stared without speaking at the three gilt-embossed certificates on heavy parchment that looked like college diplomas. Jamie could read most of the words—like "bravery" and "honor." But Kate had to explain that "posthumous" meant the Army had given the awards after their father had been killed.

The certificates referred to medals that weren't in the box. She and Kate ached to see them, but they couldn't tell their mother they'd found the Army's decoration letters. Desperate as she and Kate were to know more about their dad, even as children they'd understood their mother's pain was too deep to touch with words.

What Jamie could never understand was why nobody else—not her teachers or her friends or her friends' parents—ever talked about her father. It wasn't that she wanted sympathy—and for sure not pity. But she had needed some outside acknowledgement that she, too, once had a dad even if she'd never seen him. When she'd asked Kate why nobody talked about him, her sister shrugged and said people didn't want to make them sad because their dad was dead.

But Jamie knew, no matter what Kate said to protect her younger sister, that the silence about Lieutenant Cameron made Kate feel as lonely as it did her. Ignoring their father's death—as if he'd never existed—that's what hurt both Cameron girls, even if Jamie was the only one who'd admit it.

"I told your mother the other day," Aunt Nina's spellbinding voice brought Jamie back to the cottage, "how much you remind me of her the first time I met her."

Jamie watched the firelight play across Aunt Nina's face, the gauntness camouflaged by the high color rising in her cheeks. Jamie closed her own eyes in anticipation. She needed to pull Aunt Nina's memories inside herself. Then, later, when she needed comforting—and she would, she could sink into the remembered words like soft pillows.

"My memory of your dad at the back door with Katie running at his heels is as real to me as you are right here beside me, Jamie," she said, her eyes on Jamie but beyond her at the same time. Then she laughed, the spring sound rolling up and around Jamie. "Probably," Aunt Nina said, the laughter still in her voice, "because I was so thrilled to hear the word "rent" come out of his mouth."

Jamie blinked slowly and let the image of her father's strong face, his hair shiny dark like a panther's, fill her head.

"The summer before," Aunt Nina said tucking the maize and blue quilt under her legs, "in 1967, I cashed everything my parents left me to buy this cottage. I'd fallen in love with the big lake when I came out here during college to visit my Vassar roommate whose family lived in Holland. And I have been forever grateful to the dead alewives that stunk up the beaches in the sixties because the market for cottages dropped dramatically."

To Jamie the smell of fish blended with scents of grass and sand and water into all that was sensuous about the beach. "Fish are part of the big lake—how could they be repulsive?"

"Oh, my dear, when you couldn't go in the water without pushing through slimy, stinking white fish corpses. Even you, my water nymph, would have gagged. The coho and Chinook salmon eventually took care of them. But, besides the alewives, a few cottages north of here actually fell in during the mid-60s when the lake level rose. That also helped me afford this cottage.

"Anyway, I had a teaching job here. My plan was to get this place fixed up for the next summer's renters who'd pay more to be on the lake. Then I planned to move into the back cabin, which was heated and fairly new at the time. That first year the plumber came, the electrician, the roofer. This place needed everything. I was doing the painting myself, but I got busy teaching teenagers for the first time. I wasn't even close to done by the next June."

Jamie got up to throw another log on the fire thinking how daring it had been for Helena Judd to leave her New England roots and move almost overnight to a small Midwest town where she knew no one. But the lake had done its magic on the woman who would become Jamie's Aunt Nina. Her mother had told her that when the Spring Port High principal first read Helena Judd's Vassar resume, he'd asked only one question. Did she want the honors classes in American or English Literature?

"On impulse one day that June I wrote out a 'For Rent' sign with my phone number and nailed it to the big tree at the road. Thought it might pressure me to paint the main cottage faster if someone did call."

"But my par—" she couldn't finish the word. "They just came to the door?"

"Best laid plans—you remember that from the bonnie Scottish poet. Your dad was the one." If she'd noticed Jamie's word switch—and Aunt Nina never missed anything, she chose to give Jamie a pass. At least for now. "Not your mother."

Aunt Nina's voice quieted. "I had no idea your dad's plan was much longer range than one weekend. He wanted your mom and Katie—we called her that until sometime after you came along and she insisted on being 'Kate.' Anyway, he wanted your mom away from Ann Arbor and all the anti-war stuff while he was in Vietnam."

"I don't blame him."

"Your mother didn't either, really. Once she realized she could not stop him from going." She looked into the crackling fire as if watching a scene unfold. "I can still see her hobbling up my stony dirt road in bare feet, her long hair and dangly jewelry—the perfect Michigan hippie. And here stands this straight-backed guy in pressed khaki shorts with his crisp white, short-sleeved shirt. The two of them were—I don't know, so mismatched, they were perfect."

"That's how you met Mom?"

"Yup. And, it's bizarre, I know. But—well, it was like we'd known each other in another life or something. Like love at first sight, which can happen, only for us it was best-friends-at first-sight."

"What did she look like then?"

"Oh, skinny like you with those great long legs and wide-set eyes. She had on this skimpy white tank top over cutoff jeans and your dad? He had this gleaming black hair like an Indian's—same color as Kate's. I remember how nicely cut it was because every male teacher at school was into the long hair of the peace movement. Your dad had big white teeth like you girls do."

"He was handsome, wasn't he?"

"Are you kidding? I'd have run off with him in an eyewinker. He wasn't a lot taller than your mom, but so muscular here," she gestured across her torso, "he seemed a lot bigger."

The old longing for the father she'd never known tugged at Jamie's chest. She wanted Aunt Nina to keep talking forever.

"He said he was leaving for basic training the next month, then Vietnam for a year." Aunt Nina gazed straight into the fire. "He thought they needed a beach weekend together. It wasn't until later I found out your mother had lost it the day he joined the Army.

"She'd smashed every dish in their married-housing apartment. What he'd done made her a little crazy—and I didn't blame her. He was a med student so he had to go eventually—all doctors did during Vietnam. But he could have finished his surgical residency first."

"And the war could have ended before he would have had to go."

Aunt Nina's face grew sad. "But it didn't. Your mother just hoped it would. We all wanted that damnable war to be over. But your dad? He just couldn't put up with the Michigan students burning their draft cards when other men were coming home in body bags because they weren't in college. He could not live with that injustice."

Jamie felt the warm surge of pride in her dad—even at such a terrible cost. Aunt Nina's story was moving ideas around in her head like lost pieces of a puzzle sliding into place. Some of it resonated like truths she'd always known about her dad, in spite of her mother's silence. The part about his being ramrod straight, handsome and perfectly groomed—that's what she knew from the pictures.

But the impulsiveness of joining the Army was a side of her dad she would not have expected in someone so disciplined. She was grateful to know that about him—it made her feel more his daughter. It didn't matter that his risk-taking had been for a cause he believed in while hers was to escape a nightmare she couldn't talk about. They'd both been betrayed. He by his idealism. She by a man she'd wanted to believe was like Lt. James Cameron.

For their differing reasons, they'd both taken chances with their lives. She felt connected to him by that. Maybe for the first time, she had a marrow-deep sense of belonging to a father she'd never seen. He had not meant to hurt the people who loved him any more than Jamie had. He hadn't meant to die. She hadn't meant to destroy herself either. If he'd lived, her dad would have made it up to them. They were alike in that, too. She wondered if she could live long enough to make up for what she had done.

Jamie struggled to visualize her even-tempered mother hurling dishes at a wall, one after the other. Suddenly she was overcome by a mix of envy and grati-tude at the kinetic honesty of her mother's fury. How much easier for her dad to have been blasted with plates and saucers. Jamie would welcome having dishes smashed over her head instead of enduring her mother's forced pleasantness.

Jamie's heart skipped with a quirky longing to tell her dad he'd been the lucky one. What her mother didn't say out loud hurt Jamie so much more than getting hit by splinters of flying glass.

"But, oh, how they adored each other," Aunt Nina went on. "And little Katie. If they weren't touching each other, they were snuggling her, kissing her nose. And…" Aunt Nina puffed out her upper lip as she did sometimes when she was about to tread into painful terrain.

"And?" she needed Aunt Nina to go on even if it was hard.

Aunt Nina exhaled heavily, making the same kind of steam-escaping sound Jamie did after a draining run. "Well, I was in my 30s that summer and happy as a kitten with my single life. Then your dad showed up right at that door," Aunt

Nina pointed over her chest to the back of the cottage, "and I never wanted to be in love as much as I did that summer, my dear Jamie."

She took a slow sip of coffee. "Your *parents*," Jamie could not miss Aunt Nina's deliberate stress on the noun, "were like overlapping circles of light. They left sparks on your retinas if you watched them too long."

Jamie held on to the word "parents" as she felt her skin tingle with the truth of what she'd longed to know for so long. Her eyes were weepy with joy.

"Aunt Nina, I don't need to tell you what hearing this means—what a hole in me this has always been. You know Kate and I could never ask about…about our *parents*," now Jamie stressed the word. She caught Aunt Nina's barely noticeable approving nod.

"But never say 'never,' Jamie."

Jamie eyebrows went up on their own. "If I haven't learned any thing else in AA, I've learned that. 'Never' is way too far out for alcoholics who have to live in today. But, please, go on. I don't want you to end this story. You let them rent the cabin?"

"Heavens girl, I'd have given them this place free and moved into the cabin myself to keep them around those few days. Together they were raw electricity. Being with them was a high—not your kind, kiddo," her grey eyes sidled toward Jamie. "A real high. Money was the last thing on my mind."

"They didn't pay you?"

Aunt Nina looked up in surprise. "I think I've jumped ahead. Your mom's never told you how she and Katie ended up living in the cabin when your dad went to Vietnam?"

"Only that Mom's dad and nasty stepmother wouldn't help."

"Your mother's father was not such a generous person. His wife? Let's say they deserved each other. No, they had no interest in having your mom and Kate—and then you too—live with them in Florida while your dad was in Vietnam. Your dad's father died early, his mother remarried and was raising a second family in Texas. The kicker is your dad's mother actually blamed your mom for his enlisting."

Jamie pressed her palms hard against the chair arms at the impact of Aunt Nina's words. Her mother had been hurt by everyone who should have loved her best. Most of all her husband who left and then died. Jamie's muscles contracted under the pressure of guilt. She had piled her own particular agony on top of all that.

Aunt Nina sipped the now cool coffee before resuming her storyteller's tone.

"At the time, I had no idea your mother had nobody to go to. But I couldn't have said 'yes' any faster if I had known."

"Was it Mom's idea to move to Spring Port while my dad was in Vietnam?"

"You'd think so, wouldn't you," Aunt Nina said nodding. "But actually it was your dad who called after that first weekend. He wanted to rent the back cabin for the whole year he'd be gone. He said even if she agreed with the pro-testors, watching them burn the flag on the Diag would have been too much for her while he was in uniform fighting the war. Your mom hated the war in Vietnam—but she loved him a whole lot more."

Aunt Nina paused. "And then your dad said something I've never forgot-ten. 'What I'm really saying, Nina, is my family needs a friend more than a landlord.'"

Outside the wind had ceased its frantic howls and become a low, distant moaning somewhere beyond the swishy sound of raindrops on the window-panes. "You think my dad had a premonition?"

Aunt Nina stared into the fire a moment. "No, at least I didn't then. But when he came back here in the fall after basic training just before he was going overseas, I had a terrible feeling he was saying goodbye. Your mother finally told him about you during those lovely last days together. That you were his gift to her while he was gone—and don't you make that face at me, Jamie Cameron. You *are* a gift to all of us." Aunt Nina's eyes glistened in the firelight.

Jamie scrunched her body down into the loveseat, pressing her bare feet against the wicker of Aunt Nina's chair. She laid her head back so the hot tears could roll backwards into her hair. Her mother deserved so much better than she'd gotten with Jamie. She was swallowed by bottomless shame. Her mother had been so cheated in life. Her own father's rejection. Her step-mother. Then her dearest love's early death. And then Jamie.

"Mom should have remarried," Jamie said when she could trust her voice again. "It wasn't fair to be widowed so young."

"I happen to agree with you, Jamie, but…" Aunt Nina started to say some-thing, then hesitated.

"But she could never love anyone like she did my dad? That's what Kate says. I think Mom could have been happy with the right man. Remember the architect from Chicago who wanted to marry her? He used to bring Kate and me the coolest presents. He gave me my first set of swim goggles. He was crazy about Mom. She wouldn't have had to wait tables any more."

"No, certainly not. Mike Healy was his name. He was also a developer who came here to build the boardwalk condos on the harbor. He'd have moved his entire business to Spring Port for your mom."

"He used to take us to the Dairy Queen in his fancy red sports car. Kate said the car and the presents were bribes so we'd get Mom to marry him, but that she'd never marry anyone after Dad. I didn't believe it then and still don't. I remember being extra nice to Mike so he wouldn't break up with Mom because Kate was so obnoxious to him."

Aunt Nina looked at her with huge, loving eyes.

"What?"

"Mike Healy was a nice man, and he was in love with your mother and she with him. He'd have been a wonderful stepfather to you and Kate."

"Then why didn't she marry him?" Jamie felt a tinge of exasperation.

"Oh, Jamie, your mother always put you girls first. She would not do anything to make her daughters unhappy."

"We'd have been happier with a stepfather than no dad. I don't get it."

"You, yes. But—well, your mother worried about Kate. You have to understand why your sister never liked any man your mother dated. When your mom and Mike began spending a lot of time together, Kate hated him most of all. Not because Kate was mean, but because she was afraid." Aunt Nina leaned forward to cough, holding her ribcage against the jolt.

"Aunt Nina?" Jamie heard the alarm in her own voice.

Aunt Nina made a hand signal she was fine, taking several deep breaths before she went on. "I'm telling you what's really none of my business—maybe this illness in my bones has addled my brain too."

"I'll get you hot coffee," Jamie said taking the blue cup into the kitchen.

"Thanks, dear," Aunt Nina said when Jamie returned as she breathed in steam from the cup. "I want you to see the whole picture and not stay angry at Kate. She was a precocious little girl who had to grow up overnight. Looking back, I think your sister's childhood ended the day the soldiers came."

It occurred to Jamie she never thought about Kate as being a child. She'd always seemed grown-up and in charge.

"Your mother—well, sank into a depression that lasted several months after you were born. I'd go straight to the cabin after school and find your mother curled up in bed with you next to her and Katie—we called her that in those days—holding your bottle for you. Can you see why Kate would resent any man who wanted to take over later on?"

The clarity of what Aunt Nina was telling her flashed in Jamie's brain. Kate the caretaker.

"Kate had worked so hard protecting you and your mom, she didn't want some stranger taking over. Mike scared Kate more than any of your mom's other dates because Ellie really liked him."

Jamie thought about Kate coming home after school every day and starting dinner. She'd try to get Jamie to come inside and help—but she usually gave up if Jamie played deaf long enough. Kate had been a second parent to Jamie in many ways. Yes, Kate would have felt usurped by a stepfather.

"Well, I've run off at the mouth, and now it's time for my medicine. You still have your car to unpack. The rain looks like it's stopped so you won't get too wet now."

Jamie tried to imagine the kind of husband and stepfather Mike Healy would have been as she popped open the Saab's trunk. He'd have been fun, she reflected as she pulled out the heavy blue suitcase. Her mother would have been happier.

The damp air like an exotic mist caressed her face. Aunt Nina had just given her a glimpse of the passionate love her parents had for each other—of the father whose blood and fearlessness she'd inherited when the whole world acted as if she'd never had a dad. But Mike Healy as her stepfather wouldn't have changed any of that.

Her mother's loneliness—the sadness of a fractured family—it didn't have to continue. Poor Kate, always the big sister—the caretaker. With a stepfather, Kate would have had a better childhood too. Life had asked too much of Kate too early. And then her little sister grew up only to add new unhappiness to Kate's life. Jamie had no illusions about whose fault it was they'd grown apart—about whose fault it was they hadn't spoken since the trip to Grand Rapids.

She owed Kate so much. But, instead, she'd hurt her. Over and over and over.

T h e   S a n d p i p e r

JAMIE

"Come on, Girlfriend, you're walking me back to my car. We got to talk."
They were hardly out the front door of the AA Club when Jamie felt Gloria's
strong fingers tuck hard into her upper arm.

It was almost 8:30 at night, the long days of early July coloring the sky an
iridescent pale blue. With the temperature still in the 80s, only the hum of mosquitoes confirmed the evening hour. Gloria began steering her left on Bridge
Street, away from the post office parking lot where Jamie had parked her Saab.

"Hey," Jamie jerked her arm away. "What's with you, Gloria? I have to go
back and help Aunt Nina get ready for bed."

"Don't mess with me," Gloria said, her dark eyes snapping. "That woman
was doing fine by herself until you moved in. She has not gone helpless in a
week. Now move your butt before these blood-thirsty mosquitoes eat me alive."

She tried to stare Gloria down. But when Gloria narrowed her mouth and
pressed both fists against her rounded hips, Jamie knew she might as well start
walking. "You're probably parked in Holland," she said as they headed up the
hill.

"Nope. I left my car," she accented the last two words, "at work where I have
my own reserved parking space, thanks to you."

"You got your own damn—darn job. Not me."

"But who drove me to all those interviews, hmmm? Otherwise I wouldn't
have this job. And without this job, the bank wouldn't have loaned me money
to buy a car that runs. Now I drive myself to work every day where I park in the
first assigned space I've ever had. So, Girlfriend, I owe you."

"Is that why I'm walking two blocks out of my way on a hot night? So you can thank me?" Jamie had been nursing a low-grade headache all day. Now it was pounding behind her eyeballs.

"Not even close. We're walking because I don't like what I'm seeing and hearing with you lately, Girl. You been way too antsy the last few meetings, and that's a bad sign. All us No Snivelers know you're struggling. You got the cravings. You keep saying so in meetings."

"I'm *supposed* to talk about it," Jamie felt her temper flare. "And I really don't appreciate being criticized for doing what the Big Book says I should."

Gloria came to a stop and poked Jamie hard in the shoulder. "That's just what I'm talking about. You're all snotty over nothing lately. I don't know what's eatin' you since you moved in with your Aunt Nina. I understand her sickness is—well, it's getting to you. But I can smell something else goin' on too. You ticked off at your sister again? Your mother giving you the guilties?" Gloria stopped to slap a mosquito on her wrist.

"Maybe your old man from Aspen got your phone number? It doesn't matter. But what I'm seeing, and what I'm saying as your sponsor is you're getting your little pity pot all shined up so you can go out and use and then blame it on somebody else. Anybody but poor Jamie."

Gloria turned and began walking again, her pace quickened.

"I have been sober six months now, and your show of faith in me is really terrific support," Jamie spit out each syllable.

"You know what we just talked about back there? The meeting?" Gloria jerked her thumb back toward the AA Club and ignored the sarcasm. "Fourth of July's coming this weekend. Big drinking time. Everyone in the program always got toasted on the Fourth just like on every other holiday. It's the only way we alcoholics know how to celebrate."

"I was listening, too, in case you're interested. And I know all about holidays. So what's the big F deal?" Gloria was active in the Good Shepherd Baptist Church, and she abhorred profanity. Jamie knew Gloria would be offended by even the initial. But she was too mad to care.

They walked on, the only sounds coming from Gloria's high heels pecking the cement sidewalk in concert with the hard slap of her own Birkenstocks.

"You think I'm looking for an excuse to relapse, don't you?" Jamie finally had to break the silence. She hated verbalizing what she hadn't wanted to admit to herself.

Gloria's feet kept moving, her head low as if she were fighting a strong wind. They didn't talk anymore until Gloria reached the grey Victorian house with three stories of elegant white fretwork and gingerbread carvings. Overlooking downtown Spring Port, the century-old house was occupied by the two architects Gloria worked for. The wrap-around porch, with its shiny white spindles and aqua ceiling, was outlined by hanging baskets of overflowing hot pink geraniums.

Even with the heat, Jamie hadn't felt the hill, but Gloria was catching her breath as they came to a stop. Gloria looked up at the house before she spoke. "Do you think, Girlfriend, I ever thought I'd work in a place like this? Have my own key to it? Come and go when I want because they trust me? Have my own space reading 'Reserved' even though I got the oldest and cheapest car in the lot?

"Sobriety gave me this, Girlfriend, " she pointed at the imposing house. "Sobriety gave me my kids back and my self respect. If I ever drink again—just one time, just one sip of beer, it's all gone like that," she snapped her fingers hard. "I might better put a gun to my head."

Gloria turned and walked up the driveway toward the parking lot behind the house. Without looking back she said, "That's all I wanted to say."

Jamie drove the long way back to Aunt Nina's, avoiding the crowded waterfront, skirting the bars where she knew the serious drinkers would be getting a head start on the big weekend. Gloria meant well, no question. But…but now Jamie was starting to feel rocky. It was as if Gloria had stirred up dark sediment. Jamie didn't want any of it rising into awareness. Pity pot? Bullshit, she thought driving down Lakeshore. She didn't have to make up any grievances if that's what Gloria thought.

She didn't have to go back any farther than good old Jake, with his ponytail and trust fund who showed his love by keeping Jamie ripped on coke and then played hero by flying her in his Lear jet to an expensive Arizona rehab. But then there'd also been Nate, the bartender she gone to Aspen with leaving Michigan a semester short of graduation.

And Walt, another rich spoiled pothead she'd met after dumping Nathan. They'd all taken advantage of her.

And, yet, if she dared to be honest—at least with herself—these men—they weren't the cause. They were the result. "Post-traumatic stress." The term repulsed her. She had not looked at Aunt Nina's book since she shoved it under her car seat.

*   *   *

"How about helping me check out a rental property Merit might want to invest in?" Mr. Hamper had casually asked her last day of work as she was finishing an actuarial table for the agency. "Jamie, our math genius."

The bottle of red wine in his car had surprised her. But, then, what did she know at eighteen? Roger Hamper was the adult—the boss—the former Marine pilot who made her think of Lieutenant James Cameron. Then he'd driven her into the country down a long dirt road where there was no rental house—only thunder and noise and jagged pain.

She banged the steering wheel. Not now. Remembering was too dangerous. Then a different face, the strong jaw framing a sensitive mouth, came into her mind, and she was flooded with self-disgust. Dr. Keith Summers had cared about Jamie—had wanted only to help her get well. He was the first person she'd ever told about the rape—about how Roger Hamper had driven himself off the bridge before she'd been able to tell anyone. And then she couldn't. Then, whether she'd intended to or not, she'd made sure Dr. Summers could never tell anyone else.

*   *   *

"I know you wouldn't have paged me, Jamie," Dr. Summers said looking straight at her, "if it weren't important. You know we're not supposed to see patients after hours."

Since Jake had left her at the Tucson Clinic in those blurred days after Christmas, she'd spent four intense hours a week with Dr. Summers. Tall and rawboned, the staff psychologist had a head of unruly curls, the dark brown accentuated by traces of white. The women patients, who thought he looked like a younger, huskier Clint Eastwood, guessed Summers was in his early 50s. The men patients, who valued him for his intelligence, thought he was in his late 50s. They'd all told Jamie she was lucky he'd been assigned as her therapist.

"I know, Dr. Summers. I'm sorry. It's been—well, a really tough day. The cravings are so bad, I'm close to walking." Outside the darkness of the Sonora Desert began its swift descent, stretching angular shadows along the floor of the unlit office. She'd sat down in one of the two facing leather arm chairs in the corner of his office instead of the green office chair across from his desk where she usually sat.

Dr. Summers seated himself in the other leather chair, reaching up to turn on a small floor lamp behind him. She watched him settle in and begin tapping his finger tips together in his familiar listening posture.

"I've never seen you without a tie before," she said, then felt dumb for saying it. But she couldn't help noticing. He looked so different in a denim shirt and light khakis, his sockless feet in brown sandals.

"So what happened specifically today, Jamie?" he asked making her feel even sillier by ignoring her remark.

"Oh, well, a whole lot of things. But mostly Grant—he's hitting on me again and Sharon, she's got a thing for Grant, then she jumps all over my case about it. She says I lead him on, which I don't. I don't mean to anyway. And now most of the other women in group are taking her side, of course. The way it's always been for me—same old shit. Now everybody's all tense and pissed at me, and I want to bag this whole place. Just book out of here. I mean if you hadn't said you'd see me tonight, I'd be gone."

"We've been here before, Jamie," the psychologist spoke softly. "Your difficulty with male relationships. With boundaries. Today with Grant—that isn't new. You've told me you give men mixed signals—a push and a pull because you're ambivalent."

It was true. She'd always liked the challenge of attracting any man she picked out. But once she had them, she rebuffed them. "Not ambivalent at all, Dr. Summers. As soon as they want me—think I'm good enough for them, I'm not interested anymore." His smile was strong, his teeth white against his Arizona tan. "But you are right, Dr. Summers. I *don't* want any man who would want me."

"Yes," Dr. Summers said, nodding. "It's a core issue in your perception of unworthiness, Jamie. Whether you're conscious of it or not, I think you set up these dynamics—the flirting, the rejection, the jealousy from other women—to prove to yourself you're unlovable. Then you have the excuse you want to blot out your pain with alcohol and drugs. Getting high completes the cycle because you think drunks and addicts are losers so you make sure you are one."

"I am."

"An alcoholic and an addict, yes. But a loser, Jamie, you are not. It's a pattern you've been repeating for too many years."

Since I was 18, to be exact, she thought.

"Instead of enjoying your attractiveness, Jamie, you use it on men—and indirectly women, to confirm your own sense of inferiority. You're going to have to learn to love yourself before you can get beyond your addictions."

And suddenly she had begun talking—fast. All at once. Blurting it out. How she'd teased Roger Hamper that summer without really knowing what she was doing. The tight skirts she wore to work. The monogrammed ankle bracelet the sales girl told her was sexy. And then she drank the wine he offered her in his car when she knew better. He didn't force the first kiss. She'd let it happen. The tease she was already good at.

Only after that, she'd fought. Fought with all the strength in her body against the tearing hands, the grunts, the pressure of his weight—and then the pain had ripped her in two—thunder burying her screams. And she couldn't tell—not anyone ever. If she told, Joyce Hamper—Alex, his brothers—would have been left with nothing. Nothing.

A German wall clock ticked into the prolonged silence as she rocked back and forth sobbing. Rocked and sobbed, the aroma of Dr. Summers' Old Spice beginning to fill her senses.

"What an impossible burden to have carried alone for so long." His voice was like a stroke of silk. A sudden chill moved through her body, and she hugged herself trying to stay warm.

"No wonder you have goose bumps," Dr. Summers said and leaned forward to rub one palm up and down her bare arm.

Later she would admit the truth. His had been a natural gesture of comfort, of solace. Nothing more. It was she who had moved so that his hand slipped to her breast and all at once her mouth was on his, their bodies coming together in a longing deep and tender. Affectionate even.

Later that week she heard Dr. Summers was taking a year sabbatical. She thought about his note at the bottom of the grocery bag underneath the cactus. Tossed into the desert sands didn't matter. She'd always had a good memory.

You see, Jamie, we are all frail. I knew what was happening—what you were doing. Finally, finally telling the truth about being raped—and then coming on to me to prove you were the seducer. That it was your fault—the rape. Roger Hamper's death. But Jamie but it wasn't your fault—none of it. And then I did the worst thing I could have done to you—the worst thing I've ever done in my life. I let my basest instincts overpower my brain.

Jamie, it's not your fault you are a compellingly desirable woman. You never deserved to have sex forced upon you by a man you trusted to be the father you'd missed your whole life. Not what you wore—not drinking his wine—not letting him kiss you—none of that changes the fact you were raped. If you remember only one thing I ever said to you, please let it be that. Roger Hamper was the criminal. You were the innocent. You don't need to numb yourself anymore.

I have no right to ask anything of you, but I do ask you to continue with therapy. And if you can find a spot in your heart to forgive me, it's more than I deserve. I betrayed my wife, myself, my profession—but my worst sin was betraying you. These cuttings are from a Christmas cactus my grandmother was given as a little girl, so the plant is well over a hundred years old. Our family tradition is to share the plant with people of the spirit, as my mother puts it. You're the first patient I've ever wanted to give it to. Please believe in yourself—and try to forgive me. You deserve a good life. Dr. Keith Summers.

The Sandpiper

JAMIE

Jamie hadn't realized she was crying until the red of the stoplight blurred. Dr. Summers had been wrong about all of it. Her soul was too sick, too corroded to be of the spirit. And the blame for what happened on the plush carpet of his office was hers, not his. Her neediness, her selfishness, her impulsive leap to make a fresh conquest—to show him how she'd seduced Mr. Hamper—it had all been her fault.

She hadn't even known Dr. Summers was married until the note. But it wouldn't have mattered. At least God, in His infinite fairness, had seen to it that the consequences of her narcissism would be hers alone.

She was falling into insane thinking. The alcoholic pattern of black memories started to roil her brain. She pressed the accelerator. She had to get to Aunt Nina's where it was safe, no booze to go looking for. No hidden caches of drugs to blot out the image of Keith Summer's caring eyes, his fingertips tapping a healing rhythm.

Tonight, for sure, she had to give Aunt Nina her car keys. Since she'd moved in, she'd asked Aunt Nina to take the Saab keys at bedtime. It started the first night as the rain blew against the cottage windows, the fire crackling, and Jamie had sunk into Aunt Nina's recollections of her parents. Afterwards, she'd felt too emotional—too worked up by Aunt Nina's stories—to feel safe. Hearing about the father she'd never met had rocked Jamie between joy and remorse.

Aunt Nina had taken the Saab's keys from Jamie's extended hand without comment. She knew enough about recovery to understand that talking to Jamie about something so dredged in feelings was risky for someone newly sober. But Aunt Nina had also known how desperate Jamie was for every remnant of memory she could get about her mother and father. Since that night, Aunt Nina had reminded Jamie about the car keys if she forgot to hand them over before they went to bed.

Jamie eased the cottage's back door shut and moved quietly through the kitchen to Aunt Nina's bedroom where she found Aunt Nina asleep with a book across her chest, her tortoise reading glasses skewed across her thinned cheeks. Her skin always caramel from daily beach walks, even in the howls of February snow, now was tinted grey. *Why so pale and wan, fond lover, prithee why so pale?* came into her head. Jamie could almost hear Aunt Nina's voice reading the poetry in English class.

She tiptoed to the bed and carefully removed the glasses, then picked up the book. It was George McGovern's account of his daughter's long struggle with alcoholism—ending in her death, frozen, drunk, on a Minnesota street.

Aunt Nina opened one eye and grinned sleepily. "How nice to get tucked in. You're spoiling me, Jamie. Good meeting?"

"Yes. I needed it. We'll talk about it in the morning. Here are my keys," she laid them by Aunt Nina's left hand. "Did you remember your pills?"

As Aunt Nina nudged the keys under the pillow and nodded her answer, Jamie tried not to see how blue the veins in her neck had become. "It feels nice to have someone checking on me—especially someone I love so dearly." Jamie leaned over to give her a soft hug, smelling the trace of gardenia from Aunt Nina's skin cream.

"I might go for a quick skinny dip so don't fret if you hear me outside."

"Damn, if I felt three ticks better, I'd go with you. Just like we used to. Take a double swim for me. And see if old Matthew Arnold's *sea is calm tonight*—if his *moon lies fair.* God Bless, Jamie."

After scanning the shore in both directions to make sure she was alone, Jamie stripped off her clothes, dropping her shorts, tee shirt, and underwear on the thick beach towel. She ran across the sand into the water, warm from the long day's sun and flat from the windless night. She'd report to Aunt Nina in the morning that her poet's sea was calm.

Looking back at the deserted beach, she wondered why she'd bothered checking if anyone was around to see her naked body, the tender breasts outlined in the rosy haze of the sun's departed golds. There were only a handful of cottages as far as she could see north and south. Their owners seldom climbed down the long wooden stairs to the beach after the sun went down. Except on the night of July 4th itself. Then this beach would be scattered with bonfires highlighted in brilliant flashes of color as fireworks and burning sparklers streamed into the air.

She leaped through the long strand of shallow water until it got deep enough for her to dive under and begin swimming. She pulled her arms hard through the luxurious coolness, flutter kicking her legs until she skimmed past the second sandbar. She pulled her face out of the lake only when she had to have oxygen, trying to wear herself out. To cleanse herself of destructive thoughts—of hurtful memories.

"She doesn't swim like a fish, she swims better," the Camp Arbutus swimming counselor had told Jamie's mother. Later, Coach Briggs said almost the same thing. What they didn't seem to understand was that water was her element. How she became one with it in a seamlessness she never felt on land.

She thought of the hot summer day while she was in high school and Kate was home from college that they'd met up with friends at Lighthouse Beach. On impulse, Jamie had decided to get the attention of the cute blond lifeguard on his tall-laddered chair. She threw Kate a wave, then raced into the water and never stopped swimming out. She heard the whistle and swam even faster.

Kate had gone ballistic. And she did not believe her younger sister afterwards when Jamie said she'd never been in danger. What had really pushed Kate over the edge was hearing Jamie tell her afterwards what was true. That drowning was not really like dying—more like reconnecting. Car accidents. Shotguns. Plane crashes. Those were deaths, brutal and final. But drowning would be like drifting off in Aunt Nina's lap, warm and safe and loved.

Kate had screamed at her to just shut up about drowning because she was sounding as crazy as she'd acted. Feeling her naked body cut through the comforting water, Aunt Nina's cottage moving away behind her, Jamie still remembered the tiny kindling of warmth she'd felt that day. Kate really had been scared. Kate had not wanted her sister to die.

She kicked for one final sprint, then dived under, wishing she could keep the security of her water world around her on land. Here, in the deep peace of Lake Michigan, there was no pain to numb. At last she headed back toward the beach, swimming the breaststroke and watching the water form neat Vs in front of her.

By the time she could touch, stars were spread out across the sky, Orion shining his triple-studded belt. She would tell Aunt Nina in the morning the moon was fair. She pulled her legs against the shallow water until she reached the shore and began to lope across the beach to her clothes, sand sticking to her feet. Even after she'd toweled off, the long T-shirt she put back on still clung to her damp skin, her lash of blond hair dripping water down her back.

She didn't know how long she'd swum aerobically, but it hadn't siphoned off her nervous energy. She still felt too wired to sleep. She dried off before she put on her wet clothes and sandals, then dripped all the way up the steps to The Sandpiper. Behind Aunt Nina's cottage, where she went to hang her towel on the clothesline, she noticed Aunt Nina's mountain bike through the open door of the shed. Without a conscious plan, she began to wheel the bike down the dirt road, then climbed on the seat.

She looked over at the log cabin as she pedaled by, her heart trilling with the certain knowledge she'd been born out of a great love. Her feet pressed harder, picking up speed on the dirt road packed solid under the wide tires. She knew every twist and bump of Aunt Nina's driveway. She pushed forward as she approached the steep uphill knoll where she and Kate used to get off and wheel their bikes.

But now her legs were stronger and Aunt Nina's bike was better. Instead of slowing down to get off, Jamie stood up on the pedals and pumped with the full weight of her body, knowing if she hit the hill right, she could coast all the way to Olive Road. With no one coming, she'd roll right across the road to the bike path on the other side.

The dark truck approaching from the left came faster than she realized. But she was too far into the street to stop. She heard the shriek of brakes, and she frantically waved one hand at the driver trying to signal some apology. Over her shoulder, she caught a glimpse of a man in a dark baseball cap as he laid on his horn. She could almost lip read the obscenity coming from his mouth. "Sorry," she called after the disappearing red taillights on the pickup now going black. She stood on the pedals to move faster toward the path.

Passing the Michigan Power Plant's tall, skinny smokestack, she looked up at the red lights on top blinking like warning stars. The few cars on the road seemed to be either sports utility cars or pickup trucks. She was remembering that the workers at the power plant always drove trucks.

Suddenly an old car with a noisy muffler coming toward her slowed as it got closer. A bearded man leaned out the passenger window and yelled, "Nice jugs, honey." She heard raucous laughter spill from the open windows followed by a series of toots as the car continued north.

"Assholes," she said, then looked down. She'd forgotten her bra on the darkened beach. The combination of damp skin and a clinging T-shirt outlined her breasts like some girlie show. She sucked at her tongue in embarrassment as she used her right hand to pull the T-shirt loose. But the breeze from biking plastered the shirt right back against her skin.

Long before she saw the party store's parking lot lights, she'd known where she was going. The minute she coasted down Aunt Nina's driveway, she'd been headed for the convenience store that had been Sheldon's Corners, a small grocery and bakery. She and Kate used to beg Aunt Nina to let them ride their bikes there to pick up a loaf of bread or milk or anything. Mr. Sheldon was a baker, and he and his wife kept their tilted glass case filled with shelves of sugar cookies, glazed donuts, and warm rolls oozing white frosting.

When the Sheldons retired, the new owners kept the name, but turned it into a 24-hour convenience store. Aunt Nina could still buy what she'd forgotten at the Meijer's grocery store eight miles north in Spring Port. But Sheldon's best customers were no longer cottagers picking up odds and ends. The real patrons were the workers at the expanded power plant who could buy cigarettes and lottery tickets no matter what hour their shift ended.

And, of course, booze. She knew Sheldon's Party Store sold more cold beer out of the refrigerator case and liquor from behind the counter than anything else. She had no business going there any time, especially at night when she was fidgety and unsteady. Don't even get off your bike, she tried to tell herself. Turn around now! But within minutes, she had the kickstand down and stood before the counter where the liquor bottles were lined up like brown candy. She nervously tugged her shirt away from her chest.

"Can I help you?" a Hispanic man with tired eyes asked.

She touched the wet $20 bill in her shorts pocket. She wondered if her alcoholic brain had planned this when she'd stuck it there that morning while she was getting dressed.

"Yes, I'd like a bottle of…" then, like a color video going off in her head, she saw Gloria's back walking up the driveway toward her car. *I might better put a gun to my head.* Gloria's words banged against her skull.

Oh, my God, her heart thudded. What am I doing? She stood welded to the floor a moment. "No, no, no thank you," she babbled at the clerk's confused face and began to back up as if he were going to come after her. She banged open the screen with her fanny and grabbed both bike handles, tears stinging her eyes. She jumped on the pedals so fast she didn't notice the man in a dark baseball cap. He was putting gas in his black pickup.

The Sandpiper

KATE

Kate heard Pete's muffled conversation like a distant rustle tug at her sleep. She pulled the covers over her shoulders, burrowing her head into the pillow to keep the sound from waking her. He must have picked up the phone on the first ring because, even in her half-sleep, she knew she hadn't heard it.

A small square of light from his closet penetrated her eyelids followed by water sounds from the bathroom. After a time lapse, she reached her arm across the bed hoping she'd feel his warm body back beside her where it belonged.

"Pete?" she said into the pillow when her hand found only tossed sheets.

"Shhh," his voice was suddenly at her ear, his lips on her hair. "Don't wake up, Babe. I'm on my way to the emergency room."

"What time is it?" she lifted her head and looked at Pete through the darkened room.

"Almost midnight. Now roll back over and sleep. Love you."

"How long will you be gone?" she asked feeling more wide awake than she wanted to be.

"I don't know. Depends on what we find. No more talk or you won't get back to sleep.

"A car accident?"

"No. An open arm fracture for sure, maybe more, plus a possible rape. A pretty savage attack, according to the ER doc. The police are at the hospital now."

"Did they catch the guy?" Kate was trying not to get fully awake.

"Babe," Pete said kissing her on the forehead, "the cops don't even know the patient's name yet. Somebody found her unconscious with no ID. Now back to sleep."

"Love you," she mumbled, wondering momentarily if she should turn on the light and check her temperature. Then she turned over and rolled back into her pillow.

The next thing she knew the phone on Pete's side of the bed was jangling. It must have rung several times, she realized in her fog. She'd learned how to sleep through Pete's late night phone calls just as he was wired to grab the receiver on the first ring. She fumbled for the receiver.

"Kate," Pete's voice on the phone, a timbre of distress resonating.

"What's wrong?" She sat upright in bed. "What's wrong?" she asked sharply when he didn't answer right away.

"Kate," Pete said, and she stiffened against bad news. "It's Jamie."

"Jamie?" she said in shock. "What do you mean 'Jamie?'"

"The patient I came in to see—honey, it's Jamie. I couldn't believe it when I saw her. She's in tough shape. You need to bring your mom to the hospital. Now, Kate."

"Wait. Wait. The rape?" Kate's thoughts spun wildly. "Is this about the rape?"

"Honey, I haven't got time. We don't know yet. Jamie's just starting to wake up. Whatever happened, it looks like your sister damned near got herself killed fighting the bastard off."

"Oh, my Lord, Pete, my mother can't go through this again!" She felt her emotional gravel slide down a steep bank. "What was she doing out in the middle of the night?" Her mouth was turning cotton. Make this not be happening. "And now I'm supposed to tell Mother?" Please, God, make this go away, Kate prayed into the holes of panic opening up inside her.

"Yes." Pete's single word punched into her brain.

"My sister is a selfish drunk and I hate her!" Kate screamed at the phone, her words running together like dark water colors.

But it wasn't true. She'd tried for so long to hate her little sister. To exorcise the intense love she felt for Jamie because the pain she caused never seemed to end. It hadn't worked. Kate visualized the photo from Camp Arbutus, the bandage on her own knee. Jamie was part of her—and always would be.

Pete now spoke slowly, controlled anger in each syllable. "We did a blood alcohol and your sister is cold sober. It wasn't the middle of the night. She was riding a bike near Aunt Nina's when some psycho tried to rape her. The police think the dog they found guarding *your sister*," Kate heard Pete hammer the last two words, "scared the guy off. It could have been a lot worse."

"Jamie doesn't have a dog," Kate said as if that could change everything. Make it not true.

"I know that, but the police didn't. It doesn't matter. Right now all that matters is you getting your mother over here stat. She'll need to sign an op permit if Jamie doesn't wake up enough."

The phone clicked off, and Kate knew he was upset by what she'd said. What Pete didn't understand was that her angry words came from her head, not her chest. It was all around her heart where Kate felt the real pain kick in. She stared at the receiver clutched in her hand and started to cry. What if Jamie died, she covered her mouth in white horror. Jamie was her best friend—her small shadow asking only for her big sister's approval.

Kate smelled the sweat of fear on her skin as she jerked off her nightgown. She hadn't even honored her promise to see Jamie through the abortion. No, she'd weaseled out, concerned only about her own chance at motherhood— afraid to alienate God.

Jamie had been right that day. Kate was a hypocrite. She'd stepped aside not to stop the abortion, but to keep it off her conscience. To let somebody else— probably someone from AA Jamie barely knew—take her place beside Jamie at the clinic. The humid air and stink of her own flesh nauseated Kate.

She filled her lungs with air and swallowed back the tears as she dialed her mother's number, the phone tucked under her chin. She pulled a bra and underpants out of the top drawer in her dresser, listening to the ringing. Right now it wasn't Jamie, but her mother who needed whatever courage Kate could muster. Kate did not have the luxury of fear about Jamie. She had to focus her emotional energy on helping her mother endure whatever she was about to face at Waters Hospital. Kate closed her eyes in a silent prayer for strength as her mother's groggy voice answered.

"Oh, dear God, Jamie's gone, isn't she?" her mother asked before Kate had finished saying Jamie had been hurt. Kate felt the breath-sucking terror in her mother's words. How long her mother must have been waiting for this phone call. It was like having a child with a terminal illness. The question was not *if* Jamie would die, but *when*.

In five minutes, Kate had washed her face and put on a white Chicago Cubs sweatshirt over her jeans. It was ten minutes, almost two a.m., and the light traffic on U.S. 31 was moving fast. Turning east off U. S. 31 toward her mother's house, Kate had a déjà vu that pulled her into desperate hopelessness. Only that time it was her mother who had called Kate.

*   *   *

Kate could still hear her mother's broken voice spilling the awful news so fast Kate could barely follow her. Diane, one of Jamie's roommates in Ann Arbor, had called Ellie to tell her Jamie had quit school and moved out. All Diane knew was that Jamie and a bartender she'd been dating named Nathan were on their way to Colorado for the ski season.

Diane hadn't wanted to call, but she needed to make sure Jamie's mother knew her daughter had left Michigan only days into the second semester. Diane had worried about Jamie, about her drinking, since they'd lived together for over a year. None of Jamie's friends had heard from her since she'd left. No one knew how to reach her.

Kate remembered the nubby feel of sweatpants against her legs as her mother's words slowly penetrated her brain. The thudding sounds of the old furnace in their Chicago apartment ricocheted in the background.

Kate's initial shock coiled into anger when she heard her mother's suppressed choke at the other end of the line. "If no one knows where Jamie is—I mean we'd know, wouldn't we, if she was—you know, badly hurt?" her mother asked softly, grasping for a tatter of comfort.

Her mother's desperate reach for some kind of hope only made Jamie's actions slam harder against Kate's chest.

Before that phone call, Kate had gotten beyond her rage at the part Jamie played in Roger Hamper's death. Jamie's grades were so good at U of M that Kate figured she couldn't be partying that much. But Kate was wrong. Diane lived with her. Not until that frigid afternoon staring at the overcast Chicago sky, her mother crying quietly on the phone, did Kate feel hopeless about the sister she'd helped raise. The sister she loved.

What she heard in her mother's voice that winter day shut down Kate's sympathy for Jamie. Their mother had raised two daughters by herself, and Kate could not bear to watch her get hurt again by Jamie. Kate was the one who'd have to do the tough love because her mother couldn't. It was Jamie's only chance. It was the only way Kate could preserve enough stamina to help her mother. For everybody's sake, she had to put Jamie out of her life until—if—her sister got sober.

That January afternoon she'd driven the three hours north to Spring Port alone because Pete was on call. Her mother knew Kate had no time between her Northwestern graduate classes and the Tribune job. She told her not to come because Aunt Nina was with her. But Kate knew better. Her mother needed her too. She'd cried the first hour out of Chicago, unable to recognize this out-of-control Jamie as the gritty kid sister who'd bloody both knees, but keep on running.

Jamie once took a spanking for cutting the neighbor's tulips when she knew the little boy up the street had done it. No one was tougher than Jamie, and yet she continued to give in to the weakness of alcohol. Until that snowy afternoon, it never occurred to Kate that Jamie would not stay sober once she *knew* she was an alcoholic.

Brenda, the counselor Aunt Nina had found to talk to Jamie about her drinking just before Jamie left for Michigan, made it clear that Jamie couldn't drink at all because she was alcoholic. Kate and her mother and Aunt Nina had all met with Brenda and Jamie for a final family session. Brenda had actually told them Jamie had the disease of alcoholism, which Kate heard as a cop-out.

"You got it all, Jamie Cameron," Brenda had said as they left her office. "If you stay clean and sober, you can accomplish anything you want in this life."

Wiping her eyes with her sleeve as she'd passed Michigan City and turned on I-96 that day, Kate knew what she had to do. "Detach." That's what Brenda kept repeating during that closing session. "Detach with love, but detach." Well, maybe her mother couldn't, Kate had thought as she shoved a Bruce Springsteen disc into her car's player. But she could. Starting that day, she would box up her feelings about Jamie and put all her strength into her mother.

*   *   *

Kate heard an ambulance siren in the distant darkness and wondered if it was headed to the hospital. She approached the last cross street before her mother's house. Tonight was what she'd prepared herself for since the January day Jamie left the University of Michigan for the ski slopes of Colorado. No matter what Pete said about Jamie's blood alcohol, Kate's instincts told her that whatever happened to her sister on the bike path was about Jamie's addiction.

Pete's cool response to Kate's outburst only confirmed what she already knew. Pete was as naïve about Jamie's alcoholism as she had once been. He and

Brenda might call it a disease, but not Kate. That was a cheap excuse for the hell Jamie had put her mother through—and Aunt Nina and Kate too. The physician in Pete could cut Jamie some slack, but Kate could not. Her emotional bank account had to be spent on her mother.

She prayed the detachment she'd worked so hard on wouldn't fail her when she saw Jamie in the ER. She could not let herself care about Jamie because her mother cared so much. Pete could be mad at her hard-heartedness. But the one thing Kate could do for her mother was hold her own sympathy in check. Getting pissed at Jamie was better than feeling sorry for her. The worst thing she could do would be to break down when she saw Jamie.

Kate was not surprised when she saw her mother waiting under the streetlight at the corner saving Kate two minutes of driving time to the hospital. Her mother had on a knee-length khaki skirt and a long-sleeved white knit top, a black cardigan dangling from one hand.

She saw the brave pitch of her mother's shoulders and felt a heaviness in her own. This is how her mother must have greeted the soldiers that day. Just as she stood now, erect. Tall. Once again, her mother was bracing her spine for news she couldn't bear.

"Have you heard any more?" her mother asked, one hand propped on the open car door, her eyes riveted on Kate's face.

"No, Mom, I haven't."

Her mother slid in the front seat beside her, an audible burst of air telling Kate her mother had been holding her breath. She reached over and squeezed her mother's left hand where it lay lifelessly on her lap. "It's going to be all right. We have to keep the faith."

Her mother put her hand on top of Kate's. Then quietly she said, "I'm afraid I'm prayed out."

"Not you, Mom," Kate said with wishful vigor. "You're the one who taught us to hang on to God even when it seems like He's let go of us."

She felt her mother's hand squeezing hers. Kate was jolted at the hypocrisy of her own words. How quickly did she turn against God when the first spots of bright red marked her underpants?

But just then, unbidden, out of some deep crevice like a wisp of steam, a prayer for Jamie floated into Kate's head. The spontaneous prayer lifted Kate to a ledge of calm, and, for that moment, she did not doubt God was acting in her life. She turned to lay a reassuring hand on her mother's arm and saw the artery throbbing in her temple.

Her mother's thoughts were going where they shouldn't. She was seeing the battered face of her youngest child, the broken body of her beautiful daughter. Picking up the image of what Kate knew her mother was picturing made her own belly cramp. "Mom," she said softly, "I'm going to be with you for Jamie. We'll get through this together, I promise."

Tears spoke her mother's silent gratitude as they turned toward the hospital.

"I called Nina," her mother said pulling out a Kleenex to blow her nose. "Waking her seemed better than letting her find Jamie's bedroom empty."

Her mother went on, knowing what Kate wanted to ask, but wouldn't. "Nina said when she went to bed around nine, Jamie was going to take a swim. Nina didn't hear anything after that. Her pain pills, you know, knock her out." Her mother inhaled audibly before adding, "Jamie gave Nina her car keys before she went swimming." Both of them understood the woof and warp, the strength and weakness implicit in Jamie's not wanting her own keys.

"I wish she didn't have to do that, Mom. But it is a sign she's trying not to drink. I told you what Pete said about her blood levels. She was sober tonight." Kate heard herself speak the words with authority, trying to overcome her own doubts about what Jamie was doing when she was attacked.

They turned down a side street and saw the hospital straight ahead dominating the block. The Lakeshore News had recently done a story on Waters Hospital's being named one of the 100 Best Hospitals for its size in the country. Kate felt the relief of knowing Jamie was getting the best possible medical care. The tall light poles in the emergency room parking lot cast an eerie ivory glow across cars and trucks.

At this hour of night, each of these vehicles marked some family's frantic rush to get help for a loved one. The tall, angular security guard leaned down to make sure Kate had a legitimate reason to use the rectangular lot reserved for emergency-room visitors.

"Dr. Shane told me to watch for you, Mrs. Shane," the guard said after she introduced herself. "Sorry about your sister," he said waving her toward an empty spot in the line of cars closest to the ER's revolving doors.

She felt more than heard her mother's gasp. "Mom, he didn't mean any thing by that. Only that she's hurt and he's sorry." Of course that's what he meant, she told herself, pulling her car in at an awkward angle. She was putting the gear in reverse to repark it when her mother opened the door and got out.

"Your car's fine," her mother called to her and began running toward the ER entrance. Kate wanted to run after her mother, but she didn't like leaving her car that way. Then she noticed the irregular pattern of front bumpers in the row of cars facing her. Those drivers had more important concerns than how neatly they'd parked.

She did not like herself for caring about the Mazda's being lined up straight. Mostly she didn't like knowing Jamie would have abandoned her Saab with the engine running to get to Kate if she was the one injured.

No, don't do that. Kate dug fingers into her palms. She slammed the car door without looking back at the cockeyed Mazda. If she allowed herself to let in the memories of the tag-along sister Kate had loved above all else, she'd lose it and be no use to her mother.

The automatic glass doors of the emergency room swung inward, and she heard the staccato sounds of voices under stress, the loud cry of a child in pain jarring the air. A male nurse hurried past pushing an empty gurney toward the long corridor lined with examining rooms on both sides.

Near the wall at her left, she saw her mother leaning into Pete's chest, his bare arms under the short-sleeved green scrubs supporting her back. Pete looked up. But for the first time she could remember, he did not smile at the sight of her.

T h e   S a n d p i p e r

KATE

"Oh, dear God, Jamie's dead!" Kate cried out as she lurched toward the steel door jam for support, her heart expanding into her ribs until she couldn't breathe. In a flash, she saw Jamie's small face, sunburned and mischievous, the day she'd put the baby toad under the head counselor's overturned coffee cup at Camp Arbutus. Kate could not choke back the sob hurtling through her body. Her mother and Pete were mouthing words she couldn't hear as if the two of them were behind a glass wall.

Then they vanished into a mist and Jamie appeared—only this time Jamie wasn't a little girl any more. She was an adult sitting in the passenger seat on the way back from the abortion clinic in Grand Rapids, her hurt and anger burning inside the car. Like a hammer blow, Kate understood that now she could never take back the hideous words she'd shouted at Jamie in the car. It was too late for apologies.

Kate's mind spun kaleidoscopic frames, whirling images of a younger sister who might really have a disease. Maybe Jamie was not bad, but sick. In her unforgiveable selfishness, Kate hadn't cared about Jamie. All she'd cared about was that Jamie did not deserve to give their mother her first grandchild. Now Jamie was dead, and Kate didn't want to live with herself anymore.

"...Kate, Kate, honey," Pete's face was next to hers, her mother's just behind, his strong arms grabbing. "Honey, Jamie is awake and talking now. She is not going to die. Are you with me sweetheart?" Through a haze, Kate watched the blue of Pete's eyes ease into the turquoise shade she loved best—the color of his kisses, his bare foot rubbing her calf under the table, his hand holding out his water bottle on a hot run when she'd forgotten hers. She reached up to stroke the wonderful plane of his cheek, feeling the unshaven roughness.

Then his words registered and the fog vanished. "Not—not dead? Oh, praise God," she felt an overwhelming surge of relief and gratitude—and then joy. "Mother?" she asked as Pete slowly released her to her own feet. She didn't know how she'd ended up in this small room. Looking around she recognized it as the triage office across from the emergency room's admissions counter.

Her mother spoke from the doorway. "Are you all right, my dear Kate?"

"Oh, yes, yes. I'm just so stupid," she said, opening her arms to her mother's embrace. "Here I'm supposed to be *your* support and I pass out. Thank God Jamie's all right. For a minute I thought, oh, I've been such a shit to her. I've said such awful-"

"Shh," her mother said, grabbing both of Kate's hands. "It's all right. It's all right." Silently they held each other for a moment, then Kate stood back. She was wiping her face with both hands when she saw the downward pull of lines around her mother's mouth. Tonight, for the first time, her mother looked her age. Kate threw her arms back around her mother's neck and hugged hard.

"I love you so much, Mom. I can't stand to see you unhappy. Oh, Mom, what would we do if something had happened to our Jamie."

"*Our* Jamie?" her mother's voice purred. "That's the nicest thing you could say right now. Most of all I need you to pray for her with me."

Pete stood watching them, a softening of tension around the corners of his mouth. His short blond hair, textured and wiry with blunt curls, shot sparks of gold from the light behind him. He raised his eyebrows in question and Kate nodded. She was back. She was Kate. Whatever she needed to do for her mother and for Jamie, she would do. Kate Cameron Shane would not go to pieces again. Pete blew her a kiss that made the muscles in her belly jump.

"Ellie," Pete said, leading them down the corridor, his arm gently over his mother-in-law's shoulders, "grit your teeth a little. Jamie's pretty roughed up. She has a concussion right about here." He touched his head between his temple and his ear.

"That's why we couldn't wake her up right away. But no skull fracture. That's really good luck, considering what could have happened. No facial fractures either, no teeth missing, nothing like that." Pete stopped and took both Ellie's shoulders in his hands.

"I'm all right, Pete. My girl's alive—she's alive. It's all that matters." Ellie's voice was barely audible.

Pete exhaled through pursed lips. "Yes, it is. But you need to know—the way her clothes were torn—the police are calling it attempted rape. We all know Jamie is one tough customer and she proved it tonight. It looks like she risked her life to make damn sure it didn't happen."

"What do you mean?" Kate asked from behind them.

"She let him use her head—she must have bunched her body up like a kicking bag," Pete said looking straight at Kate. "The cops said she was curled in the fetal position when they found her. And if the dog hadn't scared the son of a bitch off—" he looked down at Ellie and stopped.

"You're saying we're lucky?" Ellie put a hand on Pete's chest.

"Very," he nodded. "This goon had to be wearing work boots—probably with steel toes. To fracture her arm like he did? Took more than street shoes."

Kate saw her mother's body shrink into itself. She stepped forward and took her mother's hand again, feeling the cold dampness of her palm. "Go on," her mother said after a moment, as if Kate's hand in hers was transferring new strength.

"Jamie's got a compound fracture," Pete touched his own forearm to demonstrate, "these two bones, the ulna and the radius, were broken all the way through and separated. The ulnar bone penetrated the skin about here," he touched just inside his forearm. "We need to get that cleaned up before it gets repaired so the exposed bone doesn't get infected."

Ellie nodded, putting her other hand on Pete's arm. "What would we do without you, Pete?"

"What would any of us do without each other, Ellie," Pete said. "That's what families are for." Kate flinched. Pete meant that comment for her.

Her mother braved a smile, the fluorescent lights flicking white against her olive skin. Then Kate noticed Pete pulling at the top of his ear lobe—a sign he was thinking something over. He started to speak, then caught Kate's eye watching him. He turned away and headed toward a closed door at the end of the emergency-room corridor. Whatever Pete was about to say, he'd changed his mind.

"Jamie's in here," he said opening the door to a large trauma room lined with complicated stainless-steel instruments. Kate knew from her occasional visits to the ER when Pete was on call that this was where the most serious trauma patients were taken. It was right across the hall from the ER's central nursing station where a bank of TV monitors kept track of heart rates and breathing functions. If a patient started to crash, nurses and doctors didn't have far to run.

Kate clenched her jaw against the idea of Jamie's having to be in this room—

against the image of steel-toed boots smashing Jamie's curled body. She walked behind Pete and her mother, trying to ready herself for whatever she had to see. It didn't help.

The left half of Jamie's flawless facial bones were so distorted with swelling and purple blotches, Kate had to cover her mouth not to gasp as she neared her sister's bed.

Then her mother began to make crooning sounds in her throat when she got to Jamie's side. "Oh, my poor, poor girl," her mother said as if to a small child. She gently laid her lips on Jamie's good right hand lying on top of the sheet, an IV dripping into a vein in the arm. Jamie was lying flat, her back on a rounded red board, the lurid color accentuating the brown stains of dried blood streaked through Jamie's blond hair.

Above Jamie's head, what looked like a giant white bug hung suspended from the ceiling, huge round lights shining at the end of its several legs. The bright bulbs made Jamie's mottled face look even more grotesque, like Halloween make-up. Her broken arm lay at a right angle across her abdomen. Kate could see what looked like betadine soaked through layers of bandages winding around Jamie's arm like a mummy wrap.

"Don't try to talk, honey," her mother said when Jamie's balloon lips started to open. "We just came in to tell you we love you, Jamie. We'll be right here waiting for you after your operation." Her mother looked back at Pete quickly. "Oh, does she know? About the operation?"

"Yes, Mom," Jamie's voice sounded hoarse like she was coming down with bronchitis. "I know. I'll be fine. Please just don't worry." Jamie strained to talk through her swollen mouth. "I just seem to keep causing you more trouble." Tiny tears slipped from the outside edges of her puffy eyelids. Her mother stroked Jamie's hair and made soothing sounds of reassurance.

"Kate," Jamie looked over her mother's shoulder and waved the fingers of her good hand. "Thanks for coming."

"Jamie," Kate said softly—"I feel—so, so bad about this." What really feels bad, she wanted to tell her, is blaming you for this attack—for not being there when you needed me—for not forgiving you. Kate swallowed instead. She couldn't find the courage to apologize to her own sister. Her life's best friend.

Pete's eyes watched Kate over her mother's bent back. Then his doctor's voice began speaking, and Ellie stood up to listen. "I asked Kate to rush you over here, Ellie, to sign the permission slip for Jamie's surgery. But when lady tiger here woke up on her own, she was plenty alert to sign herself."

Kate saw him look at Jamie with a flicker of admiration. "She's refused pain medication so we know she's not foggy. I told her I was calling my partner in to do the open reduction because Jamie is family."

Kate heard the deliberateness with which Pete spoke the last three words. It was the second time he'd made the point. But Kate didn't need to be reminded anymore.

"That's when your daughter got difficult," Pete said to Ellie. "She's refusing any surgery unless I do it." Pete gave Kate a quick grin. "And if I've learned one thing over the past ten years, it's that you Cameron women mean what you say."

Pete's easy tone started to relax Kate—until his words registered. "But…but couldn't you get in trouble for operating on her?" Kate heard her still wobbly voice and instantly hated her own question. She saw Jamie's eyes twitch through bruised flesh and realized how that must sound to her injured sister. But Jamie didn't know doctors can lose their licenses for operating on relatives. Oh, dear God, Kate clenched her fingers together. Not minutes ago she thought Jamie was dead. Now she was worried about Pete's practice!

"No," Pete said answering Kate, but looking right at Jamie. "That was the first thing Jamie asked me, wasn't it?" Her husband's reproof stung Kate—smarting because it was deserved. Before she could apologize to Jamie, a heavy-set nurse in marine-blue scrubs opened the door. Behind her Aunt Nina strode into the room.

"Nina!" her mother gasped. "You have no business driving yourself here at this time of night." Her mother's voice bounced off the chrome machinery.

"So how does the other guy look?" Aunt Nina asked ignoring her friend and studying Jamie's battered face without blinking. The first hint of a smile moved across Jamie's thick lips. She grabbed Aunt Nina's wrist with her good right hand and tried to lift her head off the red board.

"I didn't mean to leave—" Jamie's mouth twisted in pain at the movement. Aunt Nina put her finger over her own lips while Pete eased Jamie back onto the red vinyl board.

"It's the backboard the EMTs brought her in on," Pete answered Aunt Nina's questioning eyebrows. "Unconscious patients can't say what limbs they can or can't move, so they all get treated like spinal-cord patients until neck X-rays or a CT scan tells us differently. Jamie's tests were negative—except, of course, for that one."

Pete pointed at an X-ray attached to a light case near the door. The ghostly lines of angled bones reminded Kate of cracking dry branches over her knee to build bonfires on Aunt Nina's beach. The comparison nauseated Kate, filling her mouth with saliva. She held her breath fighting not to retch.

Her mother's glance barely grazed the X-rays before turning back to Jamie. But Aunt Nina was stepping closer to see them better. "Here," Pete said to Aunt Nina as he tapped the picture, "is where the bone cut through the skin. Jamie will have a small scar there, under her forearm. She'll have a good sized incision here," he drew a finger along his own lower arm, "where we go in to reduce the fracture. Otherwise, and assuming we knock out any bone infection with the antibiotics, once she heals, her arm will be good as new."

"Dr. Shane," the nurse said from the doorway in a half whisper as if she had a secret, "they're ready for you in surgery. And," she pointed down the hallway behind her, "the policemen?"

"Oh, I forgot," Pete said looking at his patient. "Jamie, two Spring Port police officers came to the ER right behind you. They had the dog they assumed was yours in their squad car. The man who found you near the bike path said the dog wouldn't move. He was still standing guard beside you when the ambulance got there."

"The dog? Oh, Lord, the dog!" Jamie started to sit up, then moaned with the pain of quick movement. "Yes, the dog. A big black one—oh, that terrible body odor and the pain in my head, my back—" Jamie's eyes focused on the acoustic-tiled ceiling above her as if she were seeing it all again. "Yes, yes, now I remember. I thought—it seemed like this man and the dog were both attacking me. The barking was so loud—but then I don't remember what happened."

"The dog could *not* belong to the monster who did this to you, Jamie," Kate said with sudden fury.

"Kate's right," Pete said. "Dogs stick by their owners even when they're nut cases. This dog—who has no tags on his collar—wouldn't have barked at his owner. The man who found Jamie went to see what the barking was all about and scared the attacker away. The cops already talked to him. They'll need to hear what you remember, too, Jamie."

"That dog saved me from that psycho. We have to find the owner—to let him know. To thank him. Please, we have to." Jamie sounded agitated for the first time.

"You can't get all upset when you're about to have surgery," her mother put a calming hand on her daughter's good arm.

"She's right," Pete said looking at his watch. "I'll ask the police to let you know when they find the dog's owner. You can thank them yourself. The two cops I talked to are bent on catching whoever did this to you. They think he might be the same guy who went after a woman jogger in Muskegon last year. When you're up to it, they want to talk to you."

Kate saw Jamie, the contusions darkening both her eyes, look down at her shattered arm lying useless on her chest. She knew Jamie was not strong enough to talk to the police—not after what she'd been through. Then a look she recognized appeared on Jamie's face, cutting through the swollen, discolored flesh.

It was Jamie poised at the pool's edge for the last leg of the state relay. It was Jamie taking on the playground bully who'd pushed Kate off the jungle gym. It was Jamie refusing to tell who'd cut the tulips. Now Jamie Cameron wanted the scumbag who'd done this to her locked up. Kate could have said Jamie's next words for her.

Unable to open her mouth very far, Jamie spoke one syllable at a time. "Damn straight I'll talk to the cops now. Tonight. No way that piece of shit— sorry, Mom, but he is. His feet pounding my head smelled like it. I'd know him by his B.O."

Kate saw the nurse still waiting in the doorway looking thunderstruck by such energy coming out of a broken face. Tougher than steel, the neighborhood kids had said about Jamie. "The lady tiger," Pete had called her, but now he was shaking his head. "Sorry, Jamie, but your doctor has other plans for you the next few hours. The policeman can come back in the morning."

Oh, my dear little sister, Kate felt close to tears watching Pete and the nurses ease her onto the hospital gurney. It had always been her job to take care of Jamie—to protect her. And she hadn't! Please dear God, the prayer rose unbidden as she and their mother followed Jamie to the elevator that would take her to the surgery wing on the second floor. Please, God, help Jamie through this operation. And please, please, this time give me the strength to stand by her.

Kate and her mother and Nina were sitting around a square formica table in the hospital cafeteria, the huge black hands of the wall clock reading twenty after three. They'd taken Jamie to the O.R. at 1:21 a.m. Kate had just delivered their third round of vending machine juice and crackers when she heard her husband's distinct walk. Pete had a sort of shuffle skip that reflected his naturally balanced personality always forced to hurry.

When her mother and Aunt Nina saw Kate stand up and look toward the closed cafeteria doors, they automatically turned around in their chairs. Pete still wore his green scrub cap, the rounded blue paper mask dangling from a narrow rubber band around his neck. His eyes had the subtle glint she knew meant he was happy. The surgery had gone well.

He gestured for her to sit back down and pulled up a nearby chair to join them, grabbing a cracker filled with cheese as he did. Directing his comments to her mother and Aunt Nina, Pete explained how he'd reduced the fractures, using stainless steel plates to stabilize both bones. Jamie would have a fair amount of pain the first few days, and she'd need some help taking care of herself for a while.

"It's good she's not left handed," Pete said holding up his own left arm. "But I'm not sure how much she can do for you right now, Aunt Nina."

"There's no question," her mother said with force. "We'll find someone to stay with Nina for now, and I'll bring Jamie back to my house where I can take care of her."

"Excuse me," Aunt Nina spoke in the patrician voice Kate remembered from English class whenever a student disrupted the discussion. Miss Judd had the same effect in the hospital cafeteria. The few people scattered around the tables stopped talking and looked at her.

"I'm the only one who knows what I need. Right now what I need is to take care of one of my own." She held a palm up to silence any resistance before Kate's mother could speak it. Then Aunt Nina tilted her long, narrowed neck slightly like a solicitous swan. "Wouldn't it be wonderful if once more in my life I could feel useful to someone else? Especially if it were the same someone who has chosen to see me through to the end?"

The stillness around the table was like water rolling down a metal slide. Finally Pete broke the silence. "If this lady," he pointed straight at Aunt Nina, "could drive herself down here in the middle of the night, she probably can take care of Jamie. It'll be time consuming more than strenuous. Cutting up her food, washing her hair, buttoning her buttons, fastening her bra." A quick blush flamed across Pete's cheeks. "I meant—well, that's what my women patients complain about most."

Then Pete's features grew dark. He looked down at his green paper booties dotted with brownish droplets of dried blood. "There is one more thing." Kate's heart skittered. She knew immediately what he was going to say. She'd known that was why he'd tugged his ear before surgery. It had to be about the abortion. Nothing else would make him so uncomfortable.

"Because I am now Jamie's doctor, patient confidentiality means I would not tell you what I'm about to without her permission."

Kate put her hand over her mouth to hide her fear from her mother.

Her mother pulled away from Pete as if to distance herself from whatever he was going to say. Aunt Nina's eyes never wavered. No matter how terrible the news, she would hear it straight on.

Pete looked in Kate's direction, but avoided her eyes. His fingers fidgeted with the strings on his scrub pants where a wide gold band dangled. Most surgeons didn't bother wearing wedding rings because taking them off all the time to scrub for the O.R. was a hassle. But she loved Pete for the time he took every day to knot his ring to the white ties of his scrub pants. She liked it that the nurses saw it too.

Pete was not looking at any of them when he spoke. "Jamie wants me to tell all three of you this, and she asks you to please honor her insistence that she not have to talk about it with any of you until she's ready. When the time comes, she will tell you what you want to know." He looked at each of them in turn as if confirming their tacit consent.

"What she wants you to know is that she is over five months pregnant."

The   Sandpiper

KATE

It was a sunny July Saturday and Kate should have felt lucky. Dr. Bauer himself was seeing patients. His office was staffed seven days a week for the blood studies and ultrasounds since hormone cycles didn't stop Fridays at five. And whenever the pivotal hours of ovulation hit, tests had to be run. But Dr. Bauer came in one weekend a month. The other weekends, Alice read the tests. No question, Alice knew what she was doing—but she wasn't Dr. Bauer.

For the third morning in a row, Kate hung her khaki skirt and white bikini underpants on a hook in the tiny changing cubicle of the ultrasound room. The patient who would follow her into this curtained space was probably sitting in the waiting room about to begin the ritual of pretend magazine reading. Kate couldn't remember if it was *Time* or *Newsweek* she'd just been thumbing through. The women lined up for Dr. Bauer's Saturday appearance had only one thing on their minds—and it wasn't national news.

The familiar crackle of paper rumpled under Kate as she sat on the side of the examining table, her eyes avoiding the steel stirrups at her left. For almost three years, she'd been riding a teeter-totter, her hopes soaring as she counted days and prayed. But then the spotting would begin, and she'd feel as if someone— some cross between God and Dr. Bauer—had jumped off the opposite seat and slammed her to the ground.

Dr. Bauer was writing notes on the lucite clipboard chart Alice handed him. "How about your bloating, Kate?" he asked, pressing the skin around her ankles, leaving small white indentations.

"I don't wear my rings anymore. They're too hard to get off by bed time. I haven't felt like eating lately, but you can see my weight's up to 131. Is that good?"

Dr. Bauer paused in his note-taking. "It's perfectly okay, Kate—both to lose your appetite and to retain fluids, which accounts for the five pounds. Those are common side effects of Clomid and nothing to worry about. It means your body is still responding to the drug which is what we want. What about the PMS? Still a little crabby, are you?" She felt unexpected tears scald her eyes as he helped her into the stirrups, and Alice smoothly inserted the lubricated probe. She held her breath and nodded what she couldn't say.

"That's what we like to hear," said Alice with a whoop in her voice. "The bitchier, the better, right Dr. B.?" Alice began moving the probe until the right ovary was visible on the screen.

"Well," Dr. Bauer chuckled almost to himself as he watched the monitor, "I'm not sure Pete would agree. But Alice has a point. Your hormones are in high gear, Kate, which is what we're looking for. Today," he read from her chart, "is the 13th day of your cycle—we're close to the hCG shot—but you know all about that."

"I think, Dr. B," Alice said removing the sound probe, "that Kate could teach the fertility course to your residents in Grand Rapids."

Kate pressed her feet against the stirrups to push herself into a sitting position and smiled at Alice. "A little learning can be a dangerous thing."

Dr. Bauer shook his head. "Not for you. You have a keen mind. As I'm sure your husband would tell you, we like it when patients know what's happening with their bodies. Not expecting them to become experts like you have, however!

"Now," his voice grew serious as he crossed his arms over his chest, "I know you're worried you didn't conceive the first four months on Clomid. But we're still tinkering with the dosage—which is perfectly normal. So let's stay upbeat and think this fifth month will be our lucky number."

Reflexively she put her hand on her flat abdomen. Five months—the same as Jamie's baby.

"If it doesn't happen this time, we'll talk about Perganol. You know we have a lot of guns left in our war chest. For now, let's trust what we're doing to make this pregnancy happen."

She studied her bare feet, working up courage to say what haunted her. At last she raised her eyes to his. "Dr. Bauer," she picked each word like a piece of soft fruit, "I don't know how to put this. But—well, your infertility patients who never got pregnant were right where I am at some point. What I mean is that cancer patients on chemo are always told they have a chance at a cure by taking the drugs. But the ones who take it and die anyway—they were going to die all along."

"Kate, Kate, Kate," Dr. Bauer took off his glasses and massaged his closed eyes with two fingers. "You simply must analyze less and believe more. You and Pete have great prospects for having a healthy baby. But if you don't think so, your brain will interfere with your fertility. I've been doing this a long time. Attitude can make a difference."

"Oh, honey, Dr. Bauer's right," Alice said from the end of the table. "I've seen it more than once."

"So now you're saying if I don't get pregnant, it will be my own fault." She tried to keep her voice from breaking.

Dr. Bauer put his glasses back on. "If I didn't know hormones were flooding your blood stream like white-water rafting, I'd scold you."

"Oh," she heard her own whininess. "I don't want to be such a pain. It's just—sometimes so overwhelming."

"Well," Alice said standing up and pulling off her sterile gloves, "not to change the subject or anything," she said pointedly, "but how is your sister doing? I read about it in your newspaper. What a terrible thing to happen while she's here visiting. What they said in the Lakeshore—sounds like she almost got killed."

For a moment Kate felt disoriented. All she wanted was to wallow in her own misery, but Alice was dragging her out of her self-absorption. "I guess so, yes," Kate finally clicked in. "But Jamie is tough."

A neighborhood scene popped into her head. Jamie's small blond head butting Billy Magger's pudgy belly. He'd called Kate a "stuck-up snot," and Jamie, at half his weight, had run at him like a tiny bull knocking him over backwards. Billy's reputation never recovered from that.

Seeing Jamie in the hospital had stirred all the old affection—but then Pete told them Jamie was still pregnant. In the surreal surroundings of the hospital cafeteria at three-thirty in the morning, Kate had swayed between relief and resentment—between gratitude and envy.

"My sister's arm was her worst injury—that and a concussion. She's living on the big lake with my mother's best friend who's...who's very sick. I'm going out to see them tomorrow." The last words were out of Kate's mouth before she'd known she was going to say them. Kate had promised herself she'd make amends to Aunt Nina the day she got a positive pregnancy test. The terrible irony was that Aunt Nina and her mother *had* gotten pregnancy news. It just wasn't Kate's.

"I understand from your paper," Dr. Bauer said, "the police now think it might be road rage. Some truck driver your sister rode her bike in front of? My patients tell me—you know how news travels in this town—maybe a Power Company employee leaving the late shift. I hope they catch him. Any person that volatile needs to be locked up. And they still don't have much to go on besides the stray dog."

Kate felt uneasy talking about Jamie in this private, terrifying space of her own. And hearing it from the guardians of her own long-standing dream. It seemed too much like bad luck, as if Jamie's unwanted pregnancy could hex Kate's. "Yes, well, I mean the police are holding the dog—a big lab. They're still hoping the owner turns up."

"Tell your reporter I liked the way he made the lab sound like Wonder Dog," Alice said. "Lassie or Rin Tin Tin or somebody. I must say, though, in the Lake-shore News photo, he looked like every other black dog I've ever seen."

"Now, Kate," Dr. Bauer said, his medical tone returned, relieving her of the need to continue talking about Jamie and the attack, "make sure Pete's not on call once we give you the shot. Then think soft music and roses and not follicles and hCGs."

Still distracted by the discussion about Jamie, Kate forgot to use the private side door to the hallway. She walked right out into the main reception room before she realized it. Quickly she put her head down and hurried past the several women looking at her over their unread magazines.

Monday—Tuesday at the latest—she'd get the luteinizing hormone shot. Thirty-six hours later she and Pete would begin, once again, to try and make a baby. How many times had she entered this kingdom of the possible, stroking her belly afterwards to bless the union of sperm and egg into a conception. Yet, on the 29th or 30th day—once, the worst of all, even the 38th day—her temperature dropped and the black bells peeled another failure.

Her sister, fertile as a bunny it seemed, would never hear that mournful ringing. Jake must have visited some weekend while Jamie was in the Tucson rehab. Or Jamie hooked up with another patient. She hated the unfairness of God's making it so easy for her little sister to create what she couldn't take care of but denying Kate what she wanted most.

The heat of her car's door handle reminded her she'd forgotten to leave any windows opened. The blue-white summer sun steamed the air in its slow ascent toward mid-day. She turned the key in the ignition and powered all four windows down, soothed by the slight breeze on the back of her neck. She glanced back at Dr. Bauer's office as she pulled out of the parking lot and thought about how Pete now always referred to "their" pregnancy. He'd never know how much that meant to her.

She still remembered the day in Pete's fourth year of residency when he finally agreed to see Dr. Delgado, a OB/GYN professor on Northwestern's faculty who specialized in infertility. Dr. Delgado told them the first tests were always run on the husband's sperm because it was the easiest screening, and the cause of infertility almost half the time. Pete, in his good denim shirt, his tie not quite straight, had sat motionless. Then it registered.

*　　*　　*

"You mean-"

"I *mean*," Dr. Delgado, said, his dark eyes sparkling with finality at the young orthopedic resident.

Afterwards, Pete scarcely pulled onto the boulevard heading to their tiny apartment in Wrigleyville when a grin exploded across his face. "Your husband is a stud, Babe. Sperm count and motility off the charts."

She'd recoiled as if he'd hit her. "I can't believe you said that!" she screamed across the seat at him. Pete looked over in shock. "I am obviously the failure here. You can operate all night and still impregnate a room full of women." She grew more upset as she talked. "But I'm the inadequate one, right? Is that what I'm hearing?"

The muscles in Pete's jawbone twitched in his fight to hold back. Then exhaustion ignited his temper, and his voice grated on her like hot sandpaper. "God damn it, Kate, I was trying, *trying* to be funny because jacking off in a bathroom with a Playboy centerfold is not my idea of a good time. Every damn person in the waiting room knew I was in there playing with my cock so they tried not to look at me when I came out but they all did anyway.

"So don't give me that shit. This whole thing is a waste of money we don't have. We'll have a baby without Delgado as soon as I quit working 80 hours a week and you're home once in a while."

Suddenly, he stopped talking and grabbed Kate's hand on the seat. "Hey, look, Babe, I'm sorry," his face softened. "I'm really sorry."

*   *   *

They'd never discussed his sperm count again. And until he'd started saying "our" pregnancy, it felt like Kate's problem alone. Now he'd joined her, and the sharing made all the difference.

Driving home from Dr. Bauer's office, Kate slowed as she passed the Tudor home a block from her house. She always took time to look at the huge sycamore encircled with brilliant fuchsia impatiens in the manicured front yard. Together, she and Pete would get through this. One day they would have a real family, and the baby would make them closer than ever. She looked again through her rearview mirror at the bursts of pink around the fat tree, feeling a new pulse of hope as she pulled into her own driveway.

Climbing out of the Mazda, she could hear Pete talking to someone in the backyard. She was surprised, happily, he was home. Not making rounds. Now they'd have a day together—a day they needed just for the two of them. She walked around the corner of the house in time to see a huge dog racing toward their back fence, his black head pointed up at an airborne green tennis ball. That's when she realized what she'd heard Pete saying was "Go get it, Pogo."

The Sandpiper

JAMIE

"I rode your bike to the party store to buy booze, Aunt Nina." She felt the warm sand fill the arch under her barefoot as she paced her steps to the slow rhythm of the woman beside her. "But you probably knew that already." Aunt Nina's emaciated face nodded in tempo with the stiff movements of her legs along the beach.

Despite the heat of the late July morning, Aunt Nina wore the navy University of Michigan sweatshirt Jamie had given her for Christmas one year. The thickly rolled cuffs bunched at Aunt Nina's wrists, the sweatshirt hanging like a loose dress around her thin knees. Jamie forced herself to take yoga breaths.

"Pretty much," Aunt Nina finally spoke. "I didn't have good feelings when I went to bed that night. Your going swimming didn't bother me. That's like a kite finding the wind. But you were jumpy—and had been since you moved in. I've read enough to know when you get antsy, my dear, I should pay attention."

"You couldn't have stopped me from drinking. You know that. Nobody could have."

"Nobody once you'd made your plan. But at least we could have talked about it—if those blasted pain pills hadn't knocked me out so fast. I never heard you come up from the beach that night. And I wouldn't have missed you until the next morning if your mom hadn't called. Guess I'm not much of a caretaker."

"Aunt Nina, the idea was for me to take care of you." Jamie's deep breathing helped calm her skittish emotions. "So far it's been the other way around." Jamie clicked the fingernails of her right hand against the curved plaster encasing her left arm. A large green sling neatly arranged across her chest covered most of her oversized red T-shirt. "As in who needs caretaking to tie this?" Jamie pointed at the sling. "And this?" she pulled her pony tail. "And how about this?" she snapped the elastic back of her bra with her right hand.

Aunt Nina held her attenuated fingers on the brim of her floppy straw hat as she watched Jamie's gestures, a smile lifting the corners of her pale mouth. "Jamie, you can't imagine what pleasure it gives me after all these years to do some of those things for you. It feels like the old days when I got to take care of you and Kate as little girls.

"I thought my days of usefulness were over—like Ulysses rusting *unburnished, not to shine in use...* And then here you come back with your combat wounds to make me feel needed again."

Jamie edged closer to the water where she pressed her new weight into the damp sand leaving lopsided ghosts on wheels behind her. Ahead of them a flock of seagulls squatted on a rounded scallop of beach, their heads pointed into the wind. As she and Aunt Nina got closer, the white-headed adult birds and their freckled young rose gracefully together off the sand like one low-flying glider. The gulls hovered over the water until the intruders passed, then recaptured their sunning beach with a few landing squawks.

"It's why, one of many reasons anyway, Jamie, your mother and I are fighting you so hard on this adoption thing. I know, I know," Aunt Nina raised her hands, "you don't want to talk about it any more. You've made that perfectly clear. Your mother and I understand. We know you've made your decision. But this child isn't just yours. And I don't care how shameless it is, I am invoking the privilege of the dying to force you to talk to me about this baby no matter how much you don't want to."

Jamie concentrated on the sand, pressing the balls of her feet deeper into the moisture. Aunt Nina was not playing fair. The darkness around Aunt Nina's eyes already dragged on Jamie's soul like a stone. Living with Aunt Nina was making it all the harder to lose her. Like a thirsty child, she was drinking in Aunt Nina's steadfast kindness, the humor, the arched courage, the unconditional love for a messed-up, unwed, pregnant alcoholic.

If she'd hoped Aunt Nina's sickness would make her crotchety so Jamie wouldn't have to miss her so much, she'd wasted a wish. One day at a time. Jamie'd been praying to be ready when the end came. But she never could be.

"She," Aunt Nina went on, "—and there's no doubt in my mind you have a little girl in there—has a dad somewhere."

Jamie's heart fluttered and her foot splashed hard in the fringes of water. She thought about Aunt Nina's desert cactus in its ornate Victorian bowl. Even though Christmas was months away, Aunt Nina checked the plant daily for signs of tiny buds—"just in case," as she put it. But Keith Summers must never, never be brought into this. Jamie could at least do that right.

"No," Aunt Nina said picking up on Jamie's agitation. "I'm not going to ask about the father because I don't care. But I care a great deal about the grandmother. I admire you for wanting a childless couple to have the greatest gift of all by adopting your baby. I also respect your insisting they live in another state and have no family history of alcoholism. That's all wise and well intended, Jamie dear."

"Aunt Nina. You, of all people, know why I can't..." Jamie's chest contracted.

"Oh, yes. You're unfit to raise a child because you are—what's that AA term—a "chronic relapser." I know that. But I also know you, and you will not be able to stay sober if you give your baby away. Don't argue yet." She pushed both her palms at Jamie. "I'm terminal."

Jamie shook her head against the smile wanting to surface.

"Here's what I've loved you long enough to know—and I held you the minute you were born. If you give your daughter up, you will grieve for her the rest of your life. And so will your mother."

Jamie's good hand instinctively moved to the hard swelling under the elastic waist of her shorts, her eyes stinging. It was rotten of Aunt Nina to talk in terms of "she" and allow Jamie to think of this amorphous thing as a little girl. Aunt Nina knew exactly what she was doing—which chains she was pulling.

But Aunt Nina didn't know how sick Jamie was—and had been even before the black thunderous night she'd been brutalized and then not allowed to tell. How she woke up every day craving whatever it took to keep her from imploding with despair at the mess she'd made of her life.

No, Aunt Nina could not understand how much strength it was taking hour by hour to stay sober. To keep this helpless baby under her belly button safe. Most of all, she had no idea how much love it would take to give away this baby moving inside her. Ending the pregnancy would have been so much easier for her—and far kinder to Aunt Nina and her mother. They never would have known. But in the end, Jamie had faltered.

Abortion as a woman's choice for her own body was something Jamie had not questioned until it was her turn. Until she was the one whose body carried the invisible cells on their way to becoming a little person. The power of that epiphany kept her from going back to the clinic in Grand Rapids. And yet Kate still believed Jamie had already had an abortion before. No, Kate didn't know her younger sister at all.

"I'm sorry to upset you, Jamie," Aunt Nina's voice broke in. "But I have done something behind your back, which you know isn't my style." Aunt Nina stopped abruptly. "Did we read *Henry IV* when you were in my honors English class, Jamie?"

Jamie came to a stop, confused. "What?"

"The play—Shakespeare's about Prince Hal? Anyway, it's about Henry the Fourth's young son Hal carousing his way through old merry England with the worthless, but in ways quite wonderful, Jack Falstaff. The king, Henry IV, pretty much gives up on Hal as any kind of a monarch.

"No, Jamie, don't give me that look. The cancer has *not* spread to my brain. Bear with me. It is not until Henry IV's enemies conspire against the king that Prince Hal finally acts like an adult. That's when he takes on his responsibilities—which means leaving Falstaff and the pubs behind."

In spite of herself, Jamie began to laugh. "Aunt Nina, my AA comrades have thrown some weird stuff at me over the years, but you take the cake. Shakespeare working for Bill W!"

Aunt Nina had her missionary look going. But she, too, gave into a little giggle as they began to walk again. "It's out there, I agree. But there is a punch line. When Falstaff threatens Hal by saying something like, *Banish me, banish the world,* Prince Hal answers his favorite drinking buddy in no uncertain terms. *I do and I will.*"

In a rush of recognition, Jamie didn't feel like laughing any more. Aunt Nina looked at her with raised eyebrows making sure Jamie got the point. How could she miss it? Prince Hal finally acted on the two words of Alcoholics Anonymous Jamie hated the most. Grow up.

"I called Tom Quinn," Aunt Nina went on talking as if Shakespeare had never come up, "to ask about a private adoption. Don't worry. He's been my lawyer for years, and you couldn't beat client information out of him with a stick." Aunt Nina paused to cough.

Jamie had been too distracted by the conversation to notice they'd walked past the red Mears cottage, the turning-back point for their morning beach walks. "We've gone way too far," she said and waited for Aunt Nina to catch her breath before they turned back south.

"My lungs knew it," Aunt Nina smiled bravely, "even if my eyes didn't. Anyway, Tom has a lawyer friend in Kansas City who specializes in private adoptions."

"How would you ever know that?"

Aunt Nina turned her head to face Jamie. "Do you really think you're the first single girl in Spring Port to get herself in a family way, as they say? I had more than one student come to me in the same situation. Several of them wanted to be talked out of an abortion. Their parents were the ones pushing for it."

"You—the things you've done for people—is there anyone you haven't helped in town?"

"These were young girls with no one else to turn to. When it first happened, I called Tom for legal advice. That's when he told me about his law school friend in Kansas City. The man's a Catholic who created a small foundation to help find the best adoptive parents for babies, not the other way around. The foundation pays all expenses so no money changes hands. In other words, no baby buying. The adopting parents aren't notified until the baby is one month old so the birth mother has that time to change her mind before…"

"But I can't—I can't!" Jamie shook her head wildly, her skin hot with anguish.

"You won't have to," Aunt Nina replied calmly. "The birth mother can choose to not ever see the baby. She signs the adoption papers any time she wants to. But the baby is not adopted out for 31 days. Over that month, if the mother chooses not to be involved, the foundation hires private nursing care for the baby."

"A month? Waiting a whole month?" No, for Jamie the whole thing had to be over immediately. She could never see it—*it*. She had to stay with that pronoun.

"The adoptive parents don't see the mother before the birth—don't even know the baby's been born for a month. As you can tell, Tom's friend designed it to encourage mothers to keep their babies by giving them extra time. It also spares heartbreak for the adopting parents."

"It wouldn't change one thing for me," Jamie said, wanting this conversation over. "I can barely take care of myself, let alone a baby."

"Your mother would love to help you care for this baby, and," Jamie knew Aunt Nina was hurrying her words to keep her from interrupting, "there's all sorts of good day care in Spring Port. You could get a job, maybe part time, and not have the baby by yourself all day every day."

Jamie wanted to cover her ears against Aunt Nina's breathless sentences that were making it sound almost possible. But why would Aunt Nina ever think Jamie could be Prince Hal when she was Falstaff? And had been since she went with Roger Hamper to check out an investment property.

"Do you want to know what that little guy makes me think of?" Aunt Nina pointed toward the spindly legs of a lone Spotted Sandpiper teetering back and forth as he pecked into the sand in front of them. "What you need right now?"

"Shakespeare?"

Aunt Nina smiled. "Remember the thing with feathers?"

Jamie didn't want to, but did. She watched the little bird keeping his wobbly steps the same distance in front of them. He paused between pecks at insects in the sand to look back at them. The dark line through his eyes looked like tiny sunglasses.

"*The tune without the words*," Jamie said almost to herself. The olive bird lifted his spotted belly into the air and flew low over the water. But nothing in Jamie's heart felt hopeful.

"*And never stops at all.* Don't forget that part."

Jamie didn't respond, and they walked on in silence.

"I have to be straight up with you now, Jamie." Aunt Nina finally spoke. "I don't have the luxury of dither time."

"You know," Jamie finally said still watching the sandpiper, "I'm not doing well with any of this conversation."

"I'm sorry for making you cry, but this has to be said. I love you and your mom enough, and I'm selfish enough to want your daughter's future resolved before—well, you know."

"What in hell happened to the thing with feathers when you talk like that!" Jamie pulled up the bottom of her shirt to blot her tears.

"It's exactly *what* I'm talking about. Your mother and I saw Tom last week," Aunt Nina said in her businesslike teacher's voice. "We wanted to know the legal options for your mother to adopt your baby. Hang on a minute," her scrawny hand shot up. "Your mother is desperate. She can not bear the idea of having a grandchild she'll never know."

Jamie came to a full stop and turned toward Aunt Nina. "Damn it all, don't you and my mother see how I can't bear the idea of having a child I'll never know either? But I am an alcoholic and an addict and way, way too sick up here!" She smacked her forehead with her good fist. "I'm too sick for a baby to be safe with me!"

She cursed herself for letting Aunt Nina make her think for even a split second she might be able to take care of a helpless infant. "Aunt Nina," she stared hard at the older woman's face, "there's a young mother who brings her new baby to our 5 p.m. AA meetings sometimes. When that baby starts crying,

I lose it. Totally."

She felt her heart accelerate at the remembered sound. "I can't stand it for more than five minutes and then I have to leave the room. Go outside. Go home. That crying baby makes me crazy! How in God's name, could I do that all day every day and stay sober? And if I drink, boom, this baby," she laid her hand on her belly, "is a goner. It's that simple."

The sandpiper resumed his pecking behind them. Aunt Nina turned to watch the bird a moment, then continued as if Jamie hadn't told her about the crying baby.

"Tom laid out a laundry list of reasons why your mother's adopting your baby is not the answer."

If she'd had any joy left in her, Jamie might have smiled at Aunt Nina's single mindedness. She was not to be deflected from the topic of adoption. "Oh, I can't believe you thought for one minute I'd let her."

"Believe us, your mom and I are ready to try anything—including kidnapping—before we watch you turn your child over to strangers."

Jamie felt a bitter taste in her mouth as she looked away to watch a sailboarder tilt his red sail toward the flat horizon of blue on blue.

"Tom wants you to consider asking Kate and Pete to adopt your baby."

Jamie stood frozen in place, her stomach in freefall. Had she heard right? As she turned, stunned, to see Aunt Nina's face, her peripheral vision caught a bounce of black pounding down the beach toward them. The dog's tongue began licking the lotion on Jamie's leg before some tiny gear in her memory engaged.

"Oh, no, oh…is this…is this you?" she dropped to her knees and held one ebony silk ear with her right hand, grateful to end Aunt Nina's conversation. "It is you, isn't it," she let the dog snuggle against her face as her arm encircled the wiggling dog's big head.

"This can't be the stray dog?" Aunt Nina asked, leaning over to pat the shining coat.

"I don't remember much about that awful night, but I know this boy, don't I, fella. You scared that stinking SOB off me." The dog let out two quick barks as if to show how he'd done it.

Jamie buried her head in his shoulder and laughed with a primal joy she hadn't felt in a long time.

"Well," Pete suddenly appeared beside them, "I guess you guys have met Pogo," he said in his soft North Carolina drawl.

"How on earth did you find him? Why is he here?" Jamie's heart pounded in spontaneous joy.

"I asked the policemen right away that night to let me know if the owner didn't show up. I told him I'd like to adopt the dog. But I came here first. Because if you want him, Jamie, he's yours. You certainly earned first rights to Rescue Dog here," Pete said scratching Pogo's big head.

"But the owner?"

Pete shrugged. "The cops checked everywhere and decided he's one of the camping dogs that got left behind the week before the 4th. Kids start shooting off firecrackers for days before and after. Dogs get spooked. If they don't come back before the campers pack up, they just leave their dogs behind. Happens every year the cop told me."

"How heartless!" Aunt Nina said. "But, in this case," she laid her hand on Jamie's head, "how blessed. Are you up for a dog, young lady?"

Jamie looked up at Pete and was startled to see something close to anxiety. Then she got it. Of course! Pete wanted Pogo like a kid wants candy. But he was offering him to Jamie first. It was so like Pete. She rubbed noses with Pogo one last time before she pulled herself up.

"How about sharing him, Peter? You keep him, feed him, get his shots, clean up after him, do all the dirty work and maybe I can pick him up once in a while for some beach running?"

She almost laughed at the relief illuminating Pete's eyes. "Deal!" He said it so fast even Aunt Nina chuckled. Jamie glanced at Aunt Nina in time to see a quick wink. She was thanking Jamie. Aunt Nina had seen Pete's face too. She knew how much he wanted Pogo too.

The Sandpiper

KATE

Kate walked along the wraparound deck connecting The Sandpiper with the stairs to the beach. She could see just the top of Aunt Nina's straw hat moving slowly up the steps, the yellow-gold of Pete's hair right behind her. Beyond them on the beach, Jamie was holding a piece of driftwood high in the air with her good hand.

Kate watched Jamie ease back on one foot, uncurl her arm and fling the stick over the water in a smooth arc. Even with one arm bound to her chest, the athletic grace in Jamie's movements made Kate think of a Beethoven symphony—power and melody compressed into sheer beauty. It was a gift Jamie never valued enough. A gift Kate had always envied.

She watched Jamie's rounded body cast chiaroscuro shadows on the sand. The sound of Jamie's unrestrained laughter at Pogo's water leaps brought Kate a sudden kick of loneliness. She missed Jamie. Missed her more than she wanted to admit.

Pete looked up from the steps where he held Aunt Nina's arm. His eyes took on the turquoise shade of the water as he smiled up at Kate with his whole face. Kate kissed her lips toward him and hurried down the wooden stairs to take his place. She watched Pete jog back to where the wet dog had dropped the driftwood on the sand before shaking water all over Jamie.

Pete hadn't asked why his wife needed a little private time with Aunt Nina. He was more than happy to detain Jamie on the beach for half an hour so he could throw sticks for the dog who already answered to the name Pogo.

Aunt Nina pulled off her hat as they reached the cottage. She ran a palm over the reddish stubble growing on her damp skull. "Look, it's longer," Aunt Nina pulled at the tiny fuzz covering her scalp. "Fix us some ice water, why don't you, Kate, while I make a quick bathroom stop."

Aunt Nina walked past the kitchen toward her bedroom, then paused to look back at her. "My dear Kate, you have no idea how happy I am to see your lovely face here today. No idea." Aunt Nina turned away again, then called over her shoulder, "I'd compare you to a summer's day, my dear, but it's already been done."

Kate twisted a plastic ice tray over the sink to loosen the cubes. Her insides cramped as she thought about what she needed to say. This didn't feel like a day for poetic fun. Kate had rehearsed this so much, she felt a little panicky. Her stomach gurgled. If she didn't get it out right away, she'd put it off once again.

She put their water glasses beside each other on the cable spool, sitting down on the end of the couch close to where Aunt Nina would stretch out in her wicker chaise. Then Kate changed her mind once more on how to begin. She would start by helping Joe with his story and ask Aunt Nina about the Nortier's land. The ice broken, she'd work herself into telling Aunt Nina how petty she'd been—how wrong—how neglectful.

Once Aunt Nina was settled in the chaise, the blue and yellow tulip quilt covering her thin legs, Kate leaned forward, hands on both knees, poised to speak. She stopped to take one slow sip of water from the moist glass. "Aunt Nina," she said with force, "I need to talk to you and apologize for so much I don't know where to begin."

Kate stared down at the fingers around the cold glass as if they weren't hers. She felt the shock of hearing herself crack open the topic she had just decided to put off a few more minutes. Somehow, an autonomic nerve connection in her brain had fired on its own. A deep, unconscious part of her had understood that if she didn't start with what she'd come to say, she'd never get to it.

"*Something there is,* my dear, *that does not love a wall,*" Aunt Nina said without hesitation. Kate looked over at Aunt Nina and saw it. She'd known all along, but had said nothing. Instead she'd waited for Kate. She'd known Kate would come back.

Kate's eyelids hurt. "You knew how hurt I was when you told me I couldn't get into Duke—when you tried to stop me from applying."

Aunt Nina's boned face nodded. "You should have been hurt. I was wrong, chickadee. I, who have admired your brilliance since you were three—I thought you were setting yourself up for rejection. You'd had enough setbacks—losing your dad and then your mother tuning out. No, it was never about your talent.

145

I'm a teacher who knows Spring Port High isn't the kind of school Duke pays attention to. They don't have to because of all the private-schoolers who apply."

"You were trying to protect me—and all I felt was betrayed."

"Do you remember your retort? The lines you threw back at me that day because I'd said them so often to your class?"

Kate shook her head. All she remembered was being devastated by the woman she'd trusted as a mother.

"*Ah, but a man's reach must exceed his grasp,*" Aunt Nina began, then paused.

"*Or what's a heaven for,*" Kate finished with her. "Yes, now I do. Oh, yes. And it felt good to hit you back with your own preaching about setting high goals. I was hurt, mad—all of it."

Kate grabbed Aunt Nina's hand with the vigor of release like a hot-air balloon that had been tied down too long. At last she could be honest with Aunt Nina, and it felt like coming home.

"It was the money, too, I know," Kate said. "You knew even if some miracle got me in, Mom couldn't afford it. And you assured me," Kate felt the old tinge of smugness, "that Duke doesn't give scholarships because they don't need to."

Aunt Nina looked away, out across the lake working her brow as she did when something weighed on her mind.

"Oh, that sounded snotty, didn't it."

Aunt Nina's skin smoothed into a smile as she turned back to Kate. "Just a little bit. But promise me one thing. No matter what, never forget that every dollar spent on your four years at Duke was the best possible investment anyone ever made."

Kate smiled at the funny request, but her reply was quick.

"Of course I won't forget. I knew at the time how lucky I was to go there. And I still know it. But why—why did I let such a stupid thing bother me? Let it come between us for so damned long?"

"My dear, you've been away since high school. If you'd lived here—we'd have had more time together. We'd have worked it out. Please don't beat yourself up one second longer." Aunt Nina leaned forward and rested her thin hand on Kate's leg.

Kate stared at her own estrogen-swollen fingers as she said, "I've learned that putting off something you need to say doesn't work because there never is a good time."

"It's done, then. Over. No foul, no penalty."

Kate rose and embraced Aunt Nina with gentle intensity—needing the physical closeness—the renewal. She held her close enough to feel the staggered breathing—then held her even closer. "Oh, I hate how much time I've lost with you." Kate willed herself not to cry as she finally sat back down.

"*To everything there is a season,* my chickadee. Now, today, this moment—it's all that matters." Aunt Nina raised the glass of water to her lips, and Kate saw the veins on the back of her hands bulge grey-blue through transparent skin. A slight tremor sloshed the water against the sides of the glass, and Kate reached instinctively to steady it. Then she pulled back. Aunt Nina did not want to be treated like an invalid. Kate bit the inside of her cheek to quell the heart pain of realizing what she'd missed. Aunt Nina had given her poetry and myths and love without edges.

Kate picked up her own water to regain control.

"I find I'm extra thirsty lately," Aunt Nina said putting the glass down slowly. "Now, Kate, go get me the photograph right there," she pointed at a high shelf on the bookcase. "The one in the pewter heart frame." Glad for the distraction, Kate brought over the heart that encircled her mother, Jamie, and her on the beach.

"You've seen this picture forever, Kate. But you don't see what I do. Why I've kept it right there all these years."

Kate's mother, slim in a black two-piece bathing suit, looked at the camera with an almost dazed smile. Several feet behind her a toddling Jamie had a "catch-me" expression as she looked over shoulder and headed straight for the water. The only serious face in the picture was Kate's as her little arms reached toward Jamie, worry imprinted on her face as she glanced at the camera. Kate understood.

"It tells its own story, doesn't it?" Aunt Nina asked needing no answer. "Being the oldest is hard anyway. But with no dad and your mother not together for a long time, guess who took charge?"

Now Kate couldn't stop the tears from spilling down her face as she saw herself—really saw.

"How can we not love to pieces a dear little girl like that?"

The two sat in silence, a new calmness like an aura around them. Then Kate smiled and asked, "Remember when you taught us the names for groups of birds like a gaggle of geese and muster of peacocks? Well right now—right this moment, do you know what I feel you and I are?"

Aunt Nina's whole face smiled. "Do I get any clues?"

"Okay. One. It rhymes with 'parks.'"

"Of course! An exaltation of larks. Yes. With you and Jamie and your mom, life has always been an exaltation for me. Oh, thank you for that, my dear. Now, before your one-armed sister and your husband and the new dog interrupt us, you can refill our water glasses and ask me the newspaper questions you pretended to come for."

Aunt Nina's sly glance told Kate she was, indeed, back home.

"It's pretty frivolous stuff after what we've just talked about." She put the filled water glasses back on the table.

"Even better. We can take only so much drama in one day. I'll get comfy and you fire away."

In slow-motion clips, Kate watched Aunt Nina carefully shift her hips, her eyelids twitching in pain. Kate looked away, out at the endless blue lake beyond the windows.

"Sorry if I grimaced," Aunt Nina said, responding to what she'd seen briefly cross Kate's forehead. "Don't worry, my dear. Just a few sore spots if I sit in one position too long. Now what's the question?"

Kate sat back into the cushions wishing Pete would come up from the beach before she broke down for good. She dug her fingernails into her palms for control. Aunt Nina was sicker than she'd realized.

How unimportant any news story was right now.

"Shoot, chickadee. Or lark."

"So silly to even bother you with." Kate gave a loud sigh before she went on. "Anyway, Joe O'Connor, our best reporter, wanted me to ask you."

"He's a good writer. I see his name in the paper all the time. How can I help?"

Kate pinched her arms across her waist. "This is so, oh," she pushed air out of her lungs. "I'm sorry I even brought it up. It seems stupid now."

"Stupid. Schmupid. You got my curiosity going now. Remember your Aunt Nina is a journalist wannabee—especially if Joe's doing some juicy investigative reporting." Aunt Nina tilted her head sideways and paused. "Does this have anything to do with Jamie's attacker?"

"No," Kate said running her fingers through her hair. "Nothing that exciting, believe me. Joe's been working on a story about the developer who bought your friends' cottage—the Nortiers. Now the developer wants to buy the empty lot next to it. Those huge dunes where you used to take Jamie and me to pick wild asparagus."

Aunt Nina lifted her glass, clinking the ice against the sides.

"The property's held in a family trust, but nobody can locate the owner. T. T. Lane is the name on the trust. When I told Joe you'd lived on the big lake a long time and knew the Nortiers, he asked if you had any idea who T.T. Lane is or even the Lane family. He can't find anything on them. See how dumb this is?" Kate shrugged her shoulders apologetically. "It's not even that newsworthy, and I wish I'd never brought it up."

Aunt Nina was still staring into her sweating water glass when a flurry of excited barks from the deck made them both look toward the deck. The dog's sounds were joined by Pete's and Jamie's voices floating through the screens. Moments later they appeared outside, the tail-wagging Pogo between them, his wet coat a brilliant charcoal.

Mad she'd even brought up Joe's news story, Kate felt a frisson of gratitude for the interruption. When she looked back at Aunt Nina, she was surprised to see a funny twitching motion of her eyebrows.

The Sandpiper

JAMIE

"It's the right thing, Girlfriend. Doesn't matter if you're going along with this Kansas lawyer just to please your mom and your Auntie." Gloria was sitting next to Jamie on the top of a worn picnic table at the far end of the parking lot behind the AA club. They were drinking cans of decaffeinated Diet Coke waiting for the five p.m. meeting to start. Over their heads, the August sky was iron grey with occasional blue patches making pockets of light on the pavement.

"Well, it's pretty obvious I don't make good choices on my own, Gloria."

"Yeah, well, you made a pretty good choice putting that," Gloria touched the cast on her arm, "in the way of that," she laid her warm palm on Jamie's belly. "Kept that dirty punk's boot from hurting the baby. I figured that out first time I heard about it. Almost got yourself killed protecting your child."

Jamie clicked her nails against the fiberglass cast. "Some primal drive to promote the species."

"Girlfriend, you just won't let yourself take credit for anything, now, will you? Here you almost get your head bashed in and you call it instinct. My ass, excuse the profanity. It's old fashioned mother love."

"No, Gloria, don't say that." Jamie felt her blond pony tail flip with the force of her headshake. "I can't afford to think like that for even a minute. I made a reflex move, that's all." Her heart suddenly felt bunched up like a cabbage inside her chest.

"Not what the cops said. But I can see you're getting bent out of shape so let's drop it."

"It's one thing for me to mess up my own life—but I am not going to do it to a little baby. That's why up here," she touched her temple with her good hand,

"I'm carrying somebody else's child. It's the only way I can get through this. I grit my teeth and visualize the loving, stable, sober Christian parents who will raise this baby the way I can't."

"Well, sounds like your Kansas lawyer got you just the couple you ordered. Church folks living way out in Nebraska without a drunk in the house!"

A solid bank of clouds moved slowly over the parking lot like a giant push broom sweeping the sun patches off the blacktop. "I'm scared, Gloria. After today, I can change my mind up to a month afterwards and I hate knowing that."

She watched Gloria take her time picking lint off the matte finish of her black microfiber skirt, the matching jacket folded neatly across her knees. The emerald silk blouse she wore accentuated the soft mahogany of her skin. Her hair was pulled back into a tall gold comb with the longer curled ends spilling out from behind her ears.

"I guess the way you snapped at your lawyer back there, you aren't going to think about letting your sister…"

"Dear Lord," Jamie cut her off, "you don't get it anymore than my mother and Aunt Nina do! This baby isn't good enough for Kate. You think my sister wants an unwed alcoholic's baby in her house? And when Miss Super Star career woman finally gets around to having her own perfect children, how do you think she'd feel then about raising this child with an addict's genes?

"Do you really think I could ever come back to Spring Port and stand to hear *this* baby calling Kate, 'Mommy?' Do stop me, Gloria, if I ever slip and say *my* baby because it never will be."

Gloria tapped her nails on the pop can thoughtfully. "Maybe you don't know everything about your sister."

"I know enough," Jamie felt her emotions cartwheel. "And even if for one insane moment I considered letting Kate adopt this baby—assuming she'd ever *want* to, what happens the day the child grows up to discover its crazy aunt is really its mother? How do you think that would feel?

"No, no, no. I grew up with an absent dad everyone pretended never existed. This child doesn't need to start life in one more dysfunctional, talk-show family. Not when there are so many normal couples out there looking for a baby to love."

"I hear you," Gloria said raising a palm in defeat. "But I wasn't talking necessarily forever. Just maybe letting your mom and Kate take care of *the* baby, as you put it, until you've had enough sobriety to feel ready to be a mom yourself.

Look, Girlfriend, you've still got over two months until you deliver. You might feel a whole lot different when the time comes."

"When the time comes, I'm out of here."

"I know you keep saying that, but how about your Aunt Nina?"

Jamie felt the tug of sorrow at the back of her skull. "You know I won't leave her."

Gloria flicked a buzzing fly away from her pop can. "Yes, I do. Long as you stay sober, you won't."

"What's that supposed to mean?"

"Hey. I'm your sponsor. It's my job to dog you about relapsing. So knock off with the attitude. Now I got to ask you this. Have you called Jake yet?"

"What the hell," she couldn't stop in time. "First you hound me about staying away from men for a year. You shoo them off at meetings like I'm a leper, and now you're bugging me to call the boyfriend who got me into coke!"

"Wait a sec. Did you forget everything I told you? Nobody 'got' you into cocaine. You did that all by yourself. Grow up, Girlfriend. And you know exactly why I'm telling you to call Jake. I'm saying you got to get honest and tell him now you're not coming back."

Jamie played with her earring. "I can't stay in Spring Port. Not after this," she put her hand on her middle. "Besides, I miss the mountains."

"Lots of places got mountains. But if you're planning to go back to Jake because he's rich and takes care of you, your sobriety is history. You and I both know it. I don't care if he paid to get you cleaned up. He's a boozer and he's not in the program. End of story."

"What if I love him?" she asked, knowing she never had. At least sober she hadn't.

"Yeah, right! Two horny ski bums pumped up on coke. You think that's got any thing to do with love? Where you been the last few months we've been coming here together?" she pointed at the back of the AA club. "Let's hear you tell the No Snivelers that one. I'd love to see their faces. Hey, there's Michelle. Why don't you bop over and tell her that right now?"

Jamie looked up to see the attractive doctor's wife from the 7 a.m. meeting pull her blue BMW into a space behind the club. She watched Michelle unfold a metallic heat protector and place it inside her windshield before she went into the building without seeing them. Gloria was right. The No Snivelers were hardcore AA which meant no bullshit. They walked through the harsh realities of everyday life while she still wanted to avoid discomfort. A wave of embarrassment warmed her skin as she imagined their response to her going back to Jake because she "loves" him.

"The operative word here, Jamie," she could almost hear one of them say, "is not 'love' him, but 'use' him."

"I know you got to leave Spring Port," Gloria was saying, her voice no longer scoldish. "With your sister and all. I'm afraid staying sober in this town might be too hard for you once this baby comes. I'm pretty sure *this*," she stressed the word, "baby is the reason you're sober now. Maybe, for once in your life, you been thinking about someone besides poor little Jamie."

Jamie glanced reflexively at the rounded hill of her belly under the soft black tunic stretched over it. Somehow the swelling had grown over that day. Then she glared at Gloria.

"Don't you go giving me the evil eye, Miss Jamie. I'm telling you what I see. Once the baby gets here, with all the adoption stuff to sign, your sobriety's going to be real shaky. What you cannot do is go back to the same-old same-old. So the first thing you do now is tell Jake you're not coming back there."

Gloria's voice softened, "Close that door now, Girlfriend, if you want to stay clean and sober."

Jamie thought she heard a click in Gloria's throat. When she turned, she saw Gloria's soul-rich eyes looking at her. Something in Jamie's temples began to throb. She rubbed her fingers into her eyes. "I hear you. I hear you," she said after a long minute. "But can we not talk about Jake anymore?"

"Sure," Gloria said patting Jamie's leg. "Just give me the high sign when you've made the phone call. Now I want to tell you I liked your lawyer friend today. He kept the legal mumbo jumbo simple so you knew what he was saying. My kind of lawyer, if I ever need one. Even if you do call him 'Uncle Tom.'" Gloria began to shake her head as a low rumble of laugh bubbled out her mouth. "Uncle Tom. Ain't that the best!"

Jamie wanted to laugh with Gloria, but inside everything felt sad. One thing she dreaded about leaving Spring Port was losing Gloria. She didn't know if she could make it without her. "Thank you for coming with me today, Gloria. I needed you. Having Mother and Aunt Nina there, I just couldn't have done it without you."

Gloria took a long sip from the Coke can. "You know, I learned early to separate the people who see my skin from those who see me. Say what you will. Those two ladies—your mom and your Aunt Nina—they're the real deal. You been lucky, Girl. Mighty lucky."

"Yeah, right," Jamie said flapping her open palms on the hard roundness of her girth.

"Don't even think about going there. You made that baby, and don't you go asking for sympathy cuz you're pregnant and don't want to be. Consequences, remember?"

"Well at least give me some credit for not..."

"Excuse me, Miss Jamie? First you won't take credit for risking your life to save *the* baby, and now you want me to honor you for not killing the little thing first? I'm sorry, but you don't want to hear what I got to say about abortion. You and your sister might not be friends, but she kept you from doing a terrible thing."

Jamie nodded, but she was no longer there. She was 18, violated and terrified. What if Roger Hamper's attack had made her pregnant? A life created in rape and ending in the rapist's suicide? What would she have done? Jamie would never know. At least God had spared her that.

"Fact is you didn't," Gloria said unaware of Jamie's mind wander. Gloria raised her hand for emphasis. "Fact is you didn't and that's all that matters."

An old model grey Chevy pulled into the last remaining parking space. The middle-aged man waved at them as he headed up the cement stoop into the AA Club's back door. Gloria swigged the last of her pop.

"Today you're doing good, day at a time." Gloria looked over at her. "And I have to say, you are looking mighty pretty, Girlfriend. Lordy when I was far along as you, I was a Mack truck and here you are still looking sexy in those jazzy outfits you wear."

Jamie looked down at the tunic she'd bought without sleeves so it fit over her cast and one size too large to fit the rest of her. Her height was giving her uterus room to spread out without jutting straight forward. She wouldn't have known this except for the other expecting mothers in Dr. Benson's waiting room who were surprised to hear she was in the sixth month.

The cheerful moms-to-be ignored the fact she sat in the most isolated corner of the waiting room with her head in a book trying not to talk to anyone. The last thing Jamie wanted was to chitchat about having a baby, especially with strangers wearing wedding rings—perky women who had no idea what it was like to wake up every morning aching for a drink.

But she'd made the unwelcome discovery that pregnancy created an instant sorority whose members set aside all rules of privacy. We're in this together, these women seemed to be saying, so let's talk. Talk meant hemorrhoids and heartburn and caudals.

"Jingle me when you've called Jake. Meanwhile, I'm keeping tight with you the next couple months." Gloria was climbing off the picnic table.

How about the next couple hours, Jamie wanted to reply. How about getting me through tonight while I pretend not to see Aunt Nina turn her back when the pain comes because she doesn't want me to see her grimace. Aunt Nina was doing that more lately. And each time it happened, the light went out of the room for Jamie, turning the cottage dark even in the middle of the day.

She pulled her shoulder away from Gloria as if she had to sneeze. "Sometimes, Gloria, I want to drink so bad my mouth fills with saliva. Some days I think I'm going crazy telling myself this baby isn't really in there so I can't love what doesn't exist." She twisted one of her turquoise earrings until it hurt. "If it weren't for you and AA…"

"Speaking of which, we're going to be late." Gloria said laying one quiet hand on Jamie's shoulder before moving forward. She walked beside Gloria to the back of the AA house, the sounds of voices and chairs sliding on linoleum filled the hallway they entered. Jamie looked over at a faded print too high on the wall as the framed sayings in Alcoholics Anonymous clubs always seemed to be hung.

'Let Go and Let God,' she read for the millionth time. Please she prayed, please God help me do that. And in her next breath, an unexpected floating quietude settled like a silk cape over her despair. A tiny pink bead of peace started to glow inside her.

Suddenly Jamie came to an abrupt stop. A baby wailed from the small, no-smoking room at the end of the hall.

The Sandpiper

KATE

"Was that your beeper or mine?" Pete asked reaching under his Duke tee shirt for the small black box clipped to his gym shorts. "Nope," he said pulling Pogo to a stop and pressing a button. "Not my Saturday to take call. Must be yours."

"There's something sick about a world where everybody carries a beeper," Kate said, stopping beside Pete to pull her pager from the pocket of her black nylon running shorts. "The world managed fine before when people could jog without electronic tethers. It's ridiculous for me anyway."

"You have big responsibilities at the Lakeshore News now, my love. Means being available."

"Oh, it's Joe," she read the tiny black phone number. "He must have gone in to finish his stories. You know Joe doesn't do deadlines. Obviously he needs to catch up on a Saturday when no one's around. Probably wants me to ask Aunt Nina one more time about the mysterious Lanes who own the beach property his developer wants. But we've run far enough. Let's walk from here. Even Pogo looks ready to slow down."

The black dog fell back between them. Kate leaned over to scratch his ears feeling the rhythmical smack of his strong tail against her leg. She looked up to see Pete's blue eyes crinkle at the edges as he smiled down at her. "Oh, yes," she said. "Pogo is a wonderful dog. But I'm still scared you'll get your heart broken if the real owner shows up some day."

"You're the one who breaks my heart."

He pulled her up and to him, their warm, pounding, chests pressed tight. Pete's unexpected tenderness toppled her precarious balance, and she felt a throb of passion hurl into the narrow space between them. She burrowed her face into his damp neck just as a bike bell jingled, and a tanned young woman pedaled past followed by a boy riding a small yellow bike, both of them wearing purple bike helmets.

Pete pulled Kate back from the path onto the grassy patch between the blacktop and the little forest of shimmering white pines planted in neat rows. The brown pine needles littering the grass snapped softly beneath their running shoes.

"What I really want to say is how I love you even more for letting Pogo stay." She felt the sloppy wetness of Pogo's tongue on her leg as if he understood the conversation. "You're not a dog person, I know."

"It's not that," she spoke into his shirt, not wanting to lose the feel of his solid arms around her back. "I was so afraid. It sounds silly now, but we might end up like the couples who can't have babies so they treat their pets like children."

Pete stepped back and stared down at her. "That isn't us, sweetheart. We are going to have children."

She felt tears coming in the roller coaster of her mood swings. The belly cramps from the fertility drugs were getting worse. "It's my last month on Clomid." She forced objectivity into her words. "If this doesn't work?" She tried not to whine.

"Don't jump ahead. This month isn't over. Jamie's mantra about one day at a time is not bad for us either." He took her hand as they walked, the stabilizing strength of his grip calming her like a tonic.

"It's so strange, Pete," she squeezed his hand back, "but having Aunt Nina back has made me feel, I don't know, somehow whole again. I had no idea how incomplete I've been without her."

She felt Pete lightly kiss her hand and knew what it meant. He sometimes understood her better than she did herself. He'd known, but she was the only one who could make it right again.

Kate tightened her grip. The silent communication clearer than words. The roar of a big red motorcycle pierced the air, the driver's bulky back bent over his bike. "So, my perceptive, loving husband," Kate said when the noise had faded down the road, "I think maybe it's time for me to start giving Jamie some support. And you don't have to say it," she raised her free palm. "You've thought that since she was hurt." She looked up at him and mouthed a kiss.

"Finally I'm getting it. What you and mom and Aunt Nina are seeing in Jamie—who's proving me wrong one day at a time. But it's such a blessing that

I'm afraid it's not going to last. I am just scared to be hopeful."

Then Kate grabbed Pete's head and kissed him hard on his lips tasting the salt of their mixed sweat. "You, my love," she whispered against his mouth, "are my truest blessing. My first always.

"Oh, and yes," she leaned over to run her fingernails over the wiggling dog's spine, "you're now another blessing, aren't you, boy."

Pete took her hand again as they walked on. "All Aunt Nina said to me was that you were way too hard on yourself."

"She deserved so much better from me."

"Well, she's hardly stopped smiling since you had your chat."

Aunt Nina had, indeed, laughed like a kid that Sunday on the deck as the two of them watched Pogo shake water on Pete and Jamie. Kate knew some of the laughter was an outburst of pure relief that Kate was back.

"I'm happier than Wordsworth's daffodils," Aunt Nina had announced when they went on the deck to greet the beach walkers. Pete might have suspected, but only Kate knew what she meant. Knew that what had separated Kate from Aunt Nina was now opened, clarified, cleansed. Aunt Nina laughed because her bookish Kate had returned.

Kate pulled back enough to look into Pete's face, reaching up to stroke his damp, flushed cheek. "Thank you for saying that. How come you always know how to make me feel better about myself?" She felt something stir deep inside her. Without knowing she was going to, Kate again brought her lips to his, sliding her tongue into his mouth. "Stud muffin," she said at last. "Let's go home."

Peeling off Pete's sticky shirt before their back door closed behind them, Kate ignored the demanding red light flashing on their answering machine. His hands slid up her back as he kissed her with a tugging fire. She opened her mouth until his tongue filled her throat, and she didn't care if she ever breathed again. She felt a jerk of deprivation as Pete suddenly pulled back and began to slide her shirt slowly up her torso.

She'd almost forgotten what a teal shade his eyes became when he was aroused. She felt his bright gaze caress her torso as he slowly exposed it. Holding his eyes, she scooched her wet sports bra up, one slow shoulder at a time, and dropped it on the floor. Gently, as if for the first time, he raised his hands to her breasts and stroked them until her nipples ached with wanting. She heard herself moan as Pete slid his hands under her arms, his tongue in her ear, and pulled her toward their bedroom.

It wasn't until later, when every pore in her body oozed with Pete as if their pleasured skins had melted together, that it hit her. She was too far from ovulating to get pregnant—and it didn't matter. She slid under Pete's arm as he dozed beside her, her nose buried into the pocket of his neck like a nuzzling kitten. For the first time in a very long time, she and her husband had not been making a baby. They had been making love.

She pulled on a white Ralph Lauren tee shirt and tucked it into her shorts. She began to blow dry her hair, smiling at herself in the mirror. Not even a long soaking bath, with some luxuriant scrubbing from Pete, had taken away the firefly tingles of sex under her skin.

She lifted her short dark hair with her fingers and let the hot air make it wavy. Today she felt pretty and sexy. She turned her profile the opposite way and pulled her shoulder blades together thrusting her small firm breasts forward and up.

"All right!" Pete called from the doorway, Pogo right beside him.

"Oh, you scared me. And caught me primping and posing at the same time." She turned off her hairdryer.

"That part," Pete shoved his own chest forward, "we like that, don't we, fella." Pogo sat down between them, his ears pointed straight up as if at attention. "Sure you don't want to come with us to the practice range?" Pete said in his full Southern sweetness.

"I look too nice to get all sweaty. I love you, but I'm not so sure about your sport. Then again," she grinned, "maybe I'll go with you tomorrow. I've got laundry to do anyway—and I'm thinking of making that doctored-up corn bread Aunt Nina likes so much."

Pete pulled her to him and kissed her softly, Pogo's tail swishing across the ceramic tiles as he looked up at them. "Don't go getting domestic on me. I like you better as a sexpot." He squeezed her bottom with both hands. She felt the bolt of sexual throb and smiled into his kiss knowing she was ripe for taking him straight back to bed. Then she felt the swelling pressed against her leg. He was ready too.

"I'm out of here, or I'm not going at all," Pete backed up both hands raised in surrender. "Come on Pogo. You can watch me perfect my duck hook."

"Oh, Pete, it's too hot to leave Pogo in the car."

"What? Concern from the lady," he talked to the attentive black face, "who didn't even want a dog!" Pogo looked up at her as if for an explanation.

"It's true, Pogo," she sang the next words, " '*Til there was you*. But really, Pete, you can't leave Pogo in the car."

"Honey, I park in the shade next to the range with all the windows down and I can see his head sticking out the whole time. Good enough, Mother?" She saw a quick flash of tension cut off his grin.

"Oh, I make this baby thing way too hard on you, don't I?" She put her palms together across her nose and moved her head back and forth in self-scolding. "You can't even call me 'Mother' without wincing."

"No…"

"Yes!" She inhaled deeply. "Well, that's it," she said firmly and kneeled to Pogo's level. "I am your mother, damn it, Pogo, and if we want to put you on our Christmas card, we will!" She tapped her finger on the dog's round nose, and looked up to see Pete's eyes, wary moments before, now luminous. She packed the love surging through her into one huge smile. Then she tilted her head, and said, "You know what Pogo saw—and heard—his *mother* doing this morning? You don't think that will give him the wrong idea about her, do you?"

After Pete and Pogo left, Kate hit the answering-machine button and began to straighten up the kitchen counter while she listened. She moved Jamie's Christmas cactus to a patch of sun under the skylight watching the radiance turn the leaves into emeralds. The washing machine was whirring in the utility room off the kitchen when Joe's voice came across the answering machine. "Kate, sorry to bother you on the weekend, but I think I just did something dumb."

Kate automatically reached for a pencil and note pad in the drawer under the phone. "No, actually, I know I did." She heard the noise of things falling in the background and pictured Joe's desk, one of his leaning Tower-of-Pisa piles sliding to the floor. "Shit," Joe mumbled away from the phone.

"Sorry. Little trouble here. Some man just called. Said he's an old friend of yours from college and didn't have your Spring Port phone number. I was in the middle of writing and told him without thinking. He sounded legit. But he didn't give me a name. Nothing. Hope he's who he says he is.

"Couple more things, 'til your tape shuts me off. The cops got an anonymous tip on your sister's attacker from a guy who thinks he knows him. Thinks the perp works the second shift at the Michigan Power Plant. Says the guy he knows is a hothead who drives a black Nissan pickup. Oh, and I finished the story on the Nortier development. Thanks for trying to find out from your aunt about the Lane family. Maybe this story will draw out someone who does remember them. Have a good one."

The machine started the next message, but all she heard was the click of a hang-up. The next message was Dave, Pete's golfing buddy, looking for a game that afternoon. She listened through two more hang-ups while she switched the laundry around. She was cracking eggs into the bowl of Jiffy cornbread mix when the phone rang. Wiping her right hand on the towel, she picked up the receiver, tucking it into her shoulder while she smacked open another egg.

Her hand froze in mid-air when the caller spoke. "This has to be Kate, am I not right? Jake speaking to you from Aspen. You know the Jakester as in Jamie's Jake? So how's it going' out there in the heartland? I'm telling you your sister doesn't make it easy on a guy. I've been waiting to hear from her since July, and we're getting near September."

"I'm sorry, I don't know what you're talking about." Kate stared blankly at the forgotten egg dripping in her hand.

"Sure you do, Kate." All at once his flippant tone turned serious. "So when's she coming home?"

Kate shook her head, a small stone of anger starting to clank in her chest. "I have no idea what you mean by 'home.' But if my sister wanted to talk to you, she'd have called you. Obviously you two haven't been in contact or you'd have called her yourself." She crushed the last egg into the batter.

"What was your first clue, Einstein?" Then Jake seemed to regret the sarcasm. His voice mellowed. "Look, Kate, I didn't call to pick a fight. I know you and Jamie don't jive. But that's not my deal. All I want's her phone number and I'll leave you alone."

"For sure you will do that, *Jakester!*" She slammed the phone hard in the cradle hoping it hurt his ear drum. Within seconds, it began ringing again. She measured the sour cream, and baking powder, ignoring the sound. By the time she poured the lumpy gold mixture into a thickly greased tin, the phone was ringing through its third cycle. She put the tin in the oven and snatched up the receiver.

"Forget it, Jake. And don't call back."

"Time out, Kate, please. Hear me for one minute. Just one." He began talking fast, but with unexpected sincerity. "Last Christmas your sister was in deep shit out here. Excuse the profanity, but she was."

Kate tried to remember what her mother had said about Jake back when her mother wanted to convince Kate, and herself, that Jake was not one more of Jamie's loser guys. What her mother really wanted was for Jake to be the one who could rescue Jamie. Take care of her. Keep her safe. He'd graduated from one of the Arizona colleges and owned a big place on the Aspen slopes where his mother's trust fund was letting him find himself on the ski slopes. Jamie had met him in an Aspen bar.

"The day before Christmas she did so much coke, the ER docs said her heart came close to kicking off. Like a heart attack." Kate needed to sit down at the kitchen table. She hadn't known—and neither did her mother. She'd worried for a long time about the cocaine—but kept hoping she was wrong.

"You still there?"

"Yes," she said, her bluster gone. She wished Pete were home.

"When she finally got out of the hospital, I flew her straight to the Saguaro Clinic in Tucson. A college buddy of mine spent some time there. I knew it was a top-drawer place. I wrote them a check for six months, whatever the insurance didn't cover, and ordered her this Saab convertible she'd wanted for Christmas. I had the keys delivered to her counselor and said she couldn't have them until she'd finished the program. All six months."

"Are you saying Jamie didn't want help?"

"Well," Jake took his time answering, "let's say it wasn't her first choice. Your little sister gets so damn blue sometimes—like this black cloud she can't shake. I think she gets high just to live with…I don't know, whatever it is that's eating her up."

A pin light started to flash in Kate's mind before Jake's next comment distracted her.

"Of course you're the family star, she keeps telling me."

Kate was surprised for the second time to hear Jamie had bragged about her.

"You wouldn't believe how she blows people off who tell her she's the best skier on the mountain. And we're talking friggin' damn Aspen here, Kate. Damn, you should see her scoot the moguls, all that gold hair of hers. She's something else, I tell you. Jammin' Jamie they call her out here. She stops the world when she skis. I guess every guy out here has the hots for her. But she doesn't give a shit. She still says she's a loser."

"So what did they tell you in Tucson—at the clinic. About how Jamie did there?" she ran her finger along a cactus leaf.

"Don't know. But she stayed. That's all they'd say. Besides telling me I wasn't supposed to write or call while she was in treatment. Then sometime in early April, Jamie phoned to say she needed to go to Michigan because your aunt was sick."

Kate didn't have to work much math. If Jake was telling the truth, and somehow she knew he was, he was not the father. Some time during treatment, her sister had hooked up with someone who'd gotten her pregnant. Kate couldn't help visualizing an overweight guy in a Harley Tee shirt with a snake arm tattoo.

"They told her to stay away from men for six months," Jake rambled on. "That's AA Nazi speak, if you ask me. But, whatever. I can deal with it. Then the talking heads out there tell her we can't even talk on the phone! Hell, I pay them seventy grand to get her well, and they cut me off at the knees! But what the—anyway, I woke up dreaming about her today and said to hell with the AA Gestapo."

"AA rules have to be tough because alcoholics are out of control," Kate surprised herself by the strength of her defense. She could see how vital it was for Jamie.

Jake snorted his disdain. "Whatever. Anyway, I don't know this Aunt Nina's last name. And since I'm not about to call Jamie's mother, I got your newspaper number from information. Jamie talks so damned much about you, I knew your paper's name was Lakeshore something. To be honest, it gets a little old hearing how you always took care of her and how you do everything right and she does everything wrong. And Jamie's got a real hang-up about some guy who was a good friend of yours. Says she ruined that too."

The pin light flashed back on, the beam broadening. Alex Hamper. Jamie'd started to talk about him that horrible day at Gertie's. About his dad. But Kate had been in shock. She hadn't heard anything after Jamie said the word "pregnant."

Kate twirled the cactus pot around on its white drip plate, her thoughts in conflict. For a long time her mother had said Jamie's big drinking problems began when Roger Hamper died. But Kate had scoffed—one more excuse her mother had come up with for Jamie. But what if there was something there? She pinched off the browned end of a stem trying to absorb what she was hearing.

"So how's she doin' out there in the mitten state?"

"What? Oh, good—I mean she's sober," Kate finally answered. "And it sounds like we're indebted to you—about Christmas, I mean."

Pete had seen more than one person Jamie's age come into the Cook County emergency room DOA from a cocaine-induced cardiac arrest. If Jamie's heart had come close to stopping in December, Jake had saved her life. She saw herself at Jamie's funeral and squeezed her eyes against the image.

"Thank you," was all she could say.

"Hey, I'm a hot dog, a ski bum, a boozer, yes. I am. But I care about your sister. Hell, there's so many horny women out here, but I can't help missing Jamie and all her craziness."

Kate sniffed quietly and told him she still couldn't give him Jamie's number until she talked to her sister. Jamie was helping their aunt, just like she'd told him she would. She was going to an AA meeting every day—sometimes more than one, and she had a great sponsor.

She did not mention either the pregnancy or the attack. Pete had called Jamie's broken arm 'a nightstick fracture'—caused by protecting her uterus.

"That's cool," Jake said. "Tell her the mountain's chillin' for her. Hey, and it's good to talk to you. Good to hear you and Jammin' Jamie are getting' your sister shit together. Later, Kate."

She punched off the "talk" button and sat motionless, a spectrum of changing patterns in her head. She was slowly learning that some things she thought she knew for sure, she didn't. Maybe she never had gotten them right. But getting to the truth? It could never be too late for that.

The Sandpiper

JAMIE

"The hour has come!" said the Badger at last with great solemnity. Leaning on the pillows propped against the headboard of Aunt Nina's bed, Jamie made her voice low and slightly bossy like Badger's. Beside her Aunt Nina lay on her side, her mouth eased into a smile under her stubbled hair, her eyes growing drowsy. Jamie held the worn book open with her cast, her good hand running gentle scratches along Aunt Nina's arm where it lay curled under her chin.

"What hour?" asked the Rat uneasily, glancing at the clock on the mantelpiece.

"Whose hour, you should rather say," replied the Badger.

Aunt Nina half lifted her head. "He sounds like a pompous old English teacher to me."

"If you keep interrupting Badger..." Jamie puckered her face into a scold. Aunt Nina put one silencing finger over her own lips and closed her eyes.

"Why, Toad's hour! The hour of Toad! I said I would take him in hand as soon as the winter was well over, and I'm going to take him in hand today!"

"Toad's hour, of course!" cried the Mole delightedly. "Hooray! I remember now! We'll teach him to be a sensible Toad!"

A giggle swelled like a red balloon in Jamie's mouth, and her head fell back into the pillows as the sound rumbled forth. "A sensible Toad, Aunt Nina. No wonder you wanted me to read this story to you! First Prince Hal, and now you are teaching me to be a sensible Toad!"

She felt the quiver of Aunt Nina's shrunken shoulders beside her as their laughter spilled through the bedroom's open windows until it mixed with the hum of waves like a strummed harp. When Jamie could finally go on reading, she saw the dark spots of her own tears on the opened book.

She was just reading how Badger and Rat were going to make Toad "*the most converted Toad that ever was*" when she heard the ruffled sounds of deep breathing beside her. She paused to watch Aunt Nina, trying not to think how much sleep looked like death. Carefully she put the book down beside the array of pill bottles on the bedside table and pulled the patchwork quilt up over Aunt Nina's shoulders.

A sensible toad, she thought, easing her bulky body off the bed. She tiptoed out of the bedroom closing the door quietly with her good arm. *A sensible toad* whose brain doesn't do the devil's gymnastics. The brilliant late afternoon light scattered the cottage in gold beams, the sweetness of air and the rhythm of water on sand.

Yet none of it could touch the unhappiness sucking at her soul. Oblivion. All she wanted was not to know Aunt Nina was dying. Not to know she was having a baby she could never let herself see. Jamie leaned against the kitchen counter as though she might fall through the floor, half wishing she could vanish into the sand underneath the cottage.

She yanked open the two cupboard doors over the sink scanning the shelves as if a vodka bottle might have suddenly materialized there. She rummaged through the narrow pantry shelves thinking about forgotten cooking wine. Then she remembered Aunt Nina's Percodan in the tiny brown vial. She laid her forehead against the pantry door and wept, desperation filling her like liquid slag.

The noise of tires on the dirt road made her wipe her eyes on her mocha-colored top, exposing the elasticized underwear beneath that stretched over her abdomen. The day Aunt Nina and she together couldn't zip up her biggest shorts, Gloria had taken her to Meijer's where she bought maternity shorts and pants, plus two tops, all in dark colors. Gloria had nagged her to get at least one outfit in a brighter shade. She'd assured Gloria black was easier to mix with the oversized tops she already had. And, besides, black was slenderizing. What she didn't tell Gloria was that it matched the color of her pregnancy.

She heard a car engine stop outside and walked toward the open back door where she looked out through the screen. She ducked back when she saw Kate's Mazda. Like a little kid, Jamie looked around for a place to hide, to get away from the last person she wanted to see. Then Jamie heard the excited bark and turned back toward the door. Pogo was with Kate. She threw open the screen door and Pogo was in her arms, licking her ears while she went down on one knee to embrace him.

"Getting down's the easy part, isn't it boy?" Jamie said, her good hand still scratching Pogo's head. She looked up at Kate who was watching them from behind her sunglasses. In one hand Kate held a rectangular baking tin covered with aluminum foil.

"Here," Kate held out one arm to help her pregnant sister up. Her mouth was relaxed into a peculiar softness Jamie didn't know how to read. Kate was wearing a lacey white sundress making her tanned skin even darker. Her curly black hair was tucked behind her ears where two small diamond earrings sparkled in the sunlight. Her hair smelled of shampoo as Jamie stood up, braced by her sister's arm.

"I like your dress, Kate. But you've always had good taste. I tried to copy you because I have no sense of style. And now it wouldn't matter," she looked down at her stomach missing her sister's slight grimace.

Kate made a big smile. "Thanks, Jamie. It's old, but since I can only wear it summers, it still feels new. But your outfit—you look really nice, Jamie."

"Meijer's finest" she spread her arms.

"*Why pay more?*" Kate finished the store slogan they'd grown up with. "I made Aunt Nina's gooey cornbread." She lowered her voice as they walked into the kitchen. "Is she resting?"

"She is, but she'll want to see you."

"No. I'll wait. Or come back later. I picked Pogo up from the golf range so Pete could play with his golfing buddy. He'll be gone a while."

Jamie wondered if she was seeing a special brightness in Kate's eyes talking about Pete. She hoped so, because, like everything Kate did in her life, she had found the perfect man. Jamie wasn't sure Kate knew how lucky she was. But today, at least, she seemed to.

"What smells so good?" Kate asked picking up the lid of the soup pan on the stove. "Corn chowder. Did you make this?" she asked with rounded eyes.

"I did learn a few things working for Mother, Kate." As soon as she said it, Jamie wanted to take back the defensive tone. She didn't want to start anything with Kate. Certainly not now with Aunt Nina in the next room. And Kate did seem to be friendlier for whatever reason.

"Hey, check this out," Jamie said quickly. It wasn't Kate's fault she did everything right while her younger sister did it all wrong. Jamie picked a book up from the counter beside the kitchen sink and handed it to Kate. "You'll love this! I got the chowder recipe out of the Colorado Junior League cookbook."

"I know that book. You gave one to Mom for Christmas a few years ago."

"Yeah, but I mean how about me and the Junior League?" She saw Kate's eyes involuntarily flick to Jamie's expanded girth.

"Not exactly the League's poster girl, am I?" She wanted to make Kate laugh, to make up for the jab because Kate had never worked for their mother's catering business. She knew Kate couldn't resist the image of Jamie in the Junior League for long. When Kate finally relaxed into a grin as she set the tin on the counter, Jamie was gratified. Then they were laughing together as they used to, their grievances momentarily forgotten in the high fun of lifelong friends.

"What I meant about your soup, Jamie, is how bizarre it is that I, who never bakes, decide to make cornbread for Aunt Nina the same day you make her corn chowder. Like we both read some article on corn as a cure for..." Kate stopped, and her eyes clouded. The jet sound of a cigarette boat's engine penetrated the stillness inside the cottage. Kate asked quietly, "How is she?"

Jamie felt her head pulled toward the hallway leading to Aunt Nina's bedroom. By the time she looked back, she knew Kate had seen the answer. The familiar tingle of knowing Kate's thoughts as surely as Kate had just read hers rippled through her. She'd missed the closeness their ESP used to give her. And it was not Kate who'd ruined what the two of them once had. She pulled a can of Arizona tea out of the refrigerator and handed it to Kate. She took a second one for herself and gestured for Kate to go out on the deck.

As soon as the screen slider to the deck closed behind them, Kate began talking. "You're doing, well, such a good job for Aunt Nina. Mom tells me all the time how grateful she is. I can't even imagine how hard it must be for you watching Aunt Nina get sicker by the day. I would like to do more, Jamie. Be more available to help out here."

"You want to know the truth?" Jamie held up her new, smaller cast. "Since this happened, I've needed Aunt Nina's help as much, sometimes more, than she's needed mine."

They sat down beside each other in the two wicker chaises pointed west over the lake where she and Aunt Nina watched the sun go down every night.

"That first month, when I had the big clunker cast all the way up here," she tapped her shoulder, "Aunt Nina shampooed my hair every morning. She had to zip my zippers and do my buttons until I finally got into elastic waist bands." She snapped the band of her maternity shorts and looked up see Kate's eyes blink as they rested on the bulge of Jamie's pregnancy.

Kate turned away, pressing her sunglasses against the bridge of her nose. "You opened that tea can pretty adroitly. Looks like you can move your broken arm as well as your good one." Kate leaned over to take off her white sandals and wiggle her outstretched toes. Jamie, already out of her Birkenstocks, thought about their mother's peace necklace. Maybe their mother's hippie DNA had double-helixed into both her daughters after all. At least where shoes came in. Not too much else about Kate was radical.

Then she remembered something. Hadn't Aunt Nina said their dad had no shoes on the first time she met him? Jamie liked hearing the man she was named for had knocked on Aunt Nina's door pin neat in bare feet. Maybe barefoot was genetic from both sides. She liked that too.

"I am doing well with this arm," Jamie finally said. "And you and I both know why. I have a great doctor. Pete says the cast comes off for good this week. Which is nice because it itches like crazy and scraping corn from the cob with one hand like I did today gets old fast. There's plenty of chowder left, by the way, if you want to take some home for Pete." Jamie had watched Aunt Nina labor to eat a few spoonfuls at lunch.

"You know I never turn down a meal someone else cooks. Especially one from a Junior League cookbook." All at once Pogo pushed his way between them, a small twig in his mouth as he looked back and forth at the sisters. Jamie tried to get up, but in her new slowness she was still pushing against the chaise when Kate was already hurling Pogo's stick in the general direction of the lake. The small branch landed in the dune just beyond the path to the beach where Pogo raced after it. "I never could throw," Kate said shrugging her shoulders.

"You didn't have a good stick," Jamie said now on her feet. Rummaging through a weathered blue plastic sand pail by the deck stairs, she pulled out a rectangle of dark driftwood. Pogo dropped the first retrieved stick at her feet and quivered with anticipation at the bigger piece of wood in Jamie's hand. She felt her shoulder muscles tighten and release as she hurled the wood out over the dunes until it came down on the beige-pink sand of the beach.

"Jake tells me you're the best skier on Aspen Mountain."

Kate's words caught Jamie in the back of the neck.

"It doesn't surprise me," Kate continued without a pause. "Look at you throw a stick. I'm also not surprised you don't believe it when people say so. You've never had any idea how I envy your athletic ability. Here I'm three years older and you were better at every sport. I mean who breaks state records as a freshman while I barely make the state team and I'm a senior!"

Jamie held her breath without moving.

"You're not in the human zone when you get in the water, Jamie."

169

Kate's words trickled like cool water into the crevices of her parched sense of self. She was stunned by Kate's praise. She felt the old tug of longing for Kate's approval. An urge Jamie hadn't expected pulled her towards the sister she'd lost the day Jamie left Ann Arbor with a fellow drunk and headed to Aspen.

But something ugly twisted inside Jamie and kept her from answering Kate. Her conditioned response of failure—of shame for what happened that hellish August night rose from a dark place. Jamie was not worthy of her sister's respect.

"World to Jamie," Kate finally spoke again.

"Why did you talk to Jake?" Getting Kate angry was safer. Having Kate yell at her was easier to take than her compliments. It was what she deserved. Jamie kept her face turned away from her sister, pretending to focus on Pogo as he ran back up the stairs from the beach, the driftwood clenched in his jaws.

If Kate was startled by the curt tone, she didn't show it. "He called for your phone number. And, no, I didn't give it to him. I told him nothing, except I'd give you his message. He wants to talk to you." A blue jay landed in the scrub oak beside the deck, singing his jagged trios of "thief."

"He's into cocaine," Jamie said watching the jay hop to a higher branch.

"I didn't say he wasn't."

"But you were thinking I should go back. He's rich. He can take care of me. I'd be out of here and you and Mom wouldn't have to worry about me anymore." She looked over her shoulder far enough to see Kate slump against the deck railing. She didn't answer right away.

"You never cease to amaze me, Jamie. Your insight has always been sharp—and obviously ahead of mine. I think you're right, whether I want to admit it or not. Not about leaving. But, yes, having someone besides Mom and Aunt Nina and me watching out for you. That sounds pretty good right now."

Kate picked up the wood Pogo dropped at her feet. "But I didn't come here to fight, and Jake was the one who got you into treatment or you might have…"

Jamie whipped around to face her older sister, feeling her skin blaze. "Is that what Jake told you? And of course your loser sister—this great athlete you can bullshit about—is the lying addict while this man you've never met is telling the truth? Of course that's how you'd hear Jake because it fits all the terrible things you think about me!"

"That is not true and it's not fair." Kate stepped closer to Jamie, her lips two white lines.

"And you know what else, while we're on the subject of men. If you hadn't been so damned selfish Mom would have married the man she was in love with. But she didn't want to hurt you so instead she's been alone all these years working her ass off…"

"I'm not spoiling a party, am I?"

Jamie's world spun for a moment making her squint to bring Gloria, in a purple linen dress with both hands on her hips, into focus. "Gloria! Oh, Gloria! The meeting," Jamie said, her heart thudding in a stressed arrhythmia. She gripped the deck railing to stay steady.

"I'm a little early," Gloria said. Now Jamie could see the fury on her sponsor's face.

"Sorry," Jamie said to Gloria, not sure what she was sorry for, but knowing she was, as usual, in the wrong.

Gloria ignored the apology and stepped toward Kate who now stood rigidly upright. "I'm Gloria Cook, your sister's AA sponsor. You must be Jamie's sister Kate. I didn't mean to eavesdrop, but I could have heard Jamie from the highway. Don't pay any mind to what your sister said. We alcoholics love to pick fights so we can go drinking and blame it on the other guy. The perfect excuse to get hammered."

Gloria looked over her shoulder, freezing Jamie with her stare, then turned back to Kate. "You just happened to be today's target. The only thing I heard that counts is no way Jamie's going back to Jake. It doesn't matter if he paid a million dollars for her treatment. She can't be around anyone who drinks and drugs. Not ever. Never. Bottom line."

Kate's voice was dry and uncertain as she extended her hand. "Gloria, I…I appreciate your candor. I am glad to meet you. I mean, not the best time, but, well, you know." Kate took a few steps, and picked up her shoes, her balance shaky as she slid one on.

Gloria reached out to steady Kate. "Thank you, Gloria," Kate said, putting on the second sandal. "I've heard wonderful things about you from Mother and Aunt Nina. They're both very grateful for…"

"That's good to hear, Kate," Gloria jumped in to fill the awkward gap. "And you are a lot prettier in person than that teeny little picture I see in the Lake-shore paper. Oh, my! This has to be Pogo," Gloria said, stepping away from the dog's shaking water sprays across the deck. "So has anybody found out where he came from?"

"Um, the police think the campgrounds at the state park," Kate finally answered. "The owners probably left without him. Probably after firecrackers scared him off. I guess it happens every Fourth. Nice to meet you Gloria. Come on Pogo. We have to go."

"Nice to meet you, Kate—even under *these*," Gloria eyeballed Jamie, "circumstances. Now you got to motor too, Jamie," Gloria checked her watch, "or you'll be late. I'm going to go make myself at home inside so I can hear your auntie if she calls."

"You're not going with Jamie?" Kate paused at the stairs leading to the driveway.

"Dr. Madison said yesterday Aunt Nina should not be alone anymore." Jamie spoke her first words to Kate since Gloria had arrived. But she could not bring herself to look at her older sister. "Gloria offered to stay with Aunt Nina so I could go to a meeting. I'll get my purse and check on her. Be right back."

By the time Jamie returned to the deck, still shaken by the meanness of her own outburst, Kate and Gloria had decided Kate would stay with Aunt Nina. Gloria would go with Jamie to the AA meeting. Jamie half mumbled a goodbye at Kate, saying she'd be back by six. She fought back an impulse to throw her arms around her older sister and apologize. Kate had reached out to her, and Jamie had spit back. It was how she ruined everything and everyone she came near.

Jamie was strapping on her seatbelt when the nightmare seized her, rocketing her into a frightened rage. She clamped her sweaty palms tight on the Saab's leather steering wheel and refused to look over at Gloria sitting silent on the seat beside her.

She'd driven past the log cabin and all the way down Aunt Nina's dirt road pausing at Olive Road before Gloria finally spoke. "You know, Girlfriend, given half a push, you can be a real bitch."

The   Sandpiper

KATE

Kate felt the reassuring dirt pack under her shoes as she turned into Aunt Nina's driveway. Sweat dripped under her red terry headband blurring her vision as she checked her plastic sports watch. Fourteen minutes before seven.

"Perfect timing, Pogo," she said to the dog loping beside her. Jamie and she would once again pass in the kitchen like the strangers they now were. She'd figured out exactly how long to run so there'd be no extra minutes for strained conversation. Jamie would need to leave right away for her seven a.m. AA meeting. Kate would have time to shower and dress before Aunt Nina woke up.

For the past few mornings, Aunt Nina was still asleep when Jamie came back from her meeting, and Kate had to leave for the newspaper office. Kate didn't like the change. She'd even thought about banging around in the kitchen to wake Aunt Nina up. She wanted more of the quiet time she and Aunt Nina'd had together when she first started coming so Jamie could get to her early meeting.

Sipping coffee side by side in the slanted grey-gold early light, the sparkling October air blowing through the screens, she'd felt even closer to Aunt Nina than before their parting. Before her parting, she corrected herself. Aunt Nina had never gone anywhere.

Pete said broken bones can heal stronger in the fracture line than in the un-injured bone. Kate knew it was like that for Aunt Nina and her. *Something there was*, indeed, *that doesn't love a wall.* Now with stone on stone removed, Kate could again let herself take in Aunt Nina's healing love. In the ease of those early morning talks, while they watched the ascension of seagulls, Kate was like a rain barrel after a heat wave, slowly filling with water.

For over a month, since the Saturday afternoon she'd brought cornbread to Aunt Nina, she'd driven here with Pogo at six every morning wearing her running clothes, her work clothes in a duffel. Some days she and Pogo jogged a three-mile loop along the bike path. Other days she did a speed walk along the beach keeping Pogo happy chasing his tennis ball and seagulls.

After a quick shower, she and Aunt Nina took their time watching the waves and eating their toast while Jamie went to her 7 a.m. meeting. These precious mornings alone with Aunt Nina were the only good things to come out of that awful afternoon. Aunt Nina had been too sick to eat the cornbread, and Jamie had slapped Kate's overtures of friendship back in her face.

Since that day, as far as Kate was concerned, Jamie could go back to Jake or dump him. She no longer believed either of them. Certainly not what Jake said about Jamie's feeling remorse over Alex Hamper and his father's death. Jake was a closed subject. He'd better never make the mistake of calling her again.

Kate rounded the knoll in the road and headed up Aunt Nina's driveway when the log cabin came into view through the misty fog of early autumn like a fairy-tale house that could vanish into Brigadoon. In a quirk of unexpected memory, she heard herself giggle as the sturdy shoulders underneath her lowered to let her small head pass under the doorframe.

"Daddy, Daddy, do more horsey." She could almost hear her own little voice. But her father was collapsed on the cabin floor playing possum, her mother walking somewhere nearby pretending not to see him. Then all at once his hand grabbed her mother's ankle, and the three of them were rolling in a pile on the hooked rug, their arms and legs and laughs all mixed together.

That blur of memory pushed against her fierce rancor at Jamie. Jamie never got to play horsey with their dad. Never got serenaded by his off-key version of, "You Are My Sunshine."

Jamie was pulling off her damp windbreaker, still gazing at the cabin when the white Saab appeared directly in front of her. Instinctively she jumped off the driveway, pulling the leashed Pogo with her. She'd forgotten about the poison ivy until she saw a patch of still green plants around her ankles. Whatever anger was starting to soften ratcheted tight again. She and Jamie didn't even wave to each other.

Kate quietly opened the cottage's back door, the rich, earthy aroma telling her that at least Jamie hadn't drunk all the coffee this time. She pulled off her headband and heard the bubbling sound. She was surprised to see the coffee maker perking a fresh pot, something Jamie had not bothered doing before. Then a voice called to her. "I'm afraid your sister and I drank all the coffee, Kate. I asked Jamie to start a new pot for you."

"Aunt Nina?" she followed the hoarse voice until she found Aunt Nina in the living room on her favorite wicker chaise directly facing the big lake. Jamie must have moved the chaise from its regular spot tucked up to the fireplace. Today it was close to the lake windows where Aunt Nina could see the ribbed sand of the beach extend in both directions.

The bright squares of blues and golds in the quilt covering Aunt Nina up to the shoulders almost made it look like she was getting better. Her hair had grown into small nubs of curly fuzz, and this morning her cheeks seemed to have a rosy cast. Three days before, the last morning Aunt Nina was awake before Kate left for work, her fleshless face had reminded Kate of the plastic skeleton Pete kept in his office to explain bones to his patients.

"You look so good today, Aunt Nina," Kate said with honest exuberance. "Really good." She leaned into the older woman's outstretched arms for a hug. Even Aunt Nina's arms around her neck felt sturdier. A glow of hope opened like a star lily inside her chest. "I'm so glad you're awake today. I've missed you the past two mornings."

"Angel girl, you have no idea. You have no idea what your company, what you have done for me as we've watched summer become fall together. Do you remember, Kate, the great sonnet of autumn I made all my English lit classes memorize? *That time of year thou mayst in me behold...*"

"*When yellow leaves or none or few do shake...* No. What was it? *Hang,' yes, hang upon the bough.* Oh, my word. I had no idea I remembered that! But hold that thought." She stood up. "I'm getting us some fresh coffee. Have you eaten anything?"

"Jamie tried. We'll get to that later. But first, my dear, please take off your wet shirt and put on one of my sweatshirts. You've got goose pimples."

"It's the wet sports bra underneath that gets me cold."

She grabbed a dark navy sweatshirt folded at the foot of Aunt Nina's bed and dropped her damp bra and shirt on the floor. She'd pick them up later. For now she wanted every minute she could get with Aunt Nina. She set Aunt Nina's coffee mug on the glossy white window sill, using one of the paperback books on the table beside Aunt Nina as a coaster.

"Did you move away from the fireplace to keep your little friend company?" Kate gestured toward the carved sandpiper on the sill beside Aunt Nina.

Aunt Nina looked at the spotted bird on his spindly legs and smiled. "He's dressed for winter, too, isn't he? The little brown scarf around his neck."

Kate said nothing as she pulled a small maple captain's chair up close to Aunt Nina. She took a careful sip of her steaming coffee, not wanting to think about what she knew Aunt Nina was telling her. The sonnet of autumn. The sandpiper readying itself for the cold to come.

She forced a grin and patted her front. "And here am I dressed in cold-weather navy fleece right off your bed."

"Jamie gave it to me when she first went to Michigan," Aunt Nina said turning away from the sandpiper. Kate hadn't noticed the University of Michigan seal on the front of the sweatshirt. Kate looked down at the gold letters and thought about what might have been for her sister.

"*Bare ruined choirs,*" Aunt Nina began again, her grey eyes luminescent.

"I do remember now," Kate said and forced Jamie out of her head. "That was the line our class cracked up at. A choir of naked people singing? You ruined it by telling us Shakespeare wasn't talking about singers."

Aunt Nina grinned. "You kids with all your high-octane hormones firing. It's one of Shakespeare's loveliest lines, I think. *Bare ruined choirs where late the sweet birds sang.*"

Kate shook her head. "No, it's too sad. Not unless you stick to the naked choir. It's too much about everything being past and over. A rotting church—the birds gone."

"Oh, but, my dear, the poet still hears the song of those summer birds. Like our little sandpiper's 'peet-peet,'" Aunt Nina patted Kate's hand. "We can hear him in our heads whenever we want because we know his song. Imagination. Memory. God's gifts to us as humans—among many, I might add."

Kate didn't answer right away. Instead she was hearing her father's deep baritone. "You are my sunshine, my only sunshine." Jamie never heard her dad's song. Kate looked out toward the lake and watched the wind move through the beach grass turning the green into silver.

"Aunt Nina," she finally said. "I need you to tell me something. It's bothered me since Jamie told me. Do you think…should Mother have remarried? I mean would she have been happier? Did she really love that architect from Chicago?"

Aunt Nina was looking out at the waves curling over the water like lace. She turned to look straight into Kate's eyes. "Yes, Kate, your mother did love him. He loved her too. Very much. Yes, I think in many ways she would have been happier—especially to have had his support during Jamie's troubles."

Kate studied her coffee. "Jamie's right then. Mother didn't marry him because of me. Because I hated him so much."

Aunt Nina closed her eyes a moment. "Now is not the time to pussyfoot, my dear. I don't have that kind of time. Yes, she turned him down because she would not make you that unhappy after what you'd been through. First your dad. Then she went into such a depression she could barely take care of you, let alone help you with your child's grief.

"The heart frame I showed you that day? Remember who the one was looking worried Jamie might toddle into the lake? That's an image you must keep up here," she tapped her temple, "forever. It says such a wonderful truth about you."

Kate swallowed hard. The photograph was vivid in her mind.

"You became the family caretaker because you had to. How could you trust some strange man to come in and take over your job? He might leave your family like your dad did. Your mother is a wise lady. She understood that."

Kate rubbed her fingers against closed eyelids and asked the question she knew the answer to. "Mom wouldn't have had to work so hard, would she?"

"Oh, but that's the good part of it all! No, of course not. As Mrs. Healy she wouldn't have had to work at all. But then she'd never have done Ellie's Catering and that is one of her life's triumphs. I can't think of any job I'd rather do less than cook for someone else. You either, I know. But your mother thrives on it. It taps her nurturing and creative and culinary talents. It also brings her great praise and admiration from the outside world. And who doesn't groove on that, my dear?"

Kate shook her head back and forth. "I've been an Olympic snot about the catering. It always seemed beneath her intelligence."

"Oh, Kate, you just try to do one party with her from menu to clean up. I promise you'll come away thinking chess is a snap compared to catering a hot dinner for eighty fussy people! I helped her with a wedding once, and I was a shipwreck for a week after."

Kate had never thought about catering as more than chopping and serving. But to think about organizing it all—planning the menu, shopping, coordinating different cooking times. Maybe catering did require more brain power than she'd given her mother credit for.

"Your mom's had men in Spring Port fantasizing about her for years. Her chances of remarrying have never been over. Still aren't. After I am…well, someday I hope she picks some lucky chap." Aunt Nina's voice quieted. "I like to think that will happen."

Kate suddenly found herself wanting the same thing. Wanting her mother to have a Pete of her own to grow old with. "Oh, Aunt Nina," Kate said flooded with a strange relief. "You have no idea how you have helped me see things like…well, like an adult, I guess, instead of a spoiled adolescent. I hope you know how very much I love you and how much I regret the years…"

Aunt Nina leaned forward with surprising agility to put both her hands on Kate's shoulders. "Promise me on this spot you will never, ever say or think that again. Promise? You aren't the only person who's held on to secrets they shouldn't have." Aunt Nina paused for breath before she went on.

"Dearest Kate, believe this if you believe nothing else. I never doubted your love for one second. Or that we'd find our way back to each other. From the beginning I turned it over to God. He helped me think only about our glorious years together, when you and Jamie were little and the sweet birds sang. Are you hearing me?"

Kate put one hand on Aunt Nina's tissue-thin cheek and knew her own wet eyes spoke for the voice she couldn't make work.

"Good, then," Aunt Nina said firmly. "Now let's talk about Kate for a change," Aunt Nina kissed each of Kate's palms and then leaned back in the chaise. "Not about your mother's love life or Jamie's problems and, for heaven's sake, not about my aches and pains, but you. Your new job—how's it really going? Are your dreams coming true, my dear girl?"

"Oh, but you're starting to look tired to me. Shouldn't you rest while I fix you some oatmeal?"

"I can rest and eat anytime. Right now I want to listen to your heart."

Kate looked past Aunt Nina at the endless horizon of lake and sky. Then, without knowing she was going to, she began to tell Aunt Nina everything. About Dr. Delgado. Dr. Bauer. The Clomid that didn't work. The first drips of blood every month hammering joy out of her life. How she continued to lie to everyone about not being ready to have children because she couldn't admit her failure.

How she'd wanted so much to give her mother a grandchild, and now Jamie could, but wasn't going to. How unfair it all seemed. Or maybe it was God's perfect fairness because Jamie never had a father and so He was letting her be a mother.

Aunt Nina just listened, her face accepting and kind. Slow tears appeared at the corners of Aunt Nina's eyes at particular points. But mostly she just held

Kate's hand and nodded. When Kate could talk no more, she laid her head on Aunt Nina's knees and cried without restraint.

"My darling, darling child," Aunt Nina repeated, stroking Kate's damp hair. "My darling girl." Kate didn't know how long she'd lain there when she began to feel a new lightness. It was as if saying out loud to Aunt Nina, "I can't get pregnant" had taken some of the awfulness out of it. In something close to holy, Aunt Nina seemed to pull some of the pain into herself and make it more bearable for Kate.

Neither of them moved when the phone rang. Kate didn't want to break the circle of healing she felt surrounding them. Maybe it was working its miracle on Aunt Nina too. She prayed for the phone to stop ringing, but it didn't. Finally Aunt Nina said softly, "It might be Jamie." Kate picked her head up, wiping at her face with both hands like a little girl. She walked to the end table where the old black phone kept ringing.

"This is Cecilia from Connecticut calling for my Aunt Nina. What took so long, honey?" Cecilia's voice seemed even more like molasses than the last time she'd called. "But, no, this isn't Jamie's voice answering. Is this Katie?"

"Yes, Cecilia, this is Kate," she accentuated the correct name. A scraping sound behind her caught her attention. She turned around to see Aunt Nina folding her hands under one cheek in the sign of sleep. "I'm talking quietly because Aunt Nina is resting now." Kate shook a scolding finger at Aunt Nina.

"Yes," Kate said after a pause. "Yes, she knows you do. Certainly she will call if she does. Of course. You're very kind to offer. And Aunt Nina appreciates it."

Kate edged her responses in between Cecilia's carrying on about her suitcase being packed to come "at the drop of a hat to care for my aunt." Kate thought Cecilia lingered a bit long on the possessive pronoun.

Kate turned the phone toward Aunt Nina so she could hear too. "Nina is the last of Father's family, you know. I'm her only relative. That's why I want to do whatever I can. But I certainly don't want to be in the way. I'll just keep calling every few days until she needs me to come. You tell her that for me, will you please, Katie, I mean Kate?"

"Cecilia again." Jamie spoke from the kitchen doorway.

Kate hadn't heard her sister come in. She avoided staring at Jamie's huge belly as she exchanged a quick look with her younger sister. They were both thinking the same thing. After all these years, now Cecilia wanted to stay in close touch with Aunt Nina. Both Kate and Jamie knew what Cecilia really wanted was to be the first to know The Sandpiper was officially hers.

"How was your meeting, Jamie?" Aunt Nina called from the living room, ignoring her niece's phone call. "Good, Aunt Nina." Jamie walked to the counter by the sink and poured herself a cup of coffee. "It was on gratitude. Gloria keeps reminding me I need to work on that."

Kate said her goodbyes to Cecilia and went back in the living room to kiss Aunt Nina on both cheeks. "Thank you for listening," she whispered in one ear. "I'm taking a shower now."

Kate was just putting on her mascara in Aunt Nina's bathroom when she thought she heard a glass drop. Then Jamie screamed. Kate raced through Aunt Nina's bedroom toward the living room where she saw Jamie huddled over Aunt Nina in the chaise, a coffee mug shattered on the floor, a wet circle darkening the wood. "No," Jamie's sob erupted into the stillness. "No, no, no, Aunt Nina you can't do this," Jamie gasped for air. "No. No. You can't leave me. You can't go. Please, please don't."

"Aunt Nina?" Kate spoke in high, piano-string notes. "Aunt Nina? Aunt Nina?" Then she was on her knees beside Jamie, both of them calling Aunt Nina's name like a mournful fugue, begging her to wake up, stroking Aunt Nina's face, her arms, her head as it lay back against the chaise.

In the same instant, they both fell forward into Aunt Nina's lap. Kate felt Jamie's strong good arm across her shoulders squeezing like a vise. Then her younger sister's body began heaving sobs from a depth Kate had never heard before.

The Sandpiper

KATE

She watched herself in the oval mirror over the bathroom sink, re-tucking her ivory silk blouse into the slim black skirt, smoothing it across her flat belly. Finishing her last round of Clomid at least had stopped the swelling, her skin no longer squishy to press. She shook her head hard against the thought, not strong enough to go there right now.

She looked at the dark hollows of her cheeks. Today only her eyes were puffy. She felt lightheaded, needing this to be over. And today, of all days, Pete would have to get called in for an open femur fracture. The frail 80-year old woman's surgery could wait until the service was over. But no longer.

She sat down on the edge of her mother's tub, hoping nobody needed the only main floor bathroom in Ellie's home. She laid her forehead between her knees and wept. Sitting between her mother and Pete in the front pew, the First Congregational Church filled into the balcony, she'd been stunned by the smallness of her own thinking.

How could she have believed she and her mother and Jamie were the only people who'd miss Aunt Nina? Behind her through the church, she had felt the stir of sadness, grief flowing down the aisles toward the altar's banks of daisies and wildflowers like a water leak.

The scattered sounds of weeping had tugged at her own tears. Even Reverend James faltered in his eulogy. "Nina Judd's passion for life and learning lives on in everyone gathered here today," he'd opened strongly. Then he stopped. Kate could almost hear hearts beating in the last row of the balcony during the stillness. His congregation understood. Their grey-haired minister needed to collect himself.

"Extraordinary woman…an intellectual with a wicked wit…a generous woman who chose to do her good works quietly, behind the scenes, for God's glory, never her own."

From behind the carved mahogany lectern, he talked about the many lives she'd enriched—her students, her friends. Then Reverend James said something to the packed audience about how they should celebrate Helena Judd's life by loving each other in the today.

His words triggered a spontaneous recall that made her flesh tingle. It was as if Aunt Nina began to whisper to Kate the last lines of the sonnet she'd quoted the morning she died. Unbidden, Shakespeare's closing couplet came to Kate word by word as she felt her mother's body start to tremble beside her.

Kate reached one arm around her mother's shaking shoulders and repeated the two lines so quietly only her mother could hear. *This thou perceivest which makes thy love more strong, To love that well which thou must leave ere long.* Her mother's hand had grabbed hers and held on. At that moment Kate finally understood she needed to love her mother well enough to tell her about the baby she and Pete wanted—and weren't having.

She blinked back tears as she heard Gloria Cook and Sandy Quinn talking to her mother somewhere beyond the bathroom door. Gloria was leaving, but first she'd made Jamie go put her feet up on the couch in the den. Now Gloria and Aunt Sandy were telling her mother to go sit down with Jamie for a few minutes, Aunt Sandy ordering her friend Ellie "to stay out of the kitchen."

Kate could hear more distant conversation coming from the kitchen, the voices merged with the clattering sounds of china and the hum of running water. Her mother's friends from The Sandpiper Club were cleaning up the light supper they'd fixed for Aunt Nina's family and close friends after the church reception.

Cecilia and her dour husband Wilson were Aunt Nina's only family members by blood. But after greeting the hundreds of people who lined up in the church basement after the service, Cecilia had told Ellie she was too "emotionally exhausted" for another gathering. Ellie Cameron hadn't even pretended to be disappointed Cecilia wasn't coming.

From the moment her mother had seen Kate come into her kitchen that terrible morning, it was as if a plug had been pulled. Her mother had accepted Kate's mournful embrace listlessly, the energy in her body drained off. Jamie had stayed back at The Sandpiper with Aunt Nina and waited for Pete. His nurse cancelled his office patients and Pete had driven straight to the cottage.

He would manage the details of death.

Jamie's job had been to phone Cecilia. But she didn't. Instead she'd asked Pete call for her. Jamie had tried to explain that she just could not deal with Cecilia's theatrical breakdown. Kate was furious at Jamie for not doing her part. Kate, after all, was the one who had to make the awful drive into town to tell their mother. But in her next honest moment, Kate knew she would have asked Pete too, and for the same reason. She couldn't have taken Cecilia's histrionics either.

After the hearse had driven away, Pete helped Jamie pack up her stuff and move back to their mother's house. Cecilia and Wilson—neither of their two children could make it—flew to Grand Rapids the same day and drove a rental car straight to The Sandpiper. Jamie wanted no part of sharing quarters with Cecilia for even one night.

Kate knew her sister had been right to move out so fast. When Cecilia had first seen Jamie at the funeral home, she'd droned on about the Lord giving and the Lord taking and how she only wished Aunt Nina had told her the good news about Jamie's coming baby. Then she'd made a point of looking directly at Jamie's ringless left hand, a lopsided smirk on her face.

Jamie refused to talk to the woman after that. Kate didn't like Cecilia any better, but she had no choice. Cecilia was, after all, the last of Aunt Nina's family. Kate had to spend energy she didn't have being pleasant, despite Cecilia's inane chatter and Wilson's stiff silence.

She pushed herself up off the tub rim and blotted her eyes with Kleenex. Cecilia and Wilson were probably back at Aunt Nina's cottage already, changed out of their funeral clothes, and cramming the last piece of Aunt Nina's furniture into their Ryder van. They weren't wasting any time. They were driving the loaded truck back to Connecticut the next day.

Kate sucked in oxygen and headed into the den, the small room off the living room that had been Jamie's and her playroom when they were little. Her mother and Jamie were not resting, as she'd expected, but standing together at the far wall, their backs to the doorway. Her mother still had on the burgundy wool suit she'd worn to the service, the stylishly long jacket and short skirt showing off her slender legs.

From behind, Kate noticed the looseness of the coat across her mother's shoulders. She'd lost weight over the last hard weeks. Now she and Jamie were looking at a big rectangular print she'd never seen before hanging on the far wall. The black frame was accented by serpentine gold trim.

"A new picture?" Kate asked before she got close enough to see it was an old tinted etching of the University of Michigan campus. "Where on earth did this come from, Mom?"

"Just what I asked," Jamie said half twisting her neck. "She says it's been in the attic forever. It looks old enough to have been there that long. How did we miss it?" Jamie gave Kate a conspirator's look. "All the times we snooped around up there." Jamie was referring to the Army citations for valor they'd found, but never told their mother about. Ellie Cameron hadn't wanted her daughters to find those either. But she'd obviously done a better job hiding this framed drawing of the Michigan campus.

"I recognize the Diag," Jamie turned back to the print. "And the president's house. This is a very cool drawing. What year is it anyway?"

"I have no idea." Their mother paused, then turned and looked at them one at a time. "Your dad bought the print for me in a used book store the weekend we met. I had it framed as his wedding present."

Kate felt the hair rise at the back of her neck. Outside a flock of Canadian geese honked somewhere over the house. She pictured their dark V soaring low in the October twilight. She held herself motionless, praying her mother to keep talking. This oversized print, the gilt-edged frame, none of it was right for this small room of Laura Ashley prints and cushions. Whatever reason their mother had for dragging this print out of its secret corner in the dusty clutter of their attic, it was not about decorating.

The silence was starting to feel awkward when Jamie tapped her fingernail on the glass. "This is Mosher-Jordan where I lived freshman year."

"I don't see the dorm where I lived for my very short college career," her mother said. "Alice Lloyd. It must have been built after this drawing was done." Her mother continued in her deep alto. "It would be right about here," she touched the glass, "next to Jamie's dorm. Your dad had an apartment somewhere around here," she slid her finger up to a grey-white sprawl of building. "Here's U Hospital," she tapped the glass. "His apartment was right behind it. Not far from the Huron River."

Kate didn't want to breathe, and she felt Jamie's matching reaction. Their mother had just told them more about their father than she ever had. Neither of them dared move for fear she would abruptly change the subject as she always did if it ever came close to their father. But this felt different to Kate. Her mother had an animation in her voice, a vibrancy she'd lost the morning Aunt Nina died.

"Find me Angell Hall," her mother said leaning even closer to the drawing. "Okay. Here's Angell. This has to be State Street." Her mother's finger traced a tiny black ribbon. "And right about here," her fingernail clicked on the glass, "is where I met your dad." The sounds from the kitchen rumbled louder into the hushed space of the den.

The rich depth of their mother's voice took on an easy pace as if she talked about this all the time. "Right around here was the State Street Cafe where my roommates and I used to go after humanities for coffee and a cigarette."

"Cigarette?" Kate blurted out and immediately wished she hadn't. She didn't want anything to break the spell.

To her relief, her mother laughed her low chortle. "Your dad said about the same thing to me that day. I can still see him coming in the door. I remember the Beatles were singing 'I Want To Hold Your Hand' on the Café's radio, and here comes this gorgeous man with a huge textbook under his arm." The gold flecks in her eyes sparkled. Her daughters understood she was seeing what they couldn't.

"All I could think about was holding his hand. Then he walks right up to our table and asks if he can sit down since the place was full. He barely got settled before he said something about cancer and smoking. He was so, I don't know—compelling. He had this coal-black hair and a smile that took your breath away. My roommates and I...we just sat and stared and pretended we were paying attention to his lecture. We all put out our cigarettes just to please him."

Her mother grew quiet, and a soft smile lit her face. "Honestly, it's so vivid. I see him right now sitting across the table all clean-cut and gentlemanly—so unlike the longhaired guys in dirty jeans we were used to in those crazy days. Your dad had these huge dark eyes you couldn't look away from." She made circles with her fingers in front of her own eyes. "Almost like a holy man's.

"And he had this...this presence, I guess you'd say, about him. A self-confidence...or charisma. Whatever you call it these days. It's hard to explain. But over the years when I've read about people blindly following some fanatic into a cult, I'm more sympathetic than I probably should be."

Kate felt her spine tingle. She was seeing her mother in a way she never had before. She didn't have to ask her sister. Jamie was meeting a new Ellie Cameron too.

"Your father might as well have been a snake-charmer. At some point my roommates left, and I barely noticed. He asked if anyone had ever told me I had perfect ethmoid bones. Then he did this," her mother ran the tip of a finger along one of her cheekbones from nose to temple as if in a dream state, her daughters forgotten.

"Just that touch, and I would have followed your father into traffic. We never discussed where we were going. Just left and he took my hand as if we'd been a couple forever. It was one of those magical Indian Summer days in Michigan. We walked the whole campus."

She looked back at the etching and traced a finger clockwise around the pastel-tinted grounds and buildings. "If we had classes, I don't remember. It was his first semester in med school. And your father was not one to miss class. So maybe he didn't have any that day. Anyway, it didn't matter, he was so brilliant. His own father, your grandfather, was a farmer who died in his forties of heart disease. Your dad won scholarships that paid most of his way.

"Walking all over campus that day, I told him more about myself than I'd ever told anyone. Even my best friends in high school didn't know this about me. How rotten my stepmother was to me and how my dad just went along with it. Your dad held nothing back either.

"I moved in with him that weekend. We had a hard time separating to go to our classes. Every night we'd go to the med library." She smiled shyly. "It's how I got a four-point my one semester at Michigan. We eloped over Thanksgiving, and I got pregnant with you, Kate. We had our first fight when I told him I had gotten a waitressing job and was quitting school. We needed the money, and it gave me time to have fun getting ready for our baby."

Her mother turned to look at her daughters. "Your father had a hard time understanding that finishing school was not important to me. I think because he was the first one in his family to go to college, it meant everything to him. But not to me. My father graduated first in his law class and, well, he didn't make higher education look all that good to me."

Kate glanced at Jamie and saw what she knew she would. Fascinated gratitude. They were, at last, being given their family history. The heroes and the toads.

"Besides," their mother went on, "I was only 18 and so head over heels in love. All I wanted in the world was to be with your dad. To make his little bachelor apartment into a real home, and then be the best mother I could be to our baby. To darling you, Kate."

Then the light left her eyes. "I never imagined life without him. Nothing, not even a war in Vietnam could have the power to separate so much love. I honestly believed that, especially with you, Jamie, growing inside me. He *had* to come back to us." Outside a car door slammed, an engine turned over.

"I could not have survived your father's death without Nina," she looked toward the outside sound, exhaling a puff of air. When she spoke again, the energy had vanished. "I'm not sure how I'll do it now."

As if rehearsed, Kate and Jamie each took one of their mother's hands at the same instant. "Thank you, girls," she said looking from one to the other. "Now I think I better go out and pay some attention to my Sandpiper friends cleaning up."

"Mom?" So many questions rocketed through Kate's head. She needed to know where they got married. Who stood up for them? What did she wear and what did her father do when he found out she'd eloped? Beside her Kate could feel Jamie's longing for the same details—for the filling in of the empty pages in their lives.

"Shh, I know, girls." Ellie heaved up her narrowed shoulders with a sigh. "It was wrong of me to deprive you of your dad. But when...when it happened, the only way I could go on was to shut him away like he'd never existed. I barely functioned as it was, but it was how I survived. If I denied him, I could not die of missing him. And, for a long, long time, I thought I might."

Footsteps moved outside the half closed door, then stopped.

"Believe me," she squeezed both their hands with unexpected strength, "I never set out to keep him from you two. It just happened. Aunt Nina made me promise," she shook her head and tears made her eyes shine like amber jewels. "I mean she actually did the death-bed thing making me swear I'd tell you about your dad. And now, I can't quite believe it, but remembering...telling you about how we met...it's made me happy, not sad."

"Is this a bad time?" The three women turned as one and Tom Quinn looked around the door almost embarrassed. "No, of course not," her mother said as she dabbed sliding tears with a wrinkled handkerchief. "I just gave my daughters the first chapter on their dad. Way overdue! And it took a little extortion from Ms. Judd to get me started. But right now I have some friends out there to thank."

"Actually, I'm the last Mohican. The kitchen crew delegated me to relay their goodbye hugs and kisses. And tell you there's enough leftover casserole and fruit in your refrigerator for a week."

"Oh, I feel terrible," her mother said. "I didn't thank Sandy or any of them!"

"You'll see them again, Ellie. And I must tell you they got a real charge out of cooking for you in your own kitchen. But if you three aren't rushing off somewhere, I'd like to talk to you for a minute."

"I need an AA meeting tonight. Big time, Uncle Tom," Jamie said. Then she remembered Gloria's smartass reaction to her "Uncle Tom" and almost giggled. Jamie could never again say his name with a straight face, thanks to Gloria. "But I have until 7:30."

"Plenty of time, Jamie," the slender, silver-haired man said easily. "It's not even 6:30 yet. This won't take long."

"Well, let's sit down right here," her mother gestured toward the couch and chairs around the den.

"Actually, I've got us set up in the living room, if that's all right."

"Set up?" She and Jamie asked at the same time. Tom Quinn didn't answer, but led the way back into the living room.

The Sandpiper

JAMIE

Two thermal carafes, one white and one black, four yellow daisy mugs, and a crystal creamer and sugar bowl were already arranged on the glass-topped coffee table. "Sandy says the white pot is hot tea, the black one coffee, both decaffeinated," Tom said. "I'm having coffee. What can I pour for you three?"

Within minutes, a cup of decaf in her hand, Jamie settled into the yellow chintz easy chair, her skin enjoying the feel of the new beige silk maternity dress she'd bought to look nice for Aunt Nina. The jewel neckline with two rows of military brass buttons down the bodice gave her the unusual feel of sophistication, her blond hair pulled into a French twist. Even Kate had gone out of her way to say how elegant she looked.

She couldn't help the impish thought that between her Grace Kelly hair style and blooming pregnancy, Jake could pass her on the street and not recognize her. After their ugly final phone conversation, that wouldn't be all bad. Gloria, too, had commented on her appearance when she'd come to sit with their family at the church. She'd leaned over to make a quiet whistle and said, "You clean up all right, Girlfriend."

Jamie pulled her swollen feet, still in sheer pantyhose, on top of the overstuffed hassock covered in the same floral chintz as the chair. Kate and their mother sat next to her on the matching couch, and she noticed Kate was drinking coffee after she'd given it up for a while.

Tom Quinn situated himself in the middle of the loveseat across from them. Then he looked up at each of their faces, one by one, his mouth a severe straight line. Jamie had a sudden sick feeling something awful was about to happen. She turned quickly toward her mother, afraid she was too fragile for any more bad news.

Her mother's braced posture reminded Jamie of a child about to be spanked. Even Kate's confident smoothness seemed to turn edgy as she jerkily poured cream into her coffee. Then Jamie's heart skidded. It was about the baby. The Nebraska couple had changed their minds. She pressed one palm against her chest to slow her accelerating heartbeat.

"Is something wrong, Uncle Tom?" Voicing Jamie's thoughts as they both had since they were little, Kate leaned toward the still handsome attorney. He shook his head as he sipped the coffee, his upper lip over three long stemmed daisies, then carefully set the cup down.

"You look so serious, Tom," her mother spoke for the first time, putting words to their shared sense of foreboding.

"This is serious. But not for you ladies to look so worried about. I will get through this quickly, as I was instructed to." He raised his still pitch-black eyebrows high and pulled a pair of small wire reading glasses from his lapel pocket.

"You are not the only one, Ellie, to have been, how did you put it, 'extorted' by our friend Nina. She's been doing it to me for years—but that's treading into privileged information. You'll have to take my word for it. Helena Judd out-lawyered me every time I was supposedly doing legal work for her."

Aunt Nina's face floated into Jamie's mind, the intelligent grey eyes set off by the tiny smile lines at the corners. She saw Aunt Nina curled up beside her on the bed, her emaciated face lit up in laughter about *a sensible toad*. She could feel the frail fingers carefully buttoning her blouse over the clumsy cast. The hand held out every evening for the Saab keys. No judgments made, no questions asked. Jamie felt a moan begin to rise from deep inside, and she had to clasp a hand over her mouth to quell it.

"…adding to it I swear until the day she died." Tom Quinn pulled a manila file out from a briefcase Jamie hadn't noticed on the floor beside the love seat. "Nothing fundamental has changed here," he tapped his forefinger on the file, "from the first time I drafted it for her right after Jamie was born. Well, at least her intentions didn't change. A few details did, for good reasons as you'll see."

"I'm sorry," Jamie said. "I'm afraid I spaced out for a minute. What are we talking about here?"

"Your Aunt Nina's will, Jamie. All of it." He picked up a thick stack of papers held together with a black plastic clamp. "I met yesterday with her niece Cecilia to distribute her portion, again following Nina's very specific instructions. By now," he tapped the face of his wristwatch, "Cecilia and her husband should have packed up everything they want from the cottage. They need to be done there no later than tomorrow at 6 p.m. Another of Helena's explicit conditions."

"But surely Nina would give Cecilia more time than that to get the cottage listed?" her mother said more than asked.

Jamie thought about Cecilia's fish eyes staring at her pregnant belly and empty ring finger. "I hope she's already sold it," Jamie said. "Total strangers living at Aunt Nina's would be better than having that woman and her Darth Vader husband there."

"Jamie," her mother said in a weak scold. Then Jamie heard Kate let out a small snorting chuckle, and she was glad she'd said it. She liked it that Kate laughed.

Tom Quinn looked at his brown wingtips, pensive for a moment. It was as if he were just about to answer her mother's question, but then changed his mind. He leaned forward to open the file on the coffee table, pulling a long envelope off the top and ripping it open. "I think this is going to clarify a lot for all three of you."

He unfolded what looked like two or three sheets of white note paper written in small inked letters. "Nina wrote this herself," he turned the sheets toward them so they could see the handwriting. "It's dated September 19th—just about three weeks ago."

Jamie felt her eyes filling at the sight of the handwriting. How many love notes had Aunt Nina left her on the kitchen counter the past months if she got too tired to wait up for Jamie after an AA meeting. Always with a big lopsided heart at the end.

"She called me that day," Uncle Tom was saying, "right after she finished it, and asked if I'd come pick it up. She'd already sealed it so I haven't read it either. I am not sure exactly what she's written, although she gave me a pretty good idea that day. You know," he said looking at each of the three women in turn, "I've been Nina's friend and lawyer, and great admirer, since she first came to Spring Port in the summer of 1967. I met her when she bought The Sandpiper and hired me to do the legal work.

"So," he said slowly, "I could make some pretty educated guesses about this last will." He tapped the file again. "But, then again, considering it's Helena," he smiled at the papers in his hands as if he could see her face, "you never dare assume."

Jamie saw their lawyer friend's jaw flex as he realized he could no longer use that verb tense. "Anyway," he spoke after an inhale of breath, "her orders to me on this document were exact. She told me to open it in front of you three, which I just did, as soon as it was 'polite'…her word, not mine…after the service. I'm to read it aloud to you, then give you each your own copies."

He swallowed audibly as he took off his reading glasses and rubbed his eyes. "She also told me," he said still pressing his eyelids, "if any of you starts crying, I am to stop reading until you stop."

The distant whirr of water through the dishwasher filled the prolonged silence. Then the low roll of her mother's laughter broke the quiet in a sound Jamie realized she hadn't heard since Aunt Nina died.

"That's just so classic," her mother said, her head tossed back, her mouth smiling at the ceiling. "Nina's still calling the shots. God bless her, how will we ever know anyone like her again?" Tears began to stream past her mother's lips while she shook her head laughing and crying at the same time. Jamie watched Kate quietly reach for their mother's hand.

"Violation one, Ellie," Tom Quinn said. Jamie looked over to see the redness around his own eyes. She understood his vigorous eyelid massage.

"Well, I can't stand the suspense," Jamie said to prevent her own collapse. "I refuse to cry or we'll never hear what Aunt Nina has to say."

"All right," her mother said, wiping her face. "Let me fill our cups while we catch our breath. But you are right, Jamie. If Nina says we can't cry, we damn well can't!"

My Dearest Ellie, Kate, Jamie—and Pete if he's not off in the emergency room fixing some old person's broken hip.

"Oh!" Kate exclaimed, her eyes squinting against tears. "Did the woman ever get anything wrong?"

Tom Quinn absently smoothed his grey paisley tie before he went on.

You precious three have been my chosen, my 'real' family, since the day I tacked up the For Rent sign, oh, so many years ago. My good friend Tom will tell you I wrote my first will the summer after that, so nothing you hear is new. Only refined. The secret I should not have kept, the apology I owe…these are my only regrets. If I could do it over, I would. But you, dear Kate, showed me the way of honesty when you unburdened yourself. Now I follow your example and ask your forgiveness.

Jamie looked over at Kate's face. She'd been angry at Kate's neglect of Aunt Nina ever since she went to college. Jamie only got angrier after the cancer was diagnosed and Kate and Pete had moved to Spring Port. But Jamie had written it off as her big sister's selfishness. Why had she never considered something might have come between Kate and Aunt Nina?

But, as with so much of her life, Jamie had been too lost to her own demons to care. Now Jamie cared very much. Whatever the trouble had been, Jamie was deeply grateful it ended before Aunt Nina died. She'd seen the light come into Aunt Nina's eyes whenever Kate came in the door. That was all that mattered. Seeing the deer-like expression on Kate's face, Jamie realized her sister had no more idea where Aunt Nina was going with this than she did.

First, whatever is left in the cottage by the time you hear this belongs to you three. I gave Cecilia first choice on what she wanted, with one exception. My library stays with The Sandpiper. Those beloved books hold our shared storehouse of memories. As I write this love letter to you three, I visualize a whole new generation of dear little faces climbing on your laps to hear the great stories of Troy and Wild Wood and Camelot.

Kate can provide those new readers, Jamie thought, refusing to look down at her own enlarged belly.

So the books stay. End of discussion.

Jamie could almost hear the sound of Aunt Nina's voice in what Tom Quinn was reading. But then, if Cecilia was not selling The Sandpiper? She looked sideways at her mother. Ellie was puckering her face against tears, the sides of her mouth flicking a quick smile at the familiar sassiness in some of Nina's words. No, her mother wasn't analyzing any thing. She was simply drinking in the unexpected joy of hearing from her dearest friend one last time.

Cecilia has had copies of my will and all its modifications since the first draft the summer after Jamie was born. To her credit, she accepted it, with only a little whining now and then. Cecilia still thinks family has to be blood. But she's wrong. And she also knew if she didn't agree to the terms, she'd get nothing. Tom will verify—but my guess is she has already signed the papers for her share.

Tom looked up and nodded. "Helena's niece had almost 30 years to get used to the idea. But, she's only human. Toward the end, she thought she could get her aunt to change her mind. Which, of course," he smiled, "means Cecilia didn't know her aunt at all!"

To ease your prickly consciences, my chosen family, I made sure to give enough money in gifts to Cecilia and her children over the years to consider myself a generous relative. These are not needy folks who have been 'cut off.' The reason I leave The Sandpiper to Ellie, Kate (meaning Pete and now Pogo, too), and Jamie, and the back cottage to Jamie alone, is that you three have made The Sandpiper yours by cherishing it as I have all these years. You three made it home for me. How could it belong to anyone else?

Jamie sat motionless, not sure what she'd heard. How could this be? Aunt Nina unrolling such a thing like a grocery list?

The Sandpiper belongs to you three because it's where you, Ellie, last saw Jim. Where you, Kate, last saw your dad. And where you, Jamie, were born. I am leaving the back cottage in Jamie's name alone. Tom has worked out the legal technicalities of sub-dividing the lot. It's important to have a place of our own. Jamie needs to know she now has one forever.

At that exact instant, Jamie felt a small limb thrust itself into her rib cage as if reaching for her heart. She laid her palm over the small lump of movement and wondered if Aunt Nina had managed that too. At the next words, Jamie knew she had.

Smart as you are Jamie, and we all know you are very, I won't pretend there's no other agenda here. But Tom is to tell you I willed the cabin to you alone when Kate and Pete got married knowing they'd have their own place to live. Giving it to you alone was done long before your pregnancy. And that's the truth, my sensible toad.

Jamie couldn't stop a gasp of pain as tears came to her eyes. She blinked hard and shook her head signaling Tom to go on. She would not cry. Aunt Nina had said she couldn't!

But, Jamie, IF you do decide you can raise your daughter on your own, you now have a place to live. This is NOT a condition. The back cabin is yours no matter what. Even if, God forbid, you relapse. Although, in that case, of course, I would come back to haunt you.

Jamie did not smile. From Aunt Nina, she knew this was not an empty threat.

Now the hard part. When I'm done confessing, you'll all three be mad at me. I've been dishonest, deceitful, manipulative, and controlling, even if out of bottomless love. For whatever pain I'm about to cause, please forgive me.

Pain? In her wildest mind, Jamie could not imagine Aunt Nina hurting anyone. Ever.

Kate, my dear, my best English student ever, with all my talk about Reynolds Price, I was the one who put the dream of Duke in your head with no thought of the consequences. To get accepted from a small-town high school like Spring Port? Unthinkable. That's why I didn't want you to apply. To get rejected. To get hurt after all your hard work. But then, chickadee, you did the unthinkable! You got in!

I will never forget the day Becky Turner, Spring Port's counselor, ran into my room to tell me Kate was our school's first student ever accepted at Duke. Counselors live for such thrills. And I did a terrible thing. Duke wasn't offering any financial help and I knew Ellie couldn't afford it. I'm sorry, but I flat-out lied and told Becky I knew of a private foundation looking for just such students.

Could she please ask the admissions people at Duke to work with me on the details? The lie came out so fast and slick, it was disarming. But Becky didn't bat an eye. She thought since I went to Vassar, I had lots of rich friends. (I do but they're in Spring Port and their richness is not in coin.)

The problem was I'd just gone in hock for an old friend, so I did the next best thing. I went to my 'rich' friends.' Your mother's good friends. Kate, my blessed booklover, our Sandpiper Club—without your mother's knowledge. And they got excited about an investment for the first time in all the years I'd been trying to teach them about the stock market. Despite their lack of interest, the rumor that we bought Walmart on the IPO is true. We started the club in 1969 not long after Jim was killed.

Kate was right. Aunt Nina had made sure the new widow in town who was barely holding on had a ready-made group of wonderful friends by starting the investment club.

Walmart went public the next year. And because it sounded like the big Meijer store in Grand Rapids we all were driving to in those days because it sold everything at good prices, we invested our whole bank account. It wasn't a lot, but enough. Five splits in the next dozen years.

Enough said. Our friends jumped at the idea of using the Walmart profits to create a foundation that could help send worthy Spring Port graduates to college. You were the first, Kate. And so far our only recipient.

Jamie felt a sudden dash of sympathy, like a tumbler of ice water dumped on her neck, as she looked at Kate's blank expression. She'd been so proud, arrogant, even, over that scholarship from Duke. Now, to have it yanked away like this in front of everybody? Jamie felt something she hardly ever had before. She felt sorry for Kate. The slight blanching around her sister's mouth was painful to see. Her mother was holding both Kate's hands, her own cheeks pale.

Tom Quinn didn't notice—or pretended not to as he went on reading in his lawyer's monotone. *Tom set up a 501(c)3 named the T.T. Lane Trust. Fool around with the letters and you'll see our mission from day one was supporting Spring Port's gifted young people. We donated all our Walmart stock. We'd have been killed in capital gains if we'd ever sold it anyway. We all got very nice tax refunds that year! Actually, none of the Sandpipers really cared about the money, and they didn't give a rip about stocks anyway. All they knew was they adored your mother and only wished their own kids were smart enough to get into Duke.*

Later, when we'd ask your mom how you were doing at Duke, she always answered modestly. She had no idea the charge we got out of your grades. You were like one of our own daughters. She'd have killed us had she known about Walmart and the trust fund. I fudged that one annual report. Didn't need to. Ellie never read them anyway. We agreed never to tell. But, Kate, now you need to know because we Sandpipers—again without your mother's knowledge—have voted to disband as an investment club. We're going to meet every month as the board of the new Sandpiper Foundation that has folded in what's still in the T.T. Lane Trust along with our entire portfolio. We've accumulated more money than we goofy women should ever be allowed to manage!

So we're not. Our first business is to offer you the job as our first director. With me gone, my Sandpiper friends have no chance of functioning as an investment club. There's one more legal twist Tom has already taken care of. I have deeded to the T.T. Lane Trust, now The Sandpiper Foundation, eight acres of land I bought long ago from my old friends Bea and Frank Nortier. (I can hear Kate's journalist's wheels spin. You see why I couldn't help you with Joe's question?) At the time, I paid more than the land was worth because the Nortiers needed money.

Jamie snuck a look at Kate and was surprised, and relieved, to see an intense interest had replaced the initial shock on her sister's face.

Your first assignment as the Foundation's director, with a stipend to be set by the board and your mother can vote on that, is researching who should buy that property from the Foundation and for what use. I know you will balance the environmental magnificence of our beloved dunes with the important financial scholarship work of The Sandpiper Foundation.

You were the first deserving student to get scholarship support from our club. Now we're asking you to make sure other gifted students bright enough to get into their dream college can go there. Having worked with these wonderful, generous, and un-businesslike Sandpiper women for over 30 years, I promise they will accept whatever you propose for the land. After all, they know how smart you are. They sent you to Duke!

Kate could not hold back a grin.

We were wrong to mislead you, Kate, and you, Ellie. But you would never have accepted our help. As I write this last letter to you, I count on your generous natures to forgive me. And when you watch the sun slide into the big lake from the deck of The Sandpiper, keep looking for the green flash. Ridiculous as your theory is, I figure that's how I'll be coming back. God bless you, my family, for filling my soul with love

and my life with joy. Yours forever and ever. Nina and Aunt Nina
   P.S. Did you think I'd go without poetry? One stanza only from Emily to tell you
why not to mourn my leaving, but to celebrate my going!
   Because I could not stop for Death,
   He kindly stopped for me;
   The Carriage held but just ourselves
   And Immortality.

Into the stillness of Ellie's living room came the calls of another flock of Canadian geese passing somewhere over the house, pointing their honking beaks northward. Jamie felt the numbed silence as they all watched Tom Quinn drink what had to be cold coffee. His throat sounded dry and tired by the end. Ellie and Kate looked stiff in their fixed positions beside each other, their eyes staring nowhere.

Aunt Nina had just given Jamie something she hadn't known she wanted. A home of her own. No loser boyfriend telling her when she could come and go. A place that belonged to her and a place she belonged to. She spread her arms across the mass of her abdomen and wept. Jamie had obeyed Aunt Nina as long as she could. She could hold the tears back no longer.

T h e   S a n d p i p e r

KATE

"I guess I should go buy weekly newspapers more often." George Lathrup swiveled in his leather office chair. Kate and Joe sat in matching side chairs on the other side of the publisher's sleek rosewood desk. "I leave town, and you two come up with the hottest story of the year. Not to mention the insider scoop."

Joe pointed a finger across his chest at Kate. "She makes the news, Mr. Lathrup. "All I do is report it."

Kate threw her hands up in a warning signal. "I hope you're not talking about what happened to my sister…" Kate stopped as a flash recall of vertigo put her back in the ER, the walls spinning. The way Pete held her mother—how he'd looked over at her—she'd thought Jamie was dead.

"No, no." Lathrup let his chair fall forward as he leaned his arms over the desk. "I did not mean to make light of what happened to her."

"I know you didn't," she said. "I'm just a little shell shocked with all that's happened. But I am very relieved the SOB's in jail. And the guy who attacked the Muskegon woman is finally behind bars so we dawn joggers don't have to worry about a serial rapist now." Besides I have Pogo now, she smiled to herself.

"Imagine," Joe said, shaking his head, "the nut case trying to kill your sister because she rides a bike in front of him!"

"How about being stupid enough to brag about it at work afterwards?" George put in. "Wasn't your sister scared to identify the guy?"

"Jamie? Scared?" Kate asked in amazement. "You don't know my sister." She felt the simmer of long absent pride. "She couldn't wait to see him up close. The police said she intimidated him, not the other way around. Jamie—my sister was plain lucky the lost dog happened to be wandering nearby." Kate doubted she'd ever know the real reason Jamie was on the bike path alone that late at night. And it didn't really matter. She had not deserved to be attacked by a lunatic.

"Speaking of the dog," Lathrup said rocking back in his chair, "that's about as good in human interest as you can get. Joe's story arrived while we were up north working out our final offer. I made copies right then for the Gaylord Weekly owners. Showed them they're getting into a happening chain of papers. A mysterious dog appears out of the night to rescue the damsel in distress. You did a job on the old heartstrings, Joe. And how many calls did Marcia say we got about the dog after his picture ran in the paper?"

Kate smoothed her mid-calf khaki skirt over her lap before answering. "One inside story we didn't write, Mr. Lathrup, concerns the dog. It's a little complicated. You see the night Jamie got hurt, she had no wallet—no I.D. She was your classic Jane Doe. Until, that is, my husband saw her in the ER. Then the police arrived with Jamie's dog, at least they assumed so, in the back of the squad car. So the cops told Pete about the dog.

"Pete said his sister-in-law didn't own a dog, but if the owner didn't show up, he'd take it and make sure he found a good home." As she related this, Kate wondered how she could have ever not wanted Pete to have his dog. Their dog. Pogo.

"I know they kept the dog at the police kennel while they tried to find the owner," Joe put in, "because they told me the station was swamped with calls to adopt him."

"After your heart-rending story, of course," Kate said elbowing Joe.

"Pulitzer stuff," he said with a casual shrug.

"But since Pete was the first to offer," Kate went on, "one Saturday morning, the cops brought him to our house and Pogo's been family ever since."

"Pogo? You mean you have the rescue dog?" George Lathrup's round cheeks puffed in surprise. "And Joe hasn't written that up for our readers?"

"See?" Joe poked a finger at her. "I've been telling her it's too good to pass up. Pete, the ER doc and all."

"No," she said with finality. "Sorry, but Joe and I have been through this already. There've been way too many Lakeshore News articles about my family already." Then she stopped. "Well, actually—the reason I asked if we could meet this morning—and, this is embarrassing. There's more."

"Wonderful," Lathrup said grinning above his red tie patterned in tiny black inkwells. "Covering your family alone might get us the Michigan Press's Blue

Ribbon Weekly this year."

She bit down on her lower lip.

"I'm teasing, Kate. Sorry. Go on, please."

Kate felt Joe's antennae spark beside her as she tried to stay objective summarizing Aunt Nina's remarkable will. How the T.T. Lane Trust was Aunt Nina's scrambling of "talent." Joe's pencil was already scratching in his long narrow reporter's notebook. She could feel his excitement grow while he scribbled, flipping filled pages as she told how Helena Judd had come to own the old Nortier lakeshore property.

When she got to the part about The Sandpiper Foundation, Joe stopped writing and stared at her. She felt her cheeks flush telling them she was the executive director, a responsibility she'd have refused from anyone but Aunt Nina.

Her tongue dry with self-consciousness, Kate began to ramble. "But now, of course, since I've had this *greatness thrust upon me*." She stopped and clapped a hand over her mouth, her eyes fixed on nothing. How could she make these two men understand what just happened? *Twelfth Night*, meaning, Aunt Nina—again ruling her head as well as her heart.

"Mr. Lathrup, Joe—I'm sorry, but this is like—like an out-of-body experience. I didn't know I remembered that line. But Aunt Nina—Helena Judd—did it all the time. Quoted poetry, literature, whatever." The two men looked at each other, their expressions puzzled.

"You both think I'm weirding out—but, well, you didn't know her. If anyone could take over someone else's brain space—she'd be the one to do it."

Kate didn't realize she was crying until she felt the coolness. She wiped at her cheeks as if the tears were someone else's. She didn't feel sad—just an overpowering awareness of Aunt Nina—as if her heart were being brushed with petals.

When she spoke again, the earlier embarrassment about her part in the foundation was gone. Instead, as she began talking about Aunt Nina's dream for young scholars, the thrill of possibilities opened like steam in her chest. In that moment, Aunt Nina's passion became Kate's.

"Think what this can mean for bright children who grow up in Spring Port with no prayer of college—for whatever reason. Money. Single parent. No family encouragement. Then some alert teacher sees something in the student and begins to feed the intellectual fire—to mentor that young mind because the teacher knows about this foundation. Knows The Sandpiper is looking for just such a young people to send to the best colleges they can get into."

It must look funny, she knew, to be talking with such sudden enthusiasm while tears streamed down her cheeks. She didn't care. If learning the truth about her Duke scholarship had been a blow, the shock had already transformed itself into something stronger. No, she hadn't paid her own way to Duke. But she now understood the greater honor was to have been sent there by so much love.

"No question." Lathrup said. "It's an incredible gift to the community—to the schools."

"It's why, much as I'd like to keep the whole story private, we can't. Putting it in the Lakeshore is going to be plenty awkward for me. But I can see how my job here," she pointed at the wooden floor, "is important to this foundation. What better way to let the parents of Spring Port know new scholarship funds are available for their kids?"

"This director's job—" George Lathrup raised one serious eyebrow. "You're not leaving me, are you?"

"No, I sure don't want to. But I have no idea what's involved running a foundation. Since the Council of Michigan Foundations happens to be head-quartered right here in Spring Port, I have already asked some of their experts to help me."

"Are we talking—this foundation, a lot of money here?" Joe asked as discreetly as he could.

"Not public information yet. But they did buy Walmart on the IPO and didn't use all the profits on their only scholarship student so far. But that's another story. Remember, Joe, when Aunt Sandy—Mrs. Tom Quinn—wouldn't let you interview her about the club? They were right in the process of convert-ing their investment club into a foundation. Nobody could talk about their plans—especially to a sharp reporter—until, well, until Aunt Nina's will was read."

Joe wiped his forehead. "Walmart IPO! Holy white eyes! And my journal-ist's 'keen' instincts told me your Sandy Quinn didn't want to be interviewed because her group had lost money in the market! Nice nose for news, Joe Boy!"

"You're telling us," Lathrup asked, "this new Sandpiper Foundation—all the women in the investment club knew about it and kept their mouths shut?"

"Only my mother didn't know. And yes they did."

Kate found herself telling the whole story back to the bogus Duke scholar-ship. She didn't even leave out the ego trip she'd ridden—or how mortified she'd been when she first heard the truth. She didn't even try to explain how her humiliation had become an epiphany. In a flash of insight, she'd understood how long she'd defined herself by her successes.

But now the scholarship plume was forever gone from her cap, and she did not feel diminished. In fact, quite the opposite. Her mother's friends had loved Ellie Cameron enough to join Aunt Nina's conspiracy so Kate could go to Duke. And now the same good women were champing at the bit to give away all the money they'd made since Kate's 'scholarship' to help others like her.

"So this makes you The Sandpiper Foundation's first scholarship winner, right?" Joe was back to taking notes.

"I sure am," she answered with unexpected pride. "Yes, I am. And if you want to write the whole bloody thing, Joe—go for it. Feel free to quote me. It's almost funny. All these years I thought I was a such big deal to win this great academic scholarship from Duke. Then, boom, find out I didn't do it at all. And now—now the bizarre thing is I think I'm happier about where the money did come from than when I thought I'd done it myself!"

Joe laughed without looking up from his notebook. "Getting into Duke from a no-name high school like Spring Port—that's a pretty big deal by itself."

The door barely opened, and Marcia Kraft's red reading glasses were partially visible through the small space. "Oh, I'm sorry, Mr. L," she said. "Kate's mother just called from Rose's-"

"What time is it?" she jumped up. "I had no idea I'd gone on so long. I'm meeting my mother for lunch twenty minutes ago. Sorry, Mr. Lathrup, Joe. Thanks Marcia."

"The land—you haven't talked about that yet," Joe followed her out the door. "I need to ask about the Nortier property? What's going to happen to it?"

Kate came to a complete stop. "For sure The Sandpiper Foundation is not selling it to a bulldozer from Chicago. Feel free to put that in your story, Joe."

He was still smiling as she turned and ran out Lakeshore's front door. She jogged east on Harbor Street, her black patent heels scraping the sidewalk. After Aunt Nina's funeral, she'd made her mother promise to have lunch with her once a week. Now she was mad at herself for losing track of time. She didn't want her mother thinking Kate was too busy. Weaving around startled pedestrians, she felt weightless—energized by what she'd just told Joe and George Lathrup.

Today over a Caesar salad with extra anchovies, she made up her mind, she would tell her mother about wanting a baby—about two years of failed infertility treatments. She might even ask her mother to come with her for an appointment and meet Dr. Bauer. Giving up on Clomid had actually given her some peace, a respite from the stress of charts and blood tests. Dr. Bauer's three-month's rest from fertility drugs had set her on a smooth plateau where hopes didn't rise only to crash at the first spotting.

The hostess recognized Kate and pointed her toward the back of the restaurant. She heard her mother's voice before she saw her. "Oh, Kate," her mother looked up as the hostess showed Kate to a corner booth. "Look who I found?"

"Sarah," Kate wanted to be pleased as she greeted her long-time friend, Uncle Tom and Aunt Sandy Quinn's daughter. "How nice."

"Be honest if I'm interrupting you two," Sarah said with genuine concern. Nothing was ever fake about Sarah Quinn. "But if not, I would love to join you. This is my one day to get away from the kids. So I was thrilled to run into Aunt Ellie outside. I've hardly seen you since you've been back, Kate—but I know how busy you are at the newspaper. This is a real treat for me."

"Me too," Kate said. This time she meant it. She would tell her mother later about the infertility and Dr. Bauer. "So how are your children?" she heard herself ask. Looking at Sarah's red-brown hair in the wedge cut she'd always had, her turned-up nose sprinkled with freckles and the mischievous mouth ready to giggle—Kate remembered how much fun they'd had growing up together. Yes, she did want to see more of Sarah from now on.

The   Sandpiper

JAMIE

The ice cube clinked rhythmically back and forth against the short glass, a metronome of hazy pleasure until Jamie floated in the bronze liquid. Her feet hung weightless above the planked floor as she watched the face staring at her from the mirror behind the bar. She started to raise her hand to wave, a friendly gesture to the watcher when the watcher waved back. Then she recognized the face—saw the pilot's wings pinned to the bare flesh of his forehead.

Jamie lurched up in bed, her clumsy body drenched in sweat. In the semi-darkness she could see Pogo's head beside her, his ears erect and alert. "Oh, Pogo," she leaned her head on his, her insides churning from the nightmare. "I scared you too." She rubbed his back, the strong texture of his coat anchoring her, pushing the terrifying dream out of her mind. "Oh, Pogo, thank heaven you're here." She said at last lifting her head from his.

She'd tried to protest when Pete and her mother wanted Pogo to come with her after she moved back to Aunt Nina's because she'd be alone. Pogo was Pete's dog—even Kate had grown attached to him. 'We'll call it his vacation with all those seagulls to chase," Pete had said to finally persuade her. Still, Jamie knew what they were thinking. Watch dog.

"Well, you did save my butt once, didn't you boy," she said, letting the dog's steadiness restore her calm. But it wasn't the protection she needed—it was Pogo's friendship. The passenger seat of the Saab was now his. And nothing pleased him more than lifting his nose to catch the wind on these late autumn days warm enough for her to put the top down. She and Pogo had not been apart in the ten days since she'd moved back to The Sandpiper.

The digital clock on the dresser in the small back bedroom read 5:10 a.m.

She would not fall asleep again. With the perspiration drying, she felt chilled. "Coffee and dog bone time, my friend," she said and got out of bed. She pulled off her damp nightshirt, pausing in the cold dawn air to study the smooth pink expansion of her belly, watching for a small foot or elbow to move under the skin. She'd welcomed the slowdown of the robust kicking the day before. Now she wished it would start again.

The baby wasn't due for another three weeks. But she was glad she was seeing Dr. Benson this morning. By the time she got to her appointment, she was sure the baby—not *hers* but *the*—would be back to somersaults.

All Jamie wanted now was for this to be over—for the Nebraska family to have their healthy baby. Then she would figure out what to do with the rest of her life. Right now all she could ask of herself was a day at a time. Then again, an hour was a good thing. The big decisions had to come afterwards. She spread her fingers over the bulging uterus. This was all she could manage today. She pulled on an old wool robe of Aunt Nina's, the front panels barely meeting, and felt the chill of the wooden floor as she walked down the narrow hall to the kitchen.

Still Aunt Nina's, she thought filling the coffee pot with water. The Sandpiper would always be Aunt Nina's no matter what the deed said. It was why she hadn't moved into Aunt Nina's big bedroom as her mother wanted her to. Instead she'd gone back to the bedroom she and Kate had grown up in. It was where she'd slept when she was taking care of Aunt Nina—when Aunt Nina was taking care of her. The little bedroom with the twin brass beds was where she belonged, at least for now. Maybe—maybe some day she really could get healthy enough to come back here and live in the cabin Aunt Nina had given her. The thought turned into a wish—and then a prayer.

She turned on the coffee maker and let Pogo out the back door before she started the affirmations Gloria insisted she practice. 'Keep thinking about the half full, Girlfriend, not the half empty.' Nothing riled Gloria quicker than Jamie's feeling sorry for herself. This morning Jamie needed the positive thoughts—needed to focus on what was going right in her life. It was the only way she could push the nightmare out of her consciousness.

Count the pluses. For the first time in her life, she had a home of her own where she could come to live any time. Sober—over ten months now, the longest she'd gone without a drink since—since Roger Hamper. Concentrate on that victory, she told herself. Shut the nightmare out of her mind. She knew it was a bad sign when recovering alcoholics dreamed about bars. And this one—with him waving at her—this one was bad.

She walked toward the front of the cottage for her first morning look at the lake, the coffee perking behind her. After her heart almost shut down at Christmas, she knew a relapse would probably kill her. Not the whiskey. She could survive a drunk. But she knew her addict too well. The alcohol would lead to cocaine with the same certainty dead flesh turned into worms. She rubbed her right foot against the scar on her other ankle and gazed out at the big lake.

Turning into the living room, Jamie came to a stop. She still wasn't used to the changes. Everything in Aunt Nina's living room was the same—and nothing was. The south wall was solid with books to the ceiling, the rows of books lined up on shelves under the windows—Aunt Nina's art gallery of beach glass and driftwood among the books. All this exactly as she'd left it. But Cecilia and Wilson had taken every piece of furniture.

Antique wicker, the good stuff like Aunt Nina's, was apparently highly prized by collectors out East. Jamie hoped Cecilia and Wilson would keep the wicker themselves—especially Aunt Nina's chaises—and not sell them to a dealer. The couch, chairs, lamps, two matching area rugs—even the loveseat she'd curled up on since she was little—all of it was gone.

Happily Cecilia and Wilson couldn't lift—or, more likely, didn't want—the old cable spool which kept its place of importance near the fireplace. Only now the naturally distressed round table, lovingly oiled to a glossy beige patina, was surrounded by Pier One rattan furniture in an ivory color.

Jamie and her mother had picked it all out in Holland the morning after Jamie asked her mother if she could move back to Aunt Nina's until the baby came. A couch, a loveseat, two armchairs lots of odd-sized cushy pillows in bright jungle colors, an assortment of small end tables and three skinny white floor lamps made the room pleasant. But it was far from the embracing charm of Aunt Nina's quilts and wicker.

Her mother had spotted a huge round off-white tasseled area rug on sale at Pier One. It felt good under Jamie's bare feet as she surveyed the room. Jamie had tried to pay for the furniture, but her mother refused. "You and Kate and I might own the cottage, but I'm the one who's going to live in it," she'd said. "I think that was Nina's plan all along."

It was funny how stunned they had been to hear Aunt Nina's own words giving them The Sandpiper. And yet, within moments, how perfectly right it seemed. Like the sandpipers coming home every spring. Of course Aunt Nina would want the three of them to have it! Their spirits, like hers, had been caressed and molded by the lake, the beach, even the little woods around the cabin. It was not just property to any of them. It was a sanctuary. A sacred place where souls came to be nourished.

Her mother had come to the same conclusion—and as quickly. In the quiet after Uncle Tom finished reading the will, her mother, tears still full in her eyes, announced she was going to sell her house and move into Aunt Nina's. It wasn't her mother's way to make rash decisions. But she, too, had felt the pull of inevitability in Aunt Nina's will. Jamie thought it must be what her mother felt the day she'd followed Jim Cameron around campus and into marriage. However impulsive it might once have seemed, Jamie now understood her mother was responding to something more like destiny.

Her mother's house was already on the market. She'd hired the builder who'd remodeled her own kitchen for catering to draw up plans for a similar addition at The Sandpiper. She was going to use the money from selling her house to make a new kitchen at the cottage that would work for her catering. She was also adding two bedrooms and bathrooms on the back of the cottage so family and guests could have their own space.

Kate had frowned about the kitchen, but Jamie knew it wasn't snobbery anymore. Kate honestly thought her mother shouldn't work such long hours on her feet. Somehow Kate finally understood that creating gourmet meals in lovely presentations was what their mother loved and was good at. It struck Jamie that if she could ever get beyond what had happened to her—if she could hang on to her skittish sobriety, maybe she'd live long enough to discover what she was good at too.

Hassling over the bill at the Pier One cash register, her mother had plucked Jamie's credit card off the counter and jammed it back into her purse. "Have we forgotten, Jamie, who owns and therefore has to furnish the back cabin? Save your money for that, my dear."

They'd started laughing at the same time. Cecilia and Wilson had gone through the back cabin like locusts. Jamie could not picture the stuffy pair living with the cabin's hand-hewn pine furniture and deep red Indian rugs. But they'd taken them all anyway. Fortunately they'd left behind the beds and mattresses in both the cottage and the cabin—but only after removing every hand-stitched quilt. Cecilia had taken every antique quilt Aunt Nina owned—except the most important one.

*   *   *

"No," she can't leave like that," Jamie shoved herself at the two young men in dark suits stooping to pick up the steel gurney, a burgundy blanket covering Aunt Nina's face. "She can't leave here like that," she sobbed as Pete tried to hold her back. "Pete, please," she wasn't hysterical like they thought. "Please, I know what I'm doing—what Aunt Nina wants. Please, one minute."

Pete nodded at the men and let go of her. She went back to the wicker chaise and grabbed Aunt Nina's favorite quilt, the pink tulips against soft diamonds of blue and yellow still smelling of lilacs. "This—this is what she wants to be covered in."

The two men stepped back, their heads down, and she heard a tiny click from Pete's throat. She pulled off the funeral home's blanket, talking to Aunt Nina's closed eyes, telling her the quilt wasn't going to be prickly like the blanket. She eased the quilt up from Aunt Nina's feet to her neck, smoothing each wrinkle as she moved it upward, talking as she worked.

"We've always loved this quilt best, haven't we? And you hate to be cold, so this will keep you toasty warm, Aunt Nina." Jamie stopped for a last look before kissing her cold forehead. Then, as gently as falling snow, she laid the quilt over Aunt Nina's face.

*   *   *

Pogo barked at the slider to come in, bringing her back to the grey autumn morning. She'd taken Aunt Nina's quilt from the back of the couch where she kept it, wrapping herself in its softness as she let the dog in. When she had tucked Aunt Nina into her colorful shroud, Jamie had meant it to go with Aunt Nina—ashes to ashes—to be returned to the big lake with her.

But at the funeral parlor, minutes after she'd walked away from Cecilia's judgmental stare, one of the young men who'd picked up Aunt Nina handed her a wrapped package. Too upset to care, Jamie had tossed it in the back of her Saab. Only later did she realize it was Aunt Nina's quilt neatly folded in tissue paper. Burying her nose in the trace of lilacs draped around her, she was profoundly grateful Cecilia had missed out on this particular treasure.

"First me," she said to Pogo as she poured coffee into one of the cherry red mugs from Pier One. Cecilia had liked Aunt Nina's collection of Fiestaware too. Inhaling the loamy smell, she sipped the hot coffee and then poured two cups of dry dog food in Pogo's white bowl. "Then you," she said, and Pogo's tail banged against the refrigerator as he began to crunch his food. "And then our 7 a.m. meeting, Pogo."

Gloria was already looking toward the door when Jamie got to the No Sniveling room. Jamie couldn't miss the smile of relief that lit up her sponsor's face. Jamie handed Gloria her coffee to hold so she could lumber into the folding chair beside her. She felt overwhelmed by sadness. Without the escape hatch of alcohol, she was an emotional pinball machine getting knocked from up to down by impacts she never saw coming. Sobriety, if never easy for her, was at least on some lucky days not all consuming. Today was not one of the lucky ones.

The bar scene had broken her sleep—and Roger Hamper had invaded her brain as he'd once torn his way into her body. The nightmare triggered the old insane thinking. Now the cravings were tearing free of the AA net she'd worked so hard to weave. Once the baby was born, she'd have no one to protect anymore and that reality terrified her. She'd never been able to stay sober for herself—not since the August night of hell and thunder.

"How you doing, Girlfriend?" Gloria asked as if reading her mind. "Here," Gloria handed back the styrofoam cup of coffee. "You look a little pasty to me."

"Bad dream," she said staring at nothing. Danielle, a chatty teenager with frizzy red hair, sat down on Jamie's other side.

"Labor's going to be your bad dream, Jamie," Danielle said with a half smirk. "Dorky you can't trade with your sister," Danielle said waving across the circle at Maudie, the funny, if crude, older woman who'd befriended the teenager.

Jamie ignored the comment until she sensed Gloria stiffen beside her. Then she turned to face Danielle. "What did you say about my sister?" She was remembering that Gloria, who rarely criticized anyone—especially if they were in the program—had once referred to this flame-haired girl as Ding Dong Danielle because she loved gossip.

"The thing she writes in the newspaper? Her picture's next to it every week. I know it's your sister. Everyone does. Forget Anonymous around this place."

Because of mouths like yours, Jamie wanted to say as she pulled her head back from the odor of the girl's unbrushed teeth. Danielle caught the motion, and her eyes narrowed slightly.

"Since you don't want this baby," she pointed at Jamie's abdomen, "you *could* let your sister have it seeing as how she can't have her own. Hey, don't give me that bug look, Jamie. I seen her leave that doc's office—the one who takes care of women who want to get PG. I drive my neighbor there sometimes when she doesn't want to go alone." Jamie felt Gloria arch across her toward Danielle.

Jerking her head back, away from Gloria, Danielle quieted her tone. "But forget it." She'd gotten Gloria's message. "I shouldn't have said nothing." Danielle picked up her satchel purse and moved across the circle to sit beside Maudie.

Jamie barely heard what was said at the meeting, passing when it came to her. She'd wanted to tell the No Sniveling group about the nightmare. The craving it had set off. About her fear knowing she was going to lose the one thing keeping her sober. But all she could think about was Kate. How could it be possible? Kate who got everything she ever wanted. Infertile? Not able to do what stray cats can?

She had to get Gloria alone. Her strong reaction to Danielle's comments meant Gloria knew something. Then Jamie remembered Gloria's telling her once that she didn't know everything she thought she did about Kate. Was this what Gloria meant?

Finally, at five after eight, the last woman had finished, and they stood to join hands and say the Lord's Prayer. Jamie barely said 'Amen' before pulling Gloria out of the room and down the hall toward the rear parking lot. She was walking swiftly toward the Saab parked at the far end of the lot when something warm touched her thigh.

"Gloria?" she asked, letting go of her sponsor's arm. Gloria stopped beside her, following Jamie's eyes down to her feet—to the dripping fluid making dark spots on the cement.

"Girlfriend," Gloria said, her voice prickly with excitement. "I think your water just broke."

The   Sandpiper

JAMIE

"I can't leave," Jamie said looking down at herself in amazement. "Pogo's in my car. I have to page Pete right away!" Jamie pointed over her shoulder at the black nose sticking out of her lowered Saab window, his licorice eyes riveted on her. "We can't leave him. We have to take my car. And," Jamie began speed talking, "you have to call Uncle Tom so he knows—but not Mother, remember, don't talk to my mother until it's all done. The papers, everything."

Gloria took Jamie's keys and got into the driver's seat. She watched her agitated sponsee work her way into the passenger side, Pogo licking Jamie's neck as she did. Jamie never stopped talking. "And Kate—you have to tell me what Danielle was babbling about back there. I have to know what that little bitch—snot," she corrected herself, "was saying."

Gloria came to an abrupt stop as they approached the huge glass doors of the emergency room. "Hold it one second here." Gloria was not smiling. "I have a life too, remember? I know we alcoholics get stuck on ourselves, but stuff it for a minute with the orders and the questions, OK?" Jamie stopped mid-sentence in her monologue.

Gloria looked hard into Jamie's eyes. "We need to check you in, and then I need to call work and tell them I'm not coming in. Then I have to see if my mom can help with the kids after school and after that there's the matter of *my* car. Remember? I just drove you here in yours which leaves mine still at the club. Other people, Jamie. Other people have needs too. Sometimes we have to think about them—even if we are going into labor."

Jamie sat rigid in the car, stung by her friend's rebuke. Then, in a flash, she was galled with shame. Gloria always told the truth.

"Now, Girlfriend," the twinkle returned to Gloria's eyes, "get out of the car and walk slow so I have time to get close to your butt and try to hide the mess you made of yourself. Today's the first time I've been glad you got all your maternity clothes in black."

A dark-haired woman behind the reception desk keyed in the information from Jamie's Blue Cross card. "You still got his insurance," Gloria said, her face unsmiling. Jamie was keeping her wet backside toward the counter while they waited. "That tells me Jake thinks you're coming back. You're using him, Jamie—and you haven't been straight with me."

Jamie looked up at the fluorescent lights, absorbing Gloria's second attack in as many minutes. Only another alcoholic could say such things to her. Gloria could because she'd done it all too. Thinking only about herself, using others, lying—hurting the people who cared about her most. Staring at the acoustic tiling, Jamie understood, as if for the first time, how good alcoholics get at selfishness. After a while, they no longer recognize the selfishness. They become it.

"World to Jamie," Gloria said.

"Oh, well, it's not always fun to hear the truth, is it? I haven't—well, really figured it out about Jake. Yes, we've had a couple screaming fights on the phone I didn't tell you about. But I did tell him what you said—that going back to him was a guaranteed relapse."

Gloria's dark eyes were unrelenting.

"But the health insurance—I needed it for this, today. And, yes, he still pays my credit card and I haven't told you that either. Sobriety doesn't fix all our bad behaviors, does it?" She looked down at her swollen abdomen and wondered what Dr. Keith Summers was doing at that moment. She'd been stone sober when she took advantage of him.

"Cameron, Jamie?" the brunette receptionist said reading from her monitor. "You were admitted here July 3, is that right?" The dark-haired woman looked up, a new interest on her face from what she was reading scrolling down the screen.

Jamie nodded, calling back the firestorm in her head, the pounding in her left arm. She saw her mother gazing down at her, fear narrowing her lips, a black sweater loose around her shoulders. Somewhere behind her mother stood Aunt Nina, frail and tired but strong. At the end of the bed Kate hovered—her eyes red-rimmed. Had she been crying? Jamie's brain was so fuzzy at the time.

Kate! Jamie put her hand on Gloria's arm. "Please Gloria. I am sorry—ordering you around, Jake—all of it. But I will get honest with him—with you,

I promise. What I need now, please, is for you to tell me about my sister—what Danielle was talking about this morning-"

Suddenly a steel band lassoed her midriff, cutting off oxygen. Jamie turned and grabbed the counter top to steady herself against the jolt. The next minutes were a blur of the wheelchair whirring beneath her, elevator doors opening and closing, people moving around her in green scrubs, a narrow bed with stiff white sheets.

She felt the gritty texture of the blood pressure wrap against her skin, a machine beeping beside her bed as it counted heartbeats. Then, as swiftly as it had started, the haze cleared, and Jamie knew with biting clarity the moment she'd feared she could not endure had come. Not the labor, for physical pain meant little to her. It was the other tearing she dreaded. She was going to amputate a part of herself. And she could never get it back.

Jamie wanted to drift into the metallic hospital sounds around her—to float beyond her consciousness into a remote place of numbness. She did not want to face the reality of how tightly she'd wound the nugget of this pregnancy into a knot of denial. A quick Arizona abortion would take care of it, she had once planned. Like having an abscessed tooth pulled or a ruptured appendix removed.

But then came the call from Spring Port. Her mother was on the Saguaro Clinic phone telling her Aunt Nina had terminal pancreatic cancer. Jamie knew immediately what she had to do. Get home to Aunt Nina as fast as she could and have the abortion in Michigan. Her sister Kate would have to help. Certainly Kate wouldn't want her unwed, alcoholic sister to have a baby in their hometown where she ran the weekly newspaper. No, Kate would especially not welcome an out-of-wedlock baby born to the sister who'd seduced her friend Alex's father. Had seduced him into suicide.

Feeling the early spasm of another contraction, Jamie closed her eyes and accepted her own sick truth. Some part of her knew all along that Kate would not go through with any part of an abortion. Yet, in the twisted machinations of her disease, she had set Kate up. If Jamie did bring an unwanted baby into the world, maybe one damaged by drugs, it would be partly Kate's fault.

If she didn't despise herself so much right then, Jamie might have actually marveled at how resourceful alcoholics can get when they need someone else to blame for their sins. Today all her plots and manipulations and self-deceptions were over. Today she was going to deliver a baby, flesh of her flesh, sinew of her sinew—and never see her own child.

"Gloria," Jamie grabbed the soft hand easing a second pillow behind her back. "Tell them to knock me out, please. Please tell them."

Gloria looked down at her, the familiar wisecracking grin back on her face, the unpleasant exchange not forgotten, but set aside for now. "Well, don't we sound like every other drunk on the planet. 'Numb this hurt for me!'"

Jamie shook her head vigorously as a new contraction seized her body. She was already adjusting to the pain of her uterus squeezing the baby down into the birth canal. Jamie found herself welcoming the body wrenching because it was so doable, so manageable. It was the leak in her heart she needed to stop.

"You're in real good hands here, Girlfriend. They'll give you what you need for pain and not a smidge more. I told them you're alcoholic."

"It's not the pain, Gloria," Jamie shook her blond head against the pillow. "I need to be out so I never...you know? I just want them to put me out and not let me wake up until it's over. *All* over." A surge of grief flushed through her veins until Jamie thought she might die from it. She wished she could die from it.

"Girlfriend," Gloria's musical voice plucked at Jamie's soul, "you don't have to tell me why you want to get knocked out. I know." Gloria pulled a tissue out of the small box beside the hospital bed and dabbed at Jamie's eyes and damp brow while she talked.

"First, I need to find a phone. Pogo, remember? My kids, my job, my car—a few little details, okay? Hey, now don't go giving me that poor hound-dog look of yours. I've said my say twice already this morning. No more picking on you. For today, anyways."

"I deserve every word. I am selfish. Totally."

"Alcoholism is the disease of selfishness. But we can recover from that too. Now what about calling your mother?"

"No!" Jamie jerked herself up from the bed. "It would kill her to see the... oh, Dear God, how can I do this?" Jamie felt a rising panic. "Please, please, Gloria, help me get through this day."

Quietly Gloria reached down and intertwined her fingers with Jamie's, forming prayer hands of blended brown and white skin, and bowed her head. "Dear Sweet Jesus, be with your servant Jamie today in her time of need. Help her surrender to your love and give her the courage to," Gloria hesitated a moment, "the courage to do what she has to do. In His Mercy, Amen."

A contraction of steel clamps started in the seconds after Gloria left. But the pressure hurtled through Jamie's body as if she weren't present. An unusual restfulness filled her. She had the sensation of sleepiness even as the labor pain tightened its grip. It was not possible, she knew, for God to act on Gloria's prayer so fast. And certainly not for a loser like Jamie. Still, she gave herself over to the peacefulness wherever it came from. She began to let go of the black stones piling up inside her.

"Here, Girlfriend," Gloria's voice floated into her soft space. Jamie opened her eyes to see Gloria holding out a covered styrofoam cup, the accordion straw angled toward her. "Drink some more water before I finish my phone calls. You know way back when you asked me to be your AA sponsor, I told you I'd stay with you through your labor. And I will."

Gloria refilled the cup with water from a white decanter, ice sounds clinking as she poured. "Now, before I go call, you keep asking about Kate. What Danielle was blabbing about, I have no idea how she knew, and it's certainly none of the Ding Dong's business. But I happened to see Kate leaving Dr. Bauer's office one Saturday morning while I was waiting for a pap smear. Dr. B's patients are pretty much women who can't get pregnant. But he still lets me come in for routine checks because he delivered both my kids, without charging me, by the way, since I was broke. He's real proud of how I got my life together. Dr. B's a good man. He'll help Kate and Pete get pregnant if he can."

"I don't understand." Jamie said, still centered in the calm aftermath of the prayer. She could not process what she was hearing. Could not fathom Kate's wanting something and not being able to get it.

"For a woman not to be able to have a baby?" Gloria said. "It happens more than you think. And it's about as private as it gets, which is why I didn't tell you, or anyone else. Nobody's business." Gloria walked around the foot of the bed, and pulled Jamie's black mesh purse off the chair as she headed to the door. "Hope you got some quarters in here," she said putting the strap over her shoulder, "I'll be back."

Jamie was still processing this news about Kate when a dark-haired woman in green scrubs suddenly materialized at her bedside. "Oh," Jamie gave a startled gasp, then read the nameplate. "Dr. Chris Jantzen. You look too young."

"I take that as a compliment. I've been in practice almost three years. And now I'm going to help deliver your baby, before too long I'd say."

As she checked Jamie's pulse and blood pressure, Dr. Jantzen was backlit by the hallway light outlining her body in a soft glow. Something about her, some higher level of tenderness made Jamie look closer. Chris Jantzen had kind eyes, honey colored with flecks like tiny searchlights that didn't miss anything. Her short brown hair was brushed back from her face.

"I like your name. Chris. It's like mine. A boy's and a girl's."

"'Jamie.' Hey, you're right. My parents wanted me to be Christina, but no way. I'm definitely a Chris."

Jamie smiled back. "No, you don't seem like a Christina, Dr. Jantzen. My dad was James Cameron."

"How nice to be named after your father. And please call me Chris."

"I will," Jamie said nodding. She had an urge to tell Chris about her dad, about Lieutenant Jim Cameron, but a crushing contraction choked off her words.

"Almost show time," Chris said calmly. "I'll be right back."

A kaleidoscope of images whirled through Jamie's brain as she breathed deeply, the contractions coming closer together now. She was seeing Kate's sunglasses pressed hard into her nose at Gertie's. 'You have no idea what I'm thinking,' Kate had said that day, her voice ice cold.

Now…only now, did Jamie understand. The unintentional cruelty of asking Kate to help her destroy a pregnancy that Kate couldn't have. Jamie felt a blistering remorse for having ever asked Kate. Even worse was her profound sorrow for her big sister. She deserved her own children. And Kate would be the wonderful mother Jamie never could be.

Then a contraction struck with such force Jamie thought of the medieval rack, criminals stretched apart inch by inch. She held the pain close to her, and, with a sense of punishing atonement, Jamie embraced the agony. As the contraction ebbed, she could picture Kate's wild eyes racing her Mazda down the clinic driveway, startled protestors stumbling out of the way.

Jamie heard her own voice, toxic with malevolence, screaming at Kate for doing what Jamie now knew she'd wanted Kate to do all along. Stop the abortion. Only Jamie had not understood the exquisite brutality of what she'd asked of Kate. If Jamie'd had any idea about Kate's infertility…but she hadn't. She never could have done such an unkindness to Kate, not even in the worst depths of her alcoholism.

Like a camera lens adjusting to a new distance, Jamie was seeing the past months differently. How Kate's eyes had carefully avoided Jamie's belly. And Jamie, who was all about herself and her little pity pot, Jamie had assumed Kate The Perfect was embarrassed for having a pregnant, unwed sister. But envy? The last thing Jamie could have imagined from Kate was envy. Oh, dear Lord, how it must have felt to Kate all these months watching Jamie's belly grow round with a baby she didn't want while Kate's own stayed flat.

The next hard contraction gripped her just when Chris came back in to check her cervix. "Good job," she said. "Let's head to delivery." Jamie barely paid attention to the two nurses wheeling her bed down the hall. She was too overcome with despair. All she'd done was pile more hurt on her big sister's already hurting heart. In penance, Jamie made herself feel every vibration spiraling pain downward through her pelvis.

"I don't blame you for crying, Jamie," Chris said from the foot of her bed. "I went from one to ten almost that fast with my first and it hurts."

Jamie heard Gloria's clompy shoes running toward them before she saw her loving face appear beside Chris's. The last thing Jamie thought before the shot kicked in was that she wasn't the only one whose perceptions were distorted. With a little refocusing, Chris would have seen that Jamie's tears had nothing to do with the pain of a dilating cervix.

T h e   S a n d p i p e r

JAMIE

The glass felt cool against her forehead where she pressed her head on the long window, her hands propped on the ledge below. In the eerie after-hours' stillness of the hospital, she hardly noticed the throbbing ache in her breasts, bound tight to stop the milk coursing toward her nipples. She ignored the soreness of stitches where her vagina had torn open for a baby who came too fast. Tired was what she felt most, tired and depressed and hopeless. Aunt Nina's thing with feathers? No, Jamie could not hear a single note of that wordless tune.

The long fluorescent lights in the hospital corridor crackled overhead. Somewhere in the distance she heard a hacking cough. She shouldn't be here, she knew. She shouldn't have climbed the back stairs to the third-floor nursery.

As a kindness, Dr. Jantzen, Chris, had put her in a semi-private room on the first-floor's medical-surgery ward, far away from new mothers and babies. Jamie's roommate, an elderly woman with emphysema, would not be breast feeding every few hours. No, she would not want to chat about her beautiful new baby and trade new-mom war stories about their labors.

They'd put Jamie out for most of it. But she did remember Gloria's face, wet with tears and smiling at the same time. telling her God was good and the baby was perfect. Nothing more than that. She thought she'd remembered Pete's voice in the background, but she wasn't sure.

Beyond the picture window, Jamie could see the border of Winnie the Pooh wallpaper encircling the bright yellow walls of the newborn nursery. In the middle of the wall facing the corridor, the hands on the round white clock read 11:03. The baby who couldn't wait to get into this world must be around eight hours old, Jamie calculated, although the anesthesia had confused her sense of time.

She began to count the tiny beds on wheels with their lucite screens on three sides, a black chart book tucked in the foot of each crib. Seven sleeping infants swaddled in flannel blankets were lined up near the windows for easy family viewing. Taped to the bassinet above each tiny head, a white card topped by a stork neatly listed in black marker the name, sex, weight, and time of birth.

She held her breath and scanned the seven cards, exhaling only when no name read 'Cameron.' Three more bassinets, however, were farther away from the window, angled so Jamie could not read the names on the cards. One of the three was empty. In the one next to it, a tiny bundle was wrapped in a blue blanket. The baby in the third distant crib was swaddled in pink. Jamie pushed her head harder against the glass trying to read even one of the three far-away cards. But she couldn't.

At the back of the nursery, a white haired woman with puffy red cheeks, reminding Jamie of Santa Claus's wife, hovered over a changing table. The nurse looked toward a sound coming from another bassinet and noticed Jamie for the first time, giving her a friendly smile. Then she went back to diapering the baby Jamie knew had come from the empty third bassinet. The blue blanket under the squirming newborn she was changing told Jamie this was a boy.

She should walk away right now, she knew. Back down the two flights of stairs to her room. But she stood transfixed, her eyes straining in their sockets to see the baby the nurse was now trying to encase in a miniature white gown. Two boys, one girl all unnamed. One of them had to be hers. How was it possible for her not to know if she was the mother of a son or a daughter?

Jamie never heard the sound of footsteps in the quiet hallway, her attention now absorbed by the tiny arms and legs waving on a changing table across the nursery. Suddenly Dr. Chris Jantzen was beside her, as if out of nowhere. "I was afraid this was where I'd find you." Chris said without preamble. "You shouldn't be here. It will only make it harder."

Jamie felt herself turn toward Chris without surprise, as if she'd half expected her. Like a sleepwalker, Jamie let the young obstetrician take her elbow and lead her toward the elevator. Looking over her shoulder at the nurse now sitting down with a small bottle to feed the freshly diapered baby boy, Jamie felt pieces of her heart tear off inside her chest.

They rode in silence, the dull whirr of the elevator beneath them. Finally Jamie looked at Chris, a long navy cardigan over her blue scrubs, a dark leather purse over one shoulder. "Why are you here?"

"Good question." Her voice was tired. "I'm off call and was almost out the door when I decided to check on you one last time. When you weren't in your bed," Chris rubbed her forehead slowly, "I knew."

"The baby you told me about, your own child, a boy or a girl?" Jamie couldn't stop herself from asking.

Chris looked at her thoughtfully for a moment. "A girl. Hannah. Look, Jamie. I need to tell you something."

The elevator dinged the first floor. Jamie followed Chris down the corridor. Through the opened door to Jamie's room they could see two nurses leaning over the older woman whose labored breathing was audible from the hallway.

"Not here," Chris said and turned back, pausing a moment. "I know," she said almost to herself. "Are you up to walking a little farther?" Jamie nodded numbly, her will to resist gone.

She didn't remember how they got there, but Jamie found herself sitting on a cushioned pew. Before her on the wall, a small brass crucifix hung over a long altar table, an open Bible in the middle. A padded kneeling bench ran the length of the altar. Along the walls and behind the altar, low-wattage coach lights spilled soft light.

"This is the quietest place in the hospital," Chris said. "Families come in here to pray. I use it to get my head together when out there," she pointed toward the door, "gets too crazy."

Jamie understood. This chapel, with its rich cranberry wallpaper and soft carpet, made Jamie feel calm too. Maybe even safe.

"Are you doing all right Jamie? You lost some blood."

"I'm all right. It's here," Jamie patted her chest where the heartbreak hurt. Chris seemed to understand the message exactly.

"I'm going to tell you something, Jamie Cameron, that only a few people will ever know. I'm 29 with a wonderful husband and a two-year old daughter I'm mad for. I love my family, my job. Life is good. But I carry one sadness that never goes away."

Chris began to twist an embroidered hanky she'd pulled out of her scrub pants. "When I was a fourth-year medical student in Chicago, I got pregnant by some dipshit. I don't even know why I ever had sex with him. One time, just one unprotected time, and what's never supposed to happen happened."

Blood pounded through Jamie's head. Once, just once with Dr. Summers. It shouldn't have happened to her either. But not Roger Hamper, thank God not that. She fought down the memory. She was far too fragile to go there now.

Chris didn't notice Jamie's reaction as her soft monotone continued. "I've always accepted choice as the last possible resort. And for me it really was. My mother's a widow on disability with MS. I'm the only child and she took out a second mortgage to help pay for med school and I still owed almost $40,000." Jamie heard Chris taking deep breaths.

"I'd just been accepted to the University of Chicago's OB-GYN residency where I'd be near Mother. The 24/7 residency meant no way could I take care of a baby by myself. But I'm a doctor sworn to preserve life?" The shimmering flecks in Chris's eyes dimmed in the muted light of the chapel.

"My roommate took me Friday, I was back in class Monday." Chris dropped her chin to her chest and slowly shook her head back and forth. "But it turned out not to be that simple."

Feet shuffled past the chapel door, hesitated, then went away. "That baby would be five next month, Jamie, and not a single day has passed when I haven't thought about that."

"You regret the abortion?"

Chris held her breath before releasing a heavy sigh. "More than I ever could have imagined. It's like a leak in my heart that will never go away. But I just didn't think I had any other option."

Jamie put her hand on Chris's arm. "I tried to have one. My sister took me to the clinic, then, at the last second, just turned around and drove away."

"She did that out of love."

"She shouldn't. I'm not worth it."

A broken puppet, Jamie suddenly collapsed her face to her knees and began to rock autistically, tears rolling down her face. Chris encircled her with both arms, pulling her close. Together they swayed back and forth in the ancient motion of grief. Jamie sank into Chris's comforting embrace and sobbed until she had no tears left.

Gently, like a parent soothing a small child, Chris began to speak again. "I'm not a very religious person. I don't get to church very often. But every day in my work I see God move in the most unexpected ways. And I know we're loved in all our failings because God can see our hearts."

Jamie looked up at the brass crucifix.

"I don't pretend to know how it hurts to give up a child you've carried inside for nine months. But ending your pregnancy would have cost you too. That's why I'm sharing my story with you. You let your child be born. I did not.

Oh, yes, I regret what I did. And will until the day I die. I don't question your reasons for letting your baby be adopted. For you, the best love is letting your child be raised by parents who can give what you cannot."

Jamie spoke in a half whisper. "I'm an alcoholic and an addict."

"You can get better." Chris answered at once.

"The father," Jamie felt herself coming unraveled, "I hardly knew him. I didn't love him. He was my therapist, a psychiatrist. It was my fault. I…I started it. He's a good man with a wife. He has no idea."

Chris nodded silently, as if processing what she'd heard. "Then," she finally spoke, "you've spared that family too."

They sat together quietly for a few minutes, Chris stroking Jamie's hair. When Jamie finally sat up, Chris handed her the embroidered hanky she'd had in her scrub pants. "You need this more than I do."

"I'll mess it up."

"It's a present."

"Thank you." Jamie unfolded it to blow her nose. "I truly do not know what I would have done if Kate hadn't driven me away that day."

"Some things we can't know. Here, hold out your arm. I'm walking you back to your room before you pass out on me."

Chris nudged Jamie to her feet and guided her down the carpeted aisle between the rows of pews. At the back of the chapel, Jamie saw a stained-glass window she hadn't seen coming in. The leaded panes depicted grazing lambs in a valley tended by a shepherd looking up. The backlighting gave the golds and blues and greens a mystical effect.

I will lift my eyes unto the hills from whence cometh my help, the Scripture passage was painted in black letters below. They reminded Jamie of the Aspen she loved. Was it possible, she suddenly wondered, if beyond the lure of skiing and partying some piece of her had been drawn to the mountains' spiritual power?

Then, just as quickly, she dismissed the thought. She followed Chris into the hallway. She was not going to con herself into thinking God and cocaine had anything to do with each other.

"Have you ever seen those WWJD bracelets people around here wear? What Would Jesus Do?" Chris asked as they turned into the medical-surgery ward. "A patient gave me one I've never put on. But I do think about the question from time to time. When you didn't abort and you didn't tell the father? Well, I think that's what they mean by WWJD."

WWJD, Jamie reflected as they reached her hospital room. What Will Jamie Do? Will she have the strength to do the one thing she has to if she wants to live? Staying sober meant life. Relapse was death. What Would Jesus Do? That was easy.

What Would Jamie Do? That was the question chilling the blood around her wounded heart.

The Sandpiper

KATE

Her running shoes felt leaden on her feet as Kate turned up Arbutus Street, every step an effort. She was already sweating from an unusual late autumn sun, one of those wondrous Indian summer days masquerading as June. It had been hot in their bedroom the night before as she'd watched the digital clock by their bed change every hour, Pete in deep sleep beside her.

Jamie was in the hospital, and their mother still didn't know. Gloria told Pete when she'd paged him to pick up Pogo in Jamie's car. But Pete didn't tell Kate until he came home after ten the night before. She'd been so happy to find Pogo in her kitchen when she got home from work, she'd only briefly wondered why he wasn't with Jamie. The baby had been her first thought, but, then, the due date was three weeks away.

The moment Pete walked through the bedroom door, his eyes tired and sad, she had known. While he pulled off his faded green scrubs, he told her the baby was healthy, Jamie was doing well. It was all he knew. He'd stopped by OB to see Jamie, but she was close to delivery. He hadn't seen the baby. Didn't even know the sex.

She and Pete had agreed to let her mother get a good night's sleep before she found out. Because what should be the most joyous of all news wasn't going to be. She pictured her mother's face when she heard she was a grandmother, but without a grandchild. Kate's breath grew short. She leaned over in the middle of the path and gulped oxygen like someone choking.

As her lungs began to fill, Kate's mind clarified and she thought through her last visit with Dr. Bauer. Cleaning his glasses with Alice smiling at his shoulder, he'd been both honest and positive. Her body needed a three-month break from any fertility drugs, he'd said calmly. Clomid didn't always work. They'd move on to Perganol shots. No big deal. He'd gone right on to congratulate her about the new foundation, "The Sandpiper isn't it?"

Alice had added her enthusiasm for college scholarships going to smart kids from poor families. At first Kate was offended by the casualness with which Dr. Bauer told her not to come back until January, and, in the meantime, to relax and let nature take its course. But as she'd driven away from his office knowing she wouldn't be back for three months, something shifted inside her. She was suddenly free. Her obsession with calendars and charts could take a rest. She didn't even have to check her basal temperature anymore.

Like a sleek hawk lifted on a burst of thermal air, Kate had felt weirdly liberated. She had no faith she'd get pregnant before January, but at least she'd have a life. She and Pete would have a life. Straight from her appointment with Dr. Bauer, she'd called George up north to tell him her dream career had altered its shape.

When she told him why she needed to work part-time, his deep voice was kind. "We both know you're my first choice to run the Lakeshore News when I'm not there, Kate. But, well, I do understand. We're lucky to have you for whatever time you can give us."

A pair of robins flew past her landing on a balsam fir branch beside the path, the bigger bird making a robust chirp. Kate could almost hear Aunt Nina's voice reading the poem to her American lit class. Even the words, Kate could actually see the words on the left-hand page of her open book. *These are the days when birds come back - A very few, a bird or two - To take a second look.* Something like that. Aunt Nina had talked about it as a spiritual, even religious poem. Kate reminded herself to look it up in one of Aunt Nina's books.

Suddenly Kate stopped. "But that's just what you want, isn't it?" she asked out loud, raising her eyes to the brilliant blue sky. "Why should I be surprised you're still in charge, you Aunt Nina you!"

A new strength kicked into Kate's bloodstream, and she sprinted toward home. She knew now what she had to do. Her Air Nikes didn't feel heavy anymore.

She barely dried her hair after a quick shower and put on a black safari dress with short sleeves. It was 8:10 a.m. when she pulled into the Waters Hospital parking lot. She, who had assiduously avoided the maternity floor on her hospital visits to Pete, now did a speed walk to the elevator and punched the round black three.

The elevator opened to a three-sided nursing station made from square panels filled with textured navy fabric and encased by soft grey metal. The two nurses behind the counter guarding entrance to the maternity wing must have been convinced by Kate's confident stride off the elevator. They didn't say anything when she came around the end of the panels to read the chalkboard of patients' names.

"My sister," she said after checking the names again, "Jamie Cameron? Her name isn't here." All at once Kate was afraid Jamie had left. That she'd come too late. "Do you know? I mean where she is?"

The nurses exchanged a quick look before the older one with short grey hair said, "If she's the one I *think* she is, she's been moved off the floor." Kate heard the condescension in the woman's voice, speaking of Jamie like an outcast. "But you'll have to get the new room number from information downstairs in the lobby on the first floor."

Kate felt a rush of the old protective adrenalin as she took in the nurse's scorn. You obnoxious bitch, she wanted to snap. Both of you with your smug little mouths. If either one of you snobs had one teaspoon of my sister's grit. Instead she said evenly, "Well, maybe I can get my husband to look it up for me. Would you mind paging Dr. Shane for me?"

She only wished Jamie were there to share the sweet discomfiture of the two women as they began shuffling papers around the desk. It was rotten of her to exploit what she knew was the high regard nurses held for doctors, especially the wonderful new Dr. Shane who treated nurses with such Southern courtesy. But these two had looked down on Jamie. That was a mistake.

Kate reacted as she had when they were little girls. She could criticize Jamie up one side and down the other. But God forbid anyone else dare say a bad word about Jamie Cameron. No one knew Jamie's faults better than Kate. But Aunt Nina's farewell letter had taught Kate some pretty humbling things about herself. Jamie had made bad choices. But big sister Kate wasn't so perfect either.

As she watched the nurses' busy hands, she wondered what made them think they could sit in judgment on other people. Then the truth came to her. "Self-righteous," Jamie had called Kate. She'd been right. Kate had judged Jamie with the same certainty these two nurses just did. And, then again, what was more self-righteous than for Kate to declare these two women judgmental?

She thought about the penitent tax collector and the sanctimonious Pharisee, how Christ honored the sinner and chastised the priest. That was the Christ she needed to remember. The one who preached against pride and called for humility. Who despised the sin, but loved the sinner. Who asked believers to forgive the other's sin so that our own might be forgiven.

"Oh, yes, here's a hospital list, Clara," the younger nurse handed the other one a clipboard. Running her finger down the sheet, the grey-haired woman read out loud, "Cameron, Jamie, room 134. That's on the first floor," she said, unable to suppress a gloat. "You have to go down to one anyway, Mrs. Shane."

"I'm sorry for the trouble, Clara and Agnes," she read the badge. "Thank you both." Kate spoke with such real kindness, the two nurses were stymied into silence.

The white muslin curtains were tightly closed on a circular rod around the first bed in room 134. Behind the rippling cloth, Kate could hear the hum of machinery and labored breathing. She walked quietly around the curtain to the second bed and saw Jamie.

Her younger sister, in a blue patterned hospital gown, lay on her side facing the window of the far wall. As Kate got closer, she could see Jamie's knees were tucked into a fetal position. She could not stop herself from leaning over to hug Jamie's back. Neither of them spoke. Finally, Kate let go and sat on the edge of the bed, letting her hand rest on Jamie's hip.

"It's weird," Jamie said, her back still turned, "I recognized your footsteps way down the hall. Must mean those young memories get engrained for good."

"I think I'd know your walk too. But I'd need to be tested."

"You shouldn't be here. Does Mom know?"

"Yes for me, no for Mom. I should be here and not yet. Pete told me."

"He wasn't supposed to."

"You're not his patient. No confidentiality to violate. He knew because Gloria called him to pick up Pogo."

Jamie rolled over on her back so the sisters could see each other's faces for the first time. Jamie's hair pulled straight back into a pony tail at her neck accentuated her carved cheeks. Her eyes looked huge, a bluish fatigue around the edges. Jamie had no makeup on, not even lipstick, but still she was lovely. "You look good, Jamie. Amazing, really." Kate repositioned her hand to Jamie's leg. Then she noticed a lumpiness across Jamie's chest.

"Ice packs," Jamie answered the question before she could ask. "They don't give shots anymore to mothers who aren't breastfeeding. Just ice them down like sprained ankles."

"Sounds awful," Kate said and grimaced.

"Everything in my life is awful right now. My boobs are the least of it."

"Is that why you didn't eat breakfast?" Kate pointed at the metal tray on the high table next to Jamie's bed. Jamie shrugged.

"Jamie, we have to talk." She worked her jaw with resolve. "No, don't turn away, please. This won't take long. But I need you to look at me. Please." Slowly, tentatively, Jamie turned back toward Kate, then scootched herself up on the bed until they were eye level.

Kate took a breath and decided to take Aunt Nina's path of skipping preludes. "Pete and I have been trying to have a baby for three years. For the last two, it's been active and expensive and very, very discouraging infertility treatment. I told Aunt Nina, well, the day she died, as it turned out. No one else."

Now it was her turn to look away. "I don't feel very good about my secrecy. It's been all about ego. Pride, whatever you want to call it. Not being able to get pregnant made me feel inferior, inadequate as a woman. I couldn't bring myself to tell people I'd failed at what everyone else could do, especially when it was the one thing I wanted most." She felt her voice begin to catch.

Jamie leaned forward and took her hand. "Believe me, Kate, the last thing in the world you are is a failure. No one knows that better than I do."

"But how awful of me," she pulled a Kleenex out of the box on Jamie's nightstand, "not to even tell Mother! All she'd want is to help." She wiped her eyes and blew her nose before she continued. "Then you tell me you're pregnant with a baby you don't want. Well, you can imagine how that felt to me."

"I had no idea…"

"How could you? It wasn't your fault, Jamie. And you want to know the really shitty truth? Part of me wanted you to have that abortion. It seemed so wrong for you to be pregnant without trying when Pete and I…but when we drove to Grand Rapids, and I looked at those clinic windows and thought about what *really* goes on inside there—I couldn't…"

"I know, Kate," Jamie said with gentleness. "I knew it that day."

"But I didn't do one thing to stop someone else from taking you back!"

"Kate," Jamie leaned forward in earnestness, "that was our blood pact. You *couldn't* tell anyone."

"Don't try to get me off the hook. You know why I really didn't tell someone? Like Mother or Aunt Nina who would stop the abortion? I didn't *want* you to have the baby I couldn't. You were right to call me a hypocrite. I am!"

Jamie's expression was a mixture of compassion and ironic humor. "Then we're a matched pair, Kate. I came to you in the first place, leaned on our Camp

Arbutus promise so ending the pregnancy could be partly your fault and not all mine."

Kate sat still, shocked, but then suddenly more relieved than she could imagine. "Are you just telling me that to make me feel better?"

With a wry grin, Jamie knocked her fist on Kate's hand where it rested on the bed. "We're not sisters for nothing, Kate."

"I guess not," Kate said, the remembered affection for her younger sister making her smile. "All that really matters now is you didn't have an ab..."

"Excuse me," a familiar looking nurse in a peach smock appeared at the foot of the bed. "Dr. Benson's making rounds for Dr. Janzen and called to say he'll be by to check Jamie in a few minutes."

"Oh, stall him. Can you?" Kate asked quickly. "Make him sign some orders or something first, please, Mrs. Vargo?" she read from the name plate knowing she'd seen the woman before.

"Didn't I meet you in the hospital cafeteria a while back?" Kay Vargo asked. "You're Dr. Shane's wife, aren't you?"

"Yes, I am. And you're right. One night when I met him here for dinner. This is my sister, Jamie, Mrs. Vargo," Kate said, the restored fondness for Jamie spilling into a pride she hadn't felt for too long.

"Nice to meet you, Jamie," Mrs. Vargo said. "I'll see what I can do with Dr. Benson, Mrs. Shane."

Kate waited until the nurse was gone before she turned to Jamie and started to speak.

"No, Kate," Jamie jumped in. "There's something you need to know. Something I should have told you a long time ago."

"Later, please," Kate spoke fast. "We don't have much time and right now nothing's more important than your daughter..."

"A girl!" Jamie gasped and huge tears pooled in her velvety dark eyes. "A girl? A girl?"

Kate covered her mouth. "You didn't know? Oh, dear Lord! Oh, Honey," she threw her arms around Jamie's shoulders, then sat back to look straight at her. "I saw the pink ribbon by your name on the chart so thought you knew! Never, I never would have told you like that. Oh, Jamie, Jamie. I am sorry."

"No, no, I'm grateful, really, to know." Jamie moved her head back and forth, her fingers kneading her thighs. "Aunt Nina was right." Jamie smiled through her tears as she took the clean tissue Kate handed her.

"If she said you were having girl, why would you have thought anything else?" Kate asked. She didn't want to miss Aunt Nina as much as she did right then.

"Now that I know," Jamie stretched the words, "I guess I can, well, think about her, you know, as real. As a real little girl."

"Oh, you're never going to *think* about her as real." Kate knew Jamie heard the strength of her intentions by the wary look on her younger sister's tired face. "You are going to *know* she is real, because you and I are going to take this little girl home, and if," Kate wasn't going to stop for air and give her younger sister time to interrupt, "Jake's the father and you want him involved in her life, fine. If not, fine. But for now we're going to introduce your daughter to her family and…"

"No, no, you don't understand!" Jamie's protest hardly slowed Kate down.

"Oh, but I do. I've finally figured out a real family doesn't have to have a mother and father and children like I used to think. We were a real family, Aunt Nina and you and mom and I. And now we have your baby too. And Pete and Pogo. Pogo loves kids."

"No, I can't—you don't understand, Kate." Jamie's voice broke.

"We're doing it together. My boss is letting me work part-time, do my column from home and The Sandpiper Foundation's office will be at my house. I can help babysit, and you have a great place to live in your own cabin with Mom just up the hill. Plus Mom's best worker just quit, and she needs your help so don't even think about saying 'no.'"

"Stop it!" Jamie half yelled. "Stop it, Kate." She grabbed Kate's arm with tensile power, then she put her face close to Kate's. Her words were clipped with fear. "And when I need that first drink? What then? What happens to the baby girl then?"

"We'll deal with it." Kate said, knowing Jamie heard the unstoppable confidence. "You've stayed away from alcohol so your daughter would be born healthy. You can do it for her now that she's here. I know how strong you are."

"But, Kate, oh, Kate. You don't, you can't understand," Jamie said, a hitch in her voice.

"Shhh, Jamie," she pulled her sister to her. "We're all going to help you. Trust me. You *can* do it. We can do it together. The Three Missketeers. Remember? Just like it used to be."

It wasn't until Kate heard Dr. Benson clear his throat that she let go of Jamie and stood up. She knew her mascara was blotted, but she didn't care. "I'm leaving." She looked back at Jamie, "I'm going to get Mom."

Dr. Benson walked between them, but as Kate turned to leave, she saw Jamie peer around the physician's back. The look of sheer terror on her younger sister's face scared Kate. Then she caught herself. There was nothing to be afraid of. Jamie had proved she could stay sober.

Kate was almost jogging down the hall, excited to meet her new niece, when an even headier thrill seized her. Her mother was about to see her first grandchild! Kate's heart kicked with joy anticipating her mother's face when she took her granddaughter into her arms.

She bounced down the stairwell to the first floor, assuring herself Jamie would be O.K. Whatever was troubling her could wait. They'd have lots of time to talk it over while they shared a precious little girl. As soon as she brought her mother back to the hospital, they'd ask Jamie if she wanted to breast feed. If she did, they'd unbind her right away. It was best for the baby. Plus the responsibility of breastfeeding would be one more reason for Jamie to stay sober.

She would find a music box of Brahm's Lullaby for Jamie to play while she nursed. Kate was not going to let her sister relapse. Not this time.

The   Sandpiper

JAMIE

"Am I glad that's the last batch of popovers so this oven can go off." Ellie Cameron turned the bake dial as she set the two hot tins on the stovetop, her face rosy from the heat. "I can't remember a warmer November, Jamie. I certainly wouldn't have put popovers on the luncheon menu for tomorrow if I had a clue we'd have this weird heat wave. Oh, but look how puffy and golden they got. These are the best popovers yet, don't you think?"

Jamie looked up from the last hard-boiled egg white she'd filled with seasoned caviar. She wiped a strand of blond hair off her face with the back of her wrist. "They're magazine ads. Truly. Aunt Nina always said you were the only person who could turn out perfect popovers and make it look easy. I'm almost done here. All I have left is sprinkling the diced yolks on these," she gestured toward the three cookie sheets filled with caviared eggs on tomato slices and toast rounds. "Where do you want them?"

"Let me see if I can make any more room here," her mother said opening the huge stainless-steel refrigerator door.

"Somehow, Mom, I can't quite see that metal monster in Aunt Nina's kitchen."

"Oh, you won't, honey. Not this one. For Aunt Nina, all my appliances will be white. And the new kitchen won't be so—so assembly-lineish as this one. Kate had never liked my kitchen after it was remodeled—and she was probably right.

"The new one at Aunt Nina's will be way different. A working kitchen for catering, but with lots of little nooks and shelves for plants and books around the appliances. I won't let it lose the dearness of Aunt Nina's little galley. I'm even trying to design it so my helpers will have some sort of lake view while we're working.

"Oh, do I hear what I think I do?" Her mother quickly washed her hands and began making a "too too too" sound as she clucked her way toward the living room.

Jamie fell against the counter, her eyes staring at her watch. Not even two hours. "Her heard us talking 'bout her namesake didn't her, honey," her mother baby-talked from the next room. "Sweet baby Helena—oh, now her's getting so mad."

Jamie listened as Helena's tiny cries escalated into the familiar shrill of colic. She rubbed her eyes, still stinging from the night before. Ten. Midnight. Two a.m. By the time she'd changed and fed and burped and rocked Helena back to sleep, Jamie'd had just over an hour to toss and turn before it started all over again. She wouldn't be on her feet now if Kate hadn't picked Helena up early that morning so Jamie could sleep.

Kate did that three or four mornings a week, swearing Helena slept angelically in her car seat next to the computer while Kate worked. It was true, daytime hours were Helena's best. But Jamie knew Kate wouldn't rat on Helena if she'd cried all morning. Her older sister adored Helena with a kind of pure affection Jamie could hardly believe. Kate should resent Helena, the 'unwanted' baby when she wanted one so badly. But it was the opposite. Kate could not show a child of her own more love than she gave her tiny niece.

Before she'd gone back to bed that morning, Jamie had used one of her precious free hours to run a fast seven miles along the bike path. Exercise had always been a combination escape and de-stressor for Jamie, both of which she desperately needed right now. She ended her runs by racing down Aunt Nina's stairs and plunging straight into the invigoratingly cold water of Lake Michigan, her jogging clothes still on. Running, and the dumbbells she worked out with on Aunt Nina's deck, had given her the extra endurance she'd needed for Helena's colic. She was leaner than when she got pregnant, but stronger.

"Gramma's got you, Punkin," she heard her mother's soft voice beneath Helena's pained wails. Jamie thought again about the Jesus bracelet. She'd tried nursing Helena until her nipples bled, but her baby never seemed satisfied. Dr. Susan Cavendish, the pediatrician, must have seen how strung out Jamie was when she suggested switching to a bottle.

"You've given your baby the good immunity for those important first weeks, Jamie," Dr. Cavendish had said. "Now you need to take care of Jamie." It wasn't until Jamie finally gave up breast feeding that she realized Helena was going to cry anyway. No matter what she ate, poor little Helena got a stomach ache. What *Would* Jesus Do? Jamie did wonder, with a twinge of guilt, what would He do if he had to walk the floor every night with a screaming baby who couldn't be comforted?

"Sweet baby, sweet baby," her mother singsonged as she came into the kitchen, jiggling the unhappy infant girl while she walked. Even crying, Helena was one of those Gerber babies with huge blue eyes and a perfect button nose that caused strangers to stop and gape. Her mother said Jamie had looked just like her. But Jamie knew this baby's face had been forged at some level of divinity higher than Jamie could ever touch.

"Here, I'll change her," Jamie said taking her daughter, "if you'll nuke her bottle in the micro." Jamie laid her face against the warm silk cheek, inhaling the sweet baby smell. She put Helena down on the soft pad her mother kept on the counter for diapering and began to ease the squirming little legs out of the pink sleeper, pausing to kiss the tiny toes on each foot.

Jamie murmured to the infant whose crying seemed to ease a bit when she recognized her mother's voice. Suddenly, through the shine of her teary blue eyes, a smile broke the small heart-shaped face, and Jamie leaned down to rub noses with her daughter. She wanted the moment to go on forever. Helena happy, smiling, knowing her mother worshipped every growing cell in her precious body.

"Let me feed the munchkin," her mother said taking the warmed bottle out of the microwave. "Now that she's stopped crying, she's Grammie's, aren't you toodle bug." Her mother held her arms out for the baby.

"All right," Jamie kissed Helena's forehead as she handed her over. "I'll put these egg trays in the garage refrigerator."

The low sun still felt warm as Jamie crossed the deck to the garage, the dry leaves crackling under her shoes. Her mother had forgotten to leave the automatic garage door up, which she usually did because her extra refrigerator was in the front of the garage. Jamie debated going back for the clicker, but decided to take a chance the single door at the back end of the garage was opened. The far door was hardly ever used so Jamie guessed her mother kept it locked. Balancing the tippy cookie sheet against her waist, she turned the knob and pushed against the door with her fanny. The door gave way at once, making Jamie stumble into the garage.

The sudden darkness blinded her and she reflexively began to wobble trying to keep the egg-piled toast slices from sliding off the tray. Suddenly her shin smacked against something hard and several of the delicate appetizers flew off the tray. "Shit," she muttered as her eyes adjusted to the dim light, and she saw the yellow plastic crate she'd tripped on.

She leaned over to check if any of the eggs were salvageable. That's when she saw a Beefeaters label through the slotted sides of the crate. Her mother had folded a blue lawn tarp across the crate like a cover. Jamie knew why. She set the tray down on an old bookcase and lifted the tarp.

Inside the yellow crate were her mother's liquor supplies for the parties when her customers wanted Ellie's Custom Catering to do it all—cater and bartend. Some of the bottles had been opened, Jamie could see, but most of them were still sealed. The red Smirnoff label over the clear liquid caught her eye. No booze smell. She stopped breathing, the WWJD bracelet vivid in her mind. She abruptly dropped the heavy canvas back over the crate.

Her feet ran to the front of the garage where she shoved the cookie sheet into the oversized refrigerator and began to pray down the craving. She begged for help against the thought of how lovely it would be to sip something that would let her sleep between Helena's fussy spells. Not to grow tense trying to rest while she waited for the next outburst, but to really sleep between the night-time bouts of colic.

"What am I doing!' she spoke out loud and rushed to the still open door at the far corner of the garage, her armpits damp with sweat. She tried to calm herself with deep yoga breaths as she swept dead leaves across the deck with her feet. She went back into the kitchen where her mother sat in the small white rocker she'd brought down from the attic when Helena was born. Ellie Cameron held her tiny granddaughter tucked in the crook of one arm while she fed her a bottle.

"You sure haven't lost your touch," Jamie said fighting back tears. Mary Cassatt, Jamie thought watching Helena's little hands clench and unclench as she suckled, her blue eyes riveted on her grandmother's smiling face. The Cassatt portrait Jamie had tried so hard to be for Helena. She gritted her teeth against the yellow crate and the release it promised.

She hadn't told her mother how close she'd come eight days earlier to phoning Uncle Tom. She wanted him to call his Kansas lawyer friend back. It had been the 30th day after Helena's birth, and the date had made Jamie frantic. By late that night, watching the clock on Aunt Nina's stove tick past midnight while she bounced her screaming baby against her chest, Jamie knew she'd waited too long.

She bent toward the rocker and kissed Helena's miniature hand. In truth, she'd crossed her Rubicon the moment the Mrs. Claus in the hospital nursery handed her the bundle from the third bassinet. The one angled so Jamie hadn't been able to read the name. The only pink one. Her mother had wept openly at her side while Kate's finger stroked the baby's soft skull coated with fine threads of gold hair.

Standing together in the newborn nursery, surrounded by Winnie the Pooh on the walls, Jamie had prayed with all her might. Please, dear God, don't let me spoil this, she'd asked silently as the four female Camerons made a tight circle locked in hands and arms. "Her name's Helena," Jamie had suddenly said as if she'd planned it all along.

"Oh, Jamie," her mother's voice broke in, "Would you mind taking the other two trays out for me? There's no way I can get them in this refrigerator." She rocked back and forth smoothly, not taking her eyes off her granddaughter.

"Sure," Jamie answered and started to ask for the garage-door opener. But then her mother would realize she'd used the other door—the back entrance near the hidden liquor supply. Why worry her unnecessarily, Jamie thought and picked up the second tray. This time Jamie made a point of not even looking toward the yellow crate in the corner as she walked past it toward the refrigerator carrying the first tray.

She slid the two trays into the garage refrigerator on the shelf below the first, and was about to shut the small back door for the last time. Then she hesitated. Before she let herself think, she pulled the unopened vodka bottle from beneath the blue tarp and stuffed it in her jeans pocket under the navy turtleneck she was wearing. It's only for security, she told herself. Like a savings account—money you spend only in an emergency. She promised herself not to touch the vodka if Helena would let her sleep.

"Jamie, it's only 4:30," her mother said when she came back into the kitchen. "Why don't I keep Helena while you go meet Gloria at your five o'clock meeting?"

Jamie grabbed a scrub brush and began nervously rinsing out the popover tins. "Oh, thanks," she said unable to look at her mother while she let the steaming water sting her hands. "But Gloria's in Detroit visiting an aunt today."

How easily the lies come back, she reflected. Like the words in a favorite old song. Gloria in fact had told Jamie she was going right from work to the 5 p.m. meeting and would look for her there if she could get away.

"Maybe tomorrow morning, then," her mother said glancing up at Jamie before returning her attention to the baby she was gently burping against her shoulder. The look on her mother's face, the expression of unconditional trust stinging Jamie with the force of a slap. How much less painful a physical blow would have been.

Jamie gave herself credit. She hadn't opened the bottle right away. She'd toughed through a crying jag with Helena around eight and then again at ten. It was not until her daughter woke with a piercing howl just before midnight that Jamie pulled Helena out of her white wicker bassinet, and then unscrewed the vodka top with her free hand. Just one little drink, she assured herself, pouring liquid into a juice glass.

Almost immediately, the roar of soothing fire in her throat began to melt her tension and she kissed Helena, flooded with affection. The crying grew bearable, almost funny, like Saturday morning cartoons. Jamie felt powerful with a heightened acuity, at full attention as if she could hear the universe pulsing around her.

A little more vodka would only enhance her awakeness, she assured herself. She'd take better care of Helena when she was alert and euphoric at the same time. A drink in one hand, Helena in the other, Jamie sat down on the living room couch and pulled up her nightie to breast feed. It took several minutes of Helena's unhappy head thrusts before Jamie remembered. She'd quit nursing two weeks before.

When she worked her way to her feet, the idea of warming a bottle in her mind, the earlier clarity seemed to migrate toward a haziness. It was like a slow fog rising over the lake. The last thing she remembered before the blackout was a baby crying somewhere in the distance.

T h e   S a n d p i p e r

KATE

The high reds of Michigan autumn had fallen, but the muted golds and russets festooned the landscape like Thanksgiving decorations, Kate thought as she turned down Hiawatha and back toward her home. Pogo's gleaming back moved effortlessly beside her, the leash slack in her hands. Her dear Pogo now went back and forth between his two homes as naturally as a New York commuter. This morning Kate needed to return Pogo to Jamie when she picked up Helena at 10.

Impulsively Kate stopped to scratch the dog's ears, telling "Mama's good boy'" she'd miss him the next few days. Maybe sharing a darling niece and one perfect dog were all the children she'd have. Kate prayed, one knee pressed hard against the bike path while Pogo licked her hand, that it would not be so. But she could not let her life be driven by wishes anymore.

Kate stood up and checked the traffic before crossing the street to her Birchbark home. She had a full life. Pete, her mother, Helena and Jamie. The Sandpiper Foundation and the Lakeshore News and Pogo. No matter what happened, or didn't happen, she'd be okay.

In her own quirky style, Aunt Nina had managed to bequeath this new serenity to Kate the morning she died. *To love that well which thou must leave ere long.* Well, life was pretty darn short. Kate intended to thrust herself into the serious business of loving her family, her very *real* family, for the brief time they had with each other on earth.

Certainly that didn't mean giving up on a baby of her own to love as she loved Helena. She'd already scheduled her January appointment with Dr. Bauer. Her mother was grateful Kate had asked her to come along. But then in bed one night, Pete, unaware Kate's mother was planning to go, said he wasn't scheduling patients the day Kate started back with her fertility treatments. Could he come with her?

Kate had been stunned, and then moved, her wet tears falling on Pete's cheek. She knew her mother would be more than willing to accompany Kate to a later appointment.

Pogo lapped the bowl of water Kate put on the kitchen floor. She poured the last cup of coffee from the pot and put a raisin bagel in the toaster. Waiting for the toaster to pop, she moved Jamie's cactus to the middle of the kitchen counter, positioning it so the striking fuschia blossoms were the first thing anyone saw coming in the door.

She'd told Jamie she'd spotted the first tiny pink buds the day after Helena was born. Jamie had scoffed, until she got home from the hospital and saw Aunt Nina's cactus, in its ornate white Victorian container, sprouting its first fuchsia leaves too. Her mother's had taken another few days, but her kitchen got less direct sun than theirs.

Kate still had no idea where the cactus cuttings came from. But Jamie had been right about the good luck. Precious Helena had come into their family. The toaster and the phone sounded at the same time. Kate grabbed the hot bagel with a napkin and reached for the telephone.

"Kate. It's Gloria. Do you...do you know where Jamie is?" The anxiety in Gloria Cook's voice knocked the wind out of Kate. The heat of the bagel singed her fingers as she squeezed it reflexively. "No. No. Gloria. What's happened?" Then she heard a shrill crying she recognized. "Helena? You have Helena?"

Kate's heart began to thud against her rib cage while Gloria talked to someone in the background. The sound of the unhappy Helena faded. "My mother's got her now. The baby's fine. Helena's fine. But Jamie isn't. In the blue bag—right there Mom," Gloria spoke away from the receiver again. "Yes, that bottle. Just warm it up. Thanks, Mom."

"Kate, sorry. I'm rattled here. Jamie showed up for No Sniveling this morning. You know our 7 a.m. women's meeting. She didn't get there until almost 7:15 and she knows I'll kick her butt if she's late. And she looked like shit. Excuse my tongue, Kate, I don't swear, but I'm shook. Jamie's looked bad before, up all night with a fussy baby. But today she's like real calm, quiet. But I hardly paid attention because—well. I'll tell you later. Everyone was just glad to see her since, you know, she can't get to our meeting too much right now.

"So then Jamie leans over and tells me she's got to pee and to keep my eye on

Helena, who's sleeping in her car seat. I am struggling myself with what I have to tell the No Snivelers when I realize I haven't heard the toilet flush. In that old AA building, you hear everything. So I tell Maudie beside me to watch the baby and I go looking for Jamie in the bathroom. Not there. Then I run into Earl and he tells me Jamie sped out of the lot ten minutes before. I didn't want to scare her mother so I'm calling you on the club phone."

Pogo laid his head on Kate's foot as if he could hear the distress pulsing through her veins. "You mean she just left the baby?" Kate felt her belly spasm in the pain she remembered from the night Diane called to say Jamie had quit school and run off with a bartender. How fast the sobriety elevator crashed, all the prayers and dreams and hopes smashed under the speeding hard steel.

"Right next to her purse. When Earl said she'd gone, I could have shot myself. Jamie's being so calm and all—that wasn't right. Not Jamie—and I should have seen it. It was like she was hypnotized or something. Is there a chance she's at your mother's house?"

Kate's thoughts raced. "No, I'm sure not. The bars—we have to check the bars."

"She didn't take her purse. She can't buy anything."

"The Sandpiper? Could she have gone back there? Maybe to sleep?" Kate asked knowing Jamie would never have just left Helena like that. "Jake. Maybe she's meeting Jake somewhere." Kate actually hoped it was so. Even Jake was better than a relapse.

"Kate, I got to be honest. I'm thinking worse. Alcoholics, when they keep on relapsing? A lot of times they get to where they just don't want to live anymore."

"What are you saying?" Kate gasped as chills shivered her body. "No, don't say that. Please."

"Kate, when I go back in the room I got to tell our group something terrible." Gloria paused.

"What? What?" Kate was now frantic.

Gloria's voice shivered. "One of our No Snivelers hanged herself last night," it came out in a choked sob. "Her husband's a doctor. Found her in the basement when he got home from night rounds. She was a great lady—Michelle. Six years of sobriety and everything to live for," now Gloria was openly crying.

"I dreaded telling Jamie. Cuz we both know alcoholics kill themselves every day. We get helpless and hopeless and think there's no other way out."

"But not Jamie! Never—Jamie would never—never leave Helena—never do that to our mother! Never! Not Jamie." She tried to fight down the hysteria pluming through her. "Please don't say that about Jamie."

"Don't you go to pieces on me, Kate. This thing with Michelle…I need your help for Jamie right now. Just accept you can't ever understand the power of this disease. Only another alcoholic can. But we don't have time for this. Kate, if Jamie were to…to harm herself, can you think of anything at all? Any way to find her before it's too late?"

"She wouldn't." Kate began to cry as Pogo stood up and nudged his head under her dangling arm. Then an image flashed in Kate's eyes. A memory. "Gloria, the beach. Call the police and send them to the beach. No, no. Call the Coast Guard first. I'm on my way." Kate dropped the phone. She and Pogo were hurtling down U.S. 31 before she realized she hadn't said what beach.

With no way to call anyone, Kate could think of only one thing to do. Kate moved into the left-hand lane and pressed the accelerator of her Mazda, checking her rearview mirror. She sped through a yellow light and pushed even harder, looking down every intersection for a patrol car. "Oh, Pogo," she said squealing her tires around the last corner and turning onto Beach Road, "the time I need to get stopped for speeding, and there's not a cop around!"

She leaned toward the windshield and strained to see the parking lot ahead of her, willing her eyes to spot a white Saab. In the distance, the tall red light-house at the end of the pier jumped off the horizon at her. She was almost there. She barely glanced at oncoming traffic before yanking the wheel left into Light-house Beach's small public parking lot. The only other car was a rusted brown pickup.

Just beyond the lot, she could see Gertie's windows boarded up, the pink neon sign dark. She started to cut her engine, then changed her mind. With her car visible from the road, she flicked on the hazard lights and left the engine running. Someone, with luck a policeman, would stop to see what was wrong.

Pogo bounded out of the front seat, and trotted along the deserted beach in front of her as she raced in the direction of the diner. Suddenly, into her unhinged thinking, came an image of Jamie in a white cotton dress, hip-sashed in red. She sat across the picnic table from Kate at the farthest end of Gertie's deck, a pot of decaf in front of her. She'd wanted privacy so she could quietly ask Kate to help her end her pregnancy. But Jamie had also started to say something about Roger Hamper. Only Kate had not listened.

She ran around behind Gertie's in the wild hope Jamie's car might be parked in the few employee spaces. No cars at all. She turned back toward the pier and the empty beach, frantic about where to go next. She took one last look at Gertie's back entrance. That's when she noticed a small protrusion of white and black from behind a woven weathered fence screening garbage bins.

Kate gasped in relief. Then horror. What if…but she saw no fumes wafting into the air. By the time she could make her feet move toward the woven partition, Pogo was already dancing around Jamie's empty car. The Saab was unlocked, the keys on the driver's seat in plain sight.

It was as if, she realized, Jamie wanted to make sure they were found. Trembling, she quickly ransacked the car for any clue to Jamie's intentions. All she found were a half-empty baby bottle and a wadded sheet of paper listing meeting times at the Spring Port AA Club.

Kate raced back around the front of Gertie's, aware her sports bra was still damp from running earlier. In the rush of adrenalin at finding her sister's car, Kate didn't feel the chill of the north wind right away as she ran toward Lake Michigan. She was torn between sheer terror at what she might find when she got to the water, and blinding optimism she wasn't too late.

Now sprinting across the spongy sand toward the shoreline, she was grateful for the sturdy Nikes she still had on. She whipped her eyes over the wide span of beach looking for? She didn't know what. The wind blew harder as she neared the lake, but she could see no one in either direction. Only a handful of seagulls circled low over the water.

"Pogo," she yelled, losing her voice to the wind. "Find Jamie. Jamie," she screamed between cupped hands. The dog never looked back at her, but continued making long arcing moves as he galloped toward the water. Ahead of her, Kate saw nothing but huge breaking waves, one overlapping the next like moving walls of white. She stared until her eyes hurt, examining the sand for anything that might suggest a swimmer. A towel. A tee shirt. Maybe a shoe or sweat pants.

Pogo didn't slow at the water's edge but plunged straight in as if a stick had been thrown. Maybe he'd seen something, recognized a scent, Kate prayed. Then feared as much in the same breath. Pogo was already running back towards her, his tail flapping with the joy of his swim. The buzz of a small airplane to the north caught Kate's attention.

She was following the plane's flight along the horizon when she thought she saw a speck of light color move against the red backdrop at the end of the pier. Kate hooded her eyes like a birdwatcher and studied the spot. This time she saw nothing but waves splashing over the grey concrete slab jutting into Lake Michigan.

The pier with its NO TRESPASSING sign was always dangerous, but especially this time of year. The wind alone could blow people into the choppy surf. Still, she had good rubber grips on her soles. And from the pier, she'd be able to see farther into the big lake.

Pogo cocked his head at her, then took off toward the pier as if he knew where she was headed. Suddenly the futility, the reckless stupidity, of what she was doing overcame her. For the first time she shivered in the cold wind. She needed to go get help. Her car's lights were still blinking in the streetside parking lot behind her. But the drivers going both ways on Beach Road didn't seem to notice. Or care.

She clapped her hands for Pogo to come back, but he was out of hearing range. Helpless, she watched the black lab lope straight toward the concrete steps leading up to the pier. She began to jog after him, for warmth more than speed this time. The blowing sand stung her cheeks as she headed into the wind.

By the time she climbed the thick metal steps, Pogo was running along the slippery concrete pier, his head swinging from side to side, exploring his new environment. "Pogo," she finally got close enough to yell over the wind. "Come. Come, Boy. I'm freezing. Jamie's not here." The abandoned Saab rose in her consciousness. "Come right now," she yelled. She could not let herself think about where Jamie might be.

Pogo was looking over his shoulder at her, poised to come back when his black nose abruptly pointed into the air. He made a funny whine and began trotting farther out on the pier. "No, Pogo, oh, no."

One summer she and Jamie had watched the Coast Guard search for a fisherman whose metal boat had capsized in Lake Michigan just south of Aunt Nina's cottage. They had been all giggly with the excitement of the boats and ropes, men on shore with walkie talkies, and divers wearing black rubber suits. Then one of the divers began walking backwards out of the lake, pulling something heavy. Before the other rescuers surrounded the diver and his find, Kate and Jamie had seen floppy blue-white legs make two small trenches in the wet sand where the divers dragged the dead fisherman to a waiting stretcher. Kate had tried to comfort Jamie on the way back to Aunt Nina's. But that night Kate threw up her dinner.

She yelled again at Pogo and started to follow him yelling for him to "Come!" Then she saw the back of Jamie's head at the far end of the pier. What she'd seen from shore was gold hair blowing free in the wind. She began shouting Jamie's name and running. Each footstep was a slide on the slippery concrete getting rhythmically drenched by waves. But Kate never took her eyes off her little sister.

"Jamie, Jamie," she felt the wind hurl her words back at her, but she kept screaming them anyway. Pogo was not thirty feet away when Jamie finally turned and saw them both. Even at long range, Kate could see the stricken look on Jamie's face as she shoved both arms forward in exaggerated go-away signals. Carefully Kate picked up her pace, each foot plant precarious, as she closed the gap between Jamie and her. Then, in one stunning motion, Jamie did a graceful dancer's leap over the edge and was gone.

Kate's scream began to rise from a pit so dark she felt her larynx might burst. The vibrations still ripping her throat, she stared in frozen horror as Pogo followed Jamie into the water. Kate's eyes blinked in nightmare cognition, and she moved, mummy-like, to the edge of the pier where Jamie had been.

Between the white spray of breaking waves, Kate saw the small black head in the water pointed straight at Jamie's bobbing blond hair. Jamie had seen Pogo jump in, Kate realized, because she was trying to make her way toward the dog. Then a wave. Then nothing. Then the heads again. Kate watched the surrealistic scene below, eyewitness to an unfolding tragedy she didn't think she could survive. But she was not the swimmer. Jamie was. If she had any chance of saving her sister's life, it would be only because Jamie would not let Kate drown.

Kate prayed to God for courage she didn't feel, and a burst of energy coursed through her bloodstream. Now. She had to go now, or she would lose her nerve. Before she could think it through, Kate took three steps backward, dug her nails into her palms for strength, and took two running steps before she cannonballed right where she'd last seen Jamie's and Pogo's heads.

The jolt of the icy water shocked her heart. For a moment she was disoriented, turned upside down somewhere under water. At the verge of panic, muscle memory took hold, and she kicked forcefully until her head broke the surface. She sucked in great gulps of air, too cold to speak, but no longer afraid.

"Shit," she heard Jamie scream above the waves, and Kate felt giddy with relief. She was right! In her own despair, Jamie might want to end her life. But she'd never let anything happen to her big sister.

The next thing Kate knew, they were swimming together, Kate half dragging her toward the shoreline, Pogo weaving up and down in front of them. Kate had an urge to ask Jamie if she remembered the World War II movie about the Nazis putting Russian POWs into ice water and then timing how long it took them to freeze to death. Her arms grew tired as the waves kept pushing her sideways, the shoreline getting no closer.

Through the leaps of water, Kate saw Jamie watching her, the raw fear on her sister's face confusing her. Jamie afraid? Jamie's not afraid of anything! Then Kate's head went heavy and her feet turned into cinder blocks, the kicking legs gone away. What she needed was to rest her face in the soft waves and sleep. Kate felt herself begin to slip under the soothing water when a sharp pain in her head jerked her toward daylight. But Kate was so very tired, and something hard hurt her and her chin hurt and all she wanted was just to sleep…sleep… sleep…

"Kate!" A voice she should know called her name, but she let it float past, her body lying down in the green pastures of the valley of the shadow where she wanted to stay forever. Jamie, this time she knew it was Jamie disturbing her rest. Jamie sobbing and coughing somewhere near her ear.

Then other voices and warm hands rubbing her legs and arms, an icy shirt peeled off her, scratchy wool wrapped tight around her arms and back, the hands still massaging her through the rough fabric. Slowly, slowly, her sleepiness ebbed. She began to remember.

"Jamie, Jamie? Where's my sister?" Kate jerked herself upright to see strange faces, anxious faces, looking down at where she sat on Lighthouse Beach, a grey Army blanket around her. A woman in a yellow parka and two others in wool jackets stood beside her, a policeman in the background on a walkie talkie.

"Kate, oh, dear God, Kate, Kate, Kate." Jamie, wrapped like a squaw in a red Indian-print blanket, was suddenly beside her, her hair plastered gold against her skull. A fourth woman appeared carrying another, heavier white blanket with one stripe each of red, green, and black at the bottom. The newest woman draped the fuzzy blanket over both Jamie's and Kate's shoulders while Jamie rocked Kate in her cold, wet arms.

"I've lived across from this beach since Pearl Harbor," the woman in the yellow parka was telling the policeman, "and I swear to God I never saw anything like it. I'm just going out the door to mail a letter when I see two people and a black dog out on the pier where no one's supposed to be ever and for sure not this time of year. I'm wondering if I should call the Coast Guard when just like that," she snapped her fingers, "they jump in the lake like it's the middle of July.

"The last one even did that dive where you hold your knees. That's when I called 911 and grabbed my beach blankets. My neighbor Mary Lou right there," she gestured at the woman beside her wearing a long grey coat, "I yelled at her and she came running down to help too.

"These others," she pointed at two other women, "they live just down the beach." Kate listened with a detached curiosity, as if she hadn't been involved. For most of the time, she knew she hadn't been.

"That little blond thing," now Mary Lou had the policeman's attention, "looked for all the world like a bluegill bobber going up and down in the waves. We thought the other one drowned, didn't we, Hazel," she said to the first woman in the rubber parka. "Then the blond one there," Kate could visualize the finger pointing toward Jamie, "she gets to the sandbar where she can touch and that's when we see she's pulled the other one, the black-haired girl, her sister, I guess, all the way from the pier. In water this temperature? Can you imagine?"

"I tell you," Hazel in the yellow parka said once more, "I've never seen anything like it in all my sixty-four years."

"You both saw three people jump?"

Kate had the impression the cop was taking notes.

"No, two people and a dog. The third one was a black dog."

"Pogo?" Kate's head whipped around to find Jamie.

Jamie looked blank a moment, her eyes dull with exhaustion. Then she forced a weak smile with lips Kate now saw were a deep blue. Jamie opened her Indian blanket, and Pogo wiggled out to begin licking Kate's face. "The mutt came back out to the sandbar wondering why we were so slow."

An ambulance siren shrilled in the background. "Are you all right, Jamie?" Kate asked, leaning around Pogo. "Your lips are blue. You're not freezing to death, are you? Remember? That Nazi movie we saw about freezing the Russians?"

"Making them tread water in the ice bath? No, no, Kate, I'm not going to die now."

It hit Kate like a jolt of electricity. She and her sister *had* almost died. *Should* have died except that Jamie was an Amazon in the water. *Would* have died if Jamie had not loved Kate so much.

"Oh, Jamie," Kate said, overcome by what her sister had done. "I love you so much." Pogo wormed himself between the sisters, burying his head in the warm space between their hips.

Jamie's jaw shook as she pinched Kate's arm. "You were a shit to jump in after me."

"I was going after Pogo."

"Like you really thought a retriever couldn't make it to shore. No, Kate, you knew exactly what you were doing."

Kate shrugged, grateful to hear the ambulance sound getting louder. "It's tough, Jamie, when someone knows your heart as well as I do. Your heart and your swimming talent."

"I can't do it, Kate," Jamie's light tone evaporated. "Helena. I could have, she might have...Kate. I'm not...Kate." She pushed her face right into Kate's. "I've been sick here," Jamie pointed at her skull "since Roger Hamper raped me."

Suddenly Kate was fully awake.

"He said we were checking a house. He had wine. But I didn't want to, I never...I fought so hard he hurt me more. That's how the chain, you know, broke."

Jamie's shoulders heaved in spasms as Kate clutched her with new strength. "Dear God, the insurance! You heard Alex telling me that. Oh my poor, dear, dear Jamie. How could I not have known? Guessed? I knew you better than that and still I listened to Alex. Dear God, Jamie. Mother was right. Your drinking did get worse after Alex's dad died. The bastard. I'm glad he killed himself. I'd kill him right now if he weren't dead-"

"Me too," Jamie sobbed.

"You don't have to hide it anymore. We'll get you good help, I promise. The best therapist in West Michigan. Oh, Jamie, so much to hold in, to carry by yourself."

Kate saw the green-and white ambulance hurl down the road.

"That's what he said. Dr. Summers." Jamie spoke so quietly, as if to herself, Kate didn't catch the name.

"Whoever that is, he's right." Kate watched the red-light twirling over the sand to where they sat. "Telling me? That's a huge step for you, Jamie." Two young men in matching green coats with red crosses on round insignias jumped out and ran toward them pulling two gurneys.

"Kate, what am I going to do?" Jamie suddenly clung to Kate like a life raft just as the medics got to her, Pogo prancing around them.

"You're going to tell these men," Kate whispered to Jamie, "that you and your big sister have some serious work to do. For each other. For Mom. For Helena."

"But Kate?"

Kate rubbed wet hair off her younger sister's forehead. "Blood oath. We're in this together. O.K.? But could we not do this swim thing again? Please?"

Then, as if from a great distance, Kate heard the rumble of Jamie's low giggles, the contagious ones. She looked up to see her sister's crying tears and laughing tears pool with water drips from her hair. With a burst of deep joy, Kate knew Jamie was on her way home.

By the time the medics had both of them strapped to stretchers, the two sisters were clutching their stomachs, convulsed in laughter. Within minutes they were speeding along in the back of the ambulance headed to the emergency room. One medic sat on a metal bench beside the two sisters with Pogo sitting upright in the front seat next to the driver.

"Oh, Jamie," Kate rolled her head toward the stretcher beside her and laid her hand on Jamie's arm. "One more thing I'd like to straighten out."
Jamie's cocoa eyes did not lose their mirth.

"Drowning is *not* a nice way to die. And don't ever forget it."

Overhead, the ambulance siren roared its way through the heart of Spring Port toward Waters Hospital emergency room where Dr. Peter Shane was putting the last twist of pink plaster on a seven-year old girl's arm.

Jackie, one of the ER nurses, leaned her head into the room and asked if he could stick around a few minutes. An ambulance was bringing in two patients they'd just pulled out of Lake Michigan.

"We know they're hypothermic, Dr. Shane. But since they either jumped or fell off the pier, we're thinking maybe fractures too."

Dr. Peter Shane checked his watch. "I don't have surgery for another half hour. Not a problem."

He followed the nurse down the hallway toward the entrance to the emergency room just as the scream of a siren sounded in the distance.

The End

Also by Susan Brace Lovell

1997

THE GOOD CAUSE IN WHICH WE ARE ENGAGED:
Blodgett Memorial Medical Center 150 Years

2000

GRAND RAPIDS TOWNSHIP: THE HISTORY

2003

PETER MARTIN WEGE: A BIOGRAPHY

2011

A DOZEN OF THE BEST:
Improvement Association 1940-2011